Quail Hill

a novel by

Barbara Morris Atcheson

Copyright © 2012 by Barbara Morris Atcheson

All rights reserved. Published in the United States
by Barbara Morris Atcheson.

This is a work of fiction. Names, characters, places, and incidents are the products of the author's imagination or are used fictitiously. Any resemblance to actual events, locales, organizations or persons, living or dead, is entirely coincidental.
No part of this book may be reproduced in any manner whatsoever without prior written permission, except in the case of brief quotations embodied in critical articles or reviews.

The author is grateful to SPCK Publishing & Sheldon Press for permission to use quotations from REASON AND REALITY by John Polkinghorne © 1991.

ISBN: 978-1-60944-037-4

Author Photograph: © Irene Sorensen

Front cover photograph:
courtesy of the Prince-Morris Family album archives

To contact the author, or obtain copies of the book, visit:
www.AtchesonBooks.com
or email: atchesonbooks@q.com

*Designed, printed, and bound by Vladimir Verano
at Third Place Press, Lake Forest Park,
on the Espresso Book Machine v.2.2.
thirdplacepress.com*

Quail Hill is published in memory of

The Rev. Mark Wayne Bailey, Ph.D.

Friend, priest, fellow writer.

and dedicated to my husband

Chuck Atcheson

with all my love.

Contents

Prologue — 3

I: Craigmoor — 9

II: Other Places — 155

III: The Trip Home — 293

Family Trees — 323

A structure in which branches divide into sub-branches, and so on for ever, is an example of what mathematicians call a fractal. Fractals are entities which look the same on whatever scale you examine them... its structure is inexhaustibly rich—whorls and dragons' claws made out of whorls and dragons' claws...you have only to blow up part of an old pattern to reveal a new pattern, approximately similar but subtly different.

~*Reason and Reality* by John Polkinghorne

Prologue

May 15, 1987

Walking away from the Vietnam Memorial, the roughness of the letters and the cool sensation of the black marble clung to her fingertips as the breeze continued to tousle her long, dark hair. She wondered when she had decided upon these actions—yesterday, last week, years ago?—but knew 'beginnings' were often difficult to establish.

Her movements seemed generated by a steady, gentle force and she focused her attention on that energy—certainly she could no longer focus on the conference—and realized her unplanned exit would cause only minor readjustments for her colleagues like the brief ruffling of birds when one of their own flies away from a crowded wire.

'Walk. Becca, walk.' She heard a voice in her head, her own voice—finally strong and trustworthy—and followed it easily. After leaving the Memorial, she caught a DC cab, returned to the Shoreham Hotel, made a few calls and left a message on Brad's answering machine saying she'd call Friday night. She completed the necessary arrangements, checked out, transferred to National Airport and boarded the flight to Boston with a minimum of fuss. Not that she understood her behavior, far from it, but most of her internal voices supported this decision.

After fastening her seatbelt, Becca leaned back and gazed out the window. She didn't know exactly why she was going to New Hampshire, but knew she needed to get back to times before loss, confusion and betrayal had left her emotionally ham-strung. Maybe the 'successful academician' part of her mind would question her later for such a rash decision, but she had to get to Craigmoor, to Quail Hill, to whatever traces she might find of her Great-Grandmother Libby. The desire to reconnect with her father's family had become irresistible like the pull to a first kiss.

She let her mind drift over the history she knew of these people who were so embedded in this country: its successes, its opportunities, its wars, arrogance, beauty, racism, sexism, abundance and wastefulness. Her family. Her country. Her home. 'How do I bring it all together,' she wondered as she closed her dark brown eyes and settled back in her seat.

Fragmented thoughts, like summer clouds, flitted by. She had Libby's names, reversed of course, but the pull felt more visceral than names. Why had her father persisted in using them? Given her mother Eleanor's animosity toward 'Rebecca Elizabeth,' why had he insisted? Especially facing what he faced. There must have been reasons he lashed Becca so firmly to the Whitman side of his family: to his Grandmother Libby who was her great-grandmother. Becca was the last baby Libby greeted, the last to inherit the label 'prettiest one yet' from Libby's lips—and only God knew how many generations *that* family tradition pre-existed all of them.

Her mind snagged on the word God and how she viewed God now: a more open, accessible and intimate reality. She visualized her Rector with her hands held high during the Easter Eucharist back in Santa Veronica, CA. Next she recalled Swami, so tall and thin, standing next to her in Bangkok, his ochre robe fluttering in the night breeze. So many images existed in the mosaic of her life and, weaving through all the pain and fear, some thread was guiding her toward hope and peace.

Landing instructions over the plane's PA system roused her from reverie. Arriving at Boston's Logan airport, she picked up a rental car and headed north into the night.

The next morning Becca's car jolted onto the narrow lane at the base of Quail Hill. Sunlight darted through the trees casting shadows on the rock-strewn fields of her great-great-grandparents' farm. She stopped in a clearing as memory met reality. In the 30 years since she'd been here, little had changed. The white farmhouse a half-mile up the rutted road still peeked over the crest of the hill like a shy child looking over a fence. Becca felt safe. A bloodhound's nose might sniff five generations of her family on this rugged hillside.

Driving on, she stopped by the house, shifted into park, set the brake and cut the engine. Across the lane stood the yellow, two-story, 'new house' (built about 1870) and behind her the big gray barn clung to the edge of the pasture. This triangle of buildings seemed like facets of a crystal. Then she noticed a difference: something missing. No huge black walnut tree: only a stump covered with flowerboxes. Becca caught her breath as though she'd been kicked in the chest. Then, inhaling carefully, she stepped slowly from the car so she wouldn't disturb the scene. In this still world Becca scanned the hills, rocks, chicken coops, orchards, fences. A horse in the big pasture by the barn watched her, switched its tail and flared its nostrils.

She gazed out over apple-blossom time on Quail Hill Farm—a sight she'd never seen—a sight Libby watched annually for 70 years. Time swirled around like dust devils in her mind as she imagined children—from generations now long dead—running, laughing and playing tag beneath the orchard's delicately blooming branches.

Becca felt someone watching her but resisted the pull of those eyes. To acknowledge another person would end this moment and make her an intruder. She smiled; the moment stretched, neutralizing the space around her. Becca felt suspended and then, like unexpected snowfall in the night, thousands of memories piled around her. Scraps of images, like fragments of songs or bits of poems, danced along the edge of her consciousness. A bird sang and, quietly, like the last leaf dropping from an autumn tree, even time slipped away.

I

CRAIGMOOR

Trees are approximately fractals... Whether you look at the whole tree, or the twigs of a branch, the patterns are at least roughly the same.

~ *Reason and Reality* by John Polkinghorne

1

February 20, 1850

Mavis adjusted her scarf, nodded to her reflection in the old family mirror in the entrance hall and said aloud "You're doing fine, Mavis Whitman." Then she carefully picked up six-week old Elizabeth Rebecca, opened the door and stepped out into the clear, cold day. She turned her face toward the sun searching for a promise of spring. Trudging up the hill her boots scrunched through last night's snow. Finally 'Libby' and her great-grandmother, Rebecca Elizabeth Tillman, could meet. Mavis' breath puffed out in little cloud shapes as she talked to her baby.

"Libby, you're going to meet your great-grandmother. Her name's Rebecca Elizabeth so you're named for her. When she was little she knew her great-grandmother. Do you suppose you'll know your great-grandchildren?"

Libby's eyes focused on her mother's face; she smiled and made soft sucking sound. Four blocks up the hill, Mavis opened the gate to her parents' small brown bungalow, walked to the door and stomped the snow from her boots as the door opened.

"Welcome little ones. Gingerbread's almost done," Margaret, Mavis' mother, said as she reached for her first granddaughter.

The pungent fragrance of molasses and spices surrounded them. Mavis' eyes flashed momentarily. Why did her mother say 'little ones?' Fine for the baby but—oh well, she sighed, greeted her mother and stepped into the room.

"How's Gram today?"

"Weaker. She'll be glad you've come. She wants to meet Libby and is pleased you and John used her names. Probably won't tell you—she's still stubborn as sin."

"Are you two fussing again?" Mavis asked lightly.

Margaret pursed her lips, "Not fussing. Just singing our song. She said grand-mothering is more fun than mothering. I expect she's right. Let's take Libby to meet her."

· Craigmoor ·

Mavis knelt by Grandma Tillman. "Gram, it's Mavis. I've brought Elizabeth Rebecca."

Gram sat dozing in her rocking chair, a blue shawl over her lap, white wispy curls escaping from under her knit cap. Breathing in sharply, she opened her steady blue eyes and smiled at Mavis.

"Sweet Mavis, I hoped you'd come today. This awful New Hampshire winter's kept you in too long." She patted Mavis' curly blond Tillman hair. "Now where's my namesake?"

Libby wiggled and cooed when Margaret placed her in Gram's arms.

"Well, Elizabeth Rebecca, you're the prettiest one yet and your names are in the right order."

Gram put her right index finger on Libby's lower lip and the baby sucked reflexively. The two blue-eyed females gazed intently at each other. Rebecca Elizabeth smiled and so did Elizabeth Rebecca, making faces across eight-decades. The old woman loosened Libby's blankets and examined her hands and feet, counting fingers and toes in a ritual as old as the species itself. Gram placed her finger in Libby's tiny hand and the baby grabbed on and made throaty gurgling sounds.

After a few minutes of this intense communion, Gram sat back and said to Mavis, "She's healthy, strong and knows how to grab. Now you must love her and teach her to let go." She sighed deeply. "Learning to love and let go: that's what life's about." She looked up at her daughter, "Margaret, I'd like my tea now."

Margaret and Mavis prepared tea as Libby slept in an old family cradle.

"You getting enough sleep?" Margaret asked.

"Yes, but not all at once. Little bits and pieces. Libby's nursing better. How're you and Gram doing? She seems clear headed but awfully weak," Mavis replied.

"Mama wanted to reach 82 and meet Libby and now she's done both. She may rally if it ever warms up. She talks about her girlhood in Virginia so much I feel I've been there." Margaret and Mavis then exchanged information about small things: seeds for summer gardens, the church guilds, people.

When they took tea to Gram, she was asleep. Mavis left soon, carrying both Libby and a basket of gingerbread. Mavis pulled abruptly away from her mother's parting hug.

"I need to get home to see Daddy when he stops by from the mill and John will come from the bank soon," Mavis blurted awkwardly. Richard, Mavis' father, visited her every afternoon on his way up the hill. Margaret both cherished and envied the relationship Richard had with their daughter.

Margaret stiffened a bit. "Walk carefully and send the basket back with your Dad." Uncomfortable partings punctuated their mother-daughter relationship.

Later, Gram wrote in her diary:

· Quail Hill ·

Dear Diary,

Mavis brought Elizabeth Rebecca to visit. 'Libby' seems strong and very quiet. I hope she isn't too reserved. Life can be difficult if one is too quiet. What will her life be? Margaret will be a good grandmother though she won't know that for a long time. Mavis looks pale. She has been cooped up too long. Does John help enough? He's a fine husband and should be an excellent father.

The sun is out but it is cold. I'm ready for spring. I've lived here in Craigmoor for 50 years but I still miss spring in Virginia. It is odd: things of childhood cling like bits of seaweed on a shell.

RET Feb 20, 1850

Her initials showed her personal flourish.

Spring flowed into summer and their gardens flourished. Gram rallied. One day in July as she weeded the porch flower boxes and Margaret snapped beans into a pot, Gram said, "I saw the most beautiful sunrise over the ocean this morning."

"It must have been a dream," Margaret stated gently.

Gram pulled off her garden gloves and threw down her trowel. "Margaret, I've done my best to expand your horizons but if you insist on limiting yourself, there is little more I can do." She turned her small, hunched body and walked slowly toward the door.

"Oh, Mama, I don't mean to doubt you."

Suddenly, Gram laughed gently. "You're a fine daughter Margaret and you'll be a wonderful grandmother." Without turning, Gram walked into the house.

Margaret treasured these words. 'Sometimes,' she mused, 'what one of us needs the other can't provide. Not simply contrariness but a matter of inexact fit; a prim mother bears a tomboy; a rugged father sires a poet. Life forces growth.'

A week later, Gram did not awaken but just lay in bed breathing quietly. Richard went to get Mavis, John and Libby. Gram roused and her eyelids fluttered briefly when the baby babbled. Rebecca Elizabeth Tillman, aged 82, rested on the edge of life, surrounded by her family. Margaret wiped her mother's face and stroked her white curls gently. At 10:15 a.m., Gram opened her eyes, focused on Margaret and smiled. Then she relaxed onto her pillow, exhaling slowly for the last time.

Margaret wept softly. Mavis stroked her Mother's head. Then Richard raised Margaret to her feet and held her close. He brushed a tear from her face with his rough miller's hand.

"Come now," he said. "We've work to do."

Gram left few things: her diaries, a locket containing a snip of Margaret's baby hair, some ancient clothes and four small pieces of linen. Prepared for burial wrapped in her blue shawl, she looked peaceful.

An Episcopalian before moving to New Hampshire, Gram attended Craigmoor's Congregational, and only, church. She had made her beliefs known to all the clergy and, while they might not have agreed with her, no one doubted the depth of her faith.

Gram's large funeral descended into cheerful chaos. The new minister tried to recount Gram's life (of which he knew little), mercifully ending his remarks when the 'cough and squirm level' reached a crescendo. The final hymn foundered: few knew the words and fewer the music. Margaret smiled. Gram always said Congregationalists couldn't do liturgy 'worth a fig' and probably watched the episode with glee. Two pallbearers, blinded by the sun when leaving the church, almost dropped the casket. Matthew Jones, at age 7 the oldest of the Jones children of Quail Hill Farm, rushed forward and blocked the fall thus averting disaster.

At the cemetery events went better. Margaret dropped two yellow roses and a handful of dirt onto the casket and tuned to gaze down the hillside to the river that bisected Craigmoor.

"It is peaceful here," Margaret murmured. Walking hand in hand with Richard, Margaret studied Mavis and John and Libby. 'Things won't always be what you want them to be' Gram would say. 'Our job is to be honest and do the best we can. Knowing that doesn't solve things, sometimes it doesn't even help, but it is true and truth is important.'

Harvest progressed; foods were dried and preserved; animal-feed gathered and stored; seeds collected, dried and placed in muslin bags. The planet continued to migrate around the sun as people repeated necessary chores. Libby grew, scooted around happily following Mavis and giggled when her father's prize setter nuzzled her face. Another winter passed.

One sunny day the next April, the family went to the cemetery to place a marker on Gram's grave. It read: Rebecca Elizabeth Tillman 1768—1850.

"She was a wise woman," Richard said.

Margaret chuckled and added, "And stubborn as a goat!"

While Mavis pulled weeds from the graves, Libby toddled after a butterfly that danced on the spring breeze. Life's daily pattern no longer included Gram but, deep within the little butterfly-chaser, segments of her lived on.

2

1855-1864

In fiercely independent New Hampshire, folks took education seriously. Thus, in 1855, when their teacher of five years announced her engagement, the Craigmoor School Board sprang into action. Meeting in John Whitman's walnut paneled office in the bank, the committee dispatched letters to Colby Junior College for Women in New London and to Dartmouth College in Hanover seeking a replacement: preferably a New Hampshire native of impeccable character.

Colby responded quickly recommending Miss Amy Middleton as a perfect candidate. After exchanging correspondence and recommendations (her many outstanding qualities included that she and her father were New Hampshire bred and born), the town finalized an agreement with Miss Middleton. She would receive a monthly stipend, be provided room and board and would be free to visit her family or study during the summer. Dartmouth's response arrived a few weeks later adding fuel to a small but vocal anti-Dartmouth contingent.

One bit of information, had it been widely known, might have ended Miss Middleton's career in Craigmoor before it began. While she was born in New Hampshire, at age six after her parents died, she moved to the home of her maternal grandparents, John and Mary Ely, in Cambridge, Massachusetts. Her grandfather, a Professor in Harvard's History Department, held radical ideas. He believed women as intellectually capable as men and expected the women around him to discuss important issues knowledgably: his wife and granddaughter obliged. Professor Ely recognized that his intellectual qualities fully manifested in Amy and his pride in her bordered on sinful.

In late August 1855, Miss Amy Middleton arrived in Craigmoor bringing one suitcase of personal effects and a footlocker of books. The welcoming committee, including John, Mavis and Libby Whitman, took her to her lodgings at the home of Louise Putnam. Slim and short with dark curly hair never totally under her control, Amy's generous black eyebrows thinned only slightly across the top of her nose. She squinted through small, round, wire-framed spectacles. Poised and centered beyond her years, little escaped the gaze of Amy Middleton.

After securing her things in her room, Amy toured Craigmoor with Louise Putnam, Mavis and Libby. They stopped at Craigmoor's one-room schoolhouse. Amy moved gracefully around the building, touching the desks and windowsills, noting the welcoming flowers, scowling intently at the books, her lips pursed in a vague smile. What she thought that first day, she never revealed. At five o'clock she returned to the Putnam's home, thus beginning her new daily pattern.

· Craigmoor ·

Walking home up the hill, Mavis commented, "Miss Middleton seems very nice."

Libby, with honey-blond curls bouncing, looked serious. "She scowls sometimes."

"Oh, Libby. She has to concentrate to see. I'm sure you'll like her."

"Maybe," Libby muttered.

Libby led an orderly mid-nineteenth century life. She played, helped with chores in the house and the garden and learned from her family and the folks in town. Every night before bed, Mavis or John read to her, told her stories of Gram or other ancestors and then knelt in prayer. The prayer pattern came straight from Gram and always ended asking God to 'work in me, around me and through me every day and night.' A bright, headstrong, slightly introverted child, Libby didn't understand that last line at all.

After starting school, Libby decided Miss Middleton only looked severe. Miss Amy praised each child and used little corporal punishment as reduced privileges kept children in line. Libby avoided most censures. Bertie Jones, three years older than she, did not.

What you'd notice first about any of the Joneses were their eyes: intense, riveting, sky-blue, often laughing eyes. Matthew, with brown wavy hair, was the oldest followed by Rachel, a honey blond. Bertie, sporting a head of dark brown curls, came next and finally platinum-headed Rose. Despite hair color differences, their eyes bound them into a tight dynastic pedigree.

Libby and Rose were the same age and shared a special friendship. Both had blond curly hair; Rose's platinum color contrasted with Libby's warm golden hues and Libby's blue eyes carried deep, warm undertones.

Dependable and wise, Matthew embodied the perfect qualities for a first-born son. The tallest Jones, Matt's shy smile won him friends easily; he studied hard and planned to be a doctor. Rachel was a sweet, bright, gangly, yet reserved, young girl. Her path seemed vague but the deep affection she shared with Toby Wills provided a solid base for her future. Bertie had his father's darker hair. A smart, clever third-child, he laughed, joked, teased and charmed his way into people's hearts. If there was mischief to be done, Bertie did it. Trouble to be found? He found it. With natural ease he tended the cows, horses, chickens, geese, orchards, and fields of the Jones' Quail Hill farm three miles southwest of the town center. Bertie considered knowledge something to serve him not something for him to serve. No punishment deterred him from being true to himself. Any sick or wounded animal took precedence over any book. Miss Middleton used, rather than fought, his natural skills. During his years at school, he fixed things that broke, built what the school needed, caught frogs for science and cleaned privies. He flirted outrageously with all females: except Libby Whitman. In truth, she was the only female he wanted to charm. One look into her serious blue eyes knotted his stomach and interrupted his breathing. Then he'd do awkward and foolish things he'd later regret.

Libby thought him cute and clever if a bit silly. With Rose Jones her best friend, Bertie automatically occupied a special place in her life.

Rose, with beauty matching her name, flirted easily. Her soft curls framed her face and her blue eyes pulled down beguilingly at the outside corners. She appeared interested in the boys who buzzed around her but, deep in her heart, she knew what she wanted.

Through the hard winters and hot summers that punctuated life in Craigmoor, both the Whitmans and the Joneses fared well. Several times diseases ripped mysteriously through town leaving pain and sorrow behind before vanishing like summer squalls. Mavis gave birth to a son, John, in 1858. Libby loved taking care of him. She also liked helping Miss Middleton teach at school and wondered about becoming a teacher.

Mavis, Miss Middleton and Libby spoke often about Colby Junior College. By the time Libby turned 13, John and Mavis had begun college savings funds for both their children. Mavis became pregnant again in 1864 when Johnny was six and Libby fourteen. The baby was due in November and, by mid July, Mavis felt worried. Pain and weakness in her back and legs plagued her. She looked gaunt. Sleep eluded her. Demon dreams pursued her. One day she handed Margaret four letters addressed simply 'John,' 'Libby,' 'Johnny,' and 'Mother and Dad.'

"Don't be negative," Margaret scoffed.

"Prudent, Mother, I'm being prudent. If it's appropriate, burn them in the spring. If not," Mavis looked out the window, "deliver them when the time is right."

Margaret stuffed the letters into her apron pocket. Mavis had inherited Gram's tendency for foreknowledge: a tendency Margaret neither shared nor understood.

On a hot, sticky day in August as Johnny weeded the vegetable garden and Libby kneaded bread dough, Mavis went to gather eggs. On her way back she stopped at the pump-house for a cup of water. She gazed down the hill toward the center of town and the river. She stood quietly absorbed in this muggy peace, thinking of John, her children and their solid home and thanked God for all of it. Her understanding of God was of a source, a power that existed internally and externally—somewhat vague but real enough. Mavis remembered that Gram said God was 'transcendent' and that memory made her smile.

Putting down her cup, she stepped from the pump-house into the hot sunlight. Mavis doubled over, gasping and grasping her belly. Earlier discomfort became ripping, searing pain. She crumpled to the ground, eggs scattering on the flagstone path. Primitive, moaning sounds erupted from her throat as blood rushed from her body.

Identifying the sound's source, Johnny raced to the house.

"Libby, come quick," he shrieked. "Something terrible is wrong with Ma."

Libby wiped her flour-covered hands on her apron preparing to calm her somewhat overly dramatic brother. One look at his face and she rushed out the door. Seeing Mavis, she stopped, turned abruptly and grabbed Johnny by the shoulders.

"Johnny, go get Grandma and Mrs. Putnam fast. Then go to the bank and get Pa." Johnny raced off as Libby ran down the path and knelt by Mavis.

"I've sent Johnny for Grandma, Mrs. Putnam and Pa," Libby said with more control than she felt. At fourteen in 1864, Libby knew a lot about life, illness and tragedy. "What can I do?" Libby understood that, until someone with more experience arrived, only she could help her mother. She moved Mavis into the shade, loosened her clothes and removed her undergarments. Blood flowed everywhere.

Mavis knew neither she nor the baby would live. It was too early for the baby and blood pumped from her body too rapidly. She tried to remain focused as Gram and Margaret had taught her. The only choice she had left was how she would die: what legacy she would pass on to Libby. She faced this truth squarely: another gift from Gram. She shuddered and gasped for strength. The concern she had felt these past months crystallized here, on the ground, next to the pump-house. 'Foreknowledge,' Gram called this and it always came uninvited. Her strength ebbing, Mavis held onto Libby's arm.

Margaret rushed around the corner of the house and saw, in one agonizing instant, that her only daughter was dying. She moved Libby aside and delivered the small dead son. Wrapping him in her apron, she put him in Mavis' arms. She kissed her daughter's forehead.

"I love you Mama," Mavis smiled weakly.

Margaret sat back and fought for composure as Mavis gestured for Libby to lean down. "Oh Libby, I love you so much. Always remember that. Mind Margaret. Love and teach your children." Mavis' feather-soft voice continued. "Take care of Pa and Johnny." Calling on every last ounce of strength, she continued. "Don't be afraid, Libby. Love…" Whatever else she wanted to say drifted off in her final, gentle breath.

John, Mrs. Putnam and Johnny arrived minutes later. Mavis and the baby lay in the shade by the pump-house. Margaret knelt on the ground next to her daughter, holding Libby and rocking back and forth. A blue butterfly landed on a nearby flower. Johnny burst into tears and ran toward the barn.

3

Revisiting memories of her own mother's death, Amy Middleton knocked on the door of the Whitman house the evening she returned from her summer travels.

"I'm so sorry," she said as Margaret opened the door. The two women hugged briefly and then went to join John, Libby and Johnny on the back porch. Amy went to each, offering her sympathy, condolences.

Libby's tight shoulders visibly relaxed as Miss Middleton gently pulled her close. "You're here." Libby murmured. "You're finally here."

"Yes, I'm here," Amy said, smiling in her slightly squinting manner. "School will start soon. Things will never be the same without your Mother but you will survive this. I know because I survived when my parents died." They walked together toward the barn.

"Mama told me not to be afraid. I try but sometimes I'm scared."

Amy took off her glasses and rubbed the bridge of her nose. "Yes, you will be and you will learn to let go of the fear: not let it paralyze you."

Later, getting ready for bed, Libby replayed their brief conversation. She relaxed onto her pillow and slept.

The new school year brought many changes. Matthew Jones attended Dartmouth College and Bertie remained on the farm so they didn't see him much in town. Miss Middleton missed his joy. Libby worked hard and began to show signs of renewed strength; Rose learned easily and kept all the boys interested; Rachel remained a bit unfocused; Johnny stagnated.

Under Miss Middleton's leadership, most students flourished. Children experienced the pleasures of reading, writing, science, math and history. They learned at different speeds and different amounts but they all learned.

John Whitman invited his widowed sister, Helen, twelve years his senior, to return to Craigmoor to care for him and his children. The moment 'Aunt Helen' arrived, life brightened with the injection of her happiness and humor. Most townsfolk applauded her; only a few of the 'anti-anything faction' believed a clergy widow should not be so jolly. Aunt Helen remained centered and happy. Spiritual (but not 'churchie') she prayed deeply, listened for direction and followed where she felt led. Now, age 50, she belonged in Craigmoor.

Helen and Jeffery Wilson had had no children: a fact that had depressed and angered Helen. Like Jacob, she wrestled with this tormenting angel and emerged a stronger, more mature person. Her youthful willfulness transformed into a profound sense of wonder at the Creator/creature bond. For Helen, God no longer existed as some arbitrary figure 'out there' but as an internal force to live into and release to the world.

· Craigmoor ·

Initially, her role as a minister's wife had perplexed her. The wife of a retired bishop told her 'we become lightening rods for the petty concerns of many people and we are also upheld by much sincere prayer. Work. Love. Trust. Leave the rest to God.' The latter became Helen's motto. After Jeff died, she grieved thoroughly, closed that chapter of her life and moved on. She kept Jeff's *Book of Common Prayer*, his *Bible* and his copy of the *Koran*.

After moving to Craigmoor during Easter season in 1865, Aunt Helen applied her formula. She worked, loved, trusted and left the rest to God. She indicated her ideas to her brother and deferred to his decisions. She cooked well, sang to herself often and read to the children every night.

The night she arrived she listened carefully to Libby's prayers. Libby knelt by her bed and hurriedly told God she was glad to be alive, asked to be forgiven for being angry with Johnny, raced through a litany of "look-after-Grandma-and-Grandpa-and-Pa-and-Johnny-while-they-sleep-amen—and-also-Aunt-Helen-amen-again." No mention of Mavis or the baby: no 'God work in me around me and through me' that integral part of nightly prayers Margaret had told Helen about but which Libby dropped after Mavis died. Helen kissed Libby gently on the forehead and prayed silently for guidance.

Next she went to Johnny's room. He addressed God solemnly, asked forgiveness for a long list of sins and omissions, begged absolution for being so tardy in going for help for his Mother (explaining he ran as fast as he could), listed dozens of people who needed protection and blessing, building to an ultimate plea that God should "look after Mama and my dead brother. Amen." He dragged himself up, flopped into his bed—tears heavy in his eyes—and turned to face the wall. Helen patted his blond hair and said aloud "Holy God, bless Johnny and protect him this night and always. Amen."

Later, Helen analyzed the challenges; Libby grieved too little; Johnny grieved too much. The former might bury and seal over grief leaving a person unable to love authentically. The latter could draw a person's energy into maudlin self-absorption. Helen smiled and shook her head, musing about the infinite number of ways people break the first commandment. "Thou shalt have no Gods before me." Not your strength or your weakness, not money or power, not your grief or your joy, not your love or your hates, not your wisdom or your foolishness. Helen marveled at the energy people expended in refusing to relax into the simple reality of 'I AM.'

The next night she slipped to her knees beside Johnny and said, "Let's pray together. Holy and loving Lord…" She stopped and Johnny slowly repeated the phrase. "I love you and thank you for my life… I miss Mama and know you are taking care of her… and my baby brother… Thank you for the beautiful day… Forgive me for being mean to Libby today… Help me to be happy again… " To this last request, he did not reply; Helen repeated and waited. Slowly he repeated the phrase. "Send your Holy Spirit to work in me around me and through me… and send your angels to protect us as we sleep. Amen." Johnny stood, hugged Aunt Helen, crawled into bed and went to sleep without tears.

In Libby's room, Aunt Helen added a short prayer after Libby finished. "Dear Lord, you know what we need before we ask. Help us to pray the prayers we are too proud or too hurt or too angry or afraid to pray. Bless and protect Mavis and Libby's little brother. Work your will in, around and through us and protect us as we sleep. Amen." Tears slid down Libby's cheeks.

Helen found her brother reading at his desk. "John," she said quietly, "this is going to work." They smiled at each other, comfortable and relaxed together.

"I'm glad you are here, Helen."

She turned and headed upstairs.

"Thank you," he added softly. Helen smiled and shrugged.

With Helen present, the Whitman house needed more living space. John and Johnny were sharing John's room while Aunt Helen camped out in Johnny's room. The attic could be converted for Johnny's use. Since Bertie Jones could build anything, John sent a note to him via his sister Rose asking if the job interested him. The next day Bertie went to the bank and arranged the details with Mr. Whitman. Aunt Helen showed him the attic; he took measurements and sketched plans for the remodel. While working on the project, Bertie walked to town with Rose three mornings a week, worked all day and headed home at about 5:00. Staying that long made him late for some farm chores but insured that he would see Libby. He wanted the job, he wanted the money and he wanted to see Libby. They were friends but a new degree of self-consciousness developed between them. Libby often blushed when talking with Bertie and he became tongue tied in a not unpleasant way. Helen watched and smiled. Libby continued to study hard and insisted, perhaps too much, that she wanted to be a teacher.

By early June, the remodeling completed, Johnny moved to the new quarters and Bertie collected his last payment from Mr. Whitman. After depositing most of the money into his newly opened bank account, he walked home whistling happily. Now 18, with money in the bank, he let a plan grow in his heart.

Helen, Libby and Johnny worked the Whitman kitchen garden.

"Lots of cultivating," Johnny, now nine, said. "Give the seeds good soil and they will break their shells and grow." Aunt Helen agreed, stood and stretched her back. "I picture the garden when I hold the seeds," Johnny added, "see the food we'll have by August." He still avoided the pump-house.

One day when Libby and Aunt Helen pumped water, Libby blurted out, "Childbirth scares me but I don't have to worry. Most teachers don't marry or have children." She grabbed the bucket of water, tuned and abruptly strode to the house.

Helen watched her niece's straight, defiant posture as she charged away. 'Certainly teaching's a fine goal,' she mused, 'but it'd be a shame for Libby to avoid marriage out of fear.'

Two days later, as Margaret and Helen sat on the porch shelling peas, Helen recounted the conversation.

"I remember feeling some fear when I was Libby's age but I've never had a child so anything I say won't count for much. I'm hoping you'll talk to her."

Margaret replied softly, "Yes, I will. Most girls have concerns about childbirth and of course for Libby…" Margaret paused and sighed. "Mavis had a premonition. She wrote some letters and gave them to me. I've not read them. Can't give them to John and the children, either. The time's never right, never will be.

"Before you came I feared you might take the children from me: usurp my role. You haven't. You include Richard and me and I thank you," she pulled the letters from her pocket and continued haltingly, "Helen, I'm helpless with these. Please take them, give them to John or you and John decide…" her voice trailed off.

Helen reached across the table and squeezed Margaret's arm gently and took the letters. "I'll deal with them, Margaret. Johnny and Libby need all of us."

After supper, Helen gave John the letters Mavis had written. He read his letter alone at his desk and an hour later rejoined the family on the porch. He looked relaxed, his eyes direct.

4

Saturday morning, John gave the children their letters.

"Mama was worried so she wrote to each of us. Nobody has read your letters. They are yours. What happens to them is up to you." He hugged Libby and patted Johnny on the head.

Libby fingered the envelope briefly before heading for the barn. After climbing to her 'special place' in the hayloft and opening the big window above the main barn doors, she settled herself in a sunny spot being careful not to sit on any newborn kittens mother cat might have buried in the hay. Libby started to read as mama cat dug three kittens from their hiding places, groomed and nursed them.

· Quail Hill ·

July 10, 1864

Dear Libby,

I'm very proud of you and grateful that you are my daughter. I love you more than I can say, more than you will know until you have your own children. You are a strong and loving young woman.

Sometimes we get moody and cross with each other. That's just the way people are; we hurt each other; it's part of living. Don't worry too much about it. Try not to be afraid; fear saps your strength. You won't always succeed but keep trying. When you feel angry or are surprised, wait before you respond. Speaking and acting too quickly can lead to harsh words and regret. Focus on being loving even when it's difficult. Gram used to say, "If you keep moving toward the light, darkness won't be able to catch you."

Your Grandma Margaret's a wonderful strong woman, a source of wisdom and support. Listen to her and Pa. He's special, too. Sometimes he's so quiet you need to listen with your eyes. Don't let his silence exasperate you; that's who he is. Ask him questions when you need to. Love Johnny a lot; he will need you.

Gram said we are each sent to life for a reason and we need to find that reason. Decisions are real. Marrying John Whitman is the best decision I ever made. I've never regretted it and I do not regret it now. Make your decisions carefully and live happily with the consequences.

You come from a long line of strong people, Libby. Remember that. Your ancestors lived through great adversity; you have that strength within you. Develop your talents. Use your gifts. Laugh and love and be joyful. Pass this on to your children, grandchildren and great-grandchildren. Life will not always be easy. It isn't meant to be.

Remember that I love you very, very much and that my love will always surround you.

Mother

Libby put the letter in her pocket and settled deeper into the hay. She turned her face to the warm sunlight. Mother cat purred loudly licking her kittens as they crawled all over each other, eyes closed, mewing softly. The cat stood, arched her back, rearranged her babies, rubbed against Libby's arm and curled up in her lap. Libby scratched her idly. 'You come from a long line of strong people. Remember that.'

Libby took a deep, slow breath, lay back and closed her eyes. Some of the fear she had carried over the last year fell away slowly like the two tears that ran down her cheeks. Libby felt surrounded by Mavis' love. She remembered Miss Middleton's visit last summer, how she felt better after that, how Aunt

Helen helped her pray again. She dozed thinking about Pa, Grandma, Grandpa, Johnny and her friends. As the cat stood and walked off, Libby jerked awake, got up and brushed hay from her skirt. Walking calmly down the stairs, Libby felt the protective shell she had built around her heart over the past year crack open and begin to fall away. With a new lightness and purpose in her step, Libby returned to the house.

After reading his letter, Johnny said Ma told him to be good and help with the chores. He became somber for a day or two.

On the anniversary of Mavis' death, the family went to the cemetery and placed fresh flowers on the grave. Libby pulled some weeds as John looked quietly at the new headstone. Johnny stood with them briefly before he ran off searching for older graves. Helen thanked God and Mavis for the healing that had begun.

Later in the afternoon, when Richard and Margaret visited the cemetery, they sat silently fingering the flowers left earlier: flowers already wilting.

"It isn't right," Richard sighed, "Mavis dying before us. But it's what is."

He took Margaret's hand; they walked to town together moving slowly, their backs bent.

5

During 1865, following General Lee's surrender to General Grant on April 9th, many Craigmoor men returned from war carrying scars in either body or mind. Most men got on with their lives. Some did not return. One of those was Toby Wills, Rachel Jones' beau.

That July in Cambridge, while Amy was visiting her grandparents during the summer vacation from school, shipping returned to normal bringing Mary Ely's nephew (thus Amy Middleton's cousin) Frederick, now Captain, Russell, home to Boston for the first time in years. Two days after sending word that 'I acquired an interesting small book in my recent travels,' he arrived for dinner. The Elys, Amy Middleton and Frederick used this newly acquired work as the focal point of their dinner table conversation. Over the years, the family had spent happy evenings pouring over the manuscripts Frederick acquired. They exchanged ideas and discussed his adventures in the Mediterranean, Africa, India and the far reaches of the Americas. Amy and her cousin shared the Russell family's dark, curly, out-of-control hair, slight builds, intense concentration and great love of books and learning. For this reunion he arrived carrying a bottle of brandy, a tin of tea from Assam and a small, recent English translation of the *Bhagavad-Gita: The Song Celestial*. Professor Ely knew of the *Gita* but did not own a copy.

"The book came to me while I was in Calcutta—a beautiful city—as I tried to hunt down elusive Holy-men who are studying Christianity and Islam as well as Hinduism looking for similarities. I had difficulty finding them. Someone always knew someone who knew someone who might know something," he chuckled, sighed and softly muttered the single word: "India." Sitting forward and looking intently at the Elys and Amy, he continued. "One evening a young boy named Gopal came up to me said 'Follow me. I know who. Come.' For some reason I trusted this lad and followed him down twisted, winding streets, enveloped in the spicy aromas of cooking. Finally, he led me into a dark room in a tidy house. There, seated cross-legged on a tiger skin, his own skin shining like bronze in the light of the oil lamp, sat a small, straight, motionless swami. My guide prostrated himself at the feet of the old man and then left silently. Someone brought me a chair. When my eyes adjusted, I could see others people meditating around the room. On an altar, lamplight flickered onto carved shapes: some human, some animal and a multi-armed dancing female: strange, delicate Hindu figures. Flowers and incense perfumed the space. My breathing was all I heard until someone began chanting. Gradually, the room filled with the voices of these men: eerie, repetitive phrases sung to hypnotic melodies on and on. I closed my eyes. Immediately I felt surrounded by a warm, golden light that fluctuated with the music. Surprised, but not frightened, by this 'bliss'—that's the best word for it—I sat there for what felt like ten minutes.

"Later, I realized the chanting had stopped and the swami and I were alone. He smiled at me, nodded and said, 'I'm glad you've come. I've been expecting you. I hope you will like this.' He patted to a small package beside him. 'Now I must go. Gopal will lead you back to your ship.' He held his hands together before his heart, bowed to me, smiled and left."

Russell took a sip of brandy and continued. "The boy reappeared and handed the package to me. I asked, 'What's this?' He replied, 'book for you from Swami-ji.' 'Do I pay?' He shrugged. 'No matter,' responded Gopal as he headed out the door. I placed some money on the floor and hurriedly followed the child as we retraced our route in the early dawn light."

Captain Russell became pensive. "In India, things like this happen. In India…" his voice trailed off. He finished his brandy and stood to leave. "You'll enjoy the book. It seems to be about war. It is and it isn't. Before Gopal left me he said 'Swami-ji said to tell you the book is about the inside of a man, the inside of all men everywhere.' Then he disappeared into early morning swarm of merchants on the dock.

"On my return voyage I read it and I find it both intriguing and puzzling. I need the mind of a History Professor to help me understand it, or maybe a Swami." He chuckled softly. "But you, Uncle John, are easier to find." After fond farewells, Russell slipped out into the night and sailed within the week.

Amy and her grandparents all read the *Gita* during the two weeks they spent relaxing on Cape Cod. The *Gita*, they learned, is a 700-verse section of a much longer text: the *Mahabharata*. Reading the translator's beautiful words, they tried to unravel what the main characters, Krishna and Arjuna, were discussing. Some of the ideas seemed familiar but they were clothed in India's strange, multi-layered culture. The young guide's words reverberated in their minds: 'The book is about the inside of a man, the inside of all men everywhere.' Grandpa Ely gave Amy the *Bhagavad-Gita* when she left to return to Craigmoor in August.

6

Three miles south of town, the Jones' Farm on Quail Hill progressed in both unique and normal ways during the summer of 1865. 'Unique' as the last summer all four Jones children worked the farm together. Matthew would go to the Massachusetts Medical College of Harvard University that fall and would live with the Elys in Cambridge. 'Normal' because weather, crops, insects, chores and livestock dominated their lives. Late evenings after sunset the family sat on the porch, resting, telling stories and reminiscing about life on this hill.

Ma and Pa Jones along with Pa's two bachelor brothers and one old maid sister bought the farm in 1840. The neat white farmhouse with its green front door stood directly across the road from the main barn. A black walnut tree grew slightly up the hill between them. The original two-room house had been enlarged twice with living space and once with a huge storage/workroom. The privy could now be reached by crossing through the workroom without going outside for more than a few yards—a blessing during hard winters. A large vegetable garden, chicken coops, orchards and pasture-land nudged to the edge of forests that tried to invade this hard-won section of hillside. At the back of the house, to the south, the land fell sharply in a steep hillside covered with blueberry bushes and brambles to the river far below. Further up hill, Pa's two brothers and his sister lived in a second, smaller house.

One afternoon, Pa stood in the barn looking down over the pastures and orchards watching Matt and Bertie leaning on the fence, talking. Pa smiled knowing that he, Ma and his family had reared these strong young men. Whistling softly, he went in to start milking.

7

"Harvest and canning," Libby sighed, wiping her face with a towel, "it's unfair, these pots boiling in hottest weather."

"I agree," Grandma Margaret replied. "After this batch of tomatoes, we'll take a break." They worked on the porch preparing the fruits and vegetables, close to the kitchen but away from the stove: any slight breeze up from the river brought welcome relief.

The long, arduous job of 'putting up' the summer harvest demanded careful, precise work: living through the winter depended on it. Mothers taught daughters these all-important lessons. Labor divided predictably between the sexes but survival depended on everyone.

After removing eight quarts of tomatoes from the boiling 'water bath' and placing them on the drain-board to cool, Margaret and Libby went to sit under the big maple tree in the back yard close to the pump house.

"It's been a difficult year," Margaret said gently.

Libby nodded. "Were you scared before you had babies?"

"Maybe a little, but happy, too. Does that idea scare you, Libby?"

"Sometimes I think if Mama'd been a teacher she wouldn't have died."

"And you wouldn't exist." Margaret watched her granddaughter closely.

"I know and that confuses me." Libby lay back on the grass.

"You know Libby, your Mama was like Gram. Sometimes they just knew things. I don't understand it. The things they 'knew' never frightened them, they'd just 'know' or 'sense' something. Your Mama wrote those letters. 'Just being prudent' that's what she said. She wasn't afraid. She wouldn't want you to be afraid."

Libby sat up. "In Mama's letter to me she mentioned my children. Is that something she 'knew'?"

Margaret shrugged. "Do you want children?"

Libby smiled faintly and said, "Whether I marry, <u>that</u> I can probably 'want' or 'decide'—if anyone asks. But having children either happens or not." She became serious. "I think about teaching: sometimes 'yes,' sometimes 'no.' Living without family around, I'm not sure I want that. But I don't need to decide till I'm seventeen." Libby stood, wiped grass from her skirt and headed for the house. "We'd better do more canning," she said.

Margaret watched Libby and decided 'she's surviving pretty well.' Rising slowly, she followed her granddaughter into the kitchen.

In early October, Patsy Hamilton married Ralph Ridgeway on a bright fall afternoon and all Craigmoor celebrated. After the bridal couple left the church,

Libby stood by the church door in the shade. Turning slowly, she saw Bertie Jones, leaning on the fence, hands in his pockets, right foot crossed over his left. He looked directly at her. Their eyes met; neither smiled, moved, or in any way acknowledged the other. Looking at each other, seconds melted into 'no-time' and 'all-time,' a strange, paralyzed, slow motion world dominated by the clear penetrating gaze of Bertie's intense blue eyes.

Two small boys in pursuit of a frolicking puppy, brushed by Libby's long skirt spinning her around, almost knocking her to the ground. Rose walked past calling, "Come on, Libby, Patsy's throwing her bouquet." Libby followed her friend. Bertie moved away from the fence and joined the crowd. Neither girl caught the bouquet.

Later, Bertie walked up to Libby and said, "Hi. How's school?"

"Fine. How's the farm?" Libby replied.

"It's good. I love it there. You should come see the fall colors."

As they talked, Libby searched Bertie's eyes. 'What happened back there? Had it only happened to her?' Libby wondered.

"You and Aunt Helen should come visit Ma. She writes poetry," he said thinking his voice too loud, his sleeves too short. Looking into Libby's eyes, he could hardly breathe.

"I don't know your Ma well."

"She doesn't come to town much. She's shy like me," he laughed a nervous laugh. "We just like looking out over the valley."

Before leaving the wedding festivities, they planned a picnic for next Sunday afternoon that would include the Whitmans, Margaret, Richard, Miss Middleton and Louise Putnam.

After church, the older adults piled into the Whitman's wagon and headed for Quail Hill; the younger folks walked. They enjoyed the vibrant fall colors, the rushing water of the river and the easy clop, clop, clop as the horse plodded along. Three miles out of town they turned onto the lane that led up to the Jones' farm. It perched a half mile above the valley. Libby had never been to the farm during the height of fall colors. Breathtaking vistas surrounded them.

The Jones family, including dogs and cats, greeted them. Pa and the men toured the buildings, fields and orchards as the women headed for the kitchen. The cows and horses were in the pastures so the children scooted in and out of the empty stalls of the milking areas. Rachel, Rose and Bertie showed where they had each carved their initials on the boards of the third horse stall. Libby and Rose went to the orchard to gather apples for pies. When they entered the house they were greeted by the sweet aroma of bread baking and chicken frying combined with the women's talk and laughter. Libby put the apples on the washboard and gazed out the window, past the vegetable garden, beyond the blueberry patch, to the valley below.

"That's why I love it here," Ma Jones remarked, standing next to Libby. "Except for the isolation and whiteouts in winter, looking out that way to the south always cheers me." She looked at Libby, continuing, "I figure it's a fair price. Now you two go join the others."

With Matthew in Cambridge, Bertie and Rachel led the tour for Johnny and Libby. They ended by gathering bruised apples for the horses and cattle and then entered the main pasture through the southwest gate. Four horses ambled up the sloping field, toward the two big flat rocks midway down the hill. Bertie whistled and Big Red picked up the pace, trotted up and nuzzled Bertie's arm. Rachel, Rose and Johnny went to see the cows.

Bertie fed Big Red an apple and leaned against his right flank. "What do you think?" he asked Libby.

"It's more beautiful than you could ever describe," she replied.

He grinned. "Ma tries to catch it in poems. She comes close. Trouble is, you try to put it in words and words are smaller than the experience or the place."

"That's beautiful," Libby said softly.

Bertie blushed, pushed himself away from his horse and said, "No, Libby Whitman, that's just words. Now you," he said looking directly into her eyes, "you are beautiful." He turned and jogged up the hill calling over his shoulder, "Come on. You'll miss dinner."

Libby wiped her hands nervously on her skirt, her heart pounding and cheeks blushing. They joined the group at the house and helped arrange plates of food. Only Ma Jones noticed the high color on the young couple's faces. She pursed her lips to hide a smile. Later she wrote a brief poem called 'A Perfect Autumn Afternoon.'

Tree branches waving outside her window cast shadows across Libby's bed. She awoke with a start, heart pounding. Snatches of her dream lingered. Bertie and children stood on a hill separated from her by a big ditch. She stood by a schoolhouse watching them. Bertie picked up the smallest girl, comforting her as she sobbed.

Libby walked to the window, her skin luminous in the moonlight. Flowers in the garden bobbed in the breeze making eerie dancing-patterns on the grass. Initially everything looked gray and white. Then, gradually, soft pastel hues emerged. Libby remembered Bertie's eyes.

8

Rachel graduated in the spring of '65 leaving Rose the only Jones attending Craigmoor School. Rose and Libby studied hard and assisted Miss Middleton in the classroom. Both girls matured, becoming more focused as they helped teach. Miss Middleton watched them closely. Then one cold, slippery Friday afternoon in November, on her way to the Putnam's, Amy fell injuring her back, right hip and leg. No one saw her fall nor found her for 20 minutes. Carried to her bed and tended by the local nurse, she asked to see John Whitman. He came as soon as summoned.

"I'll not be teaching for some time," Miss Middleton said, clenching her teeth against pain, "but Libby and Rose, with help, can take over. They should check with me everyday and townsfolk can provide the needed adult presence. That's the plan I came up with lying on the icy path." She squinted up at him. "It should work."

John smiled. "We were wise to hire you. I'll consult the board. Now you rest."

The only snag in the plan played out up on Quail Hill.

"It'll mean extra work for everyone if you go live in town and teach, Rosie," Pa said. "With Matt gone, we work hard enough. Let Libby teach if she wants to."

Ma, who'd been quiet, asked, "Rosie, what do you want?"

"I want to, Ma. Libby and I've been helping so we know a little. I love teaching. It feels natural to me. It's what I've always wanted to do, all I've ever wanted to do. This may be my only chance. Miss Middleton believes I'd be a good teacher and I want to try." She stood, arrow-straight, looking into her Mother's eyes, not daring to look at Pa.

"Pa and I'll talk about it," Ma stated simply.

At that, Bertie stood and motioned to his sisters. "Come on," he said in a compelling tone and they hurried out; the old screen door slammed behind them.

"I don't like it. Rose is our youngest," Pa's jaws clamped together hard.

"I know you don't," Ma replied softly.

"I wouldn't mind if it were Rachel. It'd be real nice if it were Rachel. Since Toby died she's so lost," he mused wistfully.

"True enough," Ma reflected, "almost like the bullet that killed Toby left shrapnel in her heart, too." Ma paused. "Rachel takes good care of things, she's sweet and bright enough, but she's not a teacher—saying that isn't meanness. She's a good, loving girl: a bit unfocused. The plan for her will work out but, for now, she's with us here on the farm and happy to be. Rose is different. Not just being the youngest but just different. She wants more, like Matt. Rose keeps trying to reach out, expand and we shouldn't pen her in."

Pa glared at her. "Are you and Miss Amy whipping up some 'let's send Rose to college' plan? If so, I don't like it."

"There's no plan from me, but if Rose wants teaching, why not? Why'd we spend our lives working so hard if not to advance this family, make it better? Besides, what we're talking about is only for a few weeks and she'll be home weekends. Louise Putnam has plenty of extra room for Rose to stay there. Bertie and Rachel are both here fulltime and can handle the chores." Ma watched her husband carefully.

He pursed his lips and sighed. "You're an honest, clearheaded woman. But don't go graduating Rosie from some teacher's college quite so fast." He pushed back from the table, "I give my permission for this but nothing else," he leaned heavily on his rough hands as he stood.

Ma watched him go, sharing his confusion. He wanted the children to follow him on the farm. Bertie would, Ma knew, maybe Rachel, not Matt and maybe not Rose. It tore the heart to let a child go. Images of their life and her love for this man flipped through her mind as the clock on the shelf chimed the hour.

Miss Middleton's plan for Craigmoor's school began Monday morning.

9

21 November 1865

Dearest Amy,

Grandma and I are distressed to hear of your injury. How we would love to have you here so we could care for you. That said, Matthew's professors concur you need to remain quiet, rest, and heal. (Matthew is well regarded here both by us and by his professors.)

Your reflections on teaching delight me. The most important offering we make is ourselves: not what we know but who we are. How to think, what is important, and how to determine what is important are the qualities our students—as future citizens—need. Minds fail as rapidly by being fossilized with facts as by being adrift with no information. Sailing on the Cape teaches the need for proper balance between sail and centerboard. As your NH farmers might say: fertilize the plants and pull the weeds. Alas, some of my strengths exist entwined in my weaknesses creating a dilemma: how to kill the weeds without destroying the crop. For both yourself and your students, remain vigilant.

Now to the Gita. Fascinating. I find the hints that similarities exist among religions quite hopeful even while the differences appear stark. When Krishna and Arjuna discuss the battle I recall Jesus turning away the tempter. The real struggle is within and needs to be addressed there. Not only must our evil aspects be overcome but our good qualities need to be transcended, too. The Gita instructs us to pull back from the 'pairs of opposites,' the 'twin snares of like and dislike.' Challenging ideas.

Emerson and Walt Whitman point toward a fresher look so a few flickers of a more Universal Truth exist. We need to re-seek the profound, transformative experience of religion rather than settle for the forms that have developed and often strangle. More weeds!

Amy, dear, recover. Grandma and I are well, rattling around with cook, the other helpers and our five boarders in this huge old house: our comings and goings quite normal.

With best love,

Grandpa Ely

Amy smiled, folded the letter and put it with the *Gita* in her bedside table drawer. Adjusting her position, she began checking Libby's workbook.

10

As the schoolhouse door closed behind the final student, Rose turned to Libby and snarled, "We're here to teach not to just tell them the answers."

"I AM teaching," Libby replied indignantly. "They ask and I tell them. What's so wrong with that? All you do is keep asking them questions and they get more confused."

"No, they don't! They learn!" Rose retorted.

"I'm going to ask Miss Middleton because I think you're wrong." Libby scooped up her notebooks and headed for the door.

"Fine. She'll say I'm right." They exited and marched in silence toward the Putnam's.

Amy sat up straighter as the two young teachers stormed into her room. Sizing up the tension between them she said cheerfully, "How are both of you today? Anything interesting at school?" They stood, looking at the floor, breathing hard. "Come on. Tell me."

"Libby just tells them everything and isn't teaching. She never makes them figure things out." Rose spat the words.

"Libby, do you agree?"

"When they ask, I give them the answer, that's what they want so that's what I do and then they're happy and have learned." Defiance dripped from the final word.

"So, Rose, what do you want her to do differently?" Miss Middleton relaxed.

"I want her to lead the children, to help them figure things out, discover answers."

"Does that always work for you?"

"No, but usually they get closer to the answer."

"And sometimes, do you tell them?" Miss Middleton prodded gently.

"Yes," Rose acknowledged, "but it's better when I don't."

"Umm," Miss Middleton mused, "Libby, what subjects do you like best?"

Confused, Libby responded, "Aren't we talking about teaching?"

"We are: teaching and learning are two sides of a coin. Now, what subjects do you like best and why?"

"Math and science, and you know that. Because math is precise and science is orderly and inter-connected and you can know what you know."

"And you, Rose, same question."

"Literature and history," came the reply, "because they make me imagine other outcomes: what else could have been."

"Different students. Different preferences. Maybe different ways of teaching?"

"Isn't there a right way?" Libby sounded confused.

"There're many good ways. What you're doing works sometimes. Rose's way works a lot. It depends on the student, the subject, sometimes the time you have available."

"Then how do you know what to do?" implored Libby.

"That's what teaching's about. Sometimes you succeed. Sometimes you fail. But keep learning from your students. Watch them. Listen to what they say, look at their eyes. Respond to each one individually. Be very present for your students: yet a bit detached."

"I'm not sure I want to do that," Libby said softly.

"This is a time to try it out, see if you like it." Amy sank back onto her pillow, removed her glasses and rubbed her eyes. "I'd better rest a bit before supper."

As the girls left the room, Libby said, "You're right."

"We're both right. And wrong to fight," Rose replied.

Mrs. Putnam spent the next morning at school. That afternoon, she brought Amy tea.

"Mrs. Putnam, how are things going at school?" Amy asked.

"About the same," Louise Putnam replied, fluffing a pillow. "Libby gives them the answers and hugs them. Rose asks them questions, smiles, pats them on the head with her 'I know you can do this' look."

Amy laughed. "You have just summed them up in two sentences."

Louise smiled. "I'm a busy woman," she said, pouring tea.

11

15 December 1865

My dearest Amy,

We're pleased you are recovering rapidly. Your two young teachers will progress under your guidance. Truth be known, one can only begin where a student actually is. I often say, 'Before preparing for a journey, know where you want to go but also know exactly where you are.' Many overlook this critical detail.

Don't fret that Libby's desire for teaching may be inappropriate for her. Having this experience provides an unmatched opportunity to discover her true talents. The young are amazingly resilient and able to channel energy into new ventures. If our Hindu brothers and sisters are correct (for me a big IF), she'll have all the opportunities her soul needs to learn the lessons she must learn.

Speaking of Hinduism, the Gita's beauty haunts me though I'm not altogether comfortable within it. The parts seem bizarre, the whole sound. I glimpse powerful Unity within the disparate offerings. Strange. The Bible presents Jesus saying 'let those who have eyes, see; those with ears, hear.' Things I see and hear as I venture into Eastern Religions seem unusual, yet true. Often I pull back, retreating into the safety of my known, thus comfortable, culture. But life calls us to seek, to dare, to expand and grow—so I move forward cautiously.

Your last letter hints that you are a bit frustrated by Craigmoor's generally conservative character. Tension always exists between the forces pushing the boundaries for more freedom and the forces maintaining order. Society should avoid both chaos and inflexibility. There is a Chinese proverb something like this: 'It is impossible to open a door so little that only good comes in.' There's wisdom here yet I don't endorse the status quo for its own sake.

I ramble -- a vice of professors, a prerogative of age.

Warmest love,

Grandpa Ely

Amy read the letter sitting in a chair in her room. She would return to school in January. Rose and Libby worked as a team now, each using her natural skills and working to broaden and diversify her abilities. Both students showed growth though differences separated them.

During one meeting Libby blurted out, "Miss Middleton, I'm not sure I should be a teacher." Libby sat, back straight, hands folded in her lap, staring at a point on the floor midway between them. Amy studied her carefully.

"There are many reasons to teach: many kinds of teachers. Why are you wondering?"

Libby shrugged. "Rose is better. I get frustrated by my own," she searched for the right word, "intensity maybe: or bad habits. I loved the idea of teaching. After Mama died, I studied hard and I do love studying and helping you, but real teaching's been different."

"How 'different'?" Amy watched and listened.

"I want the children to understand and be happy. I can't switch like you and Rose can, teaching this way, teaching that way. I want to spend lots of time with each child. For me, learning's easy but teaching's hard. Johnny says I get like a dog scratching a flea: 'here is the answer, learn it.' I'm not sure I'd be very good all alone with a whole classroom to myself. It's a big responsibility and it feels lonely."

"The life of teaching can be lonely but there are many rewards." Miss Middleton took off her glasses and rubbed her eyes. "I need to qualify that because some of the rewards are subjective and personal. We're all different when it comes to what gives us satisfaction." She put her glasses back on. "Have you talked to Aunt Helen, your father, your grandparents?"

"Aunt Helen says go to college and then decide. Papa says if I go, I should teach. Grandma's quiet. Grandpa would probably say 'follow your strengths.' He says that a lot."

"It's good advice," Amy responded. "The issue, then, is to define your strengths and decide what will use them best. For now, relax. You are teaching well and you and Rose together form a splendid team. We'll talk again later."

"You always know what to say," Libby replied, smiling.

"Not always. But I've good instincts and I'm well trained. And teaching is my life."

12

Rose and Miss Middleton sat down to talk after they finished dinner one evening the week before Christmas. Rose's flushed face and tightly clenched hands demonstrated unusual nervousness. Amy sat back and relaxed.

"Miss Middleton, I want to be a teacher. I've thought about it for years and now I know: I want to teach. Not just while you're recovering but always."

Amy smiled. "You'd be an excellent teacher: one of the best." Amy knew that Rose, with her beauty, would face challenges that Amy, with plain looks and glasses, never experienced. "You'll need three things: determination, your parents' permission and money."

"I've written to Matt and he supports me: said he'd help with Ma and Pa and suggested some schools."

Amy remembered Matt fondly: her favorite and most successful student. "Getting his cooperation will help, but getting your parents' permission may not be easy. My encouraging both boys and girls to consider college hasn't been well received by some folks here."

"Ma probably knows what I want. If I find out more about some schools, about costs, know more details before I bring the subject up, I'll have a better chance."

"Yes, but don't go behind your parents' backs. I doubt your father would take well to that. I'll write to Grandpa Ely. He'll have suggestions and knows about scholarships."

Over the next few months, Rose studied information about five colleges as Amy updated her files: Colby in New London, New Hampshire; Green Mountain in Poultney, Vermont; Bradford in Bradford, Massachusetts; Elmira in Elmira, New York; and Massachusetts State Teachers College for Women in Framingham, Massachusetts. Rose decided that Massachusetts State Teachers College for Women in Framingham, with its emphasis on teaching and proximity to Matt and the Elys, was the best. There were scholarships listed and, unbeknownst to Rose, Professor and Mrs. Ely had volunteered financial support. Rose, with Matt's agreement, planned to put this information before her parents during his two-week visit in mid-summer.

Miss Middleton returned to teaching in mid January 1866; Rose moved back to Quail Hill and both girls continued assisting. Rose focused hard on teaching; she watched Miss Middleton carefully, adapted her techniques and scanned the whole room often. Libby relaxed, spent more time with each child and, by concentrating on a specific child, felt less overwhelmed by the general classroom responsibilities. Both girls noted the change in the other's behavior but they did not discuss this. Their lives centered in their families, their common experience of teaching and the futures they faced. Life required order, purpose and discipline; these values provided both the foundations and fences they learned growing up in Craigmoor.

At home, Rose focused long and hard on teaching. One by one she let go of things she would not have: husband, children, home. By May, she was certain of her decision.

The girls continued to meet regularly with Miss Middleton and one spring day Rose told Libby her plan as they sat on the Putnam's front steps. Libby wasn't surprised. "Part of me wants to be angry and part of me wants to go with you. But it won't work for me. I'm not fed by teaching, by the classroom, like you and Miss Middleton are." They sat in silence. "But I'm glad for you and hope your Ma and Pa agree. Girls should go to college if they want to." Libby kicked the dust with her shoe. "Oh, Rosie, what am I going to do?" she wailed.

Rose's mouth dropped open as she blurted out, "You mean you don't know?"

Libby slowly shook her head. "Libby, your life is here in Craigmoor. And," she added putting her nose about twelve inches from her friend's face, "everybody sees your life-plan except you. I hope you figure it out!" Rose laughed, "Race you back to school," she shouted as she gathered up her skirts, ready to run. Libby ground her feet into the dirt, grabbed up her skirt and dashed forward. How dare Rose imply her life was all planned before she made decisions, Libby thought angrily. The two young women tore down the street—their legs wrestling with their long skirts—flew around the corner and into the schoolyard. They reached the school steps dead even: breathing heavily, hearts racing. Rose watched Libby's stubborn strength flare out like steam escaping from a rapidly boiling pot. Rose knew only one person could harness that.

During Matt's two-week visit in late June, the Jones family discussed Rose's desire to go to college. Ma brought up the most arguments and objections. Because Rose had prepared well, had identified funding, and had Matt's support, Ma then supported the decision. Pa ranted a bit; he felt squeezed by history's momentum. Bertie didn't like the idea. Rachel encouraged Rose to take this opportunity. After the decision was made, Matt would inform the Elys and Miss Middleton when he returned to Cambridge on July 5.

On the morning of July 4th, Rachel and Rose stood by the pasture fence and Rose said, "Thanks for supporting me Rachel. I promise, when you know what you want, I'll support you, too." Neither sister could understand the implications of that promise.

13

Banners proclaiming 'Live Free or Die' hung across Main Street for the 4th of July celebrations. By noon, everyone gathered in town for games, races and picnics.

Each unmarried girl 16 years and older provided a picnic for two to be auctioned to the town's bachelors and the proceeds went to the fund to build a memorial for those who died in the war. In theory, no one was supposed to know which girl went with which picnic; in practice, everybody did.

Rachel's picnic sold to Myron Gordon, a close friend of Toby's who shared her grief. Chuck Bradley, home from Dartmouth and a good friend, bought Rose's basket. Two bidders drove Libby's picnic to a respectable level while Bertie stood in the back, hands in his pockets, saying nothing, just watching the auctioneer and bidders. George Wentworth, the high bidder, smiled smugly. As the auctioneer raised his gavel, proclaiming loudly, "Going once…"

Bertie raised his hand and doubled the bid. The crowd gasped; Libby blushed; Rachel started laughing. Ma Jones chuckled, "Like father like son!"

The auctioneer's hand stopped in mid-air, "Did I hear you right?"

" 'Spect so," Bertie said ambling toward the table displaying the picnics. He flashed his famous smile, shrugged his shoulders and asked, "Hasn't anybody ever seen a hungry farmer?"

The crowd burst into laughter; a few applauded. As the couples wandered away to eat their picnics, Libby kept her eyes lowered. They settled onto a secluded bench by a grape arbor. As Libby unpacked the picnic Bertie said, "The least you could do, Libby Whitman, is thank me for rescuing you from George Wentworth."

"George Wentworth's a nice boy and he didn't embarrass me before the whole town."

Incredulous, Bertie persisted, "George Wentworth's a wimp. You should be pleased. Nobody's ever paid that much for a picnic."

"That's the point! You made me feel—different."

"Good. I want for you to feel 'different' and 'special' because you are," Bertie replied. "You know I never buy anything I can't pay for, never enter a race except to win and never want you to picnic with anybody but me." His gaze held her fast. "Besides, it's for a good cause; Craigmoor should honor our war dead. Now, what's in that basket? I'm starving."

As they relaxed, the grape leaves overhead rustled in the hot breeze. They talked about Matt's visit, Rose's plans. "I want farming. Rose wants teaching so I guess she should try." As Libby unwrapped cookies, Bertie asked, "What about you, Libby Whitman? Are you going to go to college and teach?" A bee buzzed by.

She looked into his eyes; he looked fragile. "Since teaching this past winter, I'm not sure it's right for me. I love learning but I'm not as good at teaching."

Bertie smiled happily, sat back and said, "You shouldn't do it if it isn't what you really, really want." He hesitated. "I never figured George Wentworth had a chance. But teaching does." He leaned forward and kissed her cheek lightly.

"I love you Libby Whitman and I always will," he said a bit hesitantly. Then he stood abruptly. "We'd better get back."

Stunned and happy Libby gathered the picnic remains and walked back to the center of town at Bertie's side. Snap dragons in all possible colors nodded by the picket fences of the neat homes. Bertie said he liked flowers but wasn't good at growing them. Libby remarked that Mavis had been a prize gardener. As they approached the square, Libby asked, "Well?"

"Well, what?" Bertie asked confused.

"How was my picnic?"

Bertie scratched his head, scrunched up his face, "Good," he said finally.

"That's all? Just good?"

"Worth every penny," he winked at her and jogged over toward the baseball diamond for the annual 4th of July game.

That evening, as they walked home Grandma Margaret said, "Penny for your thoughts."

"I think," Libby replied grinning, "enough's been spent on me for one day."

"He's a determined young man," Margaret replied.

"He's nice Grandma. He knows what he wants. The farm's everything to him."

"Not quite everything, Libby. I'd say you count a good deal."

At the house they sat together on the porch swing.

"Grandma, did you ever want to leave Craigmoor?"

Margaret reflected a moment. "No. I don't remember living in Boston. Your Gram talked about Virginia and it sounded lovely but I never wanted to go anyplace else. Once I met your Grandpa, well, I loved him. Family and home were my dreams."

"Sometimes I think about Mama and Gram just knowing things. That would be nice: to know, to take the guesswork from a decision," Libby mused.

"It didn't seem to work like that. I doubt it made things easier, maybe more complicated. And, if that ability skips another generation, we'll just have to ask your daughter how it works."

Libby laughed. "Well, I guess we will." The swing squeaked as she stood; lightening bugs lit up the darkness. "I love you Grandma," Libby said as she leaned over and kissed Margaret on the cheek.

'Yes,' Margaret smiled, 'grand-mothering is more fun.'

Later, as Margaret and Richard lay in bed, she said casually, "Bertie Jones is nice."

Richard chuckled. "As stubborn as his whole family and he'll probably do as well. They've dragged a living from that rocky hillside by hard work and sheer cussedness. But I know you, woman; don't you go marrying him to my Libby quite so fast. It takes more than one 4th of July picnic to make an engagement."

Margaret ran her fingers over his face and smiled into the night. "I wonder," she said softly, "I do wonder."

14

Two weeks later, after completing his errands in town, Bertie stepped into the bank and asked John Whitman if 'we could speak privately for a moment.' John led him into his office. Bertie settled nervously onto the edge of a chair, exhaled loudly, tightened and released his shoulder muscles. John eyed him, wary as a cat watching a new neighborhood dog.

"Mr. Whitman, our families have known each other for a long time," Bertie began his well-rehearsed speech. "Pa and my uncles built Quail Hill Farm by lots of hard work and that's what they taught all of us. Matt's going to be a doctor; he doesn't want to farm. I do. I'm a good farmer now and I'll get better and keep building up Quail Hill." He took a breath, shifted slightly and said in a rush, "Mr. Whitman, I want your permission to court Libby. I know she's considering teaching but if that's not what she wants then maybe, in a few years, she'll," Bertie looked John straight in the eyes, "consider marriage and maybe she'd consider me." He stopped. He had nothing else to say.

John Whitman leaned back, ideas tumbling through his mind like sand-grains in an hourglass. Libby had lived her life in town; being isolated up on Quail Hill, how would she manage? The world kept changing. Would hard work on a small farm continue to provide a good living? Only yesterday, it seemed, John sat in Bertie's place full of that same hope, that same virile optimism, asking to court Mavis. A wrenching sensation twisted below his heart. Libby remained his closest link to Mavis, to youth, to innocence. Libby weathered her mother's death and they had survived the shock and pain together. He wanted Mavis' advice; wanted to shout 'NO! SHE IS TOO YOUNG! GO AWAY.' Instead he asked, "What do you propose for a courtship?"

"I could come afternoons of the first Sundays of the month. Then Libby and I could spend time with the family or walk in town. Except, of course," he added, "if I'm snowed in."

John chuckled. Bertie was practical to the core. "Have you spoken to Libby?"

"No sir. I've talked to my folks and you. If you say 'no' there's no reason to bother Libby." Bertie's unpretentious words made John smile. Bertie's face broke into a big grin. "Half the town figures I'm in love with her."

John peered over the top of his glasses, "After that display on the 4th of July, I'd venture more than half." Then he got serious. "Bertie, I have the right to reject you as a suitor but I don't believe I have the right to accept you until I talk to Libby and the family. Come by next week and I'll let you know." He stood and offered his hand.

"Thank you," Bertie stood, shook hands, "I hope my bid on the picnic didn't seem out of place, sir."

"I'm glad you value Libby, but I'm your banker. You paid more than you needed to."

"But," Bertie grinned, "my bid won."

John nodded and watched him leave.

Bertie walked down Main Street whistling, hands in his pockets, shoulders relaxed. Next week he'd know. If Mr. Whitman wanted to reject him he'd have done that today. Stopping by the old wooden bridge on his way out of town, Bertie watched the water gurgling by. 'Please say yes, Libby,' he wished silently. Picturing her face and smile before him, he jogged the three miles home. Bursting into the kitchen, he picked Ma up and swung her around as flour and bread dough went flying.

"What's going on, young man?" Ma asked. He told her the news then dashed off to find Pa. Ma wondered what Bertie might do next week if Mr. Whitman said 'yes.' She gazed out the window feeling pensive about the changes that might be coming. 'Is there room in this kitchen for two wives? Does she have the strength for this life? Is Bertie ready?'

Was she ready to be a mother-in-law? A grandmother? She finished kneading the bread dough, put loaves in pans for a final rising, pumped water over her hands and went to her bedroom. She ran her fingers over the quilt on the bed she'd shared with Pa all these years. She walked to the dresser, studied her reflection, her graying blond hair, the wrinkles around her eyes and on her neck. Returning to the kitchen, she took out her notebook and began writing.

Later that night, Helen put down her sewing and replied to her brother's question, "Well, John, the point is: 'Is Bertie an acceptable suitor?' You know the Jones family better than I do."

"Helen, I don't want to let her go. She helped me after Mavis died. One day when I was deep in my withdrawn silence she said 'Papa, you must go on or go under.' She probably got that from you or Margaret or Amy but it helped me. Today, he looked so young, so full of promise and hope, seeing a secure future. No crop failures. No tragedy. No problems. Were we like that? He knows a lot about life, but is it enough?"

Helen's rocking chair squeaked rhythmically as she waited for her brother to continue: she knew that silence was the best gift she could offer him now. She remembered the Islamic proverb Jeff had told her: 'Love means walking through a snowfield and leaving no tracks.'

John stared at the floor. "He's a fine, strong young man. Stubborn. Uncomplicated. Libby's moody. She's lived in town. That farm's isolated; Bertie understands it, would she? If he courts her, nobody else will come around. Bertie doesn't lose. Helen, what should I do?"

"Talk to Richard and Margaret. If there are skeletons in the Jones' closet, they'll know. And talk to Libby. She might refuse, decide to teach, but I doubt it. He's right; half the town knows he adores her. What he may not realize is that about a third of the town knows she cares for him. Trouble is, Libby herself dances in and out of that group. She may need time to decide, John. Give her time."

Helen resumed sewing and continued to rock.

15

Saturday morning John went to visit Richard and Margaret. The house nudged forth memories of Mavis and youth. The smell of fresh bread greeted him; Margaret had two-dozen jars of apple butter set out to take to market. After exchanging greetings John asked their advice about Bertie's request. Margaret spoke first.

"He's solid. Matt wants medicine; Rose will teach. That leaves the farm for Bertie. It's a good inheritance. Rachel will be there at least for now. Libby and Bert have always been sweet on each other. He'll challenge her to choose: teaching or married life. He'll build a strong case but he won't grovel. Give Libby time to decide."

Richard spoke slowly. "Seems only yesterday you came asking me the same thing. It's hard, especially with Mavis gone. It's peculiar; sometimes a daughter needs her father more after she's married so if this leads to marriage, you'll still be needed. Bertie's a good boy. He needs to control his tongue but that's youth. The whole Jones tribe is rock-solid and granite-hard. They work like oxen up on Quail Hill. The old uncles and aunt are reclusive but there's little harm in being strange. After decades on that hill I'd become strange."

"And," Margaret added, "if Bertie wins his case, Libby'll spend decades on that hill."

"My dear wife, if your mother had insisted on her way, we'd not be having this talk because there'd have been no Mavis and no Libby. I wasn't in Gram's plans for you.

"Now, Libby and Bertie have to work this out." He turned to his son-in-law. "Thanks for asking us. I know how you feel. Man to man, anyone, even as solid as Bertie, sniffing around our Libby makes me kind of dizzy because I know what's on his mind."

"Richard!" Margaret said, blushing.

"Hush, woman. John, Bertie's doing the right thing, asking for permission and guidance. I doubt he'll press his case if you say 'no' but I won't vouch for Libby. A young girl can make a terrible mess if her family holds too tight. No matter what decision Libby makes, her road leads away. You can't stop time. 'Love her and let her go,' that's what Margaret told me when you came to court Mavis. With all that's happened, John, she was right. You can guide her but your job now is to begin to let Libby go."

Margaret smiled and kept knitting.

"Thank you both," John said. The town clock struck 10:00 as he walked home. After the noon meal, he and Libby would walk to market and talk.

As the clock struck 12:30, John said, "Come on Libby, let's go to town."

"I have to help Aunt Helen pack jars."

"Nope, not today. Johnny will do that. Today is a special time for us."

Johnny started to protest but Aunt Helen silenced him with a glance.

Libby put on her bonnet, picked up her shopping basket and followed her father out the door. John scanned the sky for signs of rain to break the mugginess. They walked in silence. Libby remembered what Mavis had written: 'Sometimes he's so quiet you need to listen with your eyes. Don't let his silence exasperate you… Ask him questions when you need to.'

Libby said quietly, "Penny for your thoughts."

John smiled. "Libby, I'm wondering, do you want to be a teacher?"

"I'm not sure. I like studying but, after helping out last winter, I don't know. I'm better when I focus my attention on a few children. Rose and Miss Middleton can keep the schoolhouse going. I'm not good at that. I might learn but I don't think I'd like it."

"That sounds pretty grownup," John said, impressed by Libby's analysis.

"I'm growing up, Papa."

"I know," John replied wistfully. He stopped and turned. "A young man came to the bank the other day to ask my permission to court you. Libby, do you want a suitor?"

Suddenly, the sun seemed too bright; the world crowded in and then retracted leaving Libby breathless. Scared and flushed she clutched her basket tightly. She wanted to flee. Bits from Mavis' letter buzzed in her head. 'Try not to be afraid… fear saps your strength… wait before you react…' Libby looked down, took a few deep breaths then looked into her father's eyes. "Who?"

"Bertie Jones," John replied.

Libby's shoulders relaxed and she smiled shyly. "Well, I guess that would be all right." She stood on tiptoes and kissed John on the cheek. "I'm happy it's Bertie, Papa. I was afraid it was George Wentworth."

"George Wentworth's a nice young man," John protested.

Libby smiled. "He's a wimp, Papa. Anyway, it's Bertie."

They strolled on. "You'll have to help me. I don't know about courtship."

"We'll both learn," John replied. "You'll get to know each other better, see if you agree on things, see the world the same way. You ask yourself 'Does he treat people well? Do I want to spend my life as his wife, have his children, be with him through everything life sends us?'"

"Aunt Helen and Grandma will guide you." They walked on. "By the way, they both said you'd need time to decide." He laughed. "You sure didn't!"

Libby tilted her head to one side, smiled up coyly. "It's Bertie. For anyone else I'd have needed time."

When they arrived at the market John said, "Let's meet later by the flagpole."

"It's a little scary," Libby said. As she walked away, John noted how much she moved like Mavis. He felt a brief, raw stab of loss. Then, as quickly as the pain came, it disappeared. He walked to the general store to learn today's local news.

16

On first Sundays, Bertie attended church and then walked home with the Whitmans. Craigmoor's youngsters followed and teased: a courting ritual a couple must handle with poise and humor. As the town watched closely, Libby and Bertie behaved admirably.

Bertie brought Aunt Helen flowers, eggs or vegetables. In April, he made a miniature sailboat for Johnny complete with sails and delicate string rigging. The afternoon he brought the boat, as they walked after dinner, Libby became moody and spoke sharply.

"Libby Whitman, what's wrong?" Bertie finally asked.

Libby spoke hesitantly. "You court the whole Whitman family, bring gifts to Aunt Helen and Johnny but you only make me cards." An unattractive petulance clung to her words.

Stopping on the old bridge, he took her hands, squeezed hard. "You are the Whitman I'm courting but family's important. Besides, your Pa might not approve of me bringing you gifts."

"Bertie, I know I sound small and mean but I wonder if I come first." She pulled her hands free. "I want you to love Johnny. He needs a big brother; he's been confused since Mama died. I know you'd love sons and be good with children. I guess I need to know it's me, Libby, you want and not just me, the healthy girl from the Whitman family."

Conflict pressed around them as they crossed the bridge.

Then Bertie spoke. "Where have you been for the past 10 years, Libby?" Libby started to speak but Bertie stopped her. "Let me talk. I've loved you since I was nine and you were six. Like, forever. We're courting; nothing's final. If I bring you things, give too much, if this doesn't work out I'll feel foolish. So I guess I hold back and you feel ignored.

"Maybe that's just me. In town, I'm a bit out of place: uncomfortable. I'm 20 and I'm trying to be a man and there's so much change—with Matt and Rose going to college—so sometimes I wonder if you want to join Rose, leave Craigmoor and Bertie Jones behind." He stopped under a sugar maple, reached up and grabbed a branch. "Rose wants to teach but I can't imagine not wanting children, a family, a home. I guess that's about it."

"Bertie, Rose may want a family but she wants teaching more. Matt's not rejecting the farm; he's choosing medicine. They can't do both. Either choice takes all of you. When Rose and I were teaching, I saw that. I don't think teaching's right for me but I get scared. I love you Bertie but what if I'm up on the farm and you ignore me?"

"Libby…" Bertie tried to cut in. Libby held up her hand, eyes flashing.

"I listened to you. Now you listen to me Bertie Jones. What if you ignore me? What choice will I have then? None! N-O-N-E. So when I see presents come to everybody but me, I wonder. Maybe that shouldn't matter but it does. I'm no saint; I'm not even very patient. You talk about your life, well, what about <u>mine</u>?"

They walked slowly back across the bridge. Bertie took his cap off and ran his fingers through his hair, then said softly, "That's the first time you ever said you loved me."

"I just figured you knew," Libby said sheepishly.

"Yea, well, I guess we both have a bunch to learn about this stuff," Bertie took her hand. When they reached the house he said, "Ask your Papa if you and Aunt Helen can come up to the farm next Sunday. I'll check, too, and send word with Rose. Just you and Aunt Helen; not everybody."

"Oh, Bertie," she said, reaching up and touching his cheek. "Oh, Bertie." She grinned and walked into the house.

Bertie walked home thinking how confusing courtship seemed. But maybe that was the point. Their life, framed by their families and community, would be uniquely theirs so only they could work things out. Choosing a wife would be the most important decision he'd ever make.

· Craigmoor ·

The next Sunday, Libby and Aunt Helen drove the buggy to the farm. During a normal, relaxed day, Libby watched Bertie in his element. He, his parents and sisters showed a playful nature. Soon after she arrived, Bertie handed her a small, carved wooden replica of the Craigmoor Bridge. They said nothing, just smiled at each other.

In the afternoon, right before they headed home, Bertie and Libby walked through the main orchard. Under an old gnarled apple tree he kissed her gently and held her close. She felt the strength of his body and relaxed against him.

Later, as he helped her into the carriage and they said goodbye, she knew she belonged here, with him, and he knew it, too. Arriving home, she placed the carved miniature bridge on her dresser next to her mirror and hairbrush.

17

During the winter of 1866-67, Johnny's grades slipped further; he became angry; his relationships deteriorated. Friction increased between John and Johnny, Aunt Helen and Johnny, Miss Middleton and Johnny. He left chores half done, sassed his elders behind their backs, stole a knife from his grandfather. The town watched. In a place like Craigmoor, adolescent rebellion could do permanent damage. Richard knew Johnny stole his knife. He watched his grandson disintegrating. One May afternoon, he waited for Johnny outside school.

"Hi Gramp. What're you doing here?"

"I've come to get you; you've a job at the mill."

"Naw," came the sullen reply, "Not today." As Johnny started walking away, Richard reached over and grasped him by his wrist. A lifetime in the mill created a man of strong muscle and tenacious will. Richard's hand gripped Johnny like a vice and he walked rapidly toward the river. Richard spoke gently as he pulled his grandson along. Johnny fought, tried to pull away, dug in his heels, spat, cursed, tried to bite Richard's hand to no avail; he was dragged toward the mill. As they entered, Johnny swung his free arm at Richard who caught it securely in mid-air.

Holding the boy, Richard said simply, "Johnny, all this has to stop. I know you're hurt and angry. I know you're sassing folks and swearing. And it's going to stop." Johnny tried to break away and Richard held him in a bear hug. The boy stomped his feet and raged. Richard held him securely and kept repeating, "I'm here Johnny, and I'm not letting go." Finally Johnny's fighting dissipated and he leaned into his grandfather's chest. Slowly, he began to sob; his arms fell limply to his sides. After his tears ceased, he looked up into Richard's face.

"Gramp," he said slowly, "I ran as fast as I could. Why'd Mama have to die?" Open and wounded Johnny searched Richard's face for answers. He stood terrified before the reality of Mavis' death and his own crushing sense of guilt and inadequacy.

"Johnny, you listen to me and you listen good. Nothing and nobody could've saved your Mama. If you could have flown it wouldn't have changed things. Nobody blames you—except you. Now that's got to stop. I don't understand why she died and I sure don't like it but that's the way it is." He pulled a handkerchief from his pocket and handed it to Johnny who wiped his face. "Son, there's a world we see, touch and measure: rocks, trees. And there's a world we don't see: love, hope. Mavis loved us and we loved her and that love is still around. You can let it touch you and grow or you can get nasty and steal knives." Johnny looked up, scared. "Oh, yes, I know you took my knife and you need to give it back and do something to make up for taking it. But there's more." He put his arm around Johnny's shoulders and walked him outside by the water wheel. The river gurgled by, turning the wheel with a soothing shush, shush, shush sound. "Your Great-Grandmother Tillman told me once: 'Each soul must face the rebuff of mystery.' Probably quoting some saint. That's what this is: 'the rebuff of mystery.' Life serves up lessons. You can stay mad, sass folks, refuse to learn in school, skimp on chores: or you can change. What would your Mama want?

"Moses says 'Choose between life and death.' Well, you choose by how you live. And this town's watching. You've got choices: how to act, what to believe. I think there's something bigger than me and I believe your Mama is somehow integrated into whatever God is. I can't prove it but I choose to believe it. The world just works better that way." They stood together with the waterwheel turning rhythmically.

"That's hard, Gramp," Johnny said.

"It is," Richard replied.

Johnny reached in his pocket, brought out the knife, handed it to Richard. "I'm sorry. I don't know why I took it." Richard put the knife in his own pocket. "I'll come work at the mill when you say. Would that be right?" A shadow of the old Johnny looked up at Richard, raw and trying.

"We'll work something out. What else?"

"I'll stop sassing. Mama hated sassing."

Richard smiled, "That's a start, Johnny."

18

The next year flew by. Rose and Libby both studied and continued assisting in Craigmoor's one-room schoolhouse. Libby and Bertie spent more time together.

· Craigmoor ·

Rose grew more confident in her teaching skills: more self-reliant. Amy watched them with pride.

Amy's correspondence with her grandfather continued. In one letter, Amy chided Professor Ely that he 'was truly a Philosopher dressed up in an Historian's academic gown.'

20 May 1868

Dearest Amy,

You have found me out! Earlier, I'd have been a Philosopher. Last's century's revolutions moved me into History. 'At least in History there is something solid: the rise and fall of powers brought about by action. Philosophy just dissipates into the air, into ideas based on premises that are conditioned by—History.' Now I realize it may be the other way round: Philosophy drives History.

As a young man I'd have rejected that idea: I kept a tight reign on my mind with a set of rules. With age, I see many vantage points from which to view the world and many of them have some validity. Which may mean that neither Philosophy nor History is the driving force but something deeper, more basic and parent to both fields.

I watch Matthew: he is dedicated to Science, to Medicine and so positive about his chosen path. His energy and enthusiasm are wonderful as he focuses narrowly on his studies. I wonder: 'Can his dedication to Science and Medicine lead him anyplace other than where I've arrived by studying History?' My youthful zeal was as dedicated as his: just in another direction. Yet somehow, from or through this narrow, tight discipline I became stronger, more open, less concerned about the structures that, initially, protected me from confusion. Put another way: "If one chips away looking for 'truth' in one area, can one avoid eventually glimpsing a bit of 'Truth'? Is there, in fact, anything else to find?"

All roads may lead to Rome but one must follow some road. Many people spend their lives studying maps! The choice of road may be less important than we think, though I've strong opinions on that! (According to the Gita, I need to give up 'strong feelings' altogether!)

Do take care of yourself. Grandma and I look forward to our summer together.

With greatest love,

Grandpa Ely

Amy removed her glasses, rubbed her eyes, stood and stretched. Her back and hip still bothered her. She looked down the street and could just glimpse the school through blossoming tree branches.

19

Having completed her spring preparation for the coming fall, Amy packed her suitcase to leave for Cambridge. Rose, Libby and three other students from her first, first-grade Craigmoor class were graduating and a chapter in Amy's life closed. Now, 34, she had clearly become a middle-aged spinster. She'd willingly chosen this life but that didn't eliminate loneliness. Now her role was changing both here and in Cambridge. In Craigmoor, Amy voiced her support for women's rights and progressive political policies more openly. In Cambridge, as the Elys aged, Amy provided them with increasing emotional support. She understood the changes intellectually but the emotional implications felt complicated.

Rose came to say good-bye the day before Amy planned to leave. Standing together on the Putnam's porch, Rose fidgeted, wringing her hands nervously.

"I hope you have a good summer in Cambridge and tell Matt hello," Rose said, her voice strident. Amy saw Rose's nervousness but felt her own calm of accomplishment: Matt was in Medical School and Rose was about to start college.

"I'll tell Matt. I always have a good time with Grandpa and Grandma especially our time on Cape Cod. Anything else?"

"This is such a big step; what if I can't do it?"

Amy squinted up at her student, now taller than she, pursed her lips to suppress a smile and said simply, "If you fail you may fall a very long way."

The unexpected statement surprised Rose. Her cheeks flushed; after a moment she squared her shoulders. Amy maintained her steady gaze.

"I'm not going to fail," Rose declared forcefully.

"Good. That's much more like you and like the strength you'll need." Amy unleashed her smile and continued. "You're ready. I'll always be interested and always help if I can."

Watching Rose stride confidently down Main Street, Amy recalled her Grandfather Ely's advice: "Your primary job is to teach students. You'll like some more than others but a wise teacher keeps emotions in check: give each student your best and wish them well as they walk away."

20

After graduation, Libby worked for Mrs. Morgan two days a week. Mrs. Morgan (aging, frail and mentally alert) still oversaw her family's lumberyard and lived in one of Craigmoor's largest houses. The Morgan's had been very kind after Mavis died. Helping Mrs. Morgan's nurse increased Libby's skills: valuable knowledge for a young woman.

Bertie visited most Sundays. This 4th of July, Bertie had no competition for Libby's picnic and they spent a wonderful day together. Libby and Rose did not. Rose took little interest in Libby's budding nursing skills and Libby became distracted when Rose talked about her college plans. They disagreed about how the flags should be displayed, argued about the beauty of flowers and watched as young children ran around town, weaving recklessly among the adults.

"They should not run around like hooligans," Rose remarked.

"Rose, they're just having fun. It's the 4th of July!"

"Our National Holiday deserves dignity," Rose replied primly.

"They are children, Rose. Everybody makes noise on the 4th. You sound like an old maid," words she regretted instantly.

"Maybe," Rose began, lips quivering, "now that I'm leaving Craigmoor I can see its less pleasant qualities."

"Rose Jones, that is a truly hateful thing to say!" Libby turned her back and marched away, angry with both of them. Rose set her trembling jaw, kept her tears at bay and walked rapidly to the ball field.

Later that night, Libby wrote a note to Rose and apologized for being hurtful; Rose wrote an apology back. They didn't see each other again until the day Rose left for college.

Helen and Libby stood in the kitchen sorting tomatoes in the wilting August heat. No birds sang; the oppressive humidity made breathing laborious. Helen finally broached the unspoken subject of Rose's departure.

"When are the Joneses coming to town?" she asked.

"I'll go to the station by 2:00," Libby said curtly. She eyed the tomato in her hand, suddenly hurling it into the pot. "I hate tomatoes! I hate planting them, weeding them, pulling off suckers, picking them and canning them! I hate the way my hands smell when I work with them!" Libby ripped off her apron and charged out the door onto the porch.

Helen wiped her hands methodically, said silently 'Help me now Lord,' and followed her niece. Heat draped heavily around them. Libby's mind raced. Mavis died: moved into the unknown she could not share. Rose leaving: moving into a new adventure she would not share. Libby: staying behind. Libby flopped onto the porch swing.

"Oh, Aunt Helen, it hurts so much!"

Helen settled beside her and the swing began its familiar scritch, scritch, scritch sound.

"Partings are seldom easy, Libby, even partings that are right."

"Does it get better?" Libby asked defiantly.

"Maybe not 'better' but it gets 'easier.'"

Libby flounced around on the swing; the springs squeaked angrily. "If it gets easier then that must mean you don't care anymore and that's worse!"

Helen watched Libby charge into the blind alley where life became bleak, dark and awful. Helen recognized Libby's familiar pattern: if one thing was bad then everything became horrible ending in a dramatic, destructive, self-important, self-pity that created terrible, if often brief, interior pain. She reached for Libby's hand; Libby snatched it away angrily and stood.

"This swing has squeaked all summer and no one makes Johnny do anything. Just me. I work all the time and put up with this noise! And nobody cares what I think—you always side with Johnny!" she hissed.

"That, young lady," Helen replied, "is enough! You are neither the only one who is hot nor the only one to lose a friend. You could be going with Rose and you chose not to. You have choices. I suggest you count your blessings!" Let loose, Helen Wilson's Whitman temper could easily match Libby's but Helen controlled hers and Libby did not. "Libby, it will not be easy to say goodbye to Rose today," Helen's tone softened, "but I hope you can do it without anger. It hurts because you love her and you're taking different roads."

Libby collapsed back onto the swing. "Aunt Helen, when will I grow up? How can I be a wife? Why hasn't Bertie proposed? What's wrong with me? I don't want to be a teacher and really don't want to leave Craigmoor but I feel so tense. I'm raging inside today."

"Let's go back inside. You drink some water and relax; I'll work on the tomatoes."

"Aunt Helen, I'm not angry about the tomatoes; they were just handy."

"I know, but they do go on forever. Now, if Bertie proposes and you accept, when you move to the farm, all of you must be there. Right now, you're helping with Mrs. Morgan a few days a week. Marriage is fulltime. Every year you'll plant tomatoes, weed them, pick and put-up mountains of tomatoes."

Helen's words struck home. Libby walked over and put on her apron. "I'll work on these," she said nodding at the boiling pots, "you go ahead and fix lunch for Johnny and Papa. Sometimes, Aunt Helen, I want to stop things for a while. I hate it when I say and do such awful things. I make some progress and then something like today happens. Wham! Here's Libby, being awful again."

"If it's any consolation, saints in every religious tradition discuss this so we know we're not alone. Just try to be more loving. You've been careful in your decision about college. You and Bertie are building a solid foundation. Don't be too hard on yourself about today, just be very loving at the train." She chuckled, "Besides, tomatoes do make your hands smell awful."

Big Red pulled the wagon up to the station at 1:30. Rose, dressed formally for traveling, looked hot. Libby and Aunt Helen arrived at 2. Pa, Ma and Rachel all said their goodbyes up on Quail Hill. Bertie drove Rose to the train where friends joined them. It seemed like a holiday: people standing in the shade, doing nothing. When the distant train whistle sounded, Libby caught her breath. As she looked at Rose tears streamed down her cheeks. Rose said her goodbyes and turned to Libby last. They hugged, knocking Rose's bonnet askew.

"Oh, Rosie, I'm going to miss you so much," Libby sobbed as she reached to straighten Rose's bonnet. "I know it's right for you to go and me to stay but saying goodbye hurts!"

Rose's voice trembled, "Libby, you helped me explore teaching. We'll write and I'll be home summers." She leaned close, "Take care of Bertie. He feels left out when we're together."

Rose lifted her small traveling case and boarded the train. Bertie loaded her suitcase, got her settled and jumped back onto the platform. Libby stood beside him and took his arm. He squeezed her hand.

As the train chugged away, they waved until it disappeared around the bend with a last mournful whistle. As Libby and Bertie walked toward the wagon, she asked, "Can you come up for a visit?"

"What, in the middle of the week?!" Bertie pulled back in mock indignation, "You'll start gossip and ruin my good name."

"Oh, don't be silly, Aunt Helen will be there."

"Shucks!"

"Bertie Jones!" Libby's face colored.

"Libby, I'm heading to the bank, the store and the mill: then Big Red and I'll head home. But I'll be here Sunday." He smiled as he swung up onto the seat of the wagon.

21

Thanksgiving Day dawned cloudless, cold and blustery. Bertie had permission from his parents and John Whitman to propose today. At breakfast he snapped at Rachel, apologized, stood and left the table. Pa followed him outside.

"You all right, son?"

"I'm nervous as a cat, Pa, I feel like a frayed rope—nothing holds together. Didn't sleep more than an hour last night." They strolled across the lane, stood by the gate to the big pasture watching the horses prancing around, tossing their heads and pawing the ground nervously. "Pa, what if she says 'No'? What'll I do then?"

· Quail Hill ·

"What I did with your Ma, I made it real clear that what I was about to ask I'd ask only once. That way, if she turned me down it'd be over." Pa reached over and mussed up Bertie's hair. "But I doubt she'll turn you down so what you better worry about is what you're gonna do with a bunch of little Joneses running around."

Bertie grinned. "I'm not worried about that. Heck, I got the best Pa in the world so I'll just do what he's done."

"Thanks son but what I've done is a lot what your Ma and I worked out together. What you do will be some of what you want, some of what Libby wants." Pa looked across the fields at the mountains in the distance. "I've seen good marriages and bad and the only ones I'd give a nickel for are where both folks understand the other's important: where they work together like a good team of horses and they're stronger when they know where they're going. That's the best I know, Bert. You and Libby will have to work it out." He opened the gate, "Let's check the far corner. Sounded like foxes there last night." Finding nothing amiss, they returned to the house.

Bertie changed clothes, saddled Big Red, headed for town and joined the Whitman's at church. Afterwards, Bertie, Big Red and Libby walked up to the house. The leafless trees looked like skeletons against the bright blue sky. At the house, Bertie led Red to the barn, unsaddled him and rubbed him down.

Turkey and pies were scheduled for one o'clock. They walked up to the Morgan house so Libby could take some jam to Mrs. Morgan and her nurse Alice Wallace. They strolled back down the hill, past the cliff that fell away in a tangle of brambles and wild berry-bushes. Bertie stopped walking and leaned forward and kissed Libby gently. He took a deep breath and began.

"Libby Whitman, I'm only going to ask you this once." The emphasis on 'once' caught Libby's attention. "I've talked to my folks and your father." He took both of her hands. "I love you. I want to spend the rest of my life with you and have my family with you." He paused, breathing hard. "Libby, will you marry me?"

Libby heard the wind whistling through the bare trees; she looked into his intense blue eyes. Tilting her head to one side and pursing her lips she said, "Before I agree, I'll need two promises: one for us and one for our children."

Bertie lowered his chin slightly and squinted as Libby continued. "All our daughters and any of our sons who want to go to college will be allowed to go and we'll help them if we can."

Bertie nodded and a smile began to creep across his face.

"And," Libby went on, "we must have a house. I love your Ma and Pa but we need our own house. Somehow. From the beginning."

"College for our kids and a house. Is that it?" Bertie said with exaggerated seriousness.

"Well, all the vows, too."

He picked her up and whirled around. "We'll have a house—somehow. And I agree to the college stuff."

"Then, yes, Bertie Jones, I'll marry you," she said as the town clock struck 12:45.

"I'll need to talk to Pa about a house. It'll take time to build; it might work for Auntie Jones and my Uncles to move into the main house and us live up in that house for a while. There's room to build across the road from Ma and Pa. That'd keep us close to the barn."

"I feel we'd be better off a bit separate."

"In heavy winter we all stay in the main house."

"Yes, both you and Rose told me that. Is it scary in a winter whiteout?"

"A bit. But when we're all together it's OK. The hard thing is taking care of the livestock but we know how to do it. Don't worry, I'll take care of you," Bertie assured her.

"We'll take care of each other, Bertie." Libby smiled up at him.

Grandpa, Grandma, Amy, John, Helen and Johnny were pleased when Bertie announced their news. After dinner, Libby and Bertie sketched ideas for a house. Later, Bertie saddled Red and rode home, eager to talk to his family.

As the town clock struck midnight, Libby slipped out of bed, wrapped a blanket around her shoulders, sat by the window in the old family rocking chair and watched moonlit shadows dance in the backyard. Her backyard. Home. A dull ache formed in her chest. Deciding to marry felt right but the reality of loss chilled her. The farm seemed far away: another universe. Would she fit in? Deal with the change? The isolation? The people?

Aunt Helen appeared at her door, whispered softly, "Libby?"

"Come on in," Libby replied. Helen entered, closed the door and sat on the bed.

"I figured you might be up. Getting engaged is a big step."

"If it's right, Aunt Helen, why do I feel scared?"

"Fear often just means something's new not that it's wrong." Clouds blanketed the moon, darkening the room. "Every time an angel appears in Bible stories, the first thing he says is: 'Fear not.' Even with happy announcements, they say don't be afraid."

Libby nodded and said, "Aunt Helen, I know about taking care of children, how to sew, cook, clean, keep house, even some nursing but I don't know how to be a wife."

"You mean here," Helen patted the bed, "alone with Bertie." Libby nodded again. "There's no magic formula. You love each other. You trust each other. You'll learn together and you'll make mistakes. We all start as beginners, Libby."

22

"We'll build it," Pa said. "The farm is expanding."

They designed a large kitchen/all purpose room with a pantry and one bedroom; other rooms could be added later. The new house would stand on the crest of a hill 30 yards from the barn, north of the black walnut tree and across the lane from the main farmhouse. The northeast kitchen window overlooked the barn, the apple orchard and the northeast pasture. The Morgan Lumber Company gave them a fair price for building materials. Work would begin in the spring.

Libby embroidered linens, made a nursing notebook, copied recipes from Aunt Helen and Grandma Margaret. She assisted Miss Middleton two half-days a week, helped organize the new library and worked three days a week with Mrs. Morgan. When Bertie made mid-week trips to town, he'd visit Libby at school recess and the children flocked to them.

When good weather arrived, the Jones men began building and worked late into the night after finishing regular farm chores. Libby and Aunt Helen often visited the farm after Church. Rose returned home from mid-June to mid-August, relieving Bertie of some regular chores. The house was finished in September. Then Libby and Ma painted and put up curtains. The couple inherited some furniture and Mrs. Morgan gave them a brand new bed. Bertie made an oak table and four chairs for the kitchen. Friends gave them kitchen items, a few linens.

The second weekend in October in 1869, Elizabeth Rebecca Whitman married Albert Nicholas Jones in the Craigmoor Congregational Church. Libby wore a simple white dress and a lace-trimmed veil. Standing together before their families and the people of Craigmoor they affirmed, publicly and legally, what everyone already knew: they would live together as husband and wife through whatever life sent them, until separated by death. The townsfolk witnessed, celebrated and supported this new beginning. Spectacularly bright fall foliage created a dramatic backdrop for the simple party on the church lawn.

As they drove out of town in the Jones buggy, the trees danced in the light breeze. Up at the farm, they walked around their new house and watched the setting sun splash rust-colored light across the hills.

"Well, Libby Whitman, I guess I'd better carry you over our new threshold."

When he put her down inside Libby said, "And maybe you'd better start calling me Libby Jones, too."

"I know you're a Jones but you're still 'Libby Whitman' to me."

They spent their wedding night in their new bed in their own house on Quail Hill Farm.

23

In November, Helen, Margaret and Amy Middleton organized a ladies reading group to meet at the 'County Library,' actually Ruth Stuyvesant's extra front room. Louise Putnam, Nurse Alice Wallace and Ruth Stuyvesant were also founding members. The women wanted to read and discuss books intelligently. They established four rules: 1. No gossip, 2. Respect for the privacy of all opinions, 3. 'Consensus' would guide their choice of topics and 4. Tea would be served. At their first meeting they talked about books and ideas important to them. Amy spoke of studying the *Bhagavad-Gita* with her grandparents and Helen remarked that she and Jeff had read some of it. The other members decided they would circulate Amy's copy among themselves and hold a discussion in the spring.

Up on Quail Hill, the normal fall chores proceeded within the new Jones' family structure. Work began before sunrise and continued late into the evening. Libby and Bertie ate breakfast and dinner (the noon meal) at the main house and usually had supper in their own home. The women (Ma, Rachel, Auntie Jones and Libby) often worked together in the main house or moved as a quartet among the three Jones houses. Libby felt peripheral; the other three women had long established patterns of working together. Libby sought tasks to perform that helped without stepping on someone else's role. While the Whitman home had been sedate, the Jones farm was energetic. While harvesting apples, they romped at fever pitch from one end of the orchard to the other. In the evenings they often sat on the porch and told family stories or played another inning or two in their continuing baseball game. Libby joined in, told some of her family stories and became increasingly comfortable in the routine.

One chore they gladly turned over to her was gathering eggs. There were five chicken coops. Over the first weeks Libby realized that an increasing number of large, smooth stones turned up in nests. One morning, returning to the main house before breakfast she placed a large basket of these stones on the table and said, "Our hens remarked that whoever is laying these eggs had better either eat them or hatch them because our biddies can't do a thing with them."

The Uncles laughed and Pa said, "Why Libby, you talking to chickens already? Ma didn't start that for at least three years." Libby smiled and felt more accepted. It had been a silly joke but she took it well and the family seemed pleased. The stones never reappeared.

Winter arrived early. Vicious winds whipped the final leaves from the trees; snow pelted down constantly for days. They strung guide ropes connecting the houses to the barn, moved all the chickens to the biggest coop against the main house workroom, gathered the cows, horses, geese and cats into the barn and kept the dogs and people in the main house. The men followed the ropes carefully; getting lost in a whiteout could be fatal.

The cold, the wind and the isolation dragged Libby down and sapped her energy. Craigmoor, just three miles away, got the same snow and cold but there were more houses and more people. Libby felt suffocated. One morning after she gathered eggs, Rachel met her in the workroom, pulled two stools from under the workbench and said, "Let's sit for a minute, Libby." Rachel reached over and took her hands. "A whiteout's terrible, but it will break."

"Are they often this long?" Libby asked.

"No, not this bad." Rachel chuckled. "Maybe it's Nature's way of welcoming you to the hill, 'Show her the worst right at the start.'" She paused, "You were a good sport about Uncle's stones. Did that bother you?"

"No, but thanks for asking. Sometimes I can't figure out what my place is here; how I can fit in." Libby sighed heavily.

"Oh, Libby, you're our future!"

"Me?" Libby's eyes opened wide.

"Of course, *you*. You'll be the mother of the next Joneses. We're glad you're here, just worried that you won't like us or won't like life here. That would crush Bertie."

"I love Bertie and want to be here, but this weather scares me." Libby fought tears.

"In weather like this, Rose and I would recite poems and psalms and then she'd read to us by lamplight," Rachel offered.

"I could do that." Libby said and smiled. "Rachel thanks. Now, let's get closer to the stove. And remember, you might have children, too."

"They wouldn't be Joneses and, since Toby's gone…" Tears formed in Rachel's eyes; she shivered. "You're right, we need to get warm," she added quickly.

Later, after supper, as the winds whipped more snow around the house, Libby read a story that everyone enjoyed.

That night, with the storm raging, she and Bertie held each other in his old bed in his old room. "I dreamed about you in this bed and now here I am, next to you," he whispered. Libby smiled, snuggling close.

By morning, the storm broke. Still trapped on the hill by the snow, the family could move around outside safely.

24

In April Libby and Rachel joined the Ladies Reading group in time for the discussion of the *Bhagavad-Gita* and Amy loaned Rachel her copy to read over the summer. Riding home from the April meeting, Rachel asked Libby about it.

"Aunt Helen and Miss Middleton both like it and Aunt Helen read bits of it to me. I don't understand it very well. It talks about meditation and Aunt Helen did teach me a little bit about that, to help me quiet myself," Libby remarked.

"Will you teach me sometime?" Rachel asked.

Libby reigned in Big Red under a maple tree. "How about now? I don't know much and it won't take long." After they climbed down from the wagon and secured Red, the two young women settled themselves in the shade.

"Aunt Helen says it is just like the Psalm says: 'Be still and know that I am God.' First you sit straight, rest your hands, relax and close your eyes. Focus a little bit out in front of your forehead; free your mind of distractions and listen for God. 'You lift yourself a little toward God and create a holy, loving space for God to enter,' is what Aunt Helen says. I try to meditate twice a day but since I've been married it's hard to find the time."

"Can we try it right here?" Rachel asked.

"Sure," Libby said adjusting her posture. "Breathe easily and focus on your breath if you get distracted." Libby said a brief introductory prayer to protect them from evil.

After about 20 minutes, Libby opened her eyes, said "Amen," stood and brushed off her skirts. Rachel still sat poised and motionless. Libby walked over and called her name gently. Rachel opened her eyes with a start.

"What?"

"It's time to go, Rach."

"But we just started," Rachel said as she stood.

"Maybe 20 minutes ago," Libby remarked as they climbed into the wagon. Driving home, Libby glanced surreptitiously at Rachel. "Are you all right?" she finally asked.

"Why, yes." Rachel smiled. "I feel wonderful."

At home, Bertie unloaded the supplies they'd brought; Rachel picked up her bag, took Ma's things to the kitchen and went upstairs. She put the *Gita* by her Bible. That night she read, as usual, a chapter from the Bible and then read a small piece from the *Gita*. After her normal prayer time she sat in meditation. Within four months, meditation became part of her personal daily devotion. Quietly, unexpectedly, a new world opened for Rachel.

By June, Libby's silhouette revealed the beginning of the next generation. Ma and Rachel fussed; Bertie beamed both pleased and awed; Pa chuckled and whistled more. When Rose returned for the summer she glanced away quickly from Libby's obvious plumpness. Rose talked a lot about college and all she studied, but seemed unsure of how to participate in the summer work. Libby and Rachel invited her to join them in the new garden.

The three women often worked together on this fresh plot between the new house and the orchard. Basking in the warmer weather, they fought to enrich the rocky soil with compost.

"This is what makes the winters tolerable," Rachel said, sitting back on her heels.

Libby smiled. "Yes, it's beautiful. When will this garden be as good as Ma's?"

"Years: but it'll get better each season. New Hampshire land is tough. The thing is, we've started and, as the family grows, it'll produce more and more for us." Rachel remarked as she stood, stretched and went to get them water.

"Doesn't it bother you? Just to live in this one small place?" Rose asked dismissively.

"Be careful Rose," Libby said, wiping perspiration from her forehead. "The work we do on this 'small place' makes your new life possible. Don't bite the hand that feeds you!"

"Do I sound like that?"

"A bit. You talk about you, never ask about us." Silence stretched tautly between them.

"I feel like a stranger here, Libby: you and the new house. You and Bertie…"

"Me and Bertie - what?" Libby probed.

"You know. Married and all."

"All—what?" Libby pushed gently.

Rose flung her trowel to he ground. "It's embarrassing!"

"What's 'embarrassing'?"

"You—pregnant," Rose whispered.

"There, you said it," Libby triumphed. "Going to college is right for you; being married and expecting a baby's right for me. I want to know about school but show interest in us."

After a pause, Rose asked, "What's it like to be pregnant?"

"Like a special secret," Libby said putting her hand on her belly. "It feels a little strange to have a whole new person inside me," Libby noted Rose digging idly in the dirt. "Yes, special." They worked in silence and drank deeply of the water Rachel brought.

The next evening Bertie and Libby stood at the pasture gate, a summer breeze caressing them as flaring golden light danced over the land. "You look beautiful pregnant," Bertie said. She looked wistful, far away. "Anything wrong?"

"No, nothing's wrong. I feel peaceful but sometimes how 'alone' we are frightens me."

"I've lived here all my life so I guess I don't feel it like you do."

"No, not just here. Any place. I love you and the baby so much yet we're all separate." She searched his face.

"Libby, I don't think life should be different. It's what it is; I let it be. I work, do what needs doing and enjoy myself." He grinned, reached over and tickled her lightly behind her ear. "I leave thinking to you and Ma." He took her hand as they walked to their house for supper. Rachel waved from the porch of the main house. They waved back and smiled.

25

The whole family took Rose to the train in late August, their farewells subdued. Later, Libby, Ma, Auntie Jones and Rachel went to the Morgan home to meet with Nurse Wallace and plan for Libby's delivery. Auntie and Ma had the most experience and Rachel remembered Rose's birth. "Now," Miss Wallace said, "Libby, do you have any question."

"I trust my body and I feel fine now. But Mama…" Libby looked at Miss Wallace.

"Libby, what happened to Mavis is very rare. When that thought comes, you shoo it away and concentrate on your healthy baby. That's best for both of you." Calm and authoritative, Miss Wallace took Libby's hand and looked deeply into her eyes. "You are healthy; you have good women to help; you have a plan; you and the baby are going to be fine."

Later, as Miss Wallace watched them walk down the drive she mused, 'and if fate or nature wants things some other way, there's little more we can do.'

Heading down the hill, the group stopped at the Whitman's. Libby felt fragile. Up in her old room she sat in the family rocking chair, pulled her arms around herself and rocked slowly, breathing hard. Aunt Helen walked in, closed the door. After a moment of silence she spoke quietly, "Libby, you look lost."

Libby looked up and sighed. "As best as I can say it I don't *belong* anyplace. This room was mine and memories are here, but this isn't my home. The farm and the new house are lovely but they're not totally mine yet." She searched Helen's face.

"That'll come, Libby." Helen hesitated. "Are things all right between you and Bertie?"

"Oh, yes. He's sweet and dear. It's just I'm sort of no-place."

"Everything reacts to transplanting. It takes time to grow roots. You went through a long winter; you're doing fine."

Libby looked at her aunt. "I hope you're right. I'm pleased about the baby but tired too. There's just a lot going on and sometimes it overwhelms me. Mama said 'you come from a long line of strong people,' I better remember that more often." She stood and they went downstairs.

"Johnny," Aunt Helen said, "get the rocking chair from Libby's old room and have Bertie bring the wagon up from town."

When Bertie unloaded the rocker and put it in the corner of their kitchen, Libby beamed. "Now we can rock our baby properly," she said. Over the next few months she rested sitting in her rocker, the familiar motion soothing her.

When their anniversary came, Pa raised a toast during the noon dinner. "We've been blessed to have Libby with us for a year now and pretty soon we'll have a new Jones to welcome." He put his hand on Ma's shoulder. "Ma and I wish you love, long life, happiness, healthy children and good harvests." Everyone drank to that.

Bertie stood, thanked his parents and Libby, grinned and said, "for better or worse." Libby nodded, smiling faintly.

26

Libby went into labor on the second day of a raging whiteout. The whole Jones clan was crowded into the main house: Ma, Pa, Rachel, the Uncles, Auntie Jones, Libby and Bertie. After six hours of regular mild pains, Libby began serious labor. Bertie turned pale as his wife doubled over in the kitchen with her first major contraction. Ma took charge.

"Rachel, Auntie, get her into the bed in our room. Pa, you take the men-folk to the barn or the workroom—we'll be set up here in a while. And bring more firewood."

Bertie tried to object but Pa threw his arm around him. "Come with us son: we're not needed here." Bertie watched helplessly as Auntie and Rachel escorted Libby down the hall and settled her in Ma and Pa's big bed.

For 24 hours Libby's labor progressed as the normal winter farm chores went on almost as usual in the throes of the storm. When not working, Bertie paced and winced when he heard Libby's cries. Allowing Ma to guide her, Libby held tightly to Rachel and took short, fast breaths to suppress her cries when pains crashed in on her. When brief thoughts of Mavis assailed her, she tried to picture her mother when she was healthy and happy. Finally on January 21, 1871, during the fourth day of the storm, Ma delivered a healthy baby girl. Rachel wrapped her quickly in a warm, soft blanket and gave her to Libby. The infant cried loudly. Ma tended to Libby as Rachel pulled on her heavy outer coat and followed the safety rope to the barn.

Fifteen minutes later, Bertie bounded into the house, striped off his coat and hat, stepped out of his boots and ran down the hall. Libby, wet with perspiration and tears, holding their wailing child, smiled up at him.

"We have a lovely baby girl, Bertie," Libby said.

Bertie's eyes filled with tears as he leaned down to kiss Libby and look at their daughter. He smiled at his mother. "We're naming her Katherine and we'll call her Katy."

"So, Katherine-Katy, welcome to the Jones family of Quail Hill," Ma remarked, smiling, as she headed for the kitchen. Libby had done well and Katy looked healthy.

Thus, the next generation of the Joneses of Quail Hill had begun and, by Thanksgiving Day, 1875, four younger siblings had been added: Albert, called 'junior,' Annabelle Rose, and twin boys James and John. A second floor had been added to the new house: three bedrooms, one for boys, one for girls and one for Rachel when she stayed with them. 'Auntie Rach' entertained the children by weaving magical tales of distant places, helped Libby with the work five children required and continued her daily meditations.

The farm prospered; their savings grew. Ma, Pa, the Uncles and Auntie Jones slowed a bit but still contributed substantially to Quail Hill's success.

Matthew practiced medicine in Cambridge and still lived with Professor Ely, now a spry widower of 84. Rose taught in Cambridge, boarded at the Ely's and spent every summer on the farm. A live-in couple ran the Ely's Cambridge boarding house and kept the garden while Matthew managed the household accounts. Amy spent summers with her Grandfather including a few weeks together on Cape Cod each year.

One day in 1875 as Professor Ely and Amy walked together on the beach at the Cape, he reflected, "Amy, I've had a wonderful life and doubt I'll live much longer." Amy started to protest. "Don't talk, just listen. With Matthew, Rose and our good help, I'm well cared for. This is not the vague rambling of a doddering old man. I'm quite peaceful. My heart's weak. I've lived through a remarkable time and had an honorable career. You've carried on with teaching and that brings me joy. Your teaching brought Matt and Rose to me—new blessings at life's end.

"Amy, you will inherit everything. Possibly you'll teach in Cambridge someday. In any case, the house will be yours free and clear. As long as Matthew and Rose are boarders you'd be wise to keep it. Matthew may marry and want to buy the place." He leaned over, picked up a shell and examined it carefully before handing it to his granddaughter. "Anyway, my lawyer has my Will and knows my intentions. He'll handle the legal folderol." He looked out over the ocean. "Matthew's a good manager." He waved toward the shell. "Haven't seen one of those in three years." They walked on in silence. Amy's questions could wait. Just being together and listening to the crashing waves was enough.

27

In mid-July 1875, Captain Frederick Russell returned to Boston and joined Amy, her grandfather and Matthew for supper one hot evening. The men drank sherry; Amy sipped tea.

"Well, cousin, what news do you bring?"

Russell refilled his glass and began. "Amy, another story from India. I searched again for the elusive Swami. As I disembarked in Calcutta, I saw Gopal, the lad who'd led me on my earlier adventure, in the crowd. He smiled, raised his hands in blessing and gestured for me to follow. I nodded and moved along the quay keeping his dark body, white dhoti and walking staff in view and soon caught up with him. He smiled and said 'Swami-ji will be pleased.' He engaged a Rickshaw for us and we arrived at the Kali Temple in Dakshinewar at about 4:00 in the afternoon. After removing our shoes, we entered the red brick plaza; it felt like walking on fire. We rounded a corner and ducked into a room on the right. As I entered, a river breeze swept by and the room's dark interior offered respite from the wicked heat. Gopal dropped to his knees and crawled forward, touching his head to the ground before a small, rather odd looking man who sat, eyes closed and ramrod straight, on a tiger skin. The man opened his eyes, patted Gopal on the head affectionately. He then looked at me, smiled, clapped his hands and said, 'Ah, Captain. You've returned.' Then, turning to a disciple, he ordered tea.

"I bowed as the Swami walked toward me. His gaze fixed on me—a most intense look. We walked to another room for tea and, as we sat on cushions, I recognized him as the man I'd meditated with years ago. I bowed my head and said, 'Swami, I don't know your name but you touch my life.' He placed his hands gently on my head and I felt a tingling in my spine.

"He's called 'Sri Ramakrishna Paramahansa,' meaning 'Honored God-Krishna of the Highest Swan'—which refers to the mythical white swan said to carry Deity between heaven and Earth." Russell gazed at the ceiling and sipped sherry. "Ramakrishna studied many religions looking for similarities. Remarkably, he says he found God at the center of Islam and Christianity just as he found God at the center of various paths in Hinduism."

"I've always seen Hinduism as very polytheistic," John Ely stated, "yet, the more I learn, the more I question if that's true. Is the fragmentation in Hinduism or in my mind?"

"Uncle John, we 'see through a glass darkly' with Western eyes. Hindu 'Deities' look bizarre: Siva, the destroyer of all desire; Kali, his fierce consort; Hanuman, the monkey; Genesh, the elephant and so on. Strange. But for a Hindu, these forms represent something like a ray of color split from white light by a prism. For them, God, in final form, is absolutely other—totally beyond understanding. Thus, the mind must act as a prism to separate out, cut off or establish some 'bit' to hang onto. Then one follows this 'bit' into the immensity of Deity. Each person, Hindus believe, carries a tiny speck of the Divine: thus their greeting of 'namaste' means 'I bow to the God within you.'" He smiled. "These things do not fit into words easily."

"Cousin," Amy leaned forward, "tell us more of Ramakrishna's studies."

"He wants the world's religions to recognize their similarities and to work for love, joy and peace. He believes the hearts of all true religions are similar—no matter the outward forms. Maybe this must come from a Hindu who sees any representation of Divinity as just a ray or a spark and not the whole light."

"How does Ramakrishna believe this will happen, this, this—" Amy shrugged.

"The word 'respect' comes close," Russell continued. "He doesn't want one religion. He wants all people to accept other legitimate paths to the One True Transcendent God. Love one another. Learn from others: be open. Grow. When I pressed him on how this might happen, he smiled, nodded his head in a very Indian way and said 'Ah, no problem. If God desires it.' Then he chuckled." Russell handed the volume, *Sections from the Upanishads*, to Ely. "Before I left, Swami-ji gave me this and said 'Enjoy.' Gopal then led me to a room where we slept till morning. During the night, as the moon lit the courtyard, Swami and his disciples chanted in the distance. I sat quietly and listened to them as I basked in the Indian moonlight.

"I've read some chapters of the book. It's quite poetic, haunting refrains. When we meet again you can help me understand it." Then he stood, said good-bye and headed into the night.

After Russell left, Professor Ely turned to Matthew. "My nephew lives an interesting life, Matt. I hope you were not bored," he said, a twinkle in his voice.

"Not at all," Matthew replied, remembering talk of a monkey god and a swami who made spines tingle. Bored? Matthew smiled, shook his head and chuckled. "No, not at all," he repeated thinking how far he'd traveled from Craigmoor and Quail Hill Farm.

In December 1875, Professor Ely died at his desk with the *Upanishads* open before him, his hand resting close to a line about 'let my body be dust' next to which he had written 'from dust thou came and to dust…' At this point his writing ended.

When Ely didn't come to dinner, Matt found him slumped over his open book. After establishing that the Professor was dead, Matt marked the page in the volume and placed it on the corner of the desk. Matt knew how fortunate he'd been to know this extraordinary man who showed him how to live a successful, professional life. "Thank you my friend," he said softly.

28

The twins turned 1 in the fall of 1876 as harvest duties increased. Libby's strength had returned rapidly after her first three pregnancies but not this time. Even with Rachel's help, the work for the family of seven overwhelmed her. A full year after the twins' arrival Libby remained exhausted. On their wedding anniversary, only crumbs of fall color clung to bone-dry tree limbs. Two weeks later, gathering apples in the orchard, Libby heard Auntie Jones' voice shouting wildly as she raced down the hill toward the main house. Libby stood transfixed noting a thin plume of black smoke dancing lightly above Auntie's house. Apples fell from Libby's hands as she stared dumbly at the smoke swirling softly over the roof. Finally, breaking her paralysis, Libby went to find Junior and send him for the men.

"There's a fire up at Auntie's house," she said sadly. Junior's blue eyes widened as he raced across the fields waving his arms and shouting. Annabelle wandered onto the porch. Libby took her into the house. "You stay right here with the twins, Annabelle. Do not go outside till we come back. There'll be lots of noise but you stay here with the twins. Mama will be back. Do you understand?" Annabelle, only 4, nodded seriously as Libby rushed out.

By then, Ma, Rachel and Auntie were heading back up the hill. Rachel swerved and raced to the barn. "The milking buckets!" she cried, her long legs covering the distance rapidly. The other women followed and soon were clambering uphill, buckets in hand.

Down in the lower field, hearing the news from Junior, the men left Big Red at the plow and sprang into action. First, someone must go ring the fire bell a mile down the lane to alert other farmers who might be able to come and help. Sending one of the men could fatally undermine their ability to fight the fire. Bertie turned to Junior.

"Son, can you ride Red bareback, no bridle?" Junior nodded. "Are you sure? This is awful important."

"I rode him like that in the field a couple times, Papa."

· Craigmoor ·

Bertie unhitched Red and tossed his small son onto the horse's broad back. "The gate's open. Ride to the bell; ring it real loud and long. Send anybody who comes, up here to help. You set?"

Junior grabbed two handfuls of Red's mane. "I'm set Papa but you've got to make him go fast. He won't go fast for me."

"Hang on," Bertie ordered, "MOVE OUT, RED!" he shouted and slapped the big horse on the rump. Red startled and bolted forward, heading for the gate. Bertie ran the other direction toward the barn and the burning house. He watched Red and Junior over his left shoulder. Just out the gate, Red pulled right toward the barn. Junior yanked Red's mane to the left, shouted and kicked. The horse turned left, cantered down the road and disappeared behind his own dust.

Running uphill Bertie gasped, "Lord, I don't trouble you much but we sure could use some help right now." When he arrived the bucket brigade was in full swing: pumping and hauling bucket after bucket. Flames licked up the wall, burst through the roof, gobbled up the porch. Bertie ran to the small shed next to the Uncle's house, hauled out tools and farm equipment: saws, hatchets, axes. Ax in hand, he headed for the closest trees. If fire jumped to the trees, the whole hill could go up. The men hacked, chopped and sawed furiously hauling brush and trees away from the flames as fast as they could. Sometime during the mayhem others began arriving: wagonloads of men, women and children. Folks dove into the work. Even small hands proved useful.

Less than three hours later, the fire was out. Charred remains stood; household items sat scattered around the lawn. Felled trees and hewn branches lay in disarray. Exhausted, soot-covered people stood coughing, wiping their eyes. Pa walked down the hill to the fire bell and brought Junior and Red home. Junior went up to Bertie who reached down to muss up his hair.

"I'm real proud of you, son."

"But the house burned down, Papa!" Junior wailed.

"Yes," Bertie sighed, "we lost a house, but we saved the farm. We're strong; we'll rebuild." Bertie put his arm around Junior's shoulder. "That's what Joneses do."

Folks milled around, comforted one another, wandered off and headed home. The Joneses continued dousing the smoking ruins all night.

Libby finally got herself and all five children cleaned up, fed and put to bed. She lay alone: exhausted, numb, and too tired to sleep. Any gains she made while Rose was home for the summer melted away. She knew their savings for the children's educations would go to rebuild the house—now just charred ruins— where Auntie Jones and the two Jones Uncles lived. Everyone could crowd into the two remaining houses on the farm temporally but they would rebuild. Seven years, four pregnancies and five babies Libby had given to this place where work never ended and tragedy lurked in a spark. She felt nothing: neither fear nor anger, nothing. Her prayer life, waning recently, ceased. She stared at the ceiling watching silver moonlight shadows move coldly on the walls as the curtains swayed in the night breeze. She wondered if she would live until morning—or if it mattered.

Inexorably, Libby deteriorated. Their savings spent, she had no strength for anger. Over the next three years, she slid toward a deep, passive vortex. Habits and inertia kept her moving. The threads of her emotional stability grew thin like the worn sleeve-edge of an old sweater that finally severed altogether.

People overlooked, ignored or dismissed the signs as she withdrew more and more. Bertie decided Libby's coldness came from having so many children. Initially, Ma figured 'Libby's just too busy.' Rachel became the central figure for the children, increasing her workload as Libby declined. Libby could do what Rachel or Bertie told her to do but she avoided decisions. Her best moments came with her children; she could still smile with them.

However Libby understood her condition, the illness itself left her unable to summon aid. She lost weight, couldn't concentrate, slept fitfully and, awakened by terrifying nightmares, prowled the house until the sun rose. Her world became gray, lifeless and flat. During the summer of 1878, Rose tried frantically to help. She wrote pleading letters to Matt to come home, took special trips to town and begged Libby's father, her Aunt Helen and Grandmother Margaret to spend more time on the farm. Up on Quail Hill, Rose kept the children occupied and stayed with Libby through many long frightening nights.

Bertie felt embarrassed and angry by Libby's behavior. One evening as Rose and Bertie walked in the orchard, he blurted out, "Rosie, what's wrong with her?"

"I don't know Bert, but we have to do what we can till Matt gets here."

"I don't want Matt here!" He shouted. "Not now." He clamped his jaw shut.

Rose flared back, "Matt may be the only one who can help. He's a doctor."

"No! I do not want him to come or know how she is and that's final."

"Don't use that tone of voice with me, Albert Jones. Matt already knows about her condition because I wrote and told him. Or do you just want to wait for her funeral?" Rose's eyes flashed and her cold, angry voice allowed no contradiction.

Bertie leaned against a tree, slumped onto the ground. "Oh, Rosie, no. She can't die. She just can't." The color drained from his face. Rose sat beside him.

"Then we have to do what we can. Matt's a beginning. He'll come in September after I get back to Cambridge."

Bertie nodded mutely.

When Matt arrived, he examined Libby and talked to her for a long time. He found nothing physically wrong.

"Is Bertie hurting you?' Matt asked.

"No, Matt. We argue. He gets angry. He's never hit me. He spanks the children. I don't like that."

Matt sighed and probed no further.

Later, Ma asked simply, "What good is your education if you can't help your brother's wife? We've sacrificed so much and you say there's nothing wrong? Matthew, we are watching her die inch by inch!"

Matthew felt frustrated as he experienced what every clinician feels when confronted by a diagnostic gauntlet. "Ma," he said gently, "there're more ways to get sick than any doctors understand. We do what we can. She needs rest. And maybe to get away for awhile."

By their anniversary in October, Libby had become mute. They held no celebration. After arranging for Libby to stay with Louise Putnam, Ma bundled her daughter-in-law up and took her to town. During that ride, Ma spoke gently.

"Libby, we Joneses may seem a strange lot but we love you and want the best for you. We're not sure what to do so if you can give us any clue, anything about what you need, please, if you can, let us know; you may hold the only key." Ma wasn't sure if Libby heard her as she stared into Ma's face and then looked down at her own hands.

Aunt Helen ushered them into the kitchen of the Whitman home –Libby's childhood home—as she made tea. Helen and Ma talked, tried to include Libby. Libby wandered slowly around the room, touching surfaces lightly. At the kitchen sink she splashed water onto her face, reached for a towel. Then she turned and asked quietly, "Where is Miss Middleton?"

"She's at school now but she'll be at the Putnams by 5:00," Helen replied.

"I'd like to see her," Libby said and started walking toward the door.

Ma's eyes filled with tears. Her mind grasped this tiny thread and held on like a drowning person clings to a life-ring. She asked quietly, "Shall we take the wagon or walk?"

"Walk."

As they arrived at school, the children, including Libby's own, were leaving.

"Have you come to take us home, Mama?" Katy asked.

Libby looked confused, a bit helpless.

Ma replied. "I'm going to take you home in the wagon. Mama is staying with Mrs. Putnam and Miss Middleton for awhile."

Annabelle buried her face in Libby's skirt and asked, "How long?"

Libby knelt down and looked into Annabelle's earnest face. "We don't know. Till I'm better." Libby felt less sure than she sounded and looked up at Miss Middleton.

Amy put a comforting hand on Annabelle's shoulder. "As long as she needs, Annabelle, until she's stronger. Auntie Rach, Papa, Ma and Pa will take special care of you."

Junior stood at a distance. "Can we sleep in the big house?" he asked.

"Of course," Ma said, gathering the children and heading up to the Whitman house to get the wagon. Katy turned, waved hesitantly. Libby blew a kiss. Then she and Amy stood alone.

"I need to pick up some papers," Amy said, "then we'll go to the Putnam's."

They walked in silence. Libby went straight to the room Rose had occupied during their time of teaching, sat on the bed, removed her shoes, lay down and closed her eyes. Amy arranged a blanket over her and closed the door as she left.

Amy joined Louise for tea in the kitchen. For a year, they'd been the only two in the house.

"Well, Amy, a little time here with us should help".

"We'll do what we can, Louise," Amy replied. In all these years it was the first time they had called each other by their first names.

For the next five days Libby did little more than eat and sleep. She snuggled down into the bed, feeling safe. Sometimes she woke with a start, almost remembering a dream: almost able to face it. Almost.

John, Aunt Helen and Margaret visited daily. On the fifth day, Margaret brought gingerbread. Libby savored it, leaning onto her pillows and sighing.

"Your gingerbread is special and today I can actually taste it." Libby said, looking at her Grandmother earnestly. "Grandma, what's wrong with me?"

"I don't know and I won't say I do." Margaret replied. "You need rest, that's for sure. Women can get morose from too many babies—just sucked dry. It may be that. Matt finds nothing wrong but there's more doctors don't know than what they do. Right now you need more gingerbread." Margaret stood to leave the room.

"I'll come down," Libby said. She dressed slowly, tidied her hair. In the kitchen she ate another piece of gingerbread, drank a glass of milk. "Let's go out for a few minutes."

Bundled up against the wind, Libby and Margaret walked outside into a blustery, bright, October day. Louise Putnam's garden displayed the same order the Putnam home and Louise's life exhibited. Only a few plants still bloomed. They wandered through the flowers, vegetables and herbs. Libby breathed in deeply, leaned on Margaret's arm, fumbled with her scarf and made short staccato gestures with her free hand. After fifteen minutes, they went inside. Margaret hugged Libby, said goodbye and headed home. Libby joined Louise Putnam in the parlor where she sat sewing.

"Mrs. Putnam, your gardens are lovely," Libby remarked.

"Thank you Libby, I work hard to keep them orderly. Come sit for awhile."

Libby sat on a rocker. "Nothing in my life's orderly. Everything's scattered, broken."

"Well, 'scattered' sounds easier to repair," Louise replied gently.

"Maybe both." Libby shrugged. "Scattered, broken, some places just full of weeds."

"Weeds," said Louise brightly, "are easy. Attack and show no mercy. I love to weed. Especially when I'm angry and don't want to be public about it. Dig and rip and fling them on the compost pile. Always gives me great satisfaction." Louise smiled naughtily.

Libby scowled. "You never seem angry."

Louise put her sewing down. "Libby, if I held all my petty little feelings inside, I'd be a mess pretty quick. Now, you'd best," Louise paused, deciding whether to say 'rest' or 'help me with dinner,' and chose the latter. Libby followed her into the kitchen.

As they worked together Libby asked, "Did you disagree with him much?"

"With whom?" Louise asked.

"With Mr. Putnam."

"Well," Louise cocked her head and pursed her lips. "We disagreed but I'm not sure 'much' is accurate."

"What about?"

"How to rear children. Money. Things between a husband and wife. The usual." Louise turned to face Libby. "There's never a good time to have your mother die, Libby, but you lost Mavis at a difficult time. If she'd lived she would have taught you things and just seeing her with your father would have taught you things. Helen and John are brother and sister. That's different. A major challenge for husbands and wives is merging their different family backgrounds without either feeling too diminished. Women make more compromises but you have to work it out. I figure it's pretty 'Jones' up on Quail Hill, isn't it?"

Libby chuckled. "That's a funny way to put it but, yes, it's pretty 'Jones' up there. Bertie tries real hard, even calls me 'Libby Whitman' sometimes, but I just," tears formed in her eyes, "can't push as hard for what I want as he can: he plows over me." She paused. "He doesn't mean to. He's always fought for his own way and folks he can't charm he overwhelms."

Louise wiped her hands on her apron, intensified her gaze. "You need to push harder; stand your ground firmly; keep more space for Libby. He fell in love with you because you are special and not a Jones. It's important not to lose that 'Libby.' Don't become only 'wife' and 'mother.' Mavis would have shown you that. You stay sweet and kind but you get stronger. What's needed on Quail Hill is more 'Libby Whitman' strength."

Libby blinked. 'You come from a long line of strong people' Mavis had written. Libby heard that message. Again.

29

Libby said a simple prayer that night asking protection for herself and her family. When the dark dream came, she didn't bolt from sleep but remained in it: both as spectator and participant, ready to awaken if she needed to. The dream shifted and merged with one from years before: Libby hovered over Craigmoor school, Bertie stood beyond a chasm surrounded by children. Five of the six children looked familiar but the youngest baby girl, crying in Bertie's arms, she didn't recognize. The scene shifted and she could look down on her body as it lay, covered by a white silk cloth, on a table in a dimly lit room. Only her face was visible. Her body's eyes were closed; it didn't move: appeared paralyzed. Strange gargoyles, demon-like creatures gathered around the table gnashing their teeth, wringing their hands, gurgling menacing sounds. As she watched, the room brightened. Libby experienced no fear: just powerlessness. Her 'dream persona' sensed a figure dressed in a long white robe standing by her right shoulder. She couldn't see the figure's face, couldn't make out details. In her mind the figure said, 'Before all time you belong to me.' Gradually the scene faded: first the demons melted away like butter in the sun, then her dream body dissolved, finally the figure beside her evaporated. She woke, stared into the darkness and felt protected.

Libby rolled over and went back to sleep. The next morning she ate two eggs with toast, butter and jam.

That night in dreams she wrestled a force she could neither identify nor defeat. Alone in the total darkness of her dream she wrestled endlessly with this obscure force that always remained in control. Always the force equaled her. Always the match ended in a draw, not because her strength matched its strength but because the force didn't push beyond Libby's strength. The fight continued until, out on the horizon, a pinpoint speck of light began moving toward her. As it approached closer it became larger and larger and she was about to collide with it. Libby pulled back into her pillow, opened her eyes and said, "No!" Instantly the light disappeared, the dream ended. She lay, staring into the night, her heart pounding and wondered if she had just escaped death or just rejected God.

Libby started helping with breakfast, she took walks, visited Helen, her father, Margaret and Richard. She greeted people and smiled. One day, as Helen watched her niece walk away from the Whitman home, she recalled a memory from childhood. She'd found an injured cat under the front porch; broken and terrified, it rejected everyone except Helen and allowed her near only to bring food. Slowly, its condition improved. Scars remained, it walked with a limp but it allowed itself to be touched. When partially healed, its tail made an absurd right angle an inch higher than the cat's back. Finally fully recovered, tail held high and proud, the cat wandered away. Libby, Helen realized, while improving, still limped.

One Saturday afternoon Libby and Amy walked through town, over the bridge and up the hill on the far side of the river. Looking back down at the town, Amy asked, "How are you?"

"Better. But there are things missing: things I should understand but don't."

"You're young. There's plenty of time to learn."

"It seems so useless," Libby blurted out. "People are born and die; houses are built and burn down; summer and winter chase each other around like a dog after a cat and what does any of it mean?" Libby looked at Amy who squinted through her glasses and nodded. "Why are you nodding?" Libby demanded.

"Because I agree with you. Life can look like that." Amy's now gray-streaked black hair curled in its usual semi-uncontrolled fashion around her head.

"Miss Middleton, I need a better answer than that!" Libby said indignantly.

Amy removed her glasses, rubbed her eyes. "I'm not trying to avoid your question but I don't have a better answer. The only way to get to the other side of the field marked 'it all seems useless' is to travel through it. Ultimately, you must find your own meaning, your own joy: find what sustains you."

A cold wind whipped past them; Libby shivered. "That scares me."

"We're all afraid sometimes but, frightened or not, it's the journey we're on."

"I'm like a clock that's stopped. Where do I find 'joy'?" Libby challenged.

Amy held out her left hand with her palm up, wordlessly pointed to it with her right index finger. Watching her hand, Amy slowly brought the tip of her left index finger to form a circle with her left thumb and then opened the circle so the index finger straightened out again. Slowly she repeated the action with her middle finger, her ring finger and finally her little finger. Then she turned her hand over and rapidly wiggled all her fingers at once. Libby started to speak but Miss Middleton put her right index finger to her lips and shook her head. Then she repeated the action with her right hand. Cautiously Libby turned her left hand palm up, cocked her head and looked at Amy quizzically.

"Libby, joy is in creation."

"Oh fine, Miss Middleton," Libby sounded exasperated, "but all I do is work!"

"Be very observant while you work. Watch your hands; wiggle your fingers. Think about the yeast growing in your bread dough. Smile and sing and laugh. Are you writing poetry? You wrote lots of poetry in school."

"Not anymore. I don't have time."

"Take time," Amy challenged.

"That would be selfish," Libby retorted.

"For a woman with five growing children I'd say taking care of yourself is the very *least* selfish thing you can do! You need to be healthy and back up on Quail Hill. So you take time for yourself. It's not selfish for a musician to practice."

They walked back to town in silence.

"Will you move to Cambridge now that you've inherited the house?" Libby asked as they passed the school.

"Not anytime soon: my life's here. Did you enjoy visiting school the other day?"

Libby nodded. "Mainly I watched my children. Katy is like I was but prettier, more like Rose. Junior's like Bertie. I sat there and fell in love all over again as he squirmed, wiggled and gazed out the window. How do you put up with him?"

"How did I put up with Bertie? I keep Junior very busy and I'm a better teacher now."

"Annabelle's a puzzle. Very like my father: quiet and reserved. She looks out at the world with her big blue eyes and takes everything in," Libby remarked.

"She's worried about you. If you take better care of yourself, it'll help Annabelle, too."

When they got back to the Putnam's Amy gave Libby a small blank notebook.

"I'm serious about writing—whether it's poetry or not—take time for yourself," she said.

That night, Libby jotted notes on the prayers Mavis had taught her: prayers about God working in her, around her and through her. 'I'm not good at the part about *in me*,' she wrote.

Bertie and the children came to town for church the next day. After the service Rachel took the children up to the Whitman house for Sunday dinner. Libby and Bertie walked to the school and sat on the old swing they'd shared many times. Bertie lit his pipe, clenched his teeth tightly on the stem making his mouth a straight slit below his moustache. The November north-wind swirled lightly around them and the swing springs squeaked rhythmically.

"I'm coming home Wednesday. I'll walk with the children after school." Libby's voice was soft but sure.

"Snow's coming soon. You ready for that?" Bertie's voice cracked; his eyes flashed.

"Yes. It's time." She paused, wanted to reach for his hand but couldn't. "I never wanted this to happen. I'm better: maybe not well but better. I have some clues about how to stay healthier." She sat on the edge of the swing breathing hard.

"Okay. I'll come Wednesday and get all of you, then." He stood, reached for her hand. Tears welled up in Libby's eyes. He took his pipe out and said, "We miss you and want you back." He smiled a small tight smile. They walked arm and arm up to the Whitman house.

30

On Tuesday Libby walked up the hill to her grandparent's house. Margaret made tea.

"I'm glad you're going home, Libby. You're ready," Margaret said.

"I hope so, Grandma. I feel better."

"Mavis had troubles. Her father always saw it best. He saw it coming in you, too." Margaret took Libby's hand. "Stay closer to us. Come to town more. Thank Ma Jones and Rose. They fought for you. Without them…" she shrugged.

"I'm beginning to understand that."

Margaret chuckled. "We're all beginners. That's both the problem and the fun of life."

Libby walked down to the Whitman home. Later, as she and her father left to walk to town, Aunt Helen hugged her and said, "The best advice I know is: 'Work. Love. Trust. Leave the rest to God.'"

When Libby and John reached the edge of town, he remarked, "I'm going to pick up my new dog. Want to come?"

"Oh, yes Papa."

Up the far hill and past the cemetery they arrived at the Reynolds' place. Old man Reynolds bred strong, clear-eyed hunting setters. The new pups were seven weeks old and ready to go. Three pups ran toward them followed by their dame. John scooped up his 'pick-of-the-litter' male and they fussed affectionately at each other. A little, scrawny female held back, wiggling in the dust. It shyly sidled up to Libby who knelt down pet her. Mr. Reynolds came out of his barn and greeted them.

"They all placed now?" John asked.

"All but the runt. Doubt she'd find a bird tied to her tail." Mr. Reynolds shook his head slowly. The men looked at the puppy Libby was petting. The runt jumped up: licked her face.

"Oh, Papa," Libby exclaimed. "She's beautiful."

"Not sure I agree with you but she's loving enough."

"You want her Libby?" Mr. Reynolds asked.

Libby looked up, a soft smile on her face. She nodded. Then she scooped up the puppy, stood up and said resolutely, "Yes, Mr. Reynolds, I want her."

· Quail Hill ·

"She's yours then. Maybe she'll cheer you up some," Reynolds chuckled. A shrewd businessman, he'd both gotten rid of the runt and made a friend happy. 'Sometimes' he realized, 'you just keep winning.'

"I'll pick her up tomorrow and name her 'Princess.' Papa, I'll pay you back."

"What do I owe for her?" John asked.

"Just what she's worth, John. Nothing. 'Princess' indeed!" He shook his head.

That night, as Libby slept, on the fringe of her dream-world she saw the pinpoint of light reappear. It approached steadily, grew larger, gained speed. She knew she could stop it, open her eyes, end the experience, avoid the risk but she chose to continue. Instantly she collided with the light in an immense explosion. Self-awareness ceased. Words shattered. Light, time and space merged: universally present, eternally now. Libby disintegrated into, fused with the light: became both nonexistent and totally alive. Nothing else existed: no past or future, inside or out, self or other. Nothing remained except pure, peaceful light expanding throughout the universe, throughout her.

Gradually Libby felt herself lying in the bed. She smiled and went back to sleep. In the morning, a tranquil feeling remained.

At noon, Libby walked up to the Reynolds' farm, picked up Princess and returned to the Putnam's. After Bertie did a few errands he picked up the children at school and drove the wagon around the square. Louise and Libby stood by the front gate playing with Princess. Bertie squinted down at the young setter.

"I'm not sure I want to know but who owns that pathetic creature?" he inquired.

"I do, Bertie Jones," Libby said her face opening into a broad smile. "She belongs to me and her name's Princess." Holding Princess carefully, Libby climbed onto the front seat. "She's the sweetest puppy in the world." Katy and Annabelle both reached for the dog. "Surely you wouldn't deny us a new puppy?"

Bertie shook his head. "No, Libby Whitman, I'll not deny us a useless dog named Princess." He reached over and squeezed her hand. Junior lifted Libby's suitcase into the wagon and hopped in. "Let's go," Bertie called and Red started off. Libby waved to Louise. They drove over the bridge and turned left heading for four corners. Libby released the puppy to Katy.

That night in bed, Bertie reached to extinguish the oil lamp but Libby stopped him.

"Let the light burn," she said softly. He looked confused. "Real low, just let it burn."

Libby never wanted the lamp lit, never wanted him to see her. Now he looked over at her soft smile, her blond hair down and free around her shoulders.

"I've missed you more than I thought I could miss anyone," she said.

Bertie pulled her to him, kissed her, moved his hands over her, his desire growing. He pulled his nightshirt over his head and then removed her nightgown. Slowly he moved the sheet and blankets down revealing her shoulder, arm and body. The skin on her breasts glowed in the golden light. He ran his hand across the stretch marks on her belly allowing his hand and eyes to explore her. He kissed her neck, moved slowly down to her breast, his hands pressing into her, fingers moving tentatively. She responded with short breaths and small sighs, pulling back only to return again to his touch, moving with him. When he entered her, she buried her head in his neck and pressed toward him.

Afterward, they lay together in the sputtering light. Experiencing this raw power, risking being this close and open with Bertie, was new. Libby turned off the lamp and slept naked for the first time in her life.

In the morning, Bertie rolled over and smiled at her, his eyes dancing.

"Say it, Bertie. Whatever you're thinking, say it," she coaxed.

He propped himself on his elbow. "You're a very beautiful woman," he ran his fingers over her face. "I hope you don't get sick again." She nodded.

31

The winter passed and Libby took time for herself. Princess helped. They walked together or played while the babies napped. She often jotted words or brief ideas in her notebook. Her prayer life stirred: brief silent thanksgivings or petitions woven throughout her day. She looked more deeply: at faces, carrots, even dishwater. She listened more intently: to voices, pans rattling, cats fighting. She noticed small things: textures, smells. She queried Rachel about meditation. Rachel 'sat' twice a day using the technique learned ten years before.

"It anchors me," Rachel said. "Particularly when you were gone and I was more in charge. At night, when I went to my room I'd wonder 'How would I manage to pray and meditate if I were joining a husband?' I can focus more easily on God. I admire you and Ma."

"I'm not special, Rach. We all work hard. I'm lucky you were here when I was…"

"Ill." Rachel stated gently. "You're better now. We're family; we help each other. You'd do the same for me."

"I don't know, to care for five children not your own," Libby shook her head.

"But they *are* mine: *my* family's next generation. Whatever part of me continues will be through them."

Bright sparkling March days brought the continuous flurry of activity associated with 'sugaring season.' Big Red hauled the sleigh through the maple orchard carrying men, taps, tools and buckets. The trees snapped and whistled as breezes played in ice-covered limbs. Once the sap started to flow, the real work began: checking buckets, hauling sap to sugaring shacks, watching fires and monitoring vats to produce quality syrup. Much work fell to Junior.

One afternoon, sitting with Libby in their kitchen as the twins napped, Bertie said, "Junior's not finishing all his chores; he needs another thrashing."

"I doubt that's necessary," Libby said softly. "Let's find another way." Her heart raced but her voice stayed calm and her fingers kept knitting. Bertie stared at her; she put down her knitting. His anger and her stubbornness collided as their blue eyes locked.

"I'll not mollycoddle my son. He needs a firm hand and I'll provide it!"

"I'm not suggesting he not be punished when he needs punishing; I'm suggesting there are better ways than beating him. He just gets resentful and defies you again." Libby trod dangerous ground.

"Pa produced good sons and he never shied from whipping us," Bertie stood slowly.

"Be careful, Bertie, the fruit doesn't fall far from the tree."

Bertie leaned on the table. "And?"

"I believe we can change a pattern here that feels like 'meanness.'"

"You want to spoil my son." Bertie stated flatly.

"He is our son: my son, too. I can't stop you whipping him but he's too old for it, it isn't working and you'll regret it."

"You think Pa regrets thrashing me? Are you too soft to be a Jones?"

"That's a dreadful thing to say. I've worked ten years on this farm, given five children to this family—our family, my family. My voice will be heard!" She stood and faced him. "And 'yes,' I believe your Pa regrets some of his ways, would take back some things if he could. We all have regrets, but our chance is now. We can be both strong and smarter. Let's try to figure out how to change Junior, reduce his defiance, his rage. Or does that have to continue in the Jones legacy?" Her voice softened. "Bertie, I know you love Junior and I know you love your Pa but he did hurt you sometimes and now you're hurting Junior." She put her hand on his arm. He flinched but did not pull away. "We can figure different ways. God gave children two parents so they can balance each other, make new combinations. Your parents weren't perfect, nor were mine. Let's find better ways."

Bertie sighed, put his hand on her hand. "There may be something in what you say but for now, that's all." He pulled on his coat and headed for the barn.

Libby watched him go. As she sank into her rocker she felt dizzy. She'd both affirmed his authority and stood her ground. The twins started fussing and she walked to their crib.

"Yes," she said softly, "a bit more 'Whitman' is needed here."

Bertie didn't thrash Junior. The next evening after supper they talked while the girls and the twins started chores in the barn. Junior said he had too much work. Tempers flared. Libby washed dishes at the sink, didn't interrupt. They worked out a compromise: Annabelle, the true horse-lover, would take over feeding the horses and Junior agreed to help teach the twins their new chores. That way he would be leading them, an appropriate job for the oldest son.

"Remember," Bertie said, "when the twins start doing more, you can only give away chores you're doing." Hearing this, Libby turned and smiled at Bertie over the back of Junior's head. Bertie's expression didn't change as their eyes met. Junior dashed out and joined the evening chores.

"You may be right. Time will tell." Bertie stood, heading out.

"Thank you." Libby said softly.

Libby confused him. Their lovemaking was more passionate and she responded to him more. But she'd become less predictable.

Later that spring, Libby became pregnant for the fifth time. One Saturday in June, she looked out the window and watched a quail family crossing the field. First the hen raced from behind a protective clump of grass and darted across an open space. Chicks streaked from their hiding places one by one, dashed after her, formed a line of frantically speeding bodies strung out across the bare ground and then disappeared into the taller brush.

Libby smiled. Last year she wouldn't have noticed. She headed toward the chicken coop to gather eggs. Katy joined her walking to her right, Princess padded along to her left. Junior lagged behind holding Annabelle's hand and the twins brought up the rear, poking each other. Libby turned to speak to Junior, stopped and laughed aloud.

"What's so funny, Mama?" asked Katy.

"We are!" Libby said. "We look like Mother Quail and her chicks."

She gazed at her children, her hand resting on her belly. Looking out over the fields and past the barn to the distant mountains she relaxed into the hope of early summer: the regeneration of life. In the henhouse they put the eggs into the basket carefully; once again they were saving half the egg money for future college educations.

32

One day in July of 1879, as Libby and Rose weeded the kitchen garden above the steep blueberry patch, Libby paused and said, "Thank you for all you did last summer."

"I did what I could, Libby. Matt helped. Ma and Rachel were the strong ones. They deserve the credit for getting you help."

"I might've improved, staying here, but I'm not sure." She looked over the valley. "This baby feels right, Rose. With the twins I felt exhausted; I have energy now."

After finishing their weeding, they crossed the lane to Libby's house and sat on the porch shelling peas. By the barn, Junior and both twins scattered grain for the geese, Annabelle 'trained' Princess and Katy walked toward the main chicken coop with her egg basket.

"I'm sorry you don't have children," Libby said.

Rose smiled. "I have what I want. I can't imagine having children and teaching, too."

"It'd be nice if women could do both." Libby mused.

"The work would kill you."

"Things might change. With enough help you could do both; men do both."

"Men have wives who organize and do everything. It won't happen in my lifetime."

"Perhaps in theirs," Libby remarked, nodding toward the children. "Or their children's."

"Perhaps," Rose replied.

Libby went into labor during a whiteout in January 1880. The storm locked them all into the big house. The men made only necessary trips to the barn to attend livestock. Ma had a severe flu and Rachel attended her leaving Auntie Jones and Bertie to assist Libby. Katy watched the children. Bertie had not seen a child born and, until now, Libby hadn't wanted him present. He followed Auntie's directions: gathered supplies, wiped Libby's face with water and held her hand as her contractions intensified.

After a short labor, Libby delivered a healthy baby girl. Auntie wrapped her, cleared her mouth and handed the squalling newborn to Bertie before she attended to Libby. Libby lifted her head and watched as Bertie cradled their sixth child. He looked wide-eyed. She wanted this moment to continue so she lay back on her pillows and relaxed.

This was the baby of her dream, the child she'd seen Bertie holding on the other side of the chasm, and she knew it was their last child. Relief swept through her.

Bertie placed the child in Libby's arms. "You'd better meet our baby girl," he said.

"Hello, Amy Louise. You certainly have strong lungs," Libby remarked.

"She's beautiful, even all scrunched up."

"She's beautiful because she's ours, Bertie." Libby drifted off to sleep as Amy Louise stopped crying and sucked on Libby's fingertip.

33

When Margaret, now 84, and Richard 85, met Amy Louise for the first time, Margaret carefully inspected her great-granddaughter, counted fingers and toes and declared her the prettiest one yet.

"I knew you'd say that, Grandma," Libby grinned happily. "Once I worried 'What if my babies are ugly? What will Grandma say?'"

"Libby, a great-grandmother sees the heart and the heart of a newborn is always beautiful." Margaret placed her index fingers in the baby's tiny hands. Amy Louise gripped Margaret tightly, scrunching up her face, looking intently into Margaret's eyes. They cooed and gurgled at each other. In Margaret's mind, the introduction of another infant to another great-grandmother thirty years earlier appeared. She'd baked gingerbread that day, too. Since then, so many normal family events: births, deaths, health, illness, good years and lean.

Richard pulled up his chair, leaned close to Amy Louise, smiled and cooed. Years fell away: the infant was Mavis, then Libby, finally Amy Louise. Joy and tragedy intertwined in this moment and joy prevailed because they willed it to prevail.

Quail Hill's dog population had dwindled to Bertie's aging hunter, Big Boy, and Libby's young Princess. Even with Pa and the Uncles hunting less, the farm needed more canines.

"Junior, you ready for your own dog?" Bertie asked.

"Oh yes, Papa," Junior looked at Bertie expectantly.

"Then we better go see Mr. Reynolds."

They chose Rover, a young male that Mr. Reynolds had already started training.

"Just keep him away from your Mama's bitch. Princess should not be bred."

"I may train Princess myself as Junior trains Rover. Big Boy can help but he'll retire soon." Bertie watched for Reynolds' reaction.

Reynolds snorted a laugh. "Bert, you've got courage but no sense. Don't waste your time. Leave Princess to love the missus and play with the baby and pick yourself a new dog."

"I'll give Princess a try. If I fail, I'll be back."

"Well then, you'll be back, Bert Jones." Mr. Reynolds smiled around the pipe stem clutched tightly in his teeth.

"I can't lose. If I get Princess to hunt, fine. If not, Libby loves her, she watches the baby and plays nicely with the children. And, she didn't cost me a cent." Bertie grinned.

Junior worked seriously with Rover developing a greater sense of responsibility. Together, they progressed well. Bertie's work with Princess proved less successful. Both Bertie and Big Boy tried their best, but Princess just followed them around looking eager, happy and confused. When corrected, she'd slink off and hide. When found, she'd grovel briefly and then race off to find Amy Louise and Libby.

By the first day of hunting, Rover and Big Boy worked well together. Rover watched Junior and followed his commands, took cues from Big Boy, pointed well and remained silent. Bertie felt proud of Junior. Princess, surprisingly well behaved as they left the barn, turned tail and raced back to the house as soon as shooting began. She huddled under the porch until Libby coaxed her out with food. Loud sounds terrified her. She never hunted again.

For the rest of the season, Bertie, Junior, Big Boy and Rover hunted well adding pheasants, quails and even a few wild turkeys to the Jones' larder. The next year Bertie would get a grand new pup from Reynolds but by then, the Joneses, Reynolds, most of Craigmoor and much of New England had gained new respect for Princess.

34

July 3, 1881 dawned sultry, hot and threatening rain. Robins sang rain-calls into stagnant air thick with bugs. Tempers flared and anger exploded like fireworks in the oppressive mugginess. Everyone had extra, holiday, chores. All wanted relief from the heat, the work and the bugs. Thunder rolled in the distance creating the heightened sensitivity preceding a big storm. At 2:30, the first droplets fell. Within minutes the sky turned inky black and a fiery lightening bolt blasted into a field a few miles away followed by a shrieking clap of thunder as the leading edge of the storm began advancing up the hill.

Libby and Katy pulled clothes from the lines frantically; the men moved the horses to the barn at break-neck speed; children dropped their weeding tools and raced toward the porch seeking shelter. Loaded down with damp clothes, Libby herded the children into the house. She dropped the clothes on the table, took a deep breath, looked around and panicked.

"Annabelle," she said, "where's Amy Louise?"

Annabelle looked confused and then wailed, "Oh, Mama, I don't know. I was so scared I just ran. We were at the far end of the orchard." Annabelle buried her face in Libby's skirt.

Stunned, Libby reacted instantly. She pushed Annabelle toward Katy.

"Katy, hold Annabelle and keep everyone here. When Papa comes, send him to the orchard." Libby dashed out the door, raced through the kitchen garden toward the orchard. "Please, God, let me find her, please let her be safe," she begged as she ran. As she passed the corner of the house, she saw Princess dancing around the big oak washtub they'd left close to the northeast downspout. She would deal with Princess later. After racing the entire length of the garden and reaching the most distant corner of the orchard, she heard a faint cry. Libby turned and watched Princess fifty yard away frantically digging in the tub, pushing and pulling at some partly submerged object. Horrified, Libby recognized the material of Amy Louise's skirt in the tub.

Fear paralyzed her and the whole scene changed into an eerie, slow motion ballet. Libby felt as though she swam in molasses, every movement taking an eternity as she struggled toward the washtub. Princess's actions became trapped in the same slow-motion time warp. Libby watched individual drops of water splash from the tub: watched Amy Louise's face appear and submerge: watched Princess dive under and struggle to lift the child.

Libby staggered forward as Princess leapt from the tub, shook once, turned and thrust her head and front legs back into the water. She emerged with Amy Louise's collar in her mouth and heaved the little girl's head and shoulders over the edge of the tub, trying to wrestle her to the ground. At that moment, a bolt of lightening exploded a tree in the center of the orchard no more than 15 feet in front of Libby. The ground shook, thunder roared and the concussion smashed Libby to the ground where she lay—strange sensations pulsing through her body, unable to move, unable to hear—enveloped in the acrid aftermath of the lightening strike.

Libby watched helplessly as Princess startled, released her grip on Amy Louise and crouched low, trembling fearfully. Then the dog shook herself, stopped quivering, crept back, grabbed Amy Louise's sleeve and pulled her onto the ground. Princess licked the baby's face and began dragging her toward the house.

Normal time returned as Libby stood and raced toward the house. She caught up with Princess as the dog hauled Amy Louise up the first porch step. Tears streamed down Libby's face as she lifted her limp baby and rushed toward the door, Princess by her side. She looked down at Amy Louise as more lightening crackled and a thunder blast hurled Libby, the baby and Princess against the door. Bertie and Pa leapt onto the porch, arriving at that moment from the barn. Bertie jerked the door open and they all tumbled into the kitchen, Princess at their heels. The incident may have taken five minutes but it seemed like an eternity.

Bertie sagged as he saw Amy Louise's wet, flaccid body. In a swift, powerful move he grabbed her two feet in his left hand, held her upside down in front of him and patted her hard on the back with his right hand.

"No!" He roared, "You may not die without a fight!" Amy Louise hung limply before him. He reached his right hand around to her tummy and lower chest, pressed gently. Water poured from her mouth and she choked, sputtered and coughed.

"Breathe, baby. Breathe," he said gently. "Cough up that water. Breathe." He focused his energy into her, kneading her body gently, willing her to live. Gradually she stopped gasping and began to cry.

In the dark, confused kitchen, children cried as lightening flashed, thunder rolled and the storm slowly crept away. Once in the house, and having relinquished control of the baby, Princess scampered under Libby and Bertie's bed and huddled there until the storm ended. As Amy Louise's cry became stronger, more regular, more normal sounding, the adults and older children relaxed.

Pa lit some lamps, sat down and hugged Annabelle and the twins onto his large lap, comforting them. Junior stood next to Bertie and watched every move. Libby sank into the old family rocking chair, exhausted. Katy sat on the floor beside her, clutching her mother's long wet skirt. Libby patted Katy on the head: touching another person felt soothing. Bertie eased Amy Louise down onto Libby's lap.

"Better keep her on her tummy for awhile if she'll stay. You were brave to go rescue her," he said.

"But I didn't do anything," Libby said. "Princess did it all. Without Princess, Amy Louise would have drowned." Then Libby told the story of how the dog rescued the baby from the tub. In the flickering lamplight with the storm quieting outside, Bertie, Pa and the children heard the story of Amy Louise, the thunderstorm, the washtub and the heroism of Princess. The tale wrapped itself around the family like ivy on a chimney to be told and retold to future generations about a 'no-account dog named Princess who saved'—depending on the generation—'your mother's, your grandmother's, your great-grandmother's life by dragging her out of a washtub during one of New Hampshire's biggest storms.' After the storm, Pa crossed the road to join Ma, Rachel and Rose at the main house where he gave the first retelling of what became known as the 'Princess story.'

Bertie and Libby rocked Amy Louise through the night. By morning, the 18-month-old awoke and seemed fine. Quite verbal, but not totally fluent, Amy Louise said she followed Annabelle from the orchard but the 'big noise scare me' followed by something unintelligible, followed by something about Princess, ending with something about 'Daddy spank me for naughty.' Bertie and Libby assured her she was not spanked 'for naughty,' but whether she understood was unclear. Two things, however, became clear: first, from then on, Amy Louise hated thunder and second, no one ever considered Princess worthless again. By the afternoon of the 4th of July, all Craigmoor knew the tale. Stories often grew after big storms but few topped the saga of Princess.

Old man Reynolds shook his head. Later, people from as far away as Boston came to buy his dogs after the story of Princess insinuated itself into the fabric of market-day talk. Years later Reynolds admitted to Bertie, "That mutt did as much for my reputation as all my first class hunters. If Libby hadn't wanted her, I'd have drowned that pup feeling it was the right thing to do. And I'd have been wrong, Bertie. Dead wrong."

35

By age six, Amy Louise sometimes 'knew things.' Libby tried to suppress this tendency until Margaret weighed in.

"Libby, my mother never considered it special or spooky to know things before they happened, though she occasionally felt it a burden. To us it's strange but don't focus on it. To Amy Louise, it's part of her life. Mama said 'it's as much a part of me as my curly hair and probably less important.' So listen if she says things but don't dwell on it." Margaret watched Libby's practical nature get stretched by dreamy little Amy Louise.

The delicate apple blossoms moved silently in the early morning breeze of a cotton-candy day in May 1886. Watching the sunrise, Libby almost felt the earth pulsing in this simple, tender moment. A cock crowed as the children gathered in the kitchen. Katy set the table, Bertie and Junior returned from milking, the twins gathered eggs, Annabelle supervised Amy Louise's face washing at the pump: all the normal activities before the six children left for school. Katy was completing her next-to-the-last year in Craigmoor School as Amy Louise finished first grade. Katy planned to attend Bates College in Lewiston Maine. Junior wanted to stay on the farm. Libby and Bertie contested, for the most part good-naturedly, over the younger four children.

After Libby said the blessing and served hot cereal, Amy Louise pushed her food around, not eating.

"You need to finish breakfast to be ready for school. Aren't you hungry?" Libby asked.

"Not very hungry. Just sad," Amy Louise said, putting her spoon down.

"Why are you sad?" asked Katy. "It's a beautiful day."

"It's a sad day, too."

Libby felt chilled. "Why do you say that, baby?'

Amy Louise stood up. "Great-grandpa Richard is dying and that's sad." Her blue eyes, framed by her brown curls, looked serious. "There's nothing I can do, but I'll miss him." She wrinkled her nose. "I don't like death." She climbed the stairs to her room. They all remained silent as she left.

"She shouldn't say that," Bertie said quietly, gazing steadily at Libby.

"It may not be true but she believes it." Libby excused herself, went to the girls' room.

Amy Louise sat concentrating on buttoning her shoe: her tongue and mouth working as hard as her hands as she manipulated the buttonhook.

"Baby, why do you say great-grandpa is dying?"

"Because he is," Amy Louise replied, still focused intently on her shoe.

Libby sat for a moment, collecting her thoughts as she navigated these strange waters. "Was it a dream or a vision or a voice?"

"It was a picture when I got up this morning. I saw him and great-grandma in their house and he couldn't breathe and then he was dead and she cried." Buttoning completed, Amy Louise headed for the door.

"What time was it?" Libby asked.

"When I got up?" Amy Louise looked confused.

"No, what time was it in the picture? Did you see the clock?" Libby felt foolish.

"Let's see," the child scrunched the left side of her face into her 'working very hard' position. "The clock says 10:25. Now I'd better go finish breakfast or I'll be hungry all morning." She bounded down the stairs and dug into her cereal.

Libby followed her and started drying the dishes Katy had put in the drainer. "Bertie, I'm going to walk to town with the children: see if anybody needs anything," Libby said vaguely.

He walked close to her. "You sure? Don't encourage this nonsense."

"If it's nonsense, we'll know soon enough," she replied in a low voice. Katy and Junior watched them; the other children resumed their usual chatter. "I know we don't understand this, she's never said anything so serious: only about finding lost things and sick animals. But if it's true and I don't go, I'll feel awful. Don't cross me on this, Bert, I'm going to town."

He shook his head slowly and stretched. "Come on, Junior, we'd better hitch the wagon," Bertie said. They left for the barn.

Katy walked up close to Libby. "Is it true? What Amy Louise said?"

"I don't know. But if they need us, we'll be there." Libby hugged Katy. "And we need a few things from town."

"We always need things from town but we don't go early on a school day. We get the things we need on Saturday market days," Katy spoke pointedly. "Mama, did Grandma Mavis 'know things' like Amy Louise does?"

"Some," Libby acknowledged, "but your great-great-grandmother Rebecca Elizabeth 'knew' lots of things. As a child during the Revolution in Virginia she often knew what soldiers would live, which would die. She'd walk into a room and know if someone was ill or being unfaithful. Ask your great-grandmother Margaret about her. Now go get ready to leave."

It happened as predicted. At 10:25 Richard died in his bed. Libby was fixing tea in the kitchen and, when the clock struck 10:30, she dashed upstairs. Margaret sat on the bed, crying softly and wiping Richard's face.

Libby opened the door to the room with her left hand, put her right hand on the doorframe and froze: she simply hung in the doorframe. Richard lay dead and, while Amy Louise had predicted it, Libby rejected the reality. Death's infinite finality encased her, its strange taunting voice whispered in her ears. She wanted to rage and fling her refusal to accept this death, any death, all death back into the depths of the universe but she could not.

Gradually, imperceptibly, deep within, Libby began to surrender. As she relaxed, the fear, denial and rage fell away. Reality was what it was. Life and death coexisted in mystery beyond understanding. Heartbroken, her senses open and raw, her hand dropped from the doorframe and she moved to Margaret's side and comforted her grandmother.

'To get to the other side of the field you must go through the field,' Miss Middleton had said. To become a useful vessel for God, for Life, to blossom into someone who could facilitate love for others and for yourself, first—and then repeatedly—you had to give up your will so that love could come through. 'God working through me,' Libby realized.

She didn't hear Bertie enter the room but, when he touched her, she relaxed against him. His strong arms encircled her and Margaret, adding his strength to theirs. Outside the window, a robin sang in the maple tree: its song promising that summer would come.

36

Amy Middleton continued to spend the summer months at the Ely house in Cambridge. Amy and Rose went to Cape Cod for a few weeks and Matt would join them as his schedule permitted. Then, in late June, Rose and Matt would head for Craigmoor. Rose stayed for six weeks and Matt for two. Having Rose and Matt living in, and managing, the Cambridge house pleased Amy. These two former students were now part of her family.

"It's been a delight to have Amy Louise in school this year," Amy mused as she and Rose walked on the beach at Cape Cod.

Rose picked up a pink shell and tossed it into the surf. "All this 'knowing things' before they happen: probably the result of almost drowning. Rachel calls it mystical; I call it strange."

Amy laughed. "Yes, mysticism is a bit strange."

"I don't understand these things. Your grandfather's library is full of them. Now Amy Louise 'sees' things. It's spooky."

Amy watched the choppy waters of Cape Cod and the fluffy white clouds floating in the sky as the wind blew wisps of spray from the waves that broke and crashed on the beach. She tasted the salt carried on the breeze, adjusted her small, ever-present spectacles and asked, "Tell me about the Puritans and the Pilgrims, Rose."

Exasperated, Rose replied, "If you have something to say, Amy, just say it."

"Grandpa and I used to walk here and I'd get as frustrated with him as you get with me," Amy chuckled. "He'd smile and say 'Just follow me.' So I say, 'Tell me about…'"

"All right!" Rose cut in. "The Pilgrims were heading for Virginia, got blown off course and ended up here. They wanted land, investment, a better life. The Puritans came later"

"And what did the Puritans want to create?"

"A place where they could worship as they wanted to in peace."

"Did they succeed?"

"Well, partly," Rose now swung easily with the rhythm of the conversation. "Groups moved here to establish specific things for themselves and then, years later, their descendents ended up hanging women as witches and Quakers for their 'wrong' theology. The initial vision had good intentions but it was narrow and small." Amy looked out over the sea. "If we walk through Boston today, can we find a Roman Catholic Church?"

"Of course."

"And what would those Puritan and Pilgrim founding fathers and mothers think of that?"

"They wouldn't like it," Rose said quietly.

"Rose we fought a dreadful Revolution and a bloody Civil War to establish principles that might have choked the folks who stepped off the first ships. We're their descendents but we've changed: each generation recasts the vision." Amy stooped to pick up a shell, held it, moved it in her hands, studied it and replaced it gently on the beach. "Have you ever read anything by Saint Teresa?"

"Who? What are you talking about?" Rose's exasperation returned.

"Mysticism and your fear of it in Amy Louise, in Rachel, even in me." Amy chuckled.

"Who is Saint Teresa?" Rose finally asked.

"A mystic, a writer, the founder of an order of nuns in Spain. Grandpa studied her. He believed she experienced God in a very direct way. Back in Cambridge I'll give you her writings and Grandpa's notes on *The Interior Castle* to read in Craigmoor. I found them helpful."

"Oh, all right, I'll read some mystic to understand my niece," Rose sounded petulant.

"Amy Louise is my namesake; I need to defend her." Amy squinted a smile.

Returning to their rented cottage Rose asked, "How've you been feeling this year? Any more headaches?"

Amy hung her bonnet on the hook by the door. "Only a few," she said lightly.

"Amy, promise me you'll go for an examination while you're in Cambridge."

"Libby and Bertie certainly named the right daughter after you. Annabelle Rose is both practical and a story teller," Amy remarked.

"No, Amy Middleton. That will not work; I'll not be led off course by some story about Annabelle Rose. We are talking about your headaches. Either you tell Matthew or I will." Sometimes Rose's bulldog-strong Jones tenacity exerted itself.

"You are the most stubborn people I've ever known," Amy replied. Rose glared at her. "Oh, all right. I'll talk to Matt."

Rose smiled. "Then I'll read about Saint Teresa."

Rose kept her promise. Amy didn't.

37

Deciphering Professor Ely's notes challenged Rose. She didn't understand the specific types of prayer but some form of silent, internal opening, was described. Ely's marginal notes referenced verses in both the Bible and the *Gita*. Had anyone other than Amy Middleton given these writings to Rose, she would not have persisted. Her experience of God came through nature, the Congregational

Church and Bible stories: many of these, as a post-enlightenment teacher, she doubted. That summer, struggling with material she found strange, Rose's heart said a 'yes' that her mind never quite understood.

That fall, when Rose returned to Cambridge, she took Professor Ely's manuscript back with her but left her own notes in the drawer of her desk.

One evening at dinner she asked Matthew about Amy's headaches.

"Is she having headaches?"

Rose took a breath, started to speak, then shook her head. "Never mind."

After the mad rush of harvest, with Rose back in Cambridge and the children in school, fall brought the work of preparing for winter, buttoning up buildings, repairing and storing equipment, completing the final preserving and canning. Ma, Rachel, Auntie Jones and Libby worked together, individually or in pairs. In their spare time Ma and Libby wrote, Auntie did needlework and Rachel meditated or walked in the fields.

As Rachel grew more enigmatic, Libby tried to write about her. When she wrote about Rachel's long arms and legs and her slender build, what stuck to the paper seemed a scarecrow-caricature of the graceful woman Libby tried to portray. Rachel put people at ease yet remained slightly reserved. Rachel, Libby realized, had grown into the most peacefully calm individual she knew yet, when Libby put pen to paper, the person she described sounded cold and remote.

One early October afternoon, Libby went to the orchard, intent once again to describe Rachel. Bertie, watching her from the equipment-shed beside the barn, called to her.

"Say there, beautiful lady, would you like to take a trip with me?"

Libby looked up and laughed. "A trip to where, you flirtatious rogue?"

"Portsmouth, Boston, Cape Cod." Libby dropped her pen; her mouth fell open. Bertie roared with laughter as he jogged to the orchard and whipped off his hat. "You see, Libby Whitman, we've been married a long time and we need to see some sights beyond Craigmoor."

"Are you serious?"

"I'm almost forty and I want to take a trip. These places Rose and Matt and Miss Amy go to all the time, I want to see. Only farmers stay in one place forever and I want us to celebrate our anniversary. Just us."

"Can we afford it?"

"I can get the work covered around here and we can draw on some of Rose and Matt's payments." He paused. "We might need to borrow some egg money," he said cautiously.

Libby felt herself stiffen; she hated surprises and guarded the egg money jealously. Loudly and clearly in her head she heard Mavis' voice: 'When you are surprised—wait a moment before you respond—' They'd worked hard for years. The children were healthy: the farm in order. Suddenly the idea sounded wonderful. Libby smiled a broad, happy smile.

"Well, Mr. Jones, I guess we're worth egg money. After all, we feed the chickens."

After they talked about travel plans, Bertie asked, "What are you writing?"

"I'm trying to capture Rachel in words."

Bertie chuckled. "Might as well try to dip the moon's reflection from the pond." He shook his head slowly. "I figure she's a cross between a grasshopper and a Saint."

Libby looked at him, surprised once again by his casual ability with words. "That," she said, "is the silliest and most accurate description of Rachel I've ever heard."

They left Craigmoor ten days later for Cambridge where they stayed with Matt and Rose. They visited Lexington and Concord, saw the old North Church and Bunker Hill. They walked the Boston Commons and went to museums and art galleries. They spent a week on Cape Cod huddled before a fire as a storm rolled in—as much storm, Bertie said, as he ever wanted to experience so close to all that water. They ate seafood they'd never heard of and watched people walking on the wharf who looked, to their New Hampshire eyes, wild. They got lost and became cross with each other. With Matt and Rose they celebrated their anniversary at a fine restaurant. They climbed aboard the train for home exhausted, full of memories and ready to leave. Pulling into the station in Craigmoor they saw John, Johnny, Aunt Helen, Grandma Margaret, Rachel and their six children waiting on the platform.

Bertie turned to Libby and said, "Please thank the chickens. It's been a special trip and I'm pleased to be home. And I didn't see one big-city woman as pretty as you."

"But you certainly looked enough!"

"How's a man to know how lucky he is if he doesn't look?" Bertie's eyes sparkled as he made an elaborate shrug, both hands facing the sky.

Riding home, Libby talked of some of the things they had seen and then relaxed back into her children's chatter. The sun hung low and red over the hill as they bumped up the lane. Most fall color was gone. The smell of the earth rose around them. Libby remembered her first fall visit here so many years ago. Both within herself and in the farm, much remained the same but much had changed, too. As she stepped down from the wagon, late fall leaves crunched under her feet and Princess leapt around her joyfully.

Bertie surveyed the sky. "Suppose it'll rain tomorrow, Junior?"

Junior, now slightly taller than his father, glanced at the horizons. "Sure could." They both chuckled, both recognizing the signs.

Libby breathed in the smell of home, lingered a bit in the memory of their adventure. Bertie slipped back into the farm as into a pair of work-gloves. Looking out over the hillside, Libby wondered briefly what her life would have been had Mavis lived. Then Amy Louise grabbed her hand and pulled her toward the porch. Libby followed, smiling and talking happily with her youngest daughter.

38

Pa Jones died of a heart attack while shoveling snow in February 1892. Bertie inherited the farm and assumed leadership for managing it. The Uncles, Auntie Jones and Rachel all continued as before. Ma grieved but carried on, surrounded by her family and supported by her routine. She would need her strength during the next few years.

Ma never totally understood the unlikely events of 1893. It seemed simple. Rose invited Rachel to Massachusetts for a vacation. Rose and Katy, both now teaching in Cambridge, came to the farm during June and took Rachel back to Cambridge with them. At 48, Rachel made her first trip with centered spontaneity.

Amy and Matthew met them at the station in Boston and two day later they all went to Cape Cod for a week. Rachel always enjoyed being with Matthew. At 50, his face had grown craggy and more interesting while his eyes remained full of wonder. As brother and sister walked the beach one morning, Rachel commented on how tenderly he treated Amy. Matt stiffened, blushed, changed the subject and hurried toward the cottage.

"Matt, wait." He stopped. With sand blowing and gulls soaring overhead Rachel caught up to him. "It's not wrong to care for Amy, I didn't mean that."

He kicked a shell and looked out to sea avoiding Rachel's eyes.

"You've never told her, have you Matt?" Rachel said gently. He shook his head ever so slightly. "She'd be pleased to know. Even us 'old maids' like to know we're loved." She slipped her arm around him and they walked on.

"You probably know me as well as anyone, Rach." He paused. "Please don't..." his voice trailed off.

"Of course not," she replied. They walked on, talking about shells, his work, how Ma was doing, Rachel's trip—the small things people share in the shadow of a fragile truth.

When they returned to Cambridge the next week, Amy learned that the great spiritual leader, Swami Vivekananda, would be conducting a series of lectures in

Boston. He'd come to the United States to attend the Parliament of Religions scheduled to open in Chicago in July. The conference had been delayed so he visited Boston. Vivekananda was a disciple of Ramakrishna, the holy man Amy's cousin Captain Russell had met years ago in India so Amy suggested they attend the lectures. Rachel agreed: she wanted to understand her own meditation better. Katy and Rose seemed a bit leery but, to keep from being left out, went along. Matt joined in eagerly.

Vivekananda, a surprisingly young man, spoke eloquently to the large Bostonian crowd about the Hindu belief that human beings are essentially spirit. He emphasized that a Hindu believes every soul is a circle whose circumference is nowhere, but whose center is located in the body. Death simply moves this center from one body to another. The soul, not bound by matter, is free, holy, perfect and pure. He described parallels between Christ's teachings and Hindu beliefs and discussed the spiritual strength of India indicating that the material West needed the spiritual East for balance and wholeness.

The upcoming Chicago conference had been designed so that people of different religions could come together and know that the God experienced by the Masters of all faiths is 'One.' People need not struggle to believe certain things but the individual must strive to be, and to become, perfect. This, Vivekananda indicated, is what Christ meant by the statement 'I and the Father are one.' Jesus possessed the infinite, universal individuality and lived totally open to it. When one destroyed the 'miserable little person-individuality,' then one could live open to spirit and truth. The differences among the great religions of the world are just apparent, not real, he continued. What we see is the same transcendent truth adapting itself to new circumstances.

Rachel felt transfixed by Vivekananda. She had read righteous works, had experienced deep devotion to God but had never seen a person this holy. 'This man,' she believed, 'knows God. Others know about God, some glimpse God, St. Teresa wrote of her experiences but here stands a man open to the reality behind the universe.' His teaching offered 'the pearl of great price' she could either accept or reject. She wanted to study with him.

After the lecture, she tried to approach him but the crowd blocked her. His penetrating eyes singled her out and he moved easily to her. Rachel bowed. She could not speak. He touched her head in blessing and she raised her face to him.

"Your desire will be granted," he said. "There are obstacles but hold fast to your prayer. Your teacher has come." He bowed slightly, his hands together in the 'Namaste' blessing of India. Then he moved away. The meeting lasted a moment. No one else heard him. Bliss flooded through Rachel. She would surmount the obstacles. Her teacher had come.

Matthew and the four women attended Vivekananda's first few lectures and the women sat together one afternoon in the Ely home discussing the teachings. Amy, Rose and Katy participated in a lively conversation while Rachel said nothing.

Exasperated by Rachel's silence, Rose blurted out, "Rachel what do you think?"

"Swami is Holy. I can learn from him for he knows God. I respect him. I don't want to pick his ideas apart. I want to listen to him and study with him."

"You sound like a moon-struck schoolgirl," Rose remarked.

Rachel laughed lightly. "Perhaps so, but it is not the same experience at all. As a girl, with Toby, I had moon-struck moments. But he died. Since then, people wanted me to encourage other suitors but that never seemed appropriate. I believed a plan existed for my life and that I needed to live simply and do my chores until I found that plan."

Amy, Rose and Katy stared silently at Rachel in various states of disbelief. After a long pause, Amy asked quietly, "Do you sense 'a plan,' as you call it, now?"

Rachel nodded. She sat calmly, her hands folded in her lap. "I'll attend the Parliament of Religions in Chicago and, when Swami returns to India, I plan to go with him."

Rose stood abruptly. "You cannot be serious. That is absurd. Why, you are unfit even to consider such a voyage." Rose's anger boiled.

Amy watched, reluctant to interrupt as the Jones women debated but her mind raced. Was Rachel serious?

Rose slammed a book on the table jolting Amy back to the present.

"I'll listen to no more of this," Rose spat.

Katy looked imploringly at Amy. "Miss Middleton, help us."

Amy gazed at the tableau: Katy sat leaning forward, pleading; Rachel rested calmly in the wingback chair; Rose stood ramrod straight, the veins in her neck throbbing, her cheeks flushed above the high neck of her prim, black dress as she glared at Rachel. Wispy blond curls framed Rose's face providing the only relief. Amy knew that she, too, lived in this portrait but felt unsure of her current role. They were her students and she cared for them but they'd become more than that. Needing time, Amy carefully removed her spectacles and rubbed her eyes.

"Perhaps we could all do with tea," she suggested, replacing her glasses. "Rachel, let's see what's in the pantry and Katy, arrange some cups, please." Rachel stood and accompanied Amy to the kitchen while Katy dashed off, delighted to escape the tension in the room.

Rose stood alone. She turned and walked to the bay window overlooking the garden. 'Madness!' She thought, 'Sheer madness.' But Rose knew Rachel. She would never state a plan until she'd made a decision, a characteristic that frustrated Rose. Rachel never seemed able to make up her mind but, once she did, there was no room left to maneuver. Rose often found herself at odds with Matt and Rachel over how they made decisions. Rose looked into the garden and watched two birds chasing each other around the birdbath. 'How did they arrive here?' she wondered. 'How did we all arrive here?'

Rose remembered sunshine flooding into the classroom on her first day in first grade. Miss Middleton entered her life then and never left. Rose's life was so closely interwoven with her teacher, her mentor, now her landlord and friend she often wondered if her thoughts were her own or just the flowers and fruits of seeds Amy had planted. The life she now shared with Matt and Katy in Cambridge grew directly from their association with Amy Middleton.

Rose now felt tight, fearful and mildly angry about the exposure she had had to more inclusive worldly ideas. Suddenly she longed for Craigmoor's security, the farm, a tightly controlled code of behavior and a clearly defined, precise vision of God. Why had she ever read the *Gita*? What made her believe that Ely's notes on *The Interior Castle* held meaning? Why had she spent all these years alone, in college and teaching? Was she warping the minds of her own students: leaving them open to some dreadful future catastrophe? Rose's own freedom to teach had been paid for by her family's work. She'd repaid the money but that wasn't the point. Rachel actively fought for Rose's choice. Without Rachel's support, without her tireless years of daily, unbroken toil, Rose could not be here today. Rachel occupied a key position in Rose's life and, years ago, Rose had pledged to support her sister in some vague future decision. Certainly that old promise couldn't be called due now, could it?

Rose swayed, felt faint. She watched Katy return, watched her niece's mouth moving, heard only buzzing. Things looked small and far away; Rose's thigh muscles gave way. She grasped the chair Rachel had recently vacated and collapsed into it. Perspiration rolled down her forehead; her face turned the color of fresh milk.

"Are you ill?" Katy asked.

"Stay with me, Katy," Rose grasped Katy's hand.

Rose appeared small and frail slumped in the chair. The contrast to Rachel's serene figure sitting poised in the same location only minutes earlier struck Katy powerfully. She loved both her Aunts and felt ripped apart like an old rag. She hoped Miss Middleton could help them.

"I'm sure cook left bread in the pantry," Amy said as she and Rachel entered the kitchen. "I'll go see."

When Amy returned, Rachel, having poured boiling water in the teapot, had replenished the kettle and placed it back on the stove, moving with a gracefulness she'd not had as a child. 'Rachel, the enigmatic Jones,' Amy realized. During years of caring for her parents, her brother's children and her own chores she'd become centered. Silent and calm, Rachel exercised control over few things except herself. Focusing on God, choosing honor and duty, she'd lived a quiet, faithful life developing strength and simple courage. The awkward, gentle-faced child with spindly long legs now stood a proverbial swan among the ducks. 'And swans,' Amy mused, 'must fly.'

Returning to the sitting room, the women sipped tea, ate nut bread and spoke of flowers, the weather, when Matt might be home—anything but Vivekananda. An unexpected knock sent Amy to the front door. There stood her cousin, Captain Frederick Russell, smiling broadly.

"Amy, dear, I apologize for not having contacted you earlier but my ship limped into port last week and I've been busy arranging for repairs that will keep me on land for three months. I saw you with Matt and your friends last night but couldn't get through the crowd."

Amy felt enormous relief and relaxed visibly. "What a joy to have you here," she said leading him into the sitting room. Frederick felt the underlying tension.

"Perhaps I've come at a bad time," he murmured to Amy.

"No, no. We need your wisdom," she said quietly before introducing him.

"I've met your brother," he remarked to Rose and Rachel, "and your uncle," he said to Katy, "and, while cousin Amy has spoken of you all, I'd no idea you were in town."

Rachel smiled. "This is my first trip here, Captain. My sister and niece both live here and teach in Cambridge."

Amy poured more tea and Russell spoke quietly about Vivekananda's lecture and mentioned Ramakrishna.

"Amy may have told you, I met Ramakrishna twice. He affected me deeply. When he died the world lost an important person. His disciple, Vivekananda," Russell paused when he felt the tension rising. "But perhaps you feel differently."

Amy spoke softly. "He seems sincere but can we be sure he is totally honest?"

"A legitimate concern. Had I not been to India, I'd be more skeptical but I've met him before and a close friend supports him. I believe Vivekananda's quite honest and certainly the Parliament of Religions will be an important gathering. With the work needed on my ship, I'm heading there myself." He noticed Rose's teacup clatter into her saucer.

"Are you going to the lecture tonight?" Rachel asked, offering Russell more nut bread.

"I was hoping we could all go together," he replied, taking a piece of bread.

"How very nice, I'd be pleased to join you," Rachel replied, "but I cannot speak for others. Rose?"

Rose glared at Rachel.

Katy laughed in spite of herself. "I'll go," she blurted out.

"Then," Amy said lightly, "let's all go. Rose?"

Rose flushed. The only thing she wanted less than to hear Vivekananda again was to miss what might happen. Her curiosity defeated her pride and she nodded slowly.

After the lecture, Captain Russell introduced them to Swami who greeted each in turn and was especially attentive to Rose. The two men talked easily, obviously comfortable acquaintances. When Russell mentioned his plan to go to Chicago, Swami's face brightened.

"Marvelous. You could do me a favor by escorting Miss Jones. It's a detail I'm concerned about."

"I'd be delighted to," Frederick responded.

Vivekananda raised his hands in blessing, turned to Rachel, touched her forehead and said gently, "One challenge overcome."

Later that night, Rachel meditated full of inspiration from Swami's lectures and his blessing. At the center of her forehead, she saw a pure white light and allowed it to envelop her in a cloud-like glow. She felt calm and totally alive. 'One challenge overcome.'

39

Captain Russell's offer to escort Rachel to Chicago satisfied Matthew. After long talks with Rachel, Amy concluded that this desire to study with Vivekananda grew from meditation and her readings in Western and Eastern religions. Since Rachel believed herself called to this trip, and since Amy trusted her cousin, she supported the venture. To help Rachel through the conflicts that would, Amy believed, follow in Craigmoor, she bundled up Professor Ely's letters and notebooks (dealing with many of the world's religions, the philosophy of India and the unity he had believed existed at the heart of the major religious systems) and gave them to Rachel. Amy knew the Jones family: this might be difficult.

Matthew felt going to India was extreme but he supported Rachel's traveling to Chicago for the Conference. Perhaps he believed that closer study with Vivekananda would fulfill Rachel's spiritual hunger. Perhaps he wanted his sister to experience more of the opportunities the late nineteenth-century world offered: more than existed in Craigmoor or in books. Perhaps he understood the concept of a 'call' to something larger, something compelling: what medicine was for him.

Rachel talked to Matt and Amy about her hopes. Rose wouldn't listen. Rose couldn't conceive of loosing Rachel, or, more accurately what losing Rachel might mean to her orderly life: the stable system Rose had established that served her well. Rose struggled because she knew she owed Rachel a great deal. What right had Rose, who walked away from the family at eighteen for college and teaching, to deny Rachel's dream? What right had Rose to limit the sister who stayed home, churned butter, helped rear nephews and nieces, canned food, comforted their dying father, consoled their widowed mother and performed thousands of other necessary chores? What right did Rose have to demand that Rachel live out her life in Craigmoor? None. But that was exactly what she planned to do.

Katy, Rose and Rachel traveled back to Craigmoor in August; Rachel planned to return to Cambridge and join Captain Russell for the trip to Chicago. Letters preceded them to the farm and the issue of 'Rachel's proposed trip' already smoldered. Rachel gave Ma Professor Ely's writings. Ma watched Rachel closely. Since Toby Wills' death, Ma had seen Rachel function, grow and mature but, until now, she had not sensed that Rachel had healed. Finally, the invisible shrapnel wounds that had shattered Rachel's heart were gone. Ma sensed this strange plan might be appropriate and that fact both broke her heart and frightened her.

Rose tried to discuss the matter with Ma who simply held her finger to her lips, signaling for silence, infuriating Rose. Bertie became Rose's ally and both were incredulous that Matt and Ma could even consider this. Libby tried to reason with Rose and Bertie individually.

One evening before finishing dinner dishes, she brought the matter up with Bertie.

"We need to talk about Rachel's proposed trip."

"This is Jones business and I'm not interested in a Whitman opinion. Bad enough my daughters go to college and want to teach rather than live as respectable wives but don't interfere with this Libby," his eyes flashed.

Libby spun on her heel, marched to their bedroom, picked up the small, wooden model of the old bridge—the one he'd made for her during their courtship—from her dresser and returned to the kitchen slamming the model down on the table between them.

"We've discussed this before and I will have my say. I'm a Whitman but I'm a Jones too, and don't you forget it. What Rachel wants is permission—and financial help—to take a trip to Chicago. You should say 'yes.'"

"It isn't right! It's not the way the world should be!" Bertie wailed.

"According to whom? What 'world' are you talking about? This isn't just the Jones world, the Whitman world, the Christian or the American world. It's just the 'world.' All of it: good—bad, pretty—ugly, comfortable—foreign. We can't control it but we can learn from it, grow with it. Right and wrong aren't always clear."

Bertie stared at the floor shaking his head slowly from side to side.

Four days after returning to the farm, Rose and Rachel went walking at sunset. They wandered through the fields, stood under the apple trees, walked through the vegetable gardens and by the blueberry patch. At the main pasture gate they gazed toward the distant mountains, past Joe English hill. Rose, after 20 years of teaching, believed herself wiser than Rachel.

"I know you feel following Swami is a good idea but family comes first. You have a duty to Ma, to Bertie, to the farm. Bertie's in charge and he's looking out for you. I hope you understand," Rose tried to sound wise and firm.

"Rosie, isn't that the most beautiful sunset? I've watched thousands of sunsets here and the clear colors almost choke me. There may not be a more beautiful spot on earth than Quail Hill Farm at sunset."

Encouraged, Rose said, "Then why leave?"

"I love this farm as much as Bertie does, maybe as much as Pa did. I love it more than you or Matt ever did. I love it more than Ma ever will." Rachel watched the dusky red light retreating.

"Good, then you'll stay." Rose sounded triumphant.

"No, you don't understand. I'm not leaving to get away: I'm leaving to follow a plan."

Rose hissed, "That's sheer romantic gibberish. Have you no sense of duty? What's going to happen to Ma if you leave?"

"Whether I stay or go, Ma will grow older and die. So will you and so will I," Rachel's voice was soft and mellow like the sunset itself.

"Alone and without her daughter!" Rose spat.

"We're both her daughters."

Rose flinched, changed tactics. "You cannot do this. It'd break Pa's heart if he knew you wanted to leave Quail Hill."

"If he were alive it might break his heart; his heart broke when you left. But he recovered and he'd recover again. People are very resilient." As darkness descended, fireflies danced. "When you went to college you promised you'd support me if I ever needed your support. You are not honor bound to support my decision but do understand: I'm going to Chicago and, if things work out, I'll go to India. If that happens, you can help the family or you can be resentful and make a difficult situation worse.

"Matt's comfortable about Chicago. Bertie is being Jones-New Hampshire stubborn. If we were brothers, it'd be fine: but I'm his big sis." Rachel paused, looked out into the gathering darkness. "Leaving will be terribly painful. If you can, Rosie, make it easier. Love me enough to let me go." Rachel turned and walked briskly to the main house.

Rose leaned on the fencepost, struggling with her dilemma in the darkness. She wanted security: when she came to Quail Hill during summers, she wanted

Rachel present. She didn't want to change yet knew she must. Rachel deserved her support and she must give it: as much for herself as for Rachel. Remaining tightly closed limited her. She must open, love and let go. Otherwise she'd become an intolerant, prissy, 'old maid schoolteacher.' Rose would not do that, no matter how difficult the alternative might be. She walked to the house, to her room, crawled into the familiar, comfortable bed of her childhood, and wept.

When Rose came downstairs in the morning, Ma asked, "Want a cup of coffee?"

"Later. I'll go pick blueberries."

"No need. Rachel's out there."

"I'll go help." Rose darted out. Approaching the berry patch she saw Rachel working. "Good morning. Ma said you were here."

"I'm done." Rachel smiled, stood and walked to her sister.

"Rachel, I… I'm… I'll try." Tears spilled down Rose's cheeks. No other words came.

Rachel hugged her, "Thank you. That's all any of us can do, really. Just try. Now let's fix breakfast."

40

A few days later, after dinner at the main house, the adults assembled around the old table for an unannounced family conference. Junior and Katy took their places as adults; Annabelle, the twins and Amy Louise cleaned the kitchen, finished chores and then sat close enough to hear but out of the combat zone.

Bertie, as owner of the farm, stated why Rachel should not go to Chicago and not consider going to India. He stopped short of recommending burning the books in the Craigmoor Library but made it clear he found foreign ideas suspect.

"Rachel," he declared, attempting to end the discussion, "belongs on the farm."

Years later, Amy Louise remembered the scene like this: her Aunt Rachel's voice was calm, Bertie sounded dogmatic and her Grandma Jones looked at her hands as they lay relaxed on the table. Amy Louise knew Rachel would go to India just like she knew Grandpa Richard would die, but said nothing. Why make things worse? She watched and played with her cat.

Rachel stated that she'd go to Boston, join Captain Russell and proceed to Chicago. If she felt called to follow Swami further, she'd seek his advice and his permission.

· Craigmoor ·

Junior threw a curve into the discussion, announcing his intention to propose to Abigail Morgan and begin his family here on the farm. Bertie exploded. He had enough to deal with. As he wound down, Ma began speaking softly to no one in particular, looking down at her hands.

"I'll go with Rachel to Chicago and meet Mr. Vivekananda. I'm a good judge of character. You believe I'm an old, reclusive farmwife: true enough, but not the whole story. I see more deeply than most. If Rachel leaves, and I'm not saying whether she should or shouldn't, then Bertie and Libby and the younger children will move in with me so Junior and Abby can have the 'new house.'" (Ma still called the house built for Libby the 'new house,' which, compared to the original house, it was.) "But that decision awaits another day. For now, it's enough that I'll go with Rachel to Chicago."

She turned to Junior, "An alliance between the Joneses and the Morgans will unite two of Craigmoor's strongest families and, once your father thinks about it, he will agree. We've known Abby her whole life and she's become a lovely young woman." Ma stopped speaking and looked at Bertie. He held his jaw tightly shut. His eyes flashed; he said nothing. Libby closed her eyes, dropped her head; Rose's mouth fell open; Rachel leaned close to Ma.

"It may be a difficult trip to Chicago."

Ma smiled, patted Rachel's hand. "I didn't expect you to speak of hardships."

Then they discussed money, Junior's plans and harvest details: trimming the ragged edges from their confrontation.

Ma sighed, smiled at Bertie, stood and said, "That's all we can do for now. Thank you for not fighting me on this, son." She walked slowly down the hall to her room.

Later, as the moon broke over the horizon, Libby and Bertie headed down to the main gate of the big pasture.

"It's not right for Rachel to do this. She should stay here," he spoke to the night.

"We're here. We'll always be here."

"This is her land, too. She should stay here, not travel off somewhere."

"Bertie, we wouldn't be here if your grandfather hadn't left the old country and traveled 'off somewhere.'"

Bertie grasped the fence's top rail. "Libby, he left because the mines kept killing people. He left for something better. And this is better; this is good. This land you work and love and stick by," he sounded weary, defeated.

"We love this land. Junior loves it and Abigail will. And they'll work it and raise their family here. Not everybody's born to farm."

Bertie sighed, put his arm around Libby's shoulders. "Land is everything. People who don't understand that don't understand life on this planet or anything about God's plan. Land feeds us, supports us, protects us and it's our responsibility to return the favor. I've spent my life protecting and caring for this one rocky chunk of New Hampshire because it's worth it. Everybody needs the land. People may forget that but, in the end, if people stop caring for the land, the very earth, then they will destroy life's source." They turned and headed to their home.

"Say, what about Junior and Abby?" Bertie asked.

"Well, we've all known the Morgans forever. I worked for Abby's grandmother and she gave us our bed for a wedding present. I like Abby but she's stubborn." Libby sounded so serious that Bertie laughed.

"You're a fine one to talk."

As they entered the house, Amy Louise looked up from her book. Her mother's face was flushed and her father, while bent more than usual, smiled softly: the stiff anger from an hour ago gone. Amy Louise loved the sweetness she glimpsed between her parents.

"Isn't it past your bedtime?" Bertie asked.

"It's summer."

"True, but reading by lamplight never helped anybody's eyes."

"But Papa…"

"Furthermore, seems you may need your 'beauty sleep' what with Abby's brother Charley Morgan hanging around here all the time. Doesn't that boy have anything to do except ride his bicycle out here?"

Libby interjected, "Amy Louise is only thirteen: too young for courting I'd say."

"Maybe. But when I was fifteen like young Charley I'd been in love with you for years."

Libby blushed. Amy Louise wanted a marriage like her parents; she also wanted to go to college and to teach. She wondered what Charley Morgan wanted.

Later lying in bed Bertie said, "If she leaves, I never want to hear her name again. If she leaves, she's the same as dead. If Pa were alive, she'd stay."

Libby didn't answer. There was nothing to say. 'For better or worse.' If Bertie rejected Rachel, she'd love him through that, too.

Ma and Rachel traveled together to Boston where they met Captain Frederick Russell and all took a train to Chicago for the Parliament of Religions. During the meetings, Ma met Vivekananda several times and recognized him as a man of good character even if some of his Hindu ideas were, in her words, 'highly unusual.' Rachel arranged to join him after he finished his travels in the US and go with him to India.

It was almost two years later, during 1895, that she left Quail Hill for the last time to join Vivekananda and his followers as they headed back to India. Bertie refused to accompany her to the station. For years, he never spoke of her, never wrote to her, never read her letters. He cut himself off from Rachel and thus from the person who could have helped him understand her decision and explain how beautiful her life became. Deep within him, his response to her leaving created a small, painful pocket of resentment because he believed he had failed.

Driving away in the wagon on her last day at Quail Hill, Rachel sat quietly holding Ma's hand, etching the land, the three houses, the barn and out buildings of Quail Hill Farm into her mind. Rounding the bend in the lane, she saw Bertie, hands thrust into his pockets, shoulders hunched forward, walking toward the barn. Soon after that, only the top of the barn roof poked above the crest of the hill and, at the next turn, all the buildings were blocked by land.

Even good decisions can cause pain. Rachel hoped for greater peace but she felt raw and exposed. 'This,' she realized, 'is what a seed experiences when it breaks open and grows toward the sun's promise. Once broken, a seed cannot retreat. It either grows, faithful to its inner plan, or it dies: the brokenness must be total.' During these past twenty years of meditation when she'd tried to focus on God, tried to make her life itself prayer, her own protective shell had cracked open. Now, Rachel must give way to growth beyond her imagining.

At the station, everyone cried. Time went askew: things went too fast, then too slowly. Rachel tumbled toward her chosen destiny knowing she must not try to stop, aware her heart was breaking. After boarding and taking her seat by the window, she felt profoundly alone. As the train pulled away, Rachel seared the familiar faces and the scenes into her mind. Then, rumbling south, Rachel glimpsed an important truth: totally alone, she rested in the heart of God.

41

After Junior married Abby Morgan, Libby, Bertie and Amy Louise moved into the big house with Ma; the twins moved to the house rebuilt after the fire to live with Auntie Jones and the Uncles. Junior and Abby occupied the 'new house.' Libby often headed toward the 'new house' only to catch herself and turn toward the big house where she now lived. She felt confused, displaced, lost on the farm where she had now lived most of her life. It didn't help that Charley Morgan bicycled out frequently to see Amy Louise thus diverting the girl's attention away from Libby and Bertie. Life shifted and the readjustment proved difficult.

One day over a cup of tea, Ma asked Libby, "What kind of a mother-in-law am I?"

"A very good one."

"Did I interfere too much?"

"No."

"Ignore you?" Ma put down her tea.

"Maybe sometimes," Libby said, "but I'm so headstrong. I'd've been awful if you'd hovered."

"We might have lessened your illness."

"I doubt it. So many babies so fast. And leftover things."

"They're the most difficult," Ma said, patting Libby's hand. "Well, we've a new woman here and we'd better make her welcome."

Libby sighed. "I don't know how to be a mother-in-law."

"You didn't know how to be a wife and mother, but you learned. Let's go visit Abby."

Walking across the lane Ma announced, "Tomorrow I'm retiring from the kitchen. I'll keep my vegetable and flower gardens but as of tomorrow the kitchen's all yours."

"You don't have to do that, we're sharing it pretty well."

"I know. But I'm tired of cooking, tired of planning meals and watching them disappear. I'm going to arrange my poems. I'll sketch. Maybe," Ma laughed, "I'll just sit on the porch and rock." She saw Libby's perplexed look. "The kitchen's a burden at my age. I'm not being a martyr. The farm belongs to you and Bert and Junior and Abby. I had my turn: didn't do badly." She paused. "I'd like to understand Rachel better. Her letters are happy, content. Many Hindu things sound bizarre. I'm glad there are some English women there. About the kitchen, don't worry, I'll help with canning." Ma, usually quiet, could, once launched, dart about subjects like a hummingbird flitting among flowers.

Approaching the 'new house,' Ma turned. "First lesson in being a mother-in-law: always let them know you're coming and never enter unless invited." She hurried on. "Yoo-hoo, Abby are you here?"

Change happened everywhere. A new teacher came during Amy Louise's last two years in school and Amy Middleton retired to the old Ely house in Cambridge. After graduating from Bates College, Annabelle joined Matt, Rose, Katy and Amy Middleton and they all lived together. Amy called the Ely home 'Craigmoor South' and joked that it was only proper she continue life surrounded by the Jones clan as they had dominated her entire teaching career.

Amy's headaches intensified and she became increasingly disabled. Nurses cared for her and Matthew did his best to keep her comfortable. He read to her, talked to her, obtained medications to control her pain. As the pressure in her head increased, her capacities diminished and failed. Toward the end, she occasionally squeezed Matt's hand in silent recognition. Finally, mercifully, her labored breathing ceased.

· Craigmoor ·

She died one morning at two a.m. with Matt by her side. Looking down at her silent body he remembered the first time they'd met. He'd been thirteen, she 21 or 22. They stood by the Craigmoor Schoolhouse and her dark curly hair (defying her attempts to hold it down) formed a fuzzy halo around her head. Her dark brown eyes—appearing absurdly large through her ever-present spectacles—looked at him directly. She tilted her head, greeted him and said, "How do you do. I'm Miss Middleton, your new teacher." She held out her hand and he shook it awkwardly.

"I'm glad to meet you. I'm Matthew Jones and I want to be a doctor." Matthew recalled the amber-tinged light, the smells of early fall and his confusion.

"Well, Matthew Jones, that's a fine goal. With work, you'll achieve it." Her steady, calm voice inspired him. He loved her instantly.

He gazed now at her gaunt face surrounded by the same unruly, now white, hair and marveled at the last 40 years. Their lives had moved apart and intertwined and always they remained connected. He respected her, learned from her and tried to protect her. Her diminutive size belied her toughness. He leaned over and placed his face next to hers and whispered, "Thank you. Without you I'd not be who I am."

A physician for over thirty years, he sat quietly before death, in awe of life. Often his professional mantle distanced and protected him but not now. He sat for a long time. Then, with a sigh, he pulled the sheet over Amy's face and left the room.

The next few days he kept busy with the details of her death. Amy's Will left the house to Matthew. Each servant inherited a generous gift. Colby College received an endowment for a teaching scholarship. Specific items went to friends and students. Following a simple funeral, they buried Amy beside her grandparents. As Matt left the cemetery, Amy's death seemed like a small ripple on a still pond.

During the next few weeks, he experienced sporadic rage: feelings he'd never known. How could people laugh, eat and live normally while he endured such pain? Something like fear erupted randomly; simple things angered or confused him.

Rose grieved Amy's death, tried to help her brother but never understood the depth of his caring, the measure of his loss. Gradually, Matt regained his composure and grew less irritable as life at 'Craigmoor South' moved on.

42

When Charley Morgan, two years older than Amy Louise, attended Bates College, the decision pleased Amy Louise but bothered Bertie. Over the next two years, letters arrived faithfully and the bicycling suitor returned each summer.

Bertie growled to Libby, "Amy Louise won't be safe at Bates."

"Of course she will. Katy and Annabelle were. Charley and Amy Louise will be well chaperoned."

"If you think I'd have been deterred by some silly chaperone for two years at their age you've forgotten being young. Maybe we should send her to a girl's school: someplace away from that tennis playing, bike-riding Morgan."

Libby shook her head. For all his concerns about Katy and Annabelle remaining single and teaching, he became frantic at the idea of Amy Louise marrying.

The first year Amy Louise attended Bates further shook Libby's foundations. Her last fledgling had flown. Frequent letters helped but she bristled often. Ma, sensing Libby's restlessness, gave her the poems and other things she'd written soon after Libby and Bertie married: a time of confusion and readjustment for her.

"These might help," Ma said simply. Libby read them, realized both the universality and the particularity of her current experience. And, as is so often the case with obvious truth, these facts helped not one whit.

One late fall afternoon Libby stormed out of the 'big house,' trudged across the lane, past the 'new house,' through the orchard (tearing off, then crunching aggressively into, a succulent Winesap apple), up the hill past the rebuilt house and back down through the fields. She found no evidence of the fire, no scar from the lightening strike.

'How did it disappear?' she wondered.

Stomping through the pastures, her small, tough, familiar form aroused little curiosity but flushed some pheasants that then arced against the clear blue sky. For the twenty-eighth year she stood and watched a gaggle of honking Canadian geese fly south. She continued on with a slower stride through the fields knowing every knoll and path, the peculiarities of each gate.

From the barn, Bertie watched her start up the hill: prowling the territory, searching for some segment of herself, some missing piece of life's puzzle. When she arrived at the rock outcropping in the big pasture, he put down the plow, unhitched his horse and walked close to where she stood. She knew he'd arrived by some subtle, intuitive sense. Without looking, she reached for his hand and started talking.

"I looked in the mirror this morning and this 48 year old woman looked back. She's healthy but so intense." She put her free hand to her throat and turned. "Bertie, I'm not young any more and I don't know when it happened. It just surprised me—like picking up a glass and getting cider when you expect milk. It's strange to see babies on our front porch and they aren't ours. I can't find one bit of evidence that the fire or the storm happened." She looked puzzled. Her graying blond hair was pulled into a bun and curls escaped around her face. She tilted her head slightly to the right and looked up at Bertie quizzically.

"When you're a hundred years old and tilt your head like that, I'll melt like I always have," he grinned and kissed her cheek, touched her hair. "We've lived these years."

"You always find the right words." She looked over the field toward the distant mountains. "This farm is beautiful. Thank you for sharing it with me."

"It frames our lives: you, me and the children count the most, and we're blessed seeing all six of them grow up." He stretched, yawned. "Do you suppose there's anything to eat over in the big house?"

Libby laughed. "I can find something."

He began to move toward the plow, whistled for the horse and called over his shoulder, "I still love you, Libby Whitman!"

"I know Albert Jones. And I'll always love you." She turned and walked to the big house to fix supper in the old kitchen that now belonged to her.

43

Charley Morgan exuded confidence. A strong-willed young man, he loved people and wanted to teach. At 6' 2", with laughing blue eyes, a straight, narrow nose and high cheekbones he looked patrician. Slim and muscular in a sinewy way, he towered over the Joneses.

Charley and Amy Louise adored each other. From fall 1898 when Amy Louise entered college until Charley graduated in spring 1900, they both attended Bates College. This matured their youthful attraction into to a solid relationship founded on a deep dedication to learning and service. Amy Louise grew more self-assured, better able to stand up for her ideas; Charley curbed his headstrong tendencies.

Amy Louise, with blue eyes flashing and unruly brunette curls piled high, turned many heads. Like her Aunt Rachel, she put people at ease and worked subtly to include everyone in social situations. Her college experience at Bates, an abolitionist Baptist Co-ed College, allowed her natural intellectual talents to grow and solidified her deeply rooted progressive view of the world. Her years of college honed and disciplined her mind, deepened her faith and, as often happens, shortened her name. She became simply 'A.L.'—a sobriquet she'd carry for the rest of her life.

After graduating from Bates in 1900, Charley entered a Master's degree program in Mathematics at Harvard. He boarded in a rooming house close to campus, studied diligently, volunteered to coach tennis, rode his bike around the city, visited the Joneses at 'Craigmoor South' and wrote letters to A.L. On schedule to complete his degree in the spring of 1902, he returned to Craigmoor for the Christmas break in 1901. On December 21, 1901, Charley stood in the Jones' barn and asked Bertie's permission to propose. Then he waited and watched Bertie chew on a piece of straw as their breath froze in puffy shapes in the cold.

Bertie believed Charley was too theoretical: thought studying and teaching soft. But college had tamed his temper and he'd be a good teacher. Bertie would have preferred a man more rooted in the earth. Standing in the cold, he fought an army of conflicting emotions and wondered what John Whitman had felt when he'd asked to marry Libby. A.L. came as a special gift after Libby's illness and resuscitating her during the storm welded her uniquely onto Bertie's heart. Finally, he squinted up at the tall young man.

"What are your plans?"

"Well, sir," Charley's voice cracked. Bertie coughed and shook his head. "I'll complete my Master's Degree by June and I've applied for a position at Boston Latin School next fall. Teaching can provide a good life. Like your sister Rose and your daughters Katy and Annabelle…"

"Don't talk about my family, talk about your plans," Bertie snapped peevishly.

Charley swallowed hard. "Teaching and coaching in an excellent school like Latin and living in Boston will give us many opportunities: for advancement and for our children."

"Boston's too far." Bertie stated confrontationally.

Charley squared his shoulders, took a deep breath. "We'd be close to A.L.'s sisters Katy and Annabelle, her aunt Rose and her uncle Matt. Mr. Jones, my family has a long history here with the lumber business. We haven't been farmers but we're good New Hampshire folk. You know us. My sister Abigail and Junior are making a good life. A.L. and I would build a solid home and family. We'd come back for at least part of summers. A.L. will finish college after next term. I love her, Mr. Jones. I want what's best for her."

Bertie pursed his lips, pulled his mustache, played for time, exercised arbitrary power. Assuming that this request was coming, he and Libby had decided to allow Charley to propose; but here, in this cold barn, it seemed ridiculous to permit A.L. to consider marrying this tall, skinny, tennis-playing, mathematics-loving kid. Or anyone. Bertie walked to a stall, picked an old carrot from the bucket, fed it to one of the horses.

"The most important things to me are my family and my land and I'll give neither to people who don't understand their value. A.L. wants to teach but if she's a married woman I doubt that'd be possible. She'd be a good teacher, but she'd be a good homemaker and mother too." Charley watched intently as Bertie talked quietly, mainly to himself. "I know Morgans are good folk—bought lumber from them my whole life. Why your grandparents gave us our bed," he said softly. After a pause, Bertie riveted Charley's eyes with his own. "I'll speak to her. If she approves I'll allow you to propose: but I'll speak to her first. You'd best go now. Come day after tomorrow. We'll talk more then."

"Thank you, sir," Charley gulped, turned and walked rapidly to the barn door. Before exiting, he turned. "Thank you, Mr. Jones. I'll be back day after tomorrow." Then he charged out the door and trotted off down the lane slipping and sliding in the snow. Bertie followed him out, watched him go, remembering his own run from the town to the farm all those years ago.

The next day he spoke with A.L., felt part of himself slip away as she smiled sweetly, nodding 'yes.'

Charley proposed on Christmas Eve and slipped an antique ring on A.L.'s finger on New Year's Eve right before midnight in the 'big house' on the farm. Ma, Bertie, Libby, Charley, A.L., Abby, Junior, the twins, the Uncles and Auntie Jones celebrated together, popping corn and drinking homemade cider. At midnight, Bertie wound the clock and everybody kissed. Charley stayed overnight with his sister Abby, Junior and their two daughters.

Later, lying awake with moonlight glistening on the snow, Libby ran her fingers through Bertie's hair.

"What are you thinking?"

"You suppose this is how your father felt? How Mr. Morgan felt when Junior asked for Abigail? Darn it all, he's just not good enough: too much tennis, too much 'college man' stuff. Why, he'd starve running a farm."

"But he's going to teach. They'll have a different life: won't be like us."

"Why not teach here in Craigmoor?"

"I don't want to lose her either but we raised our children to be independent and they are. Charley's a fine man and the Morgans are good people. We've watched them grow together. They're well matched.

"You know, Aunt Helen once told me Papa worried about us courting, worried about me moving to a farm: now you don't want A.L. moving to a city. It's just a big circle."

Bertie rolled onto his side, buried his face in her neck, "And furthermore, I'm not old enough to have my youngest child marry."

"Neither am I," she mumbled, caressing him gently.

A.L. graduated with honors. Charley completed his Master's degree and accepted a position at Boston Latin. The wedding would take place on the Fourth of July, 1902, "so our anniversary will always be a Holiday," Charley said.

Bertie scoffed, "That's just to help him remember the date."

The day dawned hot and clear. Driving the family to town, Bertie wanted to gallop out the other side of Craigmoor and just keep going. He growled at Ma, at Libby, at everyone. Arriving at the church, Libby, Rose, Katy, Annabelle and A.L. went to the side-room to dress the bride. Ma remained in the buggy.

"I remember a young man a few decades ago coming to this church to claim his bride, nervous as a cat and confident his love could last a lifetime. John gave Libby to you that day Bertie, his only daughter, his closest link to Mavis. He gave her freely, holding nothing back. You do the same today, Bert. Hold nothing back."

"I'm tight as an over-wound clock."

"If your Pa were alive he'd slip you whiskey but that'd just make you sick. A.L.'s special. You don't want any man to love her like a man loves a woman. But that's the kind of love that creates and sustains life. Now, go wander the town and be back for the wedding."

"I just wish Charley weren't a foot taller than I am."

"Silly man. This family needs Morgan height just like it needed Whitman wisdom."

A.L. looked fragile and radiant in a high-necked, white cotton-lace dress with a small bustle. She wore Libby's veil on her fashionably coifed curls. Escorting her down the aisle, Bertie recalled the day he'd been the groom. 'Were we that young? That innocent? That scared?' Charley stood rigid as a fence post, his piercing blue eyes following A.L.'s every step.

Bertie remembered Libby's eyes: yes, she'd been innocent and he'd been scared. He relaxed, smiled and patted A.L. on the hand. Morgan was a good man; it was all right. When he gave her hand to Charley, he felt proud and happy. Stepping back into the pew, he took Libby's hand and squeezed it.

As the newlyweds walked down the aisle, Bertie whispered to Libby, "I just wish he weren't so dang tall."

"You're just jealous," she replied, smiling and wiping away a tear.

Outside, he asked, "Do you have a picnic in the 4th of July auction this year?"

Libby turned, looked into his deeply lined face, noted the gray in his hair and mustache, and saw her Bertie. "After all these years, would you buy it?"

"Of course." A smile played on his features. "But I wouldn't bid the same."

She tilted her head, put her hands on her hips indignantly. "What a thing to say!"

Their eyes met, just as they had so many years ago after Patsy Hamilton and Ralph Ridgeway's wedding. A feeling of power swept through her. Nothing and no one else existed: only the two of them in their secret, suspended world.

"I'd triple the bid. I'd sell everything for you for you are everything to me," he said in a mellow, serious tone.

'We're magic together,' she thought as tears filled her eyes. A child raced past, brushing against her long skirt, snapping her back to reality.

Bertie grinned. "Come on, let's join the party."

44

After a honeymoon on the coast of Maine at Pemaquid Point, A.L. and Charley moved into 'Craigmoor South' in Cambridge. The old Ely mansion—now home to Matthew, Rose, Katy, and Annabelle—adjusted to the newlyweds. During that first year of teaching and marriage, a less secure man than Charley Morgan might have chafed under the combined strength of two generations of Joneses. He loved his wife, loved his work, continued to play and coach tennis and rode his bicycle in all but the worst weather.

A.L. and Charley occupied the 'family quarters' on the main floor of the house: two bedrooms, a sitting room and the main study. The formal parlor, kitchen, pantry, china closet, dining room (with French door opening onto a side porch) completed the main floor. The second floor housed a large sitting room/study and six bedrooms off a long center hall that connected the front and back staircases. Each of the four Joneses occupied a separate bedroom. Matt used the first bedroom as a study and the three women shared the sixth, and largest bedroom, for their study. The third floor was devoted to servants' quarters and storage.

The somewhat faded, floral wallpapers in the dining room and downstairs parlor spoke of an elegant history while the rest of the house reflected refined taste highlighted by light wall colors, contrasting drapes and fragile lace curtains. The furniture bore simple lines and ten-foot ceilings lent a lofty, uplifting feel to the main floor. Light flooded in through many windows. A large barn, a side flowerbed and a kitchen garden out back completed the property. A cook, a gardener and a maid (all of whom lived on the third floor) did much of the work.

A.L. managed the enterprise learning the duties from Matt and Rose. By the end of Charley's first year of teaching, A.L. became the true head of the household. Everyone noted that things ran more smoothly with her in charge;

cook fixed more interesting meals, the house stayed cleaner, the laundry was completed on schedule and the gardens became more attractive and productive. Additionally, the books balanced and expenses were down.

One evening while playing chess with Annabelle, A.L. remarked, "I know I'd like teaching but managing this menagerie does challenge me. Mama said Great-Great-Grandma Tillman ran a big house; maybe I've inherited her skills," she said, moving her knight.

Annabelle escaped her sister's chess attack, and commented, "I agree about the Tillman skills. Keeping three women teachers teaching, a doctor happy, your new husband sane around all of us and our three house staff working well is no small feat."

"Of course," A.L. said, studying the chess board intently as a smile crept coyly across her face, "once I have children, I'll be teaching them."

Annabelle stared, reached over and grabbed her sister's hand. "Will that be soon?"

"Late fall," A.L. said simply.

Annabelle brushed chess pieces aside. "You monkey! When did you plan to tell us?"

"You ruined the board and I was winning! And I just did!" A.L. replied.

On November 10th, 1903, at three o'clock in the morning, Michael Morgan entered the world. His Great Uncle Matthew Jones delivered him assisted by his Aunt Katy. Early the next morning, Charley went to the closest telephone exchange and called Craigmoor. Max Reynolds rode out to Quail Hill to deliver the news. Bertie, who believed telephones unnecessary, changed his mind when he learned so quickly about Michael's birth and A.L.'s safe delivery.

When Charley, A.L. and Michael arrived at the farm in June of 1904, A.L. carried him first to his Great Grandmother Jones. At seven months, he sat on her lap smiling and looking around, watching everyone and everything.

"I declare," Ma said, "he's the prettiest one yet!" She smiled up at Libby. "Someone needed to say it and I'm the only great-grandmother here."

Libby looked at Michael's long, thin Morgan body so different from her own babies and then noticed the remarkable resemblance to A.L. in his face. She felt a deep tenderness for both the baby and for Ma. In so many ways, Ma had incorporated Libby's family traditions, grafting them seamlessly onto the Jones family tree. Her simple statement, 'prettiest one yet,' forged yet another voluntary, unifying bond. Michael didn't just belong to A.L. and Charley: he belonged, in a much broader sense, to the many families represented here, and, beyond them, to the entire human species. He, his cousins and other far-reaching relatives, would inherit the combined symbols from their specific families and mix them into the broader planetary pool.

All that afternoon, Libby felt deeply affected that Ma remembered and honored such a small Tillman-Whitman detail. She remembered Rachel telling her that Ma fought to get her help during her illness. She recalled how Ma subtly guided her in her early years on the farm and how she welcomed Abby and helped Libby understand her new role as mother-in-law. Libby remembered how much Mavis loved having her back rubbed; how Grandma Margaret said that after Richard died, the thing she missed most was simple, human touch. So, that evening after Ma went to bed, Libby knocked softly on her door. Ma peeked out.

"Is something wrong?"

"No, no. I just wondered if you'd like a backrub."

Ma smiled. "That would be nice." She snuggled into her feather mattress and Libby began kneading her neck and shoulders lightly. Ma relaxed under the rhythmic motion and soon fell asleep. Libby continued for a few minutes. Ma stirred but did not awaken when Libby stopped. To Libby, this seemed a small offering; to Ma, it was a great gift.

45

A.L. and Charley had a second son, Andrew Whitman Morgan, in the spring of 1909. They called him Andy.

On the farm, both Uncles and Auntie Jones had died; Junior and the twins—James and John—assumed more responsibility as Bertie slowed down. Bertie and Libby often walked the land and took short trips into Craigmoor. Each summer Bertie felt happy when the family from Cambridge arrived; each fall he felt happy when they left. With three grandchildren across the lane, his three sons on the farm, Libby by his side and Ma still alert, Bertie felt blessed.

A few weeks after naming Andy 'the prettiest one yet,' Ma died in her sleep. When Libby took in morning tea, Ma didn't respond. Libby walked to the barn where the men were milking, opened the door and stood silhouetted against the rising sun.

"Bertie," she called softly, "please come."

They walked in silence across the lane. Bertie sat on Ma's bed with his head bent low and his shoulders slumped forward. Libby felt once again the strange sensation of altered time, seemed to be swimming laboriously through the air in the room as she moved to her husband and then held him as he wept.

One day in early fall, while sitting at the breakfast table and watching the morning mist rise, Libby looked over at Bertie's lined face.

"How absurd," she said aloud.

"What?"

"We've been married 40 years and I'm not ready to be the matriarch of this place."

"Ready or not: you are. As Pa used to say: 'when your parents die, there's nobody left between you and the door.'" He stood behind her and put his hands on her shoulders, watching the familiar scene out the window. "Ma had a good life. You were special to her. Keep her poems; she was proud of them. Sometimes she caught the feel of this place, of herself, too."

"At first it looked like she played favorites: loved Matt more than you. But she loved him 'differently.' It looks like 'more' and 'less' to the young, but mainly it's just 'different.' She did a lot for me and I only understood later what a powerful force she was."

"Pa said she was the only woman he ever knew 'who didn't fight too many fights—and never avoided necessary ones.' That pleased her. She'd make Matt and me mad. We'd come home from some brawl, me, of course more than Matt, and she'd be real casual cleaning us up. Saying 'well, my,' or 'you don't say,' but she'd never take sides. One day I hollered 'Ma, why don't you tell me I was right?' And she said, 'I wasn't there and I only know what you told me. If it was a fight you needed to fight, then you fought it. If it was a fight you shouldn't have fought, well, you fought it. Fights are personal things.' She taught me a lot—about life, about values. Mostly she was happy but didn't see 'happiness' as a goal. Were things fair? Were people honest? That's what she cared about."

Looking at him without her glasses, Bertie appeared fuzzy. "I love you Bertie Jones. I loved Mama and Papa, Johnny, Aunt Helen, Ma and Pa, Matt, Rachel, Rose, Miss Middleton, Louise Putnam, our children and our grandchildren but all those loves together don't come close to the love I have for you. I just wanted you to know." It was risky, saying Rachel's name.

"Careful, you'll spoil me."

"You were spoiled when I got you."

They laughed. Then he became serious. "Is she well, Libby? Rachel?" The word sounded like glass breaking into small shards.

Libby nodded. "She's well."

"Does she know Ma died?"

"I wrote and got a letter back. It's lovely—like all her letters."

"Ma," he paused, started again hesitantly, "Ma said I was wrong about Rach. I never trusted that Swami. Maybe her letters…"

After a pause, Libby spoke softly, "I have them all. I'll put the box on the table later."

He nodded silently.

They walked onto the porch, sat in their rocking chairs. Butch, Bertie's current hunting dog, curled up by his side; Libby put on her glasses, picked up her knitting. She pictured the twists and turns of the yarn of her life: a life that often seemed like stitches of both unwanted lessons and answered prayers all mixed together. Miss Middleton used to say 'character is measured by what you do with what you get.' Libby smiled, rocked and kept knitting.

That afternoon, Bertie read Rachel's letters and began to understand her sense of 'call.' That night he wrote her a short, stilted note.

In the spring of 1915, Rose Jones retired from teaching. She planned to divide her time between Cambridge and Craigmoor. She'd work with the suffragettes to obtain women's right to vote while in Cambridge and organize her writing in Craigmoor. When she arrived at the farm, she moved into the house up the lane with her nephews, the twins James and John. They were delighted to have Aunt Rose join them and expected her to cook, clean and do all the chores they'd been doing for themselves since Auntie Jones died. After forty-plus years of teaching, Rose Jones was not about to be their 'farm wife.' One morning she stormed down the lane, burst into the 'big house' during breakfast.

"Your sons," she growled to Libby and Bertie, "are impossible!"

Bertie gulped tea, grabbed a piece of bread, plopped his hat on his head, kissed Libby and dashed out. "Their Aunt Rose," he hollered over his shoulder, "isn't much better." The screen-door banged behind him.

Libby laughed in spite of herself. "You need some tea, Rosie."

Rose lowered herself rigidly onto a chair. Libby took out Ma's bone-china cup, filled it and placed it before Rose who stared into space. A minute passed. Libby added sugar and fresh cream to the tea, handed Rose a silver spoon. Rose moved the spoon around idly in the tea. The clock ticking and the delicate tinkling of silver spoon on china hung in the room.

"I shouldn't have come back."

"This is your home."

"I don't know. All that time at college and in Cambridge when I got frightened, I'd say to myself, 'Rose Jones, there's always Craigmoor,' and I'd feel better. Summers I'd live here and it felt familiar. But maybe I should stay in Cambridge. Or maybe I don't belong anyplace. That happened to Amy. Maybe it happens to us women out on our own."

"What's happening with the twins?"

"I've taught for over forty years; I helped manage the Ely house; I established committees working for women's rights. I'm not a maid! I contribute to this farm, I'm willing to do my part but James and John treat me like a servant."

Libby stirred her tea. "That's my fault. I concentrated on the girls: they all earned college degrees and I'm proud of them. The boys followed Bert and I let them. I've always done a lot for them. If no woman's around, they make do but if a female's near they figure she should care for them. Men work outside, women work in."

"Except you do everything: the gardens, the flower beds, the chickens, gather the apples and nuts, wash, iron and sew. It doesn't look 'inside/outside' to me."

Libby pursed her lips and looked down at her rough, callused farmwife's hands. She mentally reviewed her lifelong friendship with Rose: how it had become divided by their life choices. "You can move down here, live in your old room."

Rose reached over and touched Libby's hand. "Here I am again, 'everybody-do-it-my-way-Rose.' I hate that part of me Libby but I don't much care for how my nephews treat me." She sighed. "If I move down here, that's more work for you."

"Not much." A tiny smile began in Libby's eyes. "But down here you'd live with Bert and, if you think my sons are bad, remember your brother!"

"Why is it if Matt and Bert do things, I don't mind but when it's the twins, I rage?"

"You grew up with your big brothers. You didn't grow up with the twins and you want them different. They are, but not as much as you want."

"I can't move down here, Libby. We'll work it out, somehow. And I like my room up there. The view from my bed's lovely." Rose, calmer now, sipped her tea.

"We all work hard: everyone's valuable and valued. You walk behind a plow and milk cows at dawn and dusk or you cook, clean, tend vegetables and wash clothes. We rub up against each other's rough spots and, God willing, keep loving each other as the years go by. We all pay honest prices for our lives."

"I'll do my fair-share," Rose stated, standing to leave. Rose held her slim, 65 year-old body, very straight and moved with a dancer's grace. As she left, she stood on the porch with her sharp Jones' features accentuated against the trunk of the black walnut tree, and listened to a meadowlark. A breeze caressed her face and the intense beauty of the scene relaxed her. Rose stepped off the porch, headed up the hill to the house she shared with her nephews. "I started the summer up there and I'll end it there."

The three generations of the Jones/Morgan clan supported each other in Cambridge at 'Craigmoor South.' They shared strong family ties and had similar ideas about life but the society they lived in differed from Craigmoor and was changing fast. Early twentieth century immigration altered the sights and sounds of the Boston area as increasing populations from Ireland, Italy, Asia and Eastern Europe added new flavors and ideas into the cultural mix.

True to her word, A.L. taught both boys to read long before they entered school and both excelled academically. Mike and Andy grew tall, slim and athletic. Charley encouraged music and sports in addition to schoolwork and chores. Every summer they went to Craigmoor and developed close relationships with all their grandparents.

Andy, with dark curly hair and striking blue eyes, looked like a taller version of Bertie and followed his grandfather around constantly asking questions. How does the plow work? How come we trim out so many apples? How much hay does a cow need through the winter, why do chickens scratch, how do you recognize good seed, is it going to rain tomorrow, how do you know?

"You know, Andy, you'd like farming." Bertie said.

"When I retire from engineering, I'll farm. Maybe right here."

"It doesn't work like that. The land won't wait. It's merciless on folks who don't understand it."

"But I will understand it, because you're teaching me."

"A little learning a few weeks in summer's not enough." Bertie knew Andy would stay in the city and it saddened him.

One night, lying in bed, Bertie said, "It's a joy having Andy around; his questions never stop: what about this, how does that work? He has the knack to be a great farmer but he wants to be an engineer. Junior's 'Little Al' wants the land but he doesn't learn like Andy. Looks like Mike will be a doctor the way he watches bugs, animals and fusses trying to make hurt-things well. I don't begrudge the girls their educations but I'm surprised only A.L. married. That one beau of Katy's didn't get back from the Spanish American War: really sad. The twins? What can I say?"

"Well, first, Little Al's going to learn more because he's here more and he learns by watching, not talking. Second, the twins are my doing," Libby sighed. "My being sick, they got shortchanged."

"That's silly. Heck, they didn't know the rest of the family existed till they were seven: more involved with each other than anything else. That's just twins." He chuckled. "I'd love more farm-bred grandsons but Lord pity a woman trying to compete with a twin brother!

"So, we'll pass this place on: farming, living close to the land, to Little Al. Everything's changing so fast; men live in cities, wear suits, never feel the earth or touch a newborn calf. They watch the weather to figure if they need an overcoat! It's not good. Maybe I'm getting old but somehow I should have stopped this."

"Now I'll say 'silly.' Change will happen no matter what we do. We'll leave this farm in better shape than we got it."

Beside him, bathed in moonlight, Libby's skin looked soft, her eyes gray-blue and her hair almost colorless. Bertie felt a stab of longing, not desire, but longing: for youth, missed opportunities, squandered chances. He felt the tenderness of age, of regret and of sorrow all wrapped up with his deep love for this one woman.

Four nights later, Rose slept fitfully. A breeze pushed the curtains softly. Suddenly, Rose awakened and pulled the covers up as a freak gust of wind, sounding like a dozen frightened chickens, flapped the curtains into the room. Immediately, silence surrounded her. Rose watched the mirror over the dresser on the wall directly opposite her bed. Her prostrate form and the window next to her reflected eerily. Gradually, a wispy presence developed at the foot of her bed and blocked the mirror. Rose blinked hard. An ephemeral shape brightened and solidified. Rose dropped the covers, rubbed her eyes and sat up. Then she recognized Rachel's smiling face on the figure emerging within the light. Rose stiffened.

'Don't be afraid, Rosie.' The Rachel-figure conveyed the message explicitly but whether through speech or just ideas Rose couldn't tell. Rose's muscles relaxed but part of her rational mind wanted to scream and flee.

'It's all right.' The figure's smile broadened.

"Rachel?" Rose whispered. "Is it you?" After twenty years, Rachel looked serene. She stood, her long arms close to her sides, her slim hands clasped before her breastbone, without the gawky appearance that had so plagued her youth. Her direct blue eyes, small straight nose and slightly pointed chin resembled a perfectly proportioned Madonna. The sisters smiled at each other. "You look so lovely," Rose said reaching toward the figure.

'Don't touch me, Rose. I've come to say goodbye,' Rachel smiled, 'and that I love you.'

"Oh, Rach, I love you too. I'm sorry I was so…"

Rachel held up her hand. 'Shh, shh, shh. Everything's fine. It worked out. Tell Bertie and Libby I love them and I've loved all your letters. Our family's special; all families are special.' She bowed her head in the Indian way; then, accompanied by a soft sound like a breeze through a crystal chandelier, Rachel's form dissolved. As the light dissipated, a breeze within the room puffed the curtains outward.

Rose could see the mirror again, smiled at her silver-gray reflection and slipped out of bed. Downstairs she checked the mantle clock: 2:10. She returned to her bed, sighed a silent thanks to the universe for whatever had just happened and went back to sleep.

The next day, Rose hesitantly told Libby about her vision as they sat snapping beans on the porch.

"Well, I'll be!" Libby exclaimed her eyes twinkling. "My mother and great-grandmother knew things and A.L. does sometimes but who'd ever have guessed

Rose Jones would allow herself to see such a thing! If it's true, we'll hear; if it's not, well, it was a nice vision."

The letter informing them of Rachel's death indicated she died the day Rose had the dream, but no time was specified.

'Ama Rachel died surrounded by her spiritual family in a small hut close to the Kali Temple, a place special to her. Some wanted to sink her body because of her saintliness but we believed cremation would please her more. She lived a simple, holy life.'

Her friends enclosed a small heart shaped locket Rachel had worn. Bertie recognized it as a gift from Toby Wills.

"Somewhere 'between a grasshopper and a saint,' that's what you said," Libby remarked gently as she handed the letter to Bertie.

"I guess the grasshopper was mostly gone," he replied, pulling out his handkerchief and wiping his eyes. "I'm glad I wrote."

Libby nodded.

Bertie chuckled. "And like Rachel's ghost told Rose, 'our family's special.'" He shook his head, "Imagine me quoting some spook." He walked to the kitchen pump and splashed water on his face. Libby just smiled.

46

When the United States instituted the draft in May 1917, Charley enlisted. He was too old to be drafted but believed he needed to 'do his part'—a common sentiment at the time. He left Cambridge in July 1917 to begin his training. A.L. and the boys stayed in Cambridge and carried on as normally as they could at Craigmoor South. Charley was sent to France and led his men through some rough battles. After being shot in the foot early in 1918 and recovering sufficiently to rejoin his unit, he observed the end of fighting with his company. In a letter to A.L. he recounted that they all walked to the nearest town to celebrate, crossing a slippery log footbridge high over a fast moving stream. Meeting a group of Royal Irish Rifles, who 'alternately disparaged their bad luck of meeting us fool Yankees and attempting to wheedle invitations from us to come to the US, we all got thoroughly, totally, uproariously and appropriately drunk.' Returning to camp 'in pitch blackness, we slipped and slid across that dang bridge, saved from drowning only by the goodwill of the Almighty.'

Soon after this, he was transferred and worked on treaties, particularly on the Treaty of Neuilly sur Seine—signed on November 27, 1919—until he was discharged. Charley's wounded foot caused him to limp for the rest of his life.

· Quail Hill ·

He also carried minor unseen battle scars—moments of short temper, indecision and fear—that, in the future, flared occasionally.

Charley was still in Europe in October of 1919 and missed Libby and Bertie's Fiftieth Anniversary. Libby called the War 'that European mess' and was relieved the fighting was over. The second weekend in October, a relaxed A.L., her boys—Mike and Andy—Matt, Katy and Annabelle all rode in Matt's new car up to Craigmoor for the party. Friends and family, including Charley and Abby's widowed father, also came to the Quail Hill festivities.

The women prepared a lavish feast: a turkey, potatoes with gravy, carrots and peas cooked with honey and mint, Swiss chard, relishes, freshly baked rolls with fresh churned butter and blueberry jam, two kinds of pie and a cake. Matt brought wine and took pictures.

Years later on the back of one of the surviving photos Annabelle wrote to her grandniece: "When Great-Grandpa and Great-Grandma Jones had been married fifty years, they had a party. We couldn't get all the people in one picture but your Daddy's there, sitting beside Great-Grandpa Morgan." Indeed, Michael and Andy flanked their tall, patrician Grandfather Morgan who looked out at the world soberly over his white mustache. At the end of the table, Libby and Bertie eyed the camera warily. (Later, seeing the picture, Bertie scoffed, "I look like a midget.")

After the meal and many toasts, they reminisced: about the fire, the storm and Princess saving A.L., good harvests and bad. Matt and Rose spoke of how they always knew Libby and Bertie would marry, of the 4th of July picnics, of fall colors at the farm. Rose talked about Ma's poems, "She wrote one about you, Libby. I'll see if I can find it," she went and got Ma's poems.

Junior's 24 year-old daughter Sue, now a mother herself, said, "Now, Grandpa and Grandma Jones and Grandpa Morgan you've been married fifty years so tell us your secrets."

Bertie looked at Libby, then at his granddaughter and the baby she held.

"The toughest is the 'forsake all others' part because it doesn't mean just the physical: it means everything. I'm not religious but I figured that, of the 10 Commandments, if you keep the first one, the rest take care of themselves. That 'have no other' stuff works: it focuses the heart. Libby Whitman completes me: makes me whole. When you know that, then the worst of the bad disappears in the shadow of the littlest part of the good." His eyes twinkled as he took Libby's hand. "It helps that I've loved your Grandma since I was ten."

"One time I was sick for way over a year. That was hard," Libby spoke softly. "The family pulled together: we got through and learned a lot about love: it's a verb, it's what you do."

"Yes, marriage is work and love and also a contract," Mr. Morgan, a businessman his whole life, stated. "If one of the parties isn't serious, doesn't intend to fulfill the commitment, then there's nothing there. With flawed intent, there is no bond and thus no marriage."

Libby chuckled as she watched Sue scowl and bite her lower lip. "Sue wants more roses and lace, more breathless passion. We've had plenty of that but after 50 years, all three of us know that the turkey and carrots are more important than the cake!"

Andy piped up, "Grandpa, why do you call Grandma 'Libby Whitman' sometimes?"

"My Pa said, 'Always remember Libby Whitman's different from us Joneses. She's not your sister or your Ma. Remember that. There's power in that. Keep that power—some wild, unknown space—between you. It creates struggle but gives strength.'

"He'd call my mother 'your Ma' to us kids but sometimes he called her by her full name when they talked together. That was difficult for me but I followed his advice and we've had struggle, strength and our own good helping of wild." Bertie drained his wine glass as Libby blushed. "I also followed the advice of my very wise bachelor brother."

"What's that?" Matt looked surprised.

"You said 'think of a terrible predicament: a child deformed, a leg cut off, a plague and decide who you'd want by your side. Then choose that woman.' So I did."

"That's good advice," Mr. Morgan said and raised his glass. "Let's hope future generations remember this." They all clinked their glasses for a final toast.

"So what's most important?" Mike asked.

Matt looked down at him. "What's more important your heart or your lungs: your brain or your hands? Remember it all: learn from it all," he said mussing up Mike's hair

"I've found it," Rose said, lifting an old piece of paper from the box she'd been sorting through. She began reading:

Libby

She is so young this blue-eyed motherless child
  sent to him, to us, to me.
Can she survive, with city-ways and manners mild,
  be tough as she will need to be?

Must I learn to give without reserve to one who takes
  from me my laughing, joyful son?

Will I survive as my heart breaks –
release him to this other loving one?

I drink from every mother's chalice
know she'll need me so,
I'll strive to feel no hint of malice
as in love I'll let him go.

After the party broke up and all the dishes were washed and food put away, Bertie stood and stretched. He walked over to Libby and kissed her on the neck. "You both did better than Ma expected," he said softly.

47

The Morgans and Joneses paid a small price in the war: the world a great one as many places in the old social order crumbled. Reading the newspapers on the farm, Libby recalled one of Amy's Chinese proverbs: 'One can never open a door so little that only good gets in.'

Late in November 1919, after returning to Cambridge from Craigmoor, Matt and Rose drove Matt's car across town to attend a Sunday afternoon concert. After parking, Matt stepped out, slipped on some ice, fell, hit his head and lay unconscious on the frozen ground. Rose summoned help from a passerby. Arriving at the hospital, one of Matt's former students attended him. As he continued to breathe and frequently thrashed in seizures, his physician and other doctor friends knew there was nothing they could do.

Rose stayed by his side for 75 hours. She wiped his face with a moist washcloth, held his hand, spoke to him gently. Three times she felt Rachel's presence though she neither saw nor heard her sister. No one had been closer to Matt than his family and Amy Middleton. Rose hoped he could experience them now, feel their love and use it to heal. After watching his agony for three terrible days, during which she continually willed him to live, on a crisp November afternoon, Rose finally let him go: finally said, "If it is time for you to die, then I mustn't hold you." Two hours later, still holding her right hand, he stopped breathing.

Rose sat by the bed, struggling to remain composed, her left hand clasped tightly to her mouth. A nurse brought her a cup of tea and called the doctor.

Rose drank the tea gratefully, went to the nearest mirror, sponged her face and tried to arrange her hair. The gaunt eyes that peered out from her swollen lids looked unfamiliar. She pinned her hat on and went home. A.L. fed her soup and put her to bed. Rose slept for eighteen hours: got up and planned Matt's funeral with the minister of the Congregational Church. Then she slept for another eight hours.

A.L., Katy, Annabelle, Mike and Andy were all astonished at the large crowd attending the funeral: Rose was not. She knew her brother had been a formidable intellectual presence in the Cambridge medical community; his family knew him merely as 'Uncle Matt.' After the funeral, Rose decided to move back to Craigmoor permanently. Charley would be home soon, Matt was dead: she saw no reason to remain in Cambridge.

Two days after the funeral Rose boarded a train in Boston heading home. Matt's coffin lay in the freight car with her trunks. The familiar scenery sped by: cascading water, tall trees, small communities, patches of snow. She sat, her legs crossed under a skirt so short she would scandalize Craigmoor. The idea made her smile for the first time since Matt's accident. She removed her hat and offered to help a woman traveling with three small children.

Bertie and Libby met the train, loaded the trunks and coffin onto the wagon and drove to the cemetery. The grave was ready. After watching Matt's coffin lowered into the ground, each dropped a handful of cold, stony, New Hampshire dirt onto the casket. As they left, two men shoveled soil into the gaping wound in the earth that now contained Matt's physical remains.

They rode home in silence. Rose watched the landscape, awaiting her first view of the farm. She would move into her old room above the kitchen in the big house. Still remaining in Cambridge were two generations of the Jones/Whitman/Morgan clan. Rose might visit sometimes. Fifty years after leaving for college in Massachusetts, the woman her students called 'the teacher from New Hampshire,' returned to the home of her birth.

Charley arrived home in April 1920, and would again teach at Boston Latin in the fall. During the summer Charley, A.L. and the boys planned to build a summer home in Maine on land just past Owls Head Lighthouse. At sixteen and eleven, Mike and Andy would help construct the house. In their new automobile, they reached the property bumpily. During June and part of July they camped in a tent while constructing the small, cozy 'no frills' cabin. The project brought the boys closer to their Dad while focusing Charley's energy, giving him time to heal. He neither discussed nor forgot the realities of the war. Gradually, Charley smiled and joked more, calmed his quick temper, slept better. Working with saw and plane, measuring beams, leveling windows and doors, pounding nails and raising the roof bonded Charley with his sons. A.L. cooked, cleaned and assisted:

pleased that Charley seemed more relaxed as he integrated back into the family. By mid-July, they moved into the cabin.

A.L.'s two older sisters, Katy and Annabelle, motored up to visit them in August. Jogging along in Matt's automobile, Katy navigated while Annabelle drove, maintained the car and swore frequently. Katy didn't approve of swearing except when absolutely necessary, which, driving from Cambridge to Owls Head, it often was. Annabelle's favorite cuss words were 'darn,' 'drat,' 'son of a gun' and 'balderdash.' Katy found 'balderdash' particularly offensive; Annabelle found it useful. Except for a few years when they were not at Bates College together, they had never been separated. As children, they chose different activities thus avoiding competition. They loved each other intensely, never hesitated giving the other unsought advice at inopportune moments and would have defended each other to the death. In short, they were intelligent, independent, tightly-bonded sisters.

Annabelle knew more about automobiles than most mechanics. Had she been born later, she'd have been an engineer. The trip to Maine required her skills a number of times. They jostled onto the property one hot day just before noon.

"Wonderful trip!" Annabelle announced, trudging resolutely toward A.L. and embracing her younger sister. "Grand thing, the automobile. Unlimited future."

"Then why admonish it with disreputable language?" Katy asked emerging from the car.

"Like an unruly colt, the invention doesn't yet understand its subordination to human will. Now, as an owner…"

"Part owner." Katy corrected.

"…of this vehicle, it is my duty to establish my leadership forthwith." Annabelle shook a triumphant finger toward an uncaring sky. "Where are my handsome nephews?" Annabelle strode off, blue eyes flashing, smiling broadly. Katy struggled with their valise. A.L. rushed to help her oldest sister. It wasn't that Annabelle meant to leave her sisters struggling but simply that any children, and particularly children she loved, took precedence.

At the lot's edge overlooking the rugged rock cliff, Annabelle stopped as a wave crashed below and salty spray shot onto her face. The boys sailed small boats in a protected tidal pool a few feet to her left.

"Oh, Auntie Belle, you're here!" Andy shouted happily, scrambling up the rocks with their new dog, named Seine, beside him. Aunt and nephew hugged warmly as Seine danced beside them.

"We built the cabin and I sawed and planed and everything! Seine stays real close 'cuz there are bears and moose in the woods and lots of owls hooting at night." The events tumbled out. Annabelle 'oh'd' and 'ah'd' appropriately, enthralled by Andy's enthusiasm. Michael brought up small crustaceans retrieved from the tide pool studying them intently. They climbed down the rocks to investigate the pool more thoroughly; Andy's continued chatter accompanied them. An hour later they entered the cabin, pockets and fists full of local flora and fauna.

"You're as bad as the boys," A.L. remarked.

"She's worse. They'll get bored: she never will," Katy stated, hands upon hips.

Annabelle winked at the boys. "I am a teacher not because of what Bates taught me but because of mysterious things inside me. They're jealous. To them, teaching's a noble profession: to me it's adventure and what I was born to do. I always want lots of small unidentified things to catalogue."

Andy turned to his Mother, "Auntie Belle's almost as good as my Uncles."

Annabelle whipped off her glasses, anchored Andy's chin between the thumb and forefinger of her right hand and gazed intently into his eyes.

"Andrew Whitman Morgan, the fact is that Auntie Belle *is* as good as your Uncles. 'In His own image, male and female, created He *them*.' Don't ever forget that!"

Andy cocked his head a bit quizzically. He said nothing but he never forgot.

Charley bought out Rose's interest in the Ely mansion at 'Craigmoor South.' Katy became the family's Cambridge matriarch, Annabelle remained the most outspoken, A.L. played peacemaker and continued to manage the house. Charley mellowed. The boys flourished in the security of this multigenerational, educationally based home, the intellectual opportunities in Cambridge and the deep family connections supported by summers in Craigmoor and Maine.

48

One Saturday noon the next April, Libby opened a cupboard looking for her bread bowl.

"Where's my bowl?"

Rose froze as she dried a teacup. "I rearranged some things while you were out, I hope you don't mind." Her voice strident, she put the cup down, clung to the dishcloth. "Libby, I'm almost seventy and I've never had a single cupboard in a single kitchen that belonged to me. Ma had this kitchen and you've had kitchens. I helped managed in Cambridge but 'cook' kept the kitchen. With the twins, if I moved a saltshaker they fussed. So this morning I reorganized two cupboards."

Libby laughed. "You can reorganize all of them if you want. I'm plenty tired of kitchens. Sometimes I've felt a little bit jealous of your life: what you've done, what you've seen. Never imagined you'd be jealous of my kitchen—children maybe or having a husband."

"It's all right then?"
"Just let me know where things are—I'll get feisty if I can't find things."
Rose smiled and nodded. "Then I'll really belong."
Bertie came in, reached for his cup.
"Libby, where's my cup?"
"Ask Rose. She's redoing the cupboards."
"Your cup's on the shelf to your left."
Bertie's expression turned from questioning to coy. "Fine with me. Just remember which bed you sleep in."
"Bertie!" Rose expostulated.
He finished his water and left. "Women!" he snorted as the door banged behind him.
"We're a silly triangle," Libby remarked shaking her head.
"We always have been," Rose replied retrieving the bread bowl. "Here."
"Thanks. That's a good place for it."
Rose smiled. "I thought so."

Life's important lessons often arrive in ordinary daily events. Entering their seventies, the 'silly triangle' discovered rough spots. They'd never shared a home together for this long. Before, the four relationships always remained discrete: Bertie-Libby; Libby-Rose; Rose-Bertie and Libby-Rose-Bertie. Now the interactions tugged constantly at each other like the moon's relentless pull on the seas.

Bertie and Rose prowled around Libby like two cats after the same prey. One Saturday morning in May during breakfast Bertie mentioned that he and Libby were going to town. It seemed an innocent remark: it wasn't. Rose glowered at him, wiped her mouth carefully and folded her napkin in her lap.

"Libby and I are going to market today and then to the Literary Guild meeting," she said in her 'I-am-the-teacher' voice.

"No, you're not." Bertie's jaw set resolutely in the Jones way, as did Rose's.

Libby felt a tight knot below her heart; she clenched her hands and slammed her fists down on the table sending Ma's pewter tea set flying.

"Stop this! Both of you," she exclaimed, grabbing the table edge and taking a few short breaths. "You fight over me like children over a puppy—but you shouldn't be children anymore. For months I've been trying to figure out what's going on. I feel resentful and angry when we're all together. It didn't make sense. Then I watched you two together over in the orchard and you looked so happy and loving. It made me happy. I knew what you were sharing—I've stood with Johnny like that, brother and sister easy together: special together.

"Suddenly I saw us clearly. Your love pre-dates me: what you have, I understand. What I have with each of you is different: husbands and wives bond in a different way and Rose has never done that, neither the joy nor the pain. Women's friendships are different and Bertie doesn't experience that.

"Bertie, you act like my love for Rose somehow takes away from us. It doesn't: it can't. Rose, our friendship is long and important; maybe you're jealous of what Bertie and I have. Well there it is: you made a choice, we all made choices and there've been consequences. Don't push me to choose because you'll lose, Rosie." Rose's face showed pain.

"Mama's death taught me early that life is precious. We've influenced each other. We're gifts to each other. Let's heal this, live together better and do it now." Libby pushed her chair back and stood slowly. "I'm going to gather eggs and then we are all going to town. Maybe I'll go to the Guild and maybe I won't: but I'll decide. There's enough of me to go around if the two of you stop picking at me." She put on her bonnet, picked up the egg basket and walked out the door into the bright morning. She sneezed at the sun—an allergic reaction inherited from her Great Grandmother Rebecca Elizabeth Tillman—began to hum and walked across the lane to one of the many chicken coops.

A late rooster crowed. "Seems like when Ma got after us for fighting," Bertie mused.

Rose pursed her lips. "Have I been that bad?"

"Let's just say these past few months haven't been our best."

"Maybe I shouldn't live here."

"Rose, having troubles doesn't mean you leave. Besides," he chuckled, "you sold the Cambridge house and you don't want to live with the twins."

"So, what can I do?"

"Well sis," he hadn't called her 'sis' in a long time, "let go of the schoolteacher; don't try to organize us and don't keep telling us what to do. We've done OK for the past half-century. And I'll try to leave space for you and Libby, not always hang around."

Rose smiled with an expression he'd not seen since she was sixteen: part scamp, part flirt.

"Bertie, you've mellowed."

"Heck, fifty years with Libby would've mellowed Attila the Hun!" He went out to harness the team: he still preferred horses to cars.

Rose cleared the table, picked up the now badly dented pewter tea set and washed the dishes. Libby, she reflected, had borne the children who carried on the Jones genes, the Jones legacy: an immense gift to them all. Rose rubbed her fingers over the dented pewter pot and smiled. In the aftermath of their argument, only these small dents remained.

49

As the twenties roared, the Morgan boys matured. Mike entered Dartmouth College in 1921, moved back to Cambridge and enrolled in Harvard Medical School in 1925. Andy began at Dartmouth in 1927. In the fall of his sophomore year his body ached, his energy waned. On the Tuesday night before Thanksgiving, he rode as far as Craigmoor with his roommate who was driving home to Lawrence Massachusetts.

Stepping out at the base of Quail Hill at 2:30 a.m., Andy wondered if dropping in unannounced at his grandparents' farm was as foolish as it now seemed. Snow swirled, clouds scampered playfully and partially obscured the bright moon. As he rounded the final bend below the barn, the clouds parted and the entire hillside sparkled. His breath hung like puffs of cotton candy as he stood, almost blinded by the moonlight reflected from the snow. The landscape appeared black and white, silver and gray: no color. Icicles hung glistening from the barn roof. Andy remained transfixed by this intense achromatic scene. The hillside's isolated beauty stabbed into his brain some reality beyond life and death: something eternal. A cloud drifted slowly across the sky blocking the moonlight; the vision disintegrated.

Andy readjusted his rucksack as the absurdity of his actions struck him: he could be shot. Their current dog, Princess, might bark and his grandfather or Uncle James or Uncle John come out blazing. 'Well, if I stop now I'll freeze so I'll just hope for the best.' He concentrated on Princess: 'stay calm, it's Andy' he repeated silently in his mind as he trudged around the corner and up the final hill. Moving onto the front steps, he carefully avoided the third, squeaky, tread and figured he was safe. He cracked the front door cautiously, greeted by Princess's happy, panting muzzle thrust through the slight opening. As he entered, she circled him, tail wagging gracefully, claws clicking on the wooden floor. He closed the door and swung his rucksack onto the floor. Andy knelt and the fatigue he'd been resisting for weeks closed around him. He felt the floor beneath him and the dog's warmth as she began licking snow from his face and jacket. He draped his arm around her and breathed heavily. She took his jacket collar in her mouth, whined softly and pawed him. He roused, crawled to the small original bedroom off the kitchen dragging his pack part of the way. Then he removed his jacket, cap, gloves and scarf and lay on the bed; he felt exhausted and ill. Pulling the covers up to his chin, he slept. Princess watched him settle down and then curled up close to the bedroom door. Like all her predecessors, she took the job of caring for this family seriously.

An hour later, Bertie walked into the kitchen to put the kettle on. Princess panted and thumped her tail as he approached, her paw resting on Andy's rucksack. Bertie smiled, scratched the dog's head, looked beyond her to the bedroom and saw his grandson. Andy rolled over and opened his eyes.

"Hi Gramp," he moaned.

"Well, look what blew in. Makes me wonder if we should start locking doors." Bertie chuckled happily, pulled the chair up beside the bed and sat down. Andy saw the unshaven stubble on his grandfather's lined face: he looked his eighty years. Bertie scrutinized Andy.

'Flat-expression. Sunken cheeks. Dull eyes. Boy's sick. Only question's: how sick,' Bertie's mind raced, 'and how to cure him.' He allowed no other option as he reached over and patted his grandson.

"You sleep awhile."

"I'm so tired."

"Then sleep and stop wandering New Hampshire hills in the dead of night. You said you were spending Thanksgiving with some professor in Hanover. Plans must've changed."

"Got a ride to Craigmoor last night and walked up from 'four corners.'"

"Could've saved some miles if you'd gone to your Gramp Morgan's place in town."

"I knew you'd say something like that. You know I love you both." Andy smiled.

"But Morgan's front door would've been locked and those dogs would've roused the town. Besides, your Grandma Libby's a whole lot better cook than Morgan's housekeeper," Bertie chirped happily. "You may carry the Morgan name and stand Morgan tall but Andrew Whitman Morgan you are thoroughly my grandson!" Bertie didn't usually wear his heart on his sleeve so obviously. "Now sleep, while the rest of us men do the milking. People may have holidays but cows need milking twice a day, everyday." He stood slowly, leaned over and stroked Andy's pale face. "I'm mighty glad you're here. Sleep and your Grandma and your Great-Aunt Rose'll fix lots of extras for your breakfast." In the eerie pre-dawn light Bertie walked into the kitchen, closing the bedroom door behind him.

Bertie loved milking: a peaceful, quiet, contented beginning to the day. The rhythmic ssk, ssk, ssk of the milk into the bucket gave background for the mind's reflections. Not formal prayers but wonderings, sometimes half-dead old battles better left alone and sometimes continuing struggles with whatever God is or might be.

Today while milking Bertie reflected on Andy. Surrounded by the sweet fragrance of hay, the steamy breath of men and animals, the soft chewing and mooing of the cows, he knew Andy could heal here, with him, with Libby in this balanced, grounded life. Bertie's hands worked the familiar udders gently, expertly as his mind formed a plan. He'd have to convince them, make them understand he was right. Might have to fight the doctors and teachers. "Well, I can do that" he murmured softly as the ssk, ssk, ssk sound of milking continued.

50

Andy's symptoms persisted. During Christmas break, Mike arranged for him to be examined at Harvard Medical School. Having ruled out what they could treat, the doctors recommended that Andy take time off from college and rest. If he didn't improve, more tests could be done to diagnose other illnesses for which neither treatments nor cures existed.

Andy asked to go to Quail Hill. Craigmoor's proximity to Dartmouth might allow him to visit occasionally and thus not be completely cut off from his class and friends. An extra mouth to feed on the farm wouldn't be a problem and he'd have fresh air, land to roam and as much work as he could do. Charley wanted him to stay in Cambridge.

"Here you'll be closer to medical care."

"But it's unclear what's wrong," Mike countered. Since moving back to Cambridge Mike and Charley often butted heads.

"Will they be strict enough?" Charley questioned.

"They raised us," Annabelle pointed out, "and the farm's still halfway to nowhere."

"Quail Hill's the right place," A.L. said gently. "Junior and Abby are there. James and John, Aunt Rose."

Andy called his grandparents the next morning, talked to Bertie, got his permission. After Bertie hung up the phone, he went to find Libby.

"Andy wants to come here to get well." He chuckled. "You know, milking is a fine way to start the day."

"So is he coming?" Libby asked.

Bertie wrapped his wool scarf around Libby's neck and waltzed her around the kitchen.

"Do you think I'd turn that boy down?"

"I'd better clean the bedroom and check the jam supply because nobody eats more blueberry jam than Andy."

Andy arrived in late January 1929. He spent the next few months eating, sleeping, walking the land and reading: mainly philosophy and literature. Within six weeks the blueberry jam was gone. He grew stronger and helped with chores: first around the house then in the barn and finally repairing equipment and managing livestock. Bertie watched carefully; he counted on time, nature, good food and love to promote healing. By late spring, Andy helped with milking, whistled more, groomed the horses and talked as he worked. By summer he worked all day. His face tanned, his eyes grew brighter and his muscle-tone returned.

As time and rest helped Andy heal, Bertie waged an internal war: he wanted Andy well but didn't want him to leave. Health would bring separation and not just separation from Andy. Bertie loved this relationship, this intimate companionship with youth and vitality. And he was scared. A.L. had told Libby of a dream about Andy: a dream where he was young and dead. Bertie no longer scoffed at such 'funny stuff.' This time it frightened him. He felt old. He wasn't afraid to die: he just wasn't ready. And he wanted Andy to live. So he struggled.

One day, Bertie watched Andy working with his uncles harvesting wheat, all singing happily. Bertie smiled as two tears slid down his cheeks. When work finished that day Andy found his grandfather in the barn, lifted him easily and swung him around, still singing.

"I couldn't've gotten well without you."

"Put me down! I've got things to do," Bertie commanded, struggling to free himself. "And in January you'll go back to college and leave the farm."

Andy continued holding Bertie high. "Where do you need to go?"

"I've things to do," Bertie repeated a bit peevishly. "You should stay here. Farming's important. The life's healthy."

"Engineering's important. I'm strong again and I'll farm later."

"All the College stuff, your Grandmother started." Replaced onto the floor, Bertie had to look up a good 9 inches into the face of his 5' 11" grandson. "So now you're strong again, what're you gonna do with your health? Play tennis? Sissy game."

"You don't mean that. You're just being an old curmudgeon; you want me to stay. I may be a tall, skinny Morgan but my soul is pure Whitman-Jones so I know you. Mama gets peevish just like you—and I get that way, too." Andy's blue eyes sparkled, he grinned and laughed as he draped his long arm around Bertie's shoulders. They walked out of the barn.

Bertie sputtered a bit longer then said, "Baseball's a good game. I played a mean game of baseball. Good hitter."

"We play baseball at Dartmouth, I play first base. Good hitter, too. Like you."

The stock market crash, like a distant earthquake, rocked Quail Hill only slightly. The local bank did not fail; the family had no investments on Wall Street; they had plenty of food and few debts. A large group made up of people all somehow connected to Bert and Libby gathered for a Thanksgiving dinner. They spent the day immersed in the warm steamy fragrance of turkey roasting and pies baking as children ran through the house and played games. Later, with everything cleared away and everyone gone, Libby, Bert and Rose reminisced.

Andy took this family, its history, love, strengths and foibles, for granted. Sitting here listening to their talk, his family's power dawned on him. His own recovery had been fueled by their esoteric lore, willed into reality by these people. Quietly, next to the old stove, they talked about loss and gain, success and failure, wispy memory-fragments from Wales, Scotland and Virginia, of ancestors moving, sacrificing, changing and, most recently, working this tiny chunk of New Hampshire. They spoke of Miss Middleton, her role in their family: Rose and Libby showing respect, Bertie with an edge.

"Good teacher but too much 'go to college,' change for change's sake."

"She encouraged students who wanted college, never pushed others," Rose stated.

"She essentially told me not to go to college: to marry you!"

"Well that showed wisdom." Bertie cleaned out his pipe. "Time for me to hit the hay." He stretched and headed down the hall.

Rose walked to the sink, pumped a glass of water and headed for the stairs. "Goodnight, see you in the morning."

Andy and Princess stayed on the floor next to Libby in her rocker.

"What else was important to you, Grandma?" Andy asked.

Libby smiled, rocked and rested her hand on his shoulder. "People. Ideas. Mama, Papa, Aunt Helen, Bertie, Rachel. 'Work, love, trust; leave the rest to God.' Believe in help from unseen hands. Embrace it all." She rocked forward, reached down and took his hand. "My Great-Grandmother Rebecca Elizabeth Tillman touched me: I touch you. If the touch is gentle and wise then that's an influence we pass on. Probably it's enough." She studied his hand, ran her index finger over his fingers, traced his veins. "I know that hand: it's like my Papa's." She smiled and looked into his blue eyes with her own. "I'm glad you're better. Now, let's get some sleep." He helped her up, they hugged and she kissed his cheek. "Stay healthy," she said, patting his arm. Walking toward the hall, Libby shook her right index finger in the air. "And that's an order."

Andy took Princess out briefly and then went to bed. Lying with his hands locked behind his head, staring into the darkness, scenes from this year flipped before him. Without his illness, he'd have missed this. 'Life's a funny mix,' he thought. Princess made a few soft crying sounds, feet moving jerkily, chasing 'dream-bunnies' in her sleep. Andy rolled onto his side, dropped his hand down onto the dog and patted her gently.

"It's OK, Princess," he murmured. "We're safe here."

· Craigmoor ·

51

In April 1931, Mr. Morgan died leaving the Craigmoor house to Charley and A.L. Charley decided to retire from teaching, return to Craigmoor and take over the family lumber business: it needed his attention.

In June, Andy graduated, a year late, from Dartmouth and returned to Cambridge in the fall to begin his studies at MIT in aeronautical engineering. He and Mike moved into the downstairs 'family quarters' and jointly managed 'Craigmoor South' as a boarding house.

Katy and Annabelle retired from their teaching careers in Cambridge and moved back to Quail Hill Farm joining their parent's and their Aunt Rose in the big house. Annabelle used her enormous energy to run the household. Libby still ran the kitchen.

Consistent with the Quail Hill tradition of people changing houses every few decades, James and John moved into the 'new' house with Junior and Abby while Buddy, his wife Susan and their youngest son lived in the rebuilt house up the lane. As with so many details of life, these changes were important only to the participants.

Recognizing that Mr. Morgan's death had plowed into Abby, Libby spent more time with her. One day as they worked in the main vegetable garden, Libby gestured expansively.

"Look at this farm, Abby. It's all ours: yours, mine, Susan's. We've provided the offspring. All the Jones men believe it's theirs but it's ours."

Abby laughed. "I don't know Mother Libby, it's awfully 'Jones' around here."

"The three men you currently live with—all my sons—are very full of themselves. Don't let them wear you down. You and Susan and I need to spend more time together, make sure we stay sane. Heavens, now that Katy and Annabelle are here, I've got five of my children back on this hill. But my motherhood's in 'late winter.'

"I'll take some squash in for supper. Cook it with a little onion, a tomato and some parsley. That sounds good." Libby stood. "Yes, you and Susan and I may need to form a club: 'the non-Jones women of Quail Hill Farm,' maybe a secret handshake." She chuckled as she walked across the lane. 'Yes,' she smiled, 'it's all ours.'

52

In the fall of 1933, Bertie fell one morning, took a long time getting up and he often suffered indigestion. Worried about her father, A.L. invited her parents and sisters to spend the winter in Craigmoor at the big Morgan home where she and Charley now lived. Rose and Katy accepted. Annabelle, however, said she would winter with her parents. Rose kept repeating her totally convincing arguments to Libby and Bertie and, hearing no rebuttal, announced they should move into town the next Thursday. On Tuesday, Bertie took the truck to town, returned with a crate of 20 chickens and stealthily installed them in the winter coop.

During lunch he hummed happily. After the meal he announced, "Well, Sis, you have a lot to do before you go but Libby and I'll stay here. My new chickens will need tending."

"How dare you!" Rose blurted. "We're all going to Craigmoor."

"No, you are; we're not."

"You might ask Libby."

"I don't have to." He turned to Libby. "They're Rhode Island Reds, real nice, come see." Libby took his hand, followed him through the workroom to the coop door.

"This is foolish, Bertie."

"I know. But it's what I want."

"Town's closer for a doctor."

"Why? Because," he continued a conversation with himself as they entered the coop, "I may get sick and die. Well, if that happens, I want to be here. I won't be alone. Our three sons and Abby are across the lane with Buddy and Susan and their brood up the hill. I know the arguments. But I belong here. I won't be happy living in Morgan's grand house on the hill in town and I'd make everybody miserable. I'm not going." The chickens clucked softly.

She smiled and sighed. "They're nice chickens."

"Thank you, sweetheart. Now I'm going to the barn."

"Leaving me to deal with Rose."

"You'll be nicer," he said, grinning. "See you later."

She watched him walk away, stooped and fragile, yet in command; she entered the house humming softly.

Rose exploded. "Libby you'd be crazy to stay here."

"Then I'm crazy."

"Don't let him beat you down."

"He's not beating me down." Libby stood calmly.

Rose ranted. "He'll die here, with no doctor able to come."

"With or without a doctor, we'll all die. He wants to stay so we're staying."

"And what do you want? Do you ever think about that?"

"I want to be with him."

"I don't understand you, Libby!" Rose's face flushed.

"Rose, what you do not understand is marriage." Rose glared at her. "It's not a character flaw, it's a fact. I don't understand teaching or living in Cambridge and I never imagine I do. But I know my marriage; we're staying."

Rose spoke desperately. "You may be all alone when he…"

"When he dies, if he dies. Annabelle will be here. Besides, being alone is a normal state. It's the ability to connect, to fuse, if ever so briefly, that's special and we have that, your brother and I. I'll stay with him. As long as we are both alive, I'll stay with him."

The clock ticked.

"I'll help you and Katy pack." Annabelle spoke softly and wiped her hands on her apron. "Mama, how're the chickens?"

"They're real nice chickens."

Rose walked from the room shaking her head.

Twice after heavy snows in January Bertie didn't make it to morning milking. The men always left 'Toothspot'—Bertie's favorite cow obviously named for the white marking on her side—until last. When he arrived she'd be his first. Four days after Libby's eighty-fourth birthday, Bertie felt uncomfortable as he pulled on overalls and a heavy jacket. He arrived late at the barn and began milking Toothspot. Junior, James and Buddy left to tend the milk while John began cleaning the horse stalls at the far end of the barn, whistling as he worked.

Lanterns flickering in the pre-dawn light, Bertie's hands worked the rhythmic pattern of milking. As the bucket filled, he wondered how many times he'd attended morning milking. Through the ssk, ssk, ssk of the milk hitting the bucket, he tried to create the formula: say eighty-two years, 365 days, Leap years? Boston Vacation? It was hard to keep it straight through his indigestion, this squeezing sensation. He shifted position: no change, kept milking. His left hand hurt, fingers trembled, lost their grip.

Like jaws of a huge invisible steel-toothed vice, pain crushed his chest. He pitched forward, head thrown back, neck leaning against the pattern on Toothspot's side. His eyes darted around like a trapped sparrow. Gasping, his hands hung uselessly, his fingers descending into the milk. Raw, torturing, unrelenting pain pinned him into a grotesque statue leaning against the cow. She flicked her tail, swung her head as far as she could, blinked her large brown eyes, stamped her hind foot and stepped to the side.

Bertie slid down, his hands now deep in the bucket, as pain continued clawing mercilessly at his chest. Willing all his Welch-Scots determination into saving the milk, Bertie flopped his hands from the bucket as he collapsed beneath the cow. The bucket rocked upright. He'd won.

John heard a noise.

"Papa? Are you all right?" No reply.

Bertie stared ahead, struggling for small shallow breaths. When John reached him, one of the barn cats sat licking milk from his fingers.

 John shooed the cat away, moved Bertie from his location under the cow, lifted him tenderly and carried him toward the door. Moving quickly, he raised his right leg and crashed his foot into the cross bar. The door flew open with a sharp 'bang' as it slammed back against the barn. Hearing the noise, Junior and James came running through the snow. Seeing his uncle carrying his grandfather, Buddy went to get Abby.

John trudged on through the heavy snow. Junior caught up with him, saw his father's drawn face in the early dawn light, raced ahead to open the door to the big house.

Libby heard the barn door and got to the front window just as Junior raced past the Black Walnut tree, leapt onto the porch, opened the door.

"Stay back, Mama, John's coming."

Icy wind swirled into the house, chilling Libby, as John entered with purpose and assurance. James followed, closed the door and hugged Libby protectively. John moved across the kitchen to the hall and into the big, back bedroom, placing Bertie on the bed gently. Libby shuffled along, a spider-web of fear etching across her face.

Bertie gasped, grabbed John's arm. "Milk," he murmured weakly and lapsed into semi consciousness.

That day and the next, as the wind howled and snow pelted down, he remained in pain: sometimes lucid, often confused. The next afternoon at 3:30, he asked for some milk toast.

Libby fed him, he relaxed, enjoyed the meal. His pain diminished and he slept. Annabelle and Abby attended Libby as she remained at Bertie's side.

At 9:00 p.m. Libby looked up from her book, found him watching her, smiling slyly.

"Thought you'd never stop reading," he whispered hoarsely.

"How're you feeling?" She moved her chair closer.

"Weak. Chest hurts. Felt silly pinned against Toothspot. Hands got in the milk." He shook his head and lay quietly. They held hands. There was little to say.

The wind died. Moonlight reflected from the white snow in the quiet night. Bertie slept, wakened, talked a bit, slept again. At 10, Annabelle checked on them and then went to bed. After she left, Bertie chuckled. "I never knew when

I fell in love with you that anybody like Annabelle Rose Jones would ever exist. All six of our children: unique.

"Remember my building that room in your house?"

"Yes."

"And the 4th of July picnic?"

"Of course."

"And your conditions for marrying me?"

"They weren't 'conditions'—just requests."

"Your memory's gone. They were conditions. 'I'll marry you Albert Jones if you build us our own home and promise that all our daughters, and any sons who want to, can go to college.'" He smiled. "Conditions!"

"I'd have married you anyway and you knew it."

"Did not. Could've saved a peck of money and a lot of work. Anyway, you wouldn't have," he said, his eyes laughing, his lips pursed.

She smiled. "You may be right but I doubt it."

They talked of the early years: the babies, her illness, the storm and Princess saving A.L. They sat quietly together. He slept on and off.

At 2:30 a.m., he roused. "I'd like some tea, sweetheart."

She wiped his face, kissed his stubbly cheek.

"We're still magic together, Libby Whitman."

She nodded and crossed the room. Placing her right hand on the doorframe, she turned and looked back over her right shoulder, what she saw riveted her to the spot. His eyes, his face appeared exactly as they had outside the church seventy years ago when he had leaned against the fence and held her captive with his gaze. Young and strong, her Bertie re-experienced, a moment locked in time like a bug in amber: eternal. She stood breathless, once again awestruck by his blue-eyed power. Princess scratched at a flea and the moment vanished. Bertie smiled weakly, now looking frail sunk down on his pillow.

In the kitchen she made tea remembering what had just happened: wondered if he felt it too, saw her young again. She'd ask him. 'Time's funny,' Libby reflected.

Walking quietly into the room, she placed the tea on the dresser, turned and began speaking. The lamp flickered; tree-limb shadows danced on the moonlit snow.

He lay with his head angled slightly to the right facing the window, eyes half open, mouth ajar.

Libby steadied herself on the bed frame and called his name softly. Silence. She moved closer. His chest remained motionless. She watched a long time. He did not respond when touched. His eyes looked dull. She reached up and closed them: it seemed the right thing to do.

Libby sat by the bed. She would rest a few minutes and he would want his tea. Surely he would want his tea soon. She closed her eyes: light tears and a gentle semi-sleep arrived simultaneously. An odd, familiar feeling settled around her softly like a parenthesis descending quietly, protecting her. She could function in this slightly altered state, feeling little. Part of her would sit on her shoulder and marvel at her ability to fulfill obligations, complete her duties while remaining pleasant and calm. She knew the rawness would come, the searing pain would emerge and the stark terror of Bertie's death would erupt like bats from a cave after this parenthesis lifted. For now, she thanked God for granting this reprieve, for giving this protective cocoon that distanced her from reality and held pain at bay.

At 3:30, Libby tucked the covers around Bertie, left a cup of tea on the nightstand and extinguished the light. The room appeared silvery gray. The window formed a passageway for the light to enter and a soul to leave. While she'd fixed tea, he flew out the window and escaped into eternity. She felt tall, strengthened by forces she could not explain. A single tear slid down her cheek as she leaned down and kissed Bertie's forehead. Then she walked to the front room, Princess at her side.

Moving her rocking chair to the window, she watched the barn. When the men went out she'd see their lanterns. Annabelle would be up soon. There'd be much to do. Charley and A.L. might get through by afternoon. There'd be people, confusion. Resting in her parenthetical bubble, she drifted between sleep and wakefulness. At 4:10 she saw milking lanterns flickering. She put on her coat and shawl, took Bertie's lamp from its hook and headed for the barn. She moved carefully through the cold snow. 'Madness,' she thought. 'I'm 84, my husband died two hours ago and I'm going to fetch my son, who can do what? Nothing.' But a strong force drove her on.

Opening the small side door, she stepped into the barn. Lamps flickered as her sons and grandson sat on milking stools, the measured cadence of their work mingled with the soft murmurs of the cows. This was what she sought: this awakening pattern. In the immediate aftermath of Bertie's death, she needed the assurance of nature's cyclical pattern: to experience again the early morning ritual he'd loved so much. Her whole body relaxed as the smell of hay, the warm steam from the animals and the golden lamplight enveloped her.

The men looked up. Her dark shawl hung loosely over her head; her skin looked pale. White curls framed her face like a delicate halo. She extended her hand toward her oldest son.

"Albert," she said quietly, "please come. I need you." Without waiting for an answer she turned and left.

John gasped; Buddy said, "no." Before that moment, Libby had never called her oldest son 'Albert.' She never called him 'Junior' again.

53

For Libby, the day of Bertie's funeral consisted of a series of disjointed vignettes. On the trip to town, she contrasted that beautiful, colorful fall day when she'd visited the farm as a fifteen-year-old girl with this frozen morning. Arriving at the Morgan house, she expected to trip over young Charley (now A.L.'s husband for over twenty years) as she had when visiting here during her illness. Today, although tired, she felt healthy.

Bertie's funeral filled the Craigmoor Church. Andy, Mike and his fiancée, Hildur, a lovely blond Scandinavian nurse, drove up from Cambridge. 'Funny place to meet his future bride,' Libby shook her head. People fussed, took her elbow. 'Why do people take old ladies by the elbow?' Libby wondered. Bertie's casket stood at the front of the church looking austere. Libby went outside, broke off a handful of holly loaded with red berries, walked up the aisle and put it on the casket lid.

"That helps," she said, nodding her head. "Not much, but it helps." She took her seat.

The service happened in Libby's presence: she sang at the correct times, prayed at the correct times, looked at the minister attentively but experienced her own world. She tried to count the funerals she'd attended. Great Grandmother Tillman but she'd been a baby then. Mavis. That pain lasted a long time; she had no protective cocoon that time. Grandpa Richard and Grandma Margaret: the parenthetical bubbles started then. Aunt Helen. Papa. Johnny, sweet Johnny: dying just last year in a hospital after an automobile accident, saying again "I ran as fast as I could, Libby. Honest I did." Libby had tried to comfort him but, after all those years, he couldn't let go of his childhood guilt.

She remembered other people: Rachel now ashes in the sea. Amy Middleton buried with her grandparents, the Elys—people important to this family but whom she had never met. Matt, whose service had been in Cambridge, whose body they'd buried in the Craigmoor cemetery. She glanced around the congregation. 'Why are all these children here? Is this a fieldtrip about manners at a funeral?' She wanted to scream 'Get out! You don't belong here.' But they did. In ways, of course, it was a fieldtrip: another lesson in living.

Behind her, Andy's baritone cracked and failed in the third stanza of a hymn. She turned, reached over and patted his arm. (The funny voice from a miniature, invisible Libby who sat on her right shoulder said quietly, 'Look how well Libby is doing, comforting Andy nicely.')

Part of her felt trapped: wanted to stand and scream: 'This is obscene. He cannot be dead because if he is dead then a huge part of me is dead, too.' Instead she sat calmly with children and grandchildren around her like so many flowers in a bouquet. She remained in her protective parentheses, her cocoon, cut off from reality. It didn't make sense. Cocoons gave birth to something—something new should emerge. But what? Suddenly the answer struck her: a widow. "How grotesque!" she said aloud.

Rose and John, sitting on either side of her, looked at her quizzically. She waved them off, placed her hands in theirs.

She tried to keep one memory away but it seeped in: before that altar, vowing with him, both so young, so sure, so hopeful. Now it was complete. They'd vowed 'till death do us part.' It was over. Their long complex time together had ended. 'How did we ever do it? We were children! No sane person should make vows like that with so little understanding.' She turned and looked at Mike and Hildur in the pew behind her. They sat looking at the preacher intently as he jabbered on. 'I should tell them how difficult it is, they need to know.' Then she smiled. 'The only way to get to the other side of the field is to walk through the field.' Only at the end can you see the whole, realize how awesome those vows are. 'They'll find out for themselves.'

Leaving the church, she and her children all sneezed at the sun, her genetic trait inherited from Great-Grandmother Tillman. The sneeze tied all of them together. That pleased her.

The ground at the cemetery remained frozen rock-hard: his coffin would be kept locked in the shed. Libby hated leaving him there. John stood by her side, became her strength: John the shyest and tallest of her children. He'd carried his father from the barn and now he took charge of her in a loving, supportive way. Driving home, she squinted up at John; she hadn't expected him to be the strong one. Yet he was. 'Yes. Each unique, Bertie,' she mused silently and hoped that somewhere, somehow he heard her.

54

The next day, Rose moved back to Quail Hill remarking softly, "I shouldn't have left."

"You did what you felt was best. It wouldn't have made any difference: now it's over. Don't punish yourself," Libby stated matter-of-factly. Rose pursed her lips and nodded.

In this winter of sorrow Libby mourned her husband, Rose her brother and Annabelle her father. Libby understood their emotions. With Bertie at her side she'd lived through the deaths of her father and brother. Neither of the other women understood Libby's loss. Being the last Jones sibling of her generation disoriented Rose while Annabelle moped around bereft. Just over 60, she'd never entertained a serious suitor. Her father had been the central man in her universe. She'd written to him often, sent him pressed flowers and interesting dead bugs. Libby worried about both Rose and Annabelle: her concern another buffer against personal pain.

Her nights dragged: fitful sleep peppered with nightmares. Reaching for Bertie in the darkness, his absence was shocking, his side of the bed cold. She knew both edges of grief's sword: she desperately wanted her pain to end yet knew that when it did, both Bertie and their life together, would fade, settle into the background of her life. Unless she caged herself in this gloom, healing would occur. So she lay, night after night, pulled by conflicting desires: feeling guilty and bereft when she began to feel happy, yet berating herself for staying mired in grief. Fear jumped up at unexpected moments. Staring in the darkness, relationships danced around like dust particles. Rose and all of Libby's children shared genetic ties with Bertie and those connections continued. Libby's relationship with him, based solely on mutual agreement, was over. Their marriage ended with his last breath.

During the day, her routine sustained her. She fixed breakfast, tended 'our new chickens,' sorted seeds, read, mended, ironed, cleaned and helped with dinner preparations. As the days lengthened, she slept better. On clear days, she and her current Princess walked the land either alone or accompanied by other family members, often John. A hint of color returned to her cheeks; her eyes brightened a bit.

In April, Katy moved from the Morgan house in Craigmoor back to the big house on Quail Hill. On April 15, the 87th anniversary of Bertie's birth, Libby padded into the kitchen and found Rose, Annabelle and Katy sipping tea, reading and doing small tasks, waiting for Libby to make breakfast. Libby greeted them, pumped herself a glass of water and looked out over the hillside remembering the first day she stood here with Ma.

"If we can find any flowers we'll take them to his grave today. If not, greens will have to do," she commented, staring pensively out the window. She turned, scanned the women and rested her gaze on Annabelle. "I believe I'll have breakfast in bed," she stated.

Rose, Katy and Annabelle exchanged surprised looks.

"Are you all right?" Katy broke the silence.

"Quite," Libby nodded. "I'll take my breakfast in bed from now on." She smiled faintly.

"What do you want?" Annabelle asked, perplexed.

"Whatever you fix. With coffee, not tea." Libby left the kitchen, humming.

"Well, I declare," Rose said softly.

From then on, Libby cooked no meals, washed no dishes, scrubbed no clothes. She worked in her garden, cared for her chickens, walked with Princess.

With that simple declaration on what would have been Bertie's 87th birthday, Elizabeth Rebecca Whitman Jones retired.

Her mourning continued but the initial, catastrophic phase ended. For years, small things brought waves of memory and loss: a whiff of pipe tobacco, a favorite tune, a breeze or a sunset but, over time, the pain diminished. Libby became the undisputed leader and the central figure of the family. Major decisions required her approval and her veto, though seldom, was final. She exercised power born of a lifetime of service. During that short walk from the kitchen to her bedroom on April 15, 1934, she began the last phase of her life.

55

The Cambridge forsythia bloomed late in 1934, Andy realized, completing his morning run. He bounded up the back steps and burst into the kitchen.

"Top 'o the mornin' to ya, sweet Brigid."

"For all the saints, my health and your breakfast, Andrew Morgan, don't be charging in here like a bull!" Brigid O'Shea, the cook at Craigmoor South, shook her spatula at him. Along with her husband, F.X., Brigid managed the house for the Morgan brothers. Mike, Andrew and two other young professional men all lived together. Things would change when Mike and Hildur married in June; they would take over the main-floor quarters that Charley and A.L. had occupied when the boys were growing up. Hildur planned to continue her nursing career.

Andy worked for an engineering group in Boston and Mike's medical practice flourished. Their lives remained intertwined but were separated by different schedules. Shortly after Bertie's death, Andy met a blond named Eleanor, the sister of Paul Sherwood, a young man he'd known at Dartmouth during his freshman year. The Sherwoods moved to Boston to live with relatives after the death of Paul and Eleanor's father. Mr. Sherwood lost both his fortune and his will to live in the stock market crash, dying soon thereafter of a heart attack.

Eleanor's dark eyes floated in the milky whiteness of her skin. Her delicate features were pleasant enough, but her smile set her apart. When Eleanor smiled, electricity shot through Andy. It wasn't only sexual, though it certainly was sexual, but it felt as if a curtain split and the Eleanor that nature or God had created burst through in a dazzling blast. For Eleanor, Andy was 'one of Paul's friends,' an impression that changed as Andy became a regular fixture visiting the Sherwood's current home.

Sara Sherwood, Eleanor's mother, liked Andy but wanted Eleanor to 'marry well' and restore the family to social prominence. She adjusted to her new financial situation but chaffed at the loss of social standing. After the stock market crash, Paul had left Dartmouth, lived with his mother and younger sister, worked odd jobs, never furthered his education and drifted like a rudderless boat. Eleanor, having grown up in society, loved parties, dances, music, gaiety and men's attention. She flirted much, read little, found politics and business dull and airbrushed unpleasantness from her world. Unlike her brother, she did mobilize her energy to accomplish goals. She dazzled Andy Morgan. When they met, Ellie's goal was Bruce Bradford (as much Sara's goal as Ellie's). Initially, she used Andy to further her campaign to win Bruce.

Sara Sherwood considered Bruce Bradford a quality candidate for a son-in-law: moneyed, mannered, educated and connected, he moved in the right circles, played golf and acted suitably bored. Bruce did things because he should; acted bored because he was. He considered Ellie an amusement and he enjoyed access to the Sherwood's tennis courts. Sara doted on him. He enjoyed that, too.

Watching Bruce and Andy play tennis for the first time stunned Ellie. Bruce played his usual competent, a bit angry game: always watching the spectators' reactions. Andy focused on the ball, studied his opponent's technique, complimented Bruce on good shots and beamed when he made a good shot. Charley Morgan had coached his sons well and Andy won a clear, carefully calculated, victory. As Bruce and Andy, now both very sweaty, left the court, Ellie watched Andy's crooked smile and twinkling blue eyes even as Bruce leaned down and kissed her boldly. Andy wiped his face, thanked Bruce for the game, the Sherwoods for their hospitality and headed home. He knew Ellie noticed him. He also knew that the next time he played Bruce Bradford, he'd score a decisive victory. Like Bertie, what Andy went after, he got.

56

The invitation to Michael and Hildur's wedding arrived at the farm in early May. The ceremony would take place the second Saturday in June in the Congregational Church in Worcester, MA. At supper the day the invitation arrived, Libby put down her soupspoon and said, "Something blue. A bit of lace, after all I am the groom's grandmother."

Annabelle's spoon clattered into her soup.

"At your age Belle, holding onto your eating utensils should no longer be a challenge," Libby spoke ruefully.

"You never travel," Annabelle exclaimed.

"Correction: your father never traveled. He seldom left the farm or the animals so I stayed here. He fenced his world in more than I do. I'd like to go."

· Quail Hill ·

"Then we'll both get new dresses because I won't let you go to Worcester alone," Rose declared.

In the end, Libby's dress was a pale blue, Rose's a dusty pink: both had lace collars and cuffs. The family gathered for a few days in Cambridge and drove to Worchester together. Rose and Libby rode with Andy and his date, Eleanor Sherwood who impressed Libby as an attractive, somewhat superficial, young woman.

Michael and Hildur radiated shy happiness. Libby marveled at their certitude: how could anyone make such vows? Such audacity: promising 'for better or worse' and 'till death us do part!' 'Good not to know the end from the beginning,' she decided, 'all the mistakes and confusion ahead.' Would she do it again? She'd loved Bertie completely, lived a long, full life; together they had invested in their children and the farm. But would she do it again? She knew how fortunate she'd been. Bertie had been a decent man who cared for her and their family. He'd been stubborn but not abusive. The decisions they'd made had mostly turned out well and they'd been shielded from most world shattering events. Blessed. Fortunate. Lucky.

Leaving the service, stopping on the church steps, Libby said softly, "Only the young can dare so much."

"Would you do it again?" Rose asked.

A smile brushed Libby's lips as a breeze broke the stillness of the hot afternoon. "Yes. In ways now it's easier for me than for them," she nodded toward Michael and Hildur, "because, while I know the work and the heartbreak, I know that our young love held, stayed true." She sighed. "Do you suppose Bertie's watching?" Rose shrugged; Libby smiled. Then, holding hands like the schoolgirl friends they'd always been, the two old women walked down the church steps.

In early October before the leaves turned, Rose went up for an afternoon nap. She died alone, peacefully. Annabelle checked on her at dinnertime. Rose looked relaxed, her fair skin whiter than usual, her left hand resting on the pillow next to her face.

At first Libby simply shook her head. "No, Belle, you're mistaken." Then she climbed the well-worn front staircase, went to Rose's room, sat on the bed and shook Rose's body.

"Rose, wake up! Don't do this. I'm not ready." Libby's shoulders slumped forward as she sputtered small fragments. "You mustn't… Not you, Rose… I'll never be ready…" Gazing at the floor, she twisted her linen handkerchief and wept.

57

Fall vanished. Libby wondered if trees felt pain when leaves fell, shared the thought with no one. Who'd understand, or care?

Winter's stark reality encased the farm. Cold. Ice. Wind. Snow. Isolation. Fear hovered, waiting to invade, to conquer. Princess #7 stayed close, demanding attention. Libby stumbled through numb days, trapped as on a chessboard, 'checked' by an invisible opponent. Weak but undefeated, she carried on: too stubborn to die and too wounded to enjoy life.

Five months after Rose died, Libby's world remained flat, gray, chilly. She awakened feeling the usual rhythmic 'inhale—exhale—pause' of her breathing. It depressed her. She sat up, driven by habit. Another day. She sipped the coffee Annabelle brought and nibbled a molasses cookie. She tasted a bit of spice, felt her saliva flow. Molasses cookies were her favorite. In the flavor provided by Annabelle's cookies, a pale ray of color slipped cunningly into Libby's prison. She splashed water on her face, dressed and brushed her hair, tying it with a bow at the nap of her neck.

Shuffling into the kitchen, Libby watched Annabelle take more cookies from the oven. Annabelle noted the bow in Libby's hair and smiled. Why Rose's death plunged Libby into this bleak valley mystified her children. (Had they asked, which they didn't, she could have explained.) Libby stirred her coffee idly, looked from Katy to Annabelle: felt isolated.

No one knew her anymore: the whole of her. The child with long blond curls and bruised knees, the devastated young girl when Mavis died, courtship, teaching for Miss Amy, deciding about college, pregnancies, births, being ill and recovering—all the sections of her 'self' that nobody else knew. Now, only she remembered many of the experiences of her life.

'It is,' she felt, 'the "not-being-known" that rankles. If I said that, they'd all reply "we know you Mother." Phooey! Mother isn't all of me, may not even be the best part.' True she was mother, daughter, friend, grandmother and had been wife but none of these segments were, by themselves, 'Libby.' She and Bertie and Rose—they'd known each other, as much as people can. Then just Rose and Libby. Now just Libby: the last leaf on the tree. Life began small: then expanded. Finally contracted, got smaller, less connected, less involved. Looking at Katy and Annabelle she realized, 'All they know is "Mother." Not their fault: just what is.' This was not a lesson she wanted to learn, this 'isolated-cutoff-nobody-knows-all-of-me.' Libby bristled.

She smelled the molasses cookies, loved molasses cookies and fought against eating another one. It might make her happy; she didn't want to be happy because she felt angry, hurt and cheated. Part of her chose to stay dreary and isolated. This morning, eating that first bite of cookie, color snuck in past her irritability. The ancient human battle raged internally; the universe challenged her like a chess game: 'Check.'

Spring came. Then summer. Plants and flowers that pushed from the earth as fragile shoots soon burst into vivid color and masses of tangled vegetation. Seasons regard not who observes them. Time grinds on indifferent to the use made of it. Night-stars sparkle brightly in the yawning infinity of space, oblivious to human eyes watching or wolves howling.

One morning in late June, Princess #7—often called just 'Seven'—fussed. She scratched the door, pawed at Libby and whined.

"Oh, all right, Seven," Libby stood slowly, took her sweater and sunbonnet from the rack and walked into the warm morning. The screen door squeaked open, bounced shut as the dog pranced happily onto the porch. "You can go on alone," Libby scolded but Seven just waited, panting at the foot of the steps. They walked from 8:30 until 10. They passed by the new house and went through the orchard. Libby entered the chicken coop and slid her hand gently under a hen, felt the soft downy warmth surrounding the incubating eggs. The hen clucked softly and readjusted slightly. Looking into the hen's eyes, Libby felt a jolt of recognition. Libby the old woman and Libby the young girl, that hen and the entire universe fused into one eternal reality. Everything stopped yet everything continued normally. Libby blinked, felt Bertie's laughter envelop her. Life's awe and mystery broke through to her in the hen's soft warmth. She withdrew her hand slowly and the hen settled gently onto her eggs.

Leaving the coop, Libby squinted at the sun and sneezed. Seven finished rolling on the grass, stood, shook and started off again. The young wheat danced in the breeze as the sun rose higher. In the pasture, Libby stopped at the big rock outcropping and surveyed the landscape she knew intimately and loved. Woman and dog entered the big, quiet barn where the aroma of hay and cows and horses mingled. They climbed to the loft where Libby found a patch of sun and rested in the remaining piles of last year's hay. Images of other summers and other barns flickered by. Opening her eyes, Libby saw a small owl watching from its perch under the roof. Libby blinked and said, "I belong here, too." The owl swiveled its head away. Libby chuckled.

Returning to the house, Libby took her garden basket, gloves and tools to the south vegetable patch. She settled onto her garden stool, worked deftly through the pea vines, heavy with pods, as the sun beat down. She picked rapidly, humming softly, flipping peas nimbly into her basket and leaving many for another day. After twenty minutes she had her quota. She'd no intention of the family eating many of these: too big and pasty. 'Shame I haven't been out before today,' she thought.

Libby, followed by Princess #7, moved to the west end of the house where she worked furtively. She sorted the peas into three containers: eat fresh, suitable for canning, for the animals. If Katy and Belle caught her they would have to have their annual battle of the peas. How she'd reared two daughters who ate big, pasty peas she did not understand. Well, she was back in the garden and now things would be better: from now on they'd have only the sweetest baby peas. She took her small container 'for the animals' and headed to the barn, smiling to herself. She dumped the peas in the horse 'treats' bucket. Then she and Princess headed for the big house. Libby felt tiny walking out of the barn and passing the black walnut tree. Belle had planted bright portulaca by the front walk. Libby smiled. 'How I do love flowers,' she thought.

Late that night, Libby awoke, watched the swaying curtains stir moonlight patterns on the floor. Feeling no fear, she sat on the sill of the open window completely comfortable bathed in the cold moonlight. Usually, sitting here, she felt afraid—of what? She watched the stars roaming the infinite universe. 'Infinite. God. Eternal. Impossible words,' Libby realized. Was her usual—now notably absent—fear a defense to avoid this overwhelming final mystery? What had Rose's death triggered? What happened in the chicken coop today? She'd struggled so often in what felt like this same recurring battle. Bertie said she tried to make life what it wasn't, wouldn't allow it to be what it was. But he'd fought it sometimes, too. After Rachel left, he wouldn't accept that reality for a long time and made himself miserable. Finally, he'd moved the fences in his mind to allow Rachel to be who she was.

The leaves fluttered in the night breeze. Libby sat poised and alert. This morning, in the chicken coop, she knew she'd not only moved the fences in her mind to include and accept Rose's death, she'd destroyed the fences themselves. Rachel had written about 'radical unity with God,' talked about 'living inseparably from life itself.' Maybe this was that. There was no more 'Libby here' and 'God there.' Life simply existed. She felt transparent: existing in a new peaceful, tranquil realm. Moving to bed, her back ached, her fingers hurt. Everything was the same, yet transformed. She'd write of this in her diary, try to tell her daughters: or maybe not. She fell asleep. Princess #7 groaned, scratched and sank back onto her bedding.

58

Andrew's courtship of Eleanor progressed and they married in September 1936. At 86, Libby did not feel up to the trip to the wedding. She'd met Ellie a number of times and recognized how smitten Andy was, how much they doted on each other and that made her feel positive about the union.

The peace born in Libby that summer night remained. In her diary she called it 'life without fences.' Once she tried in vain to re-establish a fence, to put something 'outside.' But she couldn't hold things away so she relaxed in the 'oneness.' Libby's personal territory began to shrink: she walked less, rarely went to Craigmoor, ate less, slept a few hours at a time, many times a day, did fewer tasks. Her children lived close and her grandchildren visited and wrote. She remained keenly alert, noted that occasionally, when Charley and A.L. visited, conversation stopped if she came in the room. No one told her why. She didn't ask.

Michael and Hildur had two sons: the first in 1936, the second in 1938. Eleanor had a baby girl, Marcia, in 1937. Libby greeted each baby as 'the prettiest one yet.' Her arthritic knees hurt but she no longer fought the pain. Season followed season like heartbeats of the earth itself.

Andrew and Eleanor's second daughter arrived in March 1940 and they named her Rebecca Elizabeth. Andy, Ellie, Marcia and 'baby Becca' would soon move to Ohio where Andy was joining in a new aircraft company. Before leaving for Ohio, Mike, Andy, Eleanor, Marcia and the baby drove to Craigmoor in June and stayed in town with the Morgans. The next day while Eleanor rested, Mike, Andy, Marcia, Becca and A.L. drove to the farm. Memories, tenacious like spring growth, spun through A.L.'s mind as they turned up the familiar lane. Rounding the final bend, they saw Katy, Annabelle and Libby sitting on the porch.

"Grandma's having a good day," Michael commented.

"She's anxious to see Marcia and meet Rebecca Elizabeth." A.L. hugged Marcia, rolled down the window and waved. Annabelle hustled down the steps to greet them. Marcia hugged her Great-Aunt Annabelle, her Great-Grandmother Libby and sat by Great-Aunt Katy.

Mike and A.L. greeted Libby and then Andy put Rebecca Elizabeth on her lap. Libby gazed intently into the baby's eyes as Becca wiggled, cooed, puckered her lips and gurgled happily.

"Well, Rebecca Elizabeth, you're the only baby in this family with brown eyes. You're brave to join us." Libby unwrapped Becca's hands and feet, counted fingers and toes. "I know they're all there, but I'll count, anyway." Becca grabbed onto Libby's index finger and pulled it to her mouth. They looked across the ninety years separating them. No fences here: Libby and Becca existed as whitecaps on the same ocean. Libby pulled hard to free her finger: after losing the battle, Becca fussed.

"She's strong. Determined," Libby looked up smiling, "and the prettiest one yet." A.L. re-wrapped her granddaughter, picked her up and took her inside. Libby looked at Mike and Andy. "You two, let's take a walk."

"Mama, should you?" Katy protested.

"I can walk. And with a doctor and an engineer beside me I should be safe." Libby retorted too abruptly. She stood and patted Katy's shoulder, knowing she'd offended her. "Unfinished business," she muttered.

"What grandma?" Andy asked.

"Just unfinished business" she said. "I still need to control my tongue." She leaned on Andy and the three of them crossed the lane. Arriving at the pasture gate she put her hand on one of the rails and turned to face these two grandsons.

"There's something going on. It may have to do with one of you so you'd best tell me."

The brothers exchanged glances. "Andy's ill, grandma." They stood quietly.

"That's all? Just 'Andy's ill?' I expect a better diagnosis than that."

"I have Hodgkin's disease. There's no cure. I might live a long time. Or not."

"Dr. Michael, what else?"

"Unfortunately, that's about it. There are some experimental treatments people are working on, nothing much yet. He may go through long periods being strong and active followed by times he's weak and sick."

Libby pursed her lips, nodded and patted Michael's hand. "Thank you. I knew there was something I wasn't being told. Knowing is better. I'm old but this is my family." She looked across the field and took Andy's hand. "Andy, we're going for a walk and Mike, you can go back and keep everybody settled. Make sure my namesake isn't totally spoiled by the time we return. Open the gate, Andy." Her voice sanctioned no debate.

Libby and Andy moved to the crest of the hill by the large granite outcropping. Libby made a funny little sound and the horse down under a maple tree snorted and trotted toward her.

"Never could whistle worth anything but that doesn't bother horses." The black mane and tail of the chestnut filly blew gently in the breeze. She took the sugar cube from Libby's hand, pawed the ground, nuzzled up to the old woman. "Go on now. You'll knock me over. Shoo." The filly trotted away.

"It all started right here more than seventy five years ago. Your grandfather stood about where you are and told me I was beautiful. I was never so flustered in my life as at that moment. You see, I believed I wanted to be a teacher, go to college, not have a family. In this field, all that changed." She paused. "He was such a good man: honest, matter of fact. This farm, his family and I were his life." She took Andy's arm again. "You know, if my mother had lived, I might've had a different life: might not have chosen Bertie's direct love and simple basic goodness. Then you wouldn't even exist and wouldn't be facing this disease. Events change things." She looked up at Andy's face, her gaze open and steady. "Sometimes you sit here on this rock, don't you?" He nodded. "Well then, we'd better sit. Help me down and help me up: the sitting I'll do myself." Her eyes smiled as they settled onto the rock. A breeze tousled the wild flowers that remained along the fence beyond horses' reach. They gazed into the distance.

"How's Eleanor taking this?"

"I can't really tell, Grandma. She won't talk about it."

"Probably trying to keep it fenced out. She'll handle it her way, the best she can."

"You may be right," Andy looked at Libby's profile. "I can't force her to change."

"No, of course not. It's just that fencing never works." She turned and met his gaze. "I've lived a long time and fencing simply doesn't work. What is: is."

Andy felt the eyes he looked through and the eyes he looked into were one reality: as if looking into Libby's eyes he viewed the vast soul of the universe, the heart of life.

"I sensed you didn't like Ellie much."

"I'm a farm wife; I judge by that. She'd not last many winters here but that doesn't matter. She's beautiful; you love her. You've shared youthful passion, that's good: healthy."

Andy looked surprised.

"Oh for heaven's sake, Andrew! Why does each generation think they've discovered passion? It's been around awhile. After all, your grandfather and I created six children: together! And our passion didn't end then, either." He blushed; she chuckled.

They looked across the field toward the distant mountains. Libby began speaking softly.

"I watched my mother die in my grandmother's arms next to our old pumphouse. Mama had a premonition she'd die and wrote letters to Papa, my brother Johnny and me. Her letter was special. It put words in my mind to use years later when she wasn't there. Couldn't have been easy writing those words, so young and pregnant. I've thanked her countless times." Libby took a deep breath, rested her head on Andy's shoulder and let the hillside's beauty sustain them.

After a few minutes, Andy leaned down and kissed her cheek. "Thank you."

She patted his arm. "We'd better get back." He helped her up. Looking at the horizon she asked, "Are you afraid of dying, Andrew?"

"No. I'd rather not but I'm not afraid, at least not for me."

A simple direct answer—he sounded like Bertie. She nodded. They stood looking over the green fields and forested hills to the mountains of this land they both loved. An old woman and a young man: grandmother and grandson, Libby and Andy, holding hands, both dying. Beyond words they lingered and shared a simple, beautiful moment. A meadowlark sang. Libby looked at Andy and smiled.

"Imagine," she shook her head slowly, "a great-grandchild of mine with brown eyes."

59

Soon after the 4th of July 1940, Libby's strength failed: she couldn't get out of bed without help. Lying alone much of the day she'd drift from memory to sleep to dream and back to reality. Having severely reduced physical abilities, while a nuisance, seemed neither more nor less acceptable than anything else. Life without fences continued.

One day while A.L. sat by her, Libby said, "My body's all used up. I can't figure out why it doesn't just stop."

"Oh, Mother, we don't want you to leave us."

"That's precisely what I'm about to do, so you'd better adjust."

A.L. saw neither fear nor challenge in her mother's penetrating blue eyes. Libby patted her daughter's hand.

"You've always been sweet, gentle. Not weak, just a bit special because of when you came to us. The fact that you inherited 'knowing things' from Great-Gram Tillman set you apart, too. But A.L. you must be strong when I die and when Andy dies." A.L. looked away. "You mustn't run from this: when his time comes, whenever that is, be strong."

"It's so unfair. I've known for a long time but I don't want it to be true. The knowing is a burden."

"The world simply is, A.L. There are some things we can change but some events overtake us, disrupt our plans. I've always done better, helped most when I've stayed centered and calm. Eleanor and the girls will need you. I know they're all off in the Midwest now in Ohio—far away. Too far from the folks they'll need."

"I'll try, Mother." They sat quietly.

A bit later, Libby figured out that she was connected to four centuries: Great-Grandmother Tillman had been born in 17-something and now Libby had greeted great grandchildren who should be in their 60's in the twenty-first century. The idea pleased her—seemed both silly and important. She shifted and groaned a bit.

"Can I do anything for you, Mother?"

"Just a little water, please."

A.L. held the glass and Libby drank. After a few swallows, she lay back on her pillows and looked at the crude replica of the old Craigmoor Bridge sitting on her dresser.

· Quail Hill ·

"He wanted to finish it, make it better. I'd never let him. 'Just like you,' I'd say, 'rough edges but all the necessary details.'" She drifted into sleep chuckling.

A.L. had no idea what she was talking about: put it down to meaningless rambling. Over the next hour, Libby's breathing became labored. A.L. gathered her sisters and brothers. They took turns wiping her forehead, holding her hand, watching and waiting.

As Libby slept, figures moved around the hazy borders of her awareness. At first what she experienced seemed like insubstantial outlines: like faces etched lightly on clear glass. Then it felt like watching a silent sunrise over a misty meadow. People she knew emerged and became three-dimensional. Bertie drifted close, moved away. A young boy, then courting, walking in the fields, holding babies, showing her his chickens as an old man: different but always the same. Gently, Rose floated in: beautiful Rose, and Mavis—how young she looked. Rachel and Matt. More real than dreaming, Libby struggled to see.

As soon as she opened her eyes, the people disappeared and were replaced by anxious 'bubble-heads' looking at her: three of them. One turned and said something but all Libby heard was buzzing. Then six faces peered down. They had names, she knew they all had names; she'd named them. But she couldn't talk. She lay helpless breathing panting little breaths. Gradually, faint representations of the etched figures appeared even with her eyes open. At the edge of her vision the white fog expanded its gleaming light within the room. The blurred outlines of Bertie, Mavis, Rose and Rachel stood behind her children. Libby smiled and closed her eyes.

Instantly, foreground and background reversed as Richard, Margaret, Papa, Johnny, Matt, Aunt Helen and Amy Middleton surrounded her. Amy leaned down and greeted her. Her mouth didn't move but Libby 'heard' her. 'That's not necessary,' Amy thought and Libby understood.

'You aren't wearing glasses,' Libby realized.

'Here, I can see clearly.'

Libby wondered how she could learn these new ways. Amy smiled. 'That's why we're here.'

'Still my teacher?' Libby wondered.

'Always.'

Brightness increased and subsided cyclically. Libby heard music, voices. Lilting waves of peace swept through her. There were lots of figures now moving gracefully. When she opened her eyes they remained, a bit dimmer, but mingling with her children as the two separate planes of her reality intertwined. Figures from the 'light world' moved gently around and through the physical, gravity-bound bodies of her children. Rose glided over and placed her arm over A.L.'s shoulder, adding her hand weightlessly onto A.L.'s and Libby's hands. A.L. relaxed; Libby's hand felt warmer.

· Craigmoor ·

Libby watched scenes from her life come into focus and fade away. There was little left to live before it would be complete: a whole of which the scenes were simply fragments. Even tiny insignificant bits held meaning and depth beyond imagining. She'd glimpsed this before: flashes of insight, moments of clarity and understanding. Certainly during these past few years 'without fences' she'd lived with increased openness but this experience surpassed anything she'd known. She lay, unable to speak or move, witnessing radiant meaning. 'I must tell them.'

Libby struggled, gasped for breath. She lifted her head and squeezed A.L.'s hand. Her eyes darted around the room like a ricocheting bullet.

"Amy…love…" Her voice faded as her strength failed. She smiled and sank back.

Instantly, Bertie and Rose beckoned her. 'It's time.' A tiny pinpoint of light began rushing toward her and expanding rapidly. Libby moved toward it. Two unknown figures, one on each side, accompanied her.

'Before all time you belong to me,' one figure conveyed. 'Come home, Libby.'

'Home?' she wondered, peacefully perplexed. 'Home' was here, this bed, this farm, this town. The figures coaxed her on with warmth and power. Bertie, Rose, Mavis, Rachel and Amy remained close but unseen, adding their love, encouraging her to—what? Fragmentary confusion spun around. Warmth and love grew huge within her, spreading out into the infinity of space. At some deep core where she connected to life, Libby smiled and surrendered. As breath moved out of her body for the last time, Libby withdrew from the physical form she'd occupied for over ninety years and her soul gently slid into another realm. The scene below her—the room, her children, the farm, the town, the world—came into proper perspective.

'Yes, home,' she understood, 'really home.' An unknown figure extended a hand; Libby willed herself forward and merged into the light.

60

During the summer of 1941, Andy brought his family back to New Hampshire to visit his parents and all the aunts, uncles and cousins in New England. Up at the farm, Andy felt the loss of his grandmother keenly. Her personality, even in old age, had been such a huge part of his life and this place. He retraced the walk they'd taken together last summer: felt close to her sitting on the big rock. He'd written letters to his daughters and Eleanor and had given them to A.L. She put them in an envelope, added them to a box of Libby's things that was pushed into a far corner of the attic in the big house, behind a chimney and under the eaves.

Quail Hill

Andy's health fluctuated. With every Hodgkin's attack he lost strength. His emotions felt like soup: chunks of anger, frustration, rage, helplessness and peace in a broth of daily life. He needed to discuss things with Eleanor, consider options and talk about the future. He'd try to be sensible, matter-of-fact, look life in the eye and not blink. They never got around to it.

On Tuesday they visited the cemetery: Libby and Bertie side by side, John, Mavis and Johnny a few plots away, Richard and Margaret over by his Great-Great-Great-Grandmother Tillman, the original Rebecca Elizabeth. At least Andy believed she was the original—maybe there'd been others. When he tried to tell Eleanor about these people she became distracted.

"Graves are morbid. Are the girls safe?" she asked.

He took her hand. "Sweetheart, they're fine, the whole place is walled-in and it is Craigmoor," he chided her. "Ellie, we need to talk, make plans. You'll be left in charge but they're my daughters, too." Ellie tried to pull away; he clutched her hand. "Save the insurance money for college. They're Joneses, Whitmans and Morgans: women like Gram and Mama."

"No!" Ellie pulled free. "No!" She shook her head forcefully. "I will not talk about this, not here, not now. Andy," her lip trembled and she fought for control, "what do you want from me? I may have to bury you here, in this ground, but not today. You are alive. We are alive. Our two little girls are alive and we need you. Don't talk like this. I can't do it. Maybe you New Hampshireites can but I can't." She stepped back, tears flowing down her cheeks. He moved toward her but she shook her head, held up her hands to stop him, turned and ran toward the gate.

He'd been wrong to bring up the topic here but maybe the location didn't matter. Marriage, two people from different backgrounds with different temperaments, trying to mesh their lives into a team, a couple, a family, seemed terribly complex. Grandpa called Grandma 'Libby Whitman.' 'Smart man my granddad,' Andy thought. He kept trying to plan for later but all he knew was living. Things would work out somehow. His parents would be there after he was gone; Ellie's mother would be there. He put his hands in his pockets and walked down the hill toward the maple trees to get the girls. Marcia skipped up to him, embraced his legs and smiled. Becca was squatting down studying something intently. Andy looked down the hill to the town, across the river and toward the distant mountains enjoying the singular beauty of this one small place.

Suddenly the butterfly that had been sitting on a tall blade of grass in front of Becca hopped into the air and fluttered off. The delighted toddler giggled, stood and began a zigzag pursuit of the illusive Monarch. Andy walked to Becca, laughing. He scooped her up and she squealed gleefully as he tossed her into the air. 'Life,' he knew, 'with all its confusion and challenges, is precious and wonderful.'

II

Other Places

The fundamental aspect of the Fall is the moral act of the rebellious refusal of creaturely status, the desire 'to be like God'

~Reason and Reality by John Polkinghorne

1

May 1969

Icy water closed overhead as the huge shark brushed Becca's side. 'Oh, God,' she thought, 'so now I choose: drown or be eaten.'

Unimaginable terror paralyzed her. She'd never understood risks, appreciated consequences until now. Everything pointed toward this frozen moment: for what? To die one of two ludicrous deaths? Eyes bursting, her body screamed for oxygen; paralyzed lungs shrieked for air. But movement, any movement, and the giant shadowy man-eater would strike, mouth ripping, teeth slashing sending blood—her blood—flooding into the surrounding water. Finally, reflexes as ancient as the shark itself took over. In one last desperate surge for life, she thrust her arms explosively overhead, powering toward the surface.

Pain shot through her right hand and arm, reverberating everywhere. Her eyes jerked open: stared into darkness. Her hand had smashed the wall so hard her knuckles bled. Her heart pounded.

"Oh damn!" she said aloud. She'd dreamed this each night since learning Greg's MIA status five days ago. Slowly the walls and ceiling came into focus and pictures, window and drapes emerged. 'Well,' she decided, 'shades of gray beats total darkness.' Lying quietly, the Hawaiian scenes spun in her mind like pictures in a continuously repeating tape-loop. Fragments of childhood memories appeared—trapped in a carnival 'Fun House,' wet disgusting strands slithering by—and flashed by interspersed with the Hawaii pictures. Back in childhood, she'd screamed and the grotesque drama ended when someone led her out. Now, no rescuers would materialize as the tape-loop kept playing.

Hawaii. Three months ago: light years away. His smile and well-honed charm initially reassured Becca. They'd been warned things might be tense. Plucked from Vietnam and dropped into Hawaiian R&R, reunited with wives who were worried about their men, their kids, leaky faucets and unpaid bills in a society that increasingly painted them and their husbands as 'enemies,' created stress. Greg looked normal; he acted weird. Had she seen it coming? How can you judge letters from a war zone? What about dope? Other drugs? Their sex raged furiously. Rough and angry, it hit her limits. When she felt like his dirty, hidden joke, 'mutual consent' ceased to be a relevant term. Then, under the palm trees, over fresh pineapple after a morning swim, he dropped the comment like a weather report.

"Becca, I don't want to be married anymore." He stared into his coffee. "Things are different now, I'm different. See a lawyer. Settle things, will you?"

Her plane would leave in five hours, his somewhat later. They fought a monstrous, ugly, vicious verbal-brawl that now kept repeating slowly in her mind over and over again. Why? Why? But never an answer that made sense. Just the recurrent 'I'm different.' How did it come to this? What the hell went on in 'Nam?

Becca closed her eyes tightly and focused on her appointment with the attorney. He'd said, "Forget it. Every guy in 'Nam is nuts. Wait till he gets home, he'll come back for his clothes. See me then if you need to." Feeling patronized, she'd left the office angry but hadn't contacted another lawyer.

Now, just as she'd begun adjusting to Greg not wanting to be married to her, had almost pushed her love for him and her anger, if not away, at least into a manageable place in her life, he's listed MIA. She felt sick, raw, trapped and terrified. 'Drown or be eaten.'

She rolled over and turned on her bedside light, reached for a book, saw her bloody hand.

"Well, at least I can bleed even if I can't feel." She walked to the bathroom, washed her hand and applied some antibiotic ointment. She stared at her nude body in the mirror and wondered if she'd ever trust again. Returning to bed, she opened the book.

"Three hours of Alistair MacLean, then work." The sound of her own voice stabilized her: tentatively anchoring her to reality.

At 7:45 she walked into the graduate-student office she shared with her friend Rich Brent at the Seattle Veterans' Administration Speech Pathology Clinic; they were students together at the University of Washington and both held VA Traineeships. He looked up from his book, gulped some coffee.

"The dream again?" he asked. Becca nodded. "Looks like it. Go do something to your face."

"Any suggestion? Perhaps a mask or surgery?" Her voice dripped sarcasm.

"Just try a little lipstick, some eye make up," he said quietly. "Take some time. We'll talk later." She nodded, sighed and headed for the women's room.

Rich had served in 'Nam in some unit that probably never officially existed. He understood. When she'd returned from her trip to Hawaii three months ago, he knew something was wrong and the next night, with his wife Jenny, listened to the whole messy story over pizza and beer on their patio. The day after that, a pile of mystery novels appeared on her desk with a note: 'We're here for you. Call anytime. At 3:00 a.m. try Alistair MacLean first: then call. Jenny.' After which Rich scrawled, 'We love you but self immolation isn't a spectator sport.'

Except for the Brents, only the lawyer knew about the divorce talk. Most others saw 'Becca and Greg: perfect couple.' Now that he was MIA people either avoided her or dripped maudlin, hand wringing pity. Rich simply said, "It must feel like leopards chewing at your guts." It might feel like that if she ever felt anything again. Awake, she remained coiled and numb. She snarled like an angry wolverine at small things, but felt nothing.

Her heels clicked on the terrazzo floor as she re-entered the small office, in better control now. Rich handed her coffee.

"You need coffee and you need help. This isn't something to handle alone."

"Great." She snatched the coffee as her brief composure snapped. "Just great. I look like hell and I'm crazy, too. Any other happy morning messages?"

"You're impossible."

She sank into her chair. "Rich, what the hell am I supposed to do? Join some MIA wives' group? 'Hi, I'm Rebecca Elizabeth Morgan Chadwick, my husband, the bastard who wants a divorce when he gets his ass home from nightmare land, was just declared MIA. How do you like them egg rolls, Mr. Goldstone?' Or do I sashay into some shrink's office and ask 'Does Dr. Bigbottom recommend the water or the shark?'"

"You slam any door you're shown. Lord woman! Others may be dealing with this, other people may be able to help."

"So I find another red and purple polka dotted flea on the planet. Then what? We compare spots and hold hands waiting for the dog tags and body bags? The only thing keeping me this sane is working, studying, seeing patients." She slammed a book open.

"You are the most defensive person I know." Rich shook his head.

"By the way," she said softly into her text, "one of those mysteries helped last night. Thanks."

"High drama at 3:00 a.m. is only a bandage."

They both studied. Rich and Jenny liked the woman hidden in the barbed-wire ball Becca currently presented to the world. They knew she needed help but weren't sure she'd allow anybody through her porcupine defenses.

2

Nightmares got worse. Amorphous shapes pressed down. She couldn't breathe. Screaming figures leapt at her and, when confronted, grew docile, but attacked again when she turned her back. Greg mired in ooze, eyes gaunt, perfect smile. She prowled her apartment at night like some caged nocturnal animal: drank too much coffee, ate little. Becca felt imprisoned by events, history and her own warped worldview. Taught by her mother that seeking help revealed weakness, she had, regrettably, learned the lesson well. One small grace she recognized even in her darkest moments was that both her family and Greg's lived far away. Becca couldn't have handled their combined pathology. She could barely handle her own.

The Brents went camping with their kids between semesters and when Rich walked into the office on Monday morning a week later he found Becca with her nose in a book.

"Hi kid."

"Hi." She looked up, her face cadaverous, dark circles framing her brown eyes; her hands appeared bony, bird-like. Rich closed the door, swung into his chair. His time away brought perspective: she'd deteriorated badly. He dialed Jenny's office number: a Medical Social Worker, her connections would be helpful.

"Hi, Jen," he said softly into the phone. "Becca needs to see someone good today." He watched, concerned that Becca would spring at him but she just sat picking at her fingernails while Jenny had him on hold. "That's fine. Harvey. Two o'clock. Got it. Thanks Jen." Rich sprawled across his desk making his body a large barrier between Becca and the window.

"How was camping?" Her voice sounded vague.

"Wonderful. Just what we all needed." He stretched, remained casual. "Right now we are going to focus on what you need. You've got an appointment with a Dr. Harvey at 2:00. Jenny says he's good. Now I'm taking you out for breakfast and then we'll go to the U for our eleven o'clock class. At 1:45, I'm dropping you at Dr. Harvey's. When did you eat last?"

"I don't really remember. We can't go though; there are clients scheduled."

"You," he said simply, "aren't working today and my job is to get you to Dr. Harvey. I'll deal with the stuff here." He reached for the phone and buzzed the secretary. "Hey beautiful, did you miss me?" He paused and laughed. "Change of schedule: Brent and Chadwick are leaving and 'the Chad' won't be back today. I'll return by 2:00. Anybody up the ladder gives you grief, I'll see 'em later. Any complaints from the younger generation about putting in an honest day's work, they answer to me, too. All reports on my desk by four thirty." He listened and smiled. "So long, and thanks." He turned to Becca. "Let's get you some food."

"Harvey." Her voice sounded clinical. "Elwood P. Dowd's invisible six-foot rabbit: 'giant pooka' to be exact. Lord, Brent, you know how to pick 'em. You hired me a shrink named after a goddamned monster bunny without asking permission!" She stood, grabbed her jacket and briefcase. Her clothes hung from her like Spanish moss on a dying tree. "So, let's fatten me up for the kill." Even painfully thin, she moved toward the door with a dancer's grace. "I'll go wash my face."

Rich caught her arm. "I'd rather you freshen up at the restaurant, at ground level." She shot him a challenging look. "Sorry, Becca. No third floor windows without me present."

She smiled. "I'm too vain to splatter myself all over the pavement."

"Probably true but, until I turn you over at Dr. Rabbit's office, I'm not taking chances." She still had spunk. They went to the hall and she jabbed the call button for the elevator.

At 1:40, Rich parked in the 'passenger load zone' outside Harvey's office building, flipped the car into park, set the brake and stretched. "Suite 201. Have fun."

Becca huddled in her seat, stared out the window. "What if I don't go?"

"Then you catch a bus home now rather than later." Rich looked up at the pattern of tiny holes in his VW Bug's ceiling. "Becca, in 'Nam I watched a young kid's face explode because he didn't hear my warning. I could've called louder but I was too fucking scared. Felt guilty as hell. Confessed to a priest. The good Padre said, 'Rich, you did what you reasonably could. You tried; you acted; you reached out. Now you need to let it go. Keep doing that in the future.'" He turned to Becca. "I'm doing what I reasonably can, Bec. I can't walk in that door for you but I've got you here on time."

She squinted at him, her chin tilted up to the left; she bit her lower lip. Without a word she uncrossed her arms, opened the door and stepped from the car. As she slammed the car door an order arose inside her—'Walk, Rebecca.' She stepped forward tentatively. 'Walk. Open the door. Keep moving.' She stumbled into the elevator, ignored the muzak, found 201 and entered. Five minutes after filing out forms, a rosy faced, slightly balding, white-haired man appeared at the door—the 'blood-brain barrier' between the real and the therapeutic worlds—and called her name. Wordlessly, he ushered her into his office.

"I'm Leon Harvey," he said holding out his hand.

She shook it. "That figures." The room, eight by ten with two skinny windows on the far narrow wall, contained two leather-looking reclining chairs. Two walls were paneled in a rich mahogany and the other two painted a soothing taupe. A tidy desk sat in the corner. "Jesus, how can you work at a desk that neat?" The question burped out, called for no answer and got none. She clutched her briefcase and moved around cautiously like a cat exploring a new space. She studied a picture hanging on the longer, paneled wall: blues, browns, reds and splotches of white: gobs of paint with no discernible pattern. Becca turned.

"Which chair is mine?" She tried to sound casual: felt stupid.

"Whichever you want."

She plopped into the chair on her left, dropped her briefcase onto the floor. She stared at her hands; her fingertips fidgeted. Harvey sat down. She glanced at him. His face seemed open, neutral. Suddenly, Becca pushed her chair back into the reclining position, crossed her arms and stared at the ceiling. Slowly a tear erupted and slid down her cheek. She snatched a Kleenex from the box on the side table and wiped her eyes.

"There's just too damned much." Her voice, though breaking, sounded strong. Dr. Harvey sat back and waited.

3

Life separated into four compartments: graduate school, clinical work, the essentials of living (eat, sleep, bathe) and Dr. Harvey. The first three sustained her life while the fourth challenged growth. Exploring her relationship with Greg during this horrific time led to investigating other events and relationships. It didn't take long to get to Andy, Eleanor, Marcia and Biff—Eleanor's second husband and Becca's stepfather. Once she started down this slide, stopping could be dangerous.

One clear memory seen through her own two and a half year old eyes helped her focus on the task. Andrew stood at the foot of a slide in a swimming pool. Little Becca sat at the top of the slide with Marcia behind her offering gentle support. Eleanor stood in the water a little to the left of Andy, smiling.

"Come to Daddy, Becca, come to Daddy." She pushed off and hurtled down, gaining speed. He caught her, swooped her up, and tossed her into the air in one smooth, giant motion. Becca saw his eyes, his smile, felt his strong hands lifting her, heard her own excited squeal.

Five months later, everything changed. They carried Andy away. He smiled and waved propped up on the stretcher. She never saw him again. He never came home. A huge hole developed in her world, a space he had occupied: now an empty, aching void. Life became a frantic struggle to control, keep things stable, avoid pain. The 'tunnel.' And now, twenty-five years later, she encountered a new tunnel.

Her face often felt numb, frozen, expressionless. A detached homunculus sat on her right shoulder, watched and commented. 'Look at Becca studying. See her developing research. Watch her working with brain-injured patients, sounding wise. Look! She cooks, eats, bathes and dresses. She reads, drives and climbs stairs. She looks sane.'

Quail Hill

Her dreams got worse. She and Harvey grappled with them. Images, fears, rage emerged. What if Greg died? Lived? Returned injured? Healthy? Never was found? In a desperate moment of logical clarity Becca went to Nordstrom's and bought a simple, tailored black dress; if a funeral happened she'd give no one cause to scorn. She hung the dress in her closet then indulged in a long hot bath, pulled on a nightshirt and crawled into bed intending to read a journal article she'd copied at the library that afternoon.

Uninvited, memories of their courtship appeared. She remembered her first glimpse of Greg through the peephole of the apartment she shared with her roommates in Georgetown: a blind date who arrived as a tall, singularly handsome man smiling coyly on the other side of the door. His square jaw, clear dark eyes and Marine crew cut matched his perfect name: Gregory Alan Chadwick, III. The whole thing seemed slightly unfair because, while she watched his initial reaction to her, her reaction to him had been hidden. Becca tried to end this reverie by reading but somehow 'Language Retrieval Strategies for External Traumatic Head-Injury Cases' could not compete with her 'first date' memories. She turned off the light and settled into a pre-sleep 'positive images' scenario Harvey had suggested; she visualized her great-great-grandparent's farm on Quail Hill at the height of fall colors bathed in the light of the setting sun.

Four days later, she got the news. Greg's remains and 'dog tags' had been recovered four hundred yards from the crash site. Fragile, like a harmonically driven crystal wineglass, Becca knew she might shatter into a million small, sharp shards, virtually disintegrate into basic molecular units. This Humpty-Dumpty threat felt close and terrifying. Thankfully, a giant parenthesis erected itself around her.

She called the Brents, Greg's family, her family; prepared her clothes, began packing her suitcase and made plane reservations with remarkable focus and outward calm. The next afternoon she kept her appointment with Harvey.

The moment he saw her he knew. What is it in the human species, he wondered, that produced in some people, during periods of immense stress, eyes that looked into your deepest hidden center to reveal your own nakedness? Such eyes did not mock, but simply knew and accepted. Today, Becca had such eyes. Following her down the hall, Harvey sensed that were she a Yogi, a Dervish, a Religious she might attain this state after years of prayer and practice. But Becca, catapulted into this territory unwillingly, might well smash back lower than she'd ever been, hurl helplessly to other places like Alice down the rabbit hole. They entered the room and sat. Becca stared at the ceiling.

"Deceptive," she said.

"What's deceptive?"

"The ceiling, the world, you, me." She paused. "He's dead, Harvey. Remains and dog tags recovered four hundred yards from the crash site." A long silence.

"I'm very sorry, Becca. How are you?"

She rolled her head to the side, looked at him unblinking. "I'm alive, Harvey. Sad, confused, relieved, angry, scared, guilty." Her eyes changed, narrowed, her facial muscles tightened, her voice hardened. "Enraged. Four hundred fucking yards! He was alive." Her guttural voice felt like acid thrown in his face. "What the hell does this mean 'remains and dog tags'? Is that supposed to comfort me? How the hell did he die?" Her body curled forward, her clenched hands pressed to her mouth.

She vaulted from her chair, prowled the room touching things randomly like an autistic child. "He was alive. He got almost a quarter of a mile from the crash. After Hawaii I wished him pain. I wanted him hurt like I hurt, I wanted him to feel the knife of betrayal." She spun around. "Remains!? How much of his body? What parts? They saw off his jaw to identify his teeth?"

"Becca....."

"Becca what? Am I hallucinating? What the hell happened? I wished this stuff Harvey. I hated and now I get this. Did I do this?"

"No, of course not, but the fear…"

She cut him off. "How the hell do you know? Maybe it works like that. Maybe God's a joke. Maybe we're alone in the universe and we get to play these same lousy tapes forever. Maybe even after death it just goes on." She sat down hard in the chair at his desk. "Let's change the subject."

"To what?"

"Clever, Harvey, very therapeutic. Let's talk about the funeral. Let's talk about the new black dress 'Becca-the-wonderful-widow' will wear. Let's talk about the prayers, the tears, the presentation of the flag. Let's talk about two pathological families meeting in the Southern Ohio heat for a 'nice family gathering.' Let's talk about repression and denial, about the mother and the sister sticking a symbolic sock in 'Becca-the-Brat's' mouth if she dares speak the truth." She stopped, put her elbows on the desk and held her head in her hands. "Shit, Harvey. What is the truth and how am I gonna get through this?"

"When do you leave?"

"In two days. The exact date for the funeral hasn't been set. I'll come back as soon as I can. The heat in August is vicious back there. I have work to do here and, Harvey, they really are all nuts. I won't play their games anymore so it'll be rough going." She paused, looked at him pleadingly, "Oh God, Dr. Harvey, what's in that body-bag?"

4

As the plane took off, Becca relaxed against the window and watched as SeaTac, Puget Sound and Mount Rainier slid into the background. She'd arrive in Cincinnati this afternoon. The next week might be very bumpy. She tried to foresee danger points, imagined handling situations calmly, hoped she'd avoid clashes with her mother, Eleanor, and her mother-in-law, Josephine Chadwick. She drifted to sleep, dreamed of her great-grandparent's farm, saw her two great-aunts. Katy looked concerned as Annabelle resolutely shoved her foot into her left boot and said firmly, 'Let's not just stand here, let's help the girl.'

Becca awoke smiling and saw the dim reflection of her own face on the airplane window. She figured God, as many people seemed to conceive of God, probably didn't exist, but she believed in her dreams and she believed in foreknowledge. Now, she knew she'd have strength. Things would be all right: not perfect but, with Great-Aunt Annabelle's help, she'd get through.

"Mother," Nancy Chadwick Goddard, Greg's sister, said as she guided the car out of the airport parking lot, "is organizing things with her best Prussian-General, velvet-glove style." Becca groaned and sank into the Cadillac's considerable plush. "I know the feeling but there it is. Prepare yourself."

"Thanks Nancy. I figured as much. I hope it won't be a total circus."

"It will. He was your husband but Mother never let go of him."

"That's not news," Becca snapped. "Nancy, I've been a Chadwick for a number of years." Becca was two months older than Nancy and they'd become good friends during her relationship with Greg. Becca twisted her wedding band. She'd remove it after the funeral. He was dead but there had been no divorce. An idea burped up from her unconscious: maybe she hadn't seen the request for divorce coming because maybe it wasn't really Greg's idea. Maybe his mother, Josephine, pressured him. Becca tried to push this away but it wouldn't go. Even now, she battled with Josephine Chadwick for Greg.

As they pulled into the long driveway winding uphill to the large brick home, Nancy said, "This won't be easy. Mother may come on strong but your relatives are no picnic either. I love you but he was my brother and I'm in mourning, too. I've been a Chadwick all my life and…"

"Putting me in my place. Look, we were married. No, don't interrupt me. Your mother put terrible pressure on Greg. I was not the woman she wanted for him but I'm the wife he chose. Okay, now it's over. He's dead. But I will not be treated like hired help. This is my husband's funeral and I will have some say here."

· Other Places ·

Becca stepped from the car and leaned back against the door as it closed. Her heart pounded and she felt dizzy. Wisteria arched over the front door. Becca loved this house but visits here could turn Kafkaesque at any minute. 'Okay, Great-Aunt Annabelle, help now!' Instantly her legs strode confidently up the walk as the front door opened.

Josephine Chadwick appeared fresh and cool in a medium gray linen dress, her silver hair swept into a French twist. She wore almost no makeup and the death of her oldest son etched new and unfamiliar lines in her face. They hugged wordlessly, clinging to each other for a moment. Becca genuinely liked Josephine. Without Greg between them, they might have had an interesting older/younger woman friendship.

Inside, family and friends gathered; food and drink overwhelmed tables; people milled around. Some of the Chadwicks' politically connected acquaintances came and went. Greg's younger brother, Tim, took her suitcase upstairs. Josephine called to Becca as she and Tim ascended the long staircase.

"You might prefer Nancy's old room: fewer memories."

Becca hesitated. Greg's room had always been 'their' room. If she belonged anyplace in this house, she belonged there.

"That's kind of you, but I'd be more comfortable in Greg's room." They looked at each other, both waited. 'If she plans to order me out,' Becca thought, 'wave some secret stash of letters from Greg in my face then she'd better do it now.'

"Of course, it's your choice."

"Thank you." Becca smiled thinly. She felt wicked, triumphant and sad. She and Josephine were a lot alike.

Tim turned toward Greg's bedroom.

"Nobody's been in here for a long time."

"Well, it isn't a museum and it's where Greg and I always stayed. It's sad to be here without him."

"I hate that he died. Mother says to be strong but I don't feel strong."

Becca hugged him briefly, sixteen to twenty-nine being an awkward age difference.

"Greg was proud of you Timmy. He felt you had lots of talent, that you handled things at your age better than he had. None of us is strong all the time. It's terribly sad he died. We'll never forget him."

"He was too young to die."

"Yes, but he lived a lot and he was doing what he wanted to do. He loved being a Marine Officer. Now, I need to freshen up; I'll be down in a few minutes."

The week progressed as a surrealistic montage. At times Becca felt present and relaxed: then events screamed by. She pogo-stick-jumped from lucid and calm to bordering on out-of-control. Clarity switched to blur in an instant; almost normal behavior changed to deep agonizing tears instantly. The oppressive heat surrendered briefly during afternoon thunderstorms. After these she'd walk in the yard, smelling the fresh rain. It bothered her that Greg would never again smell fresh rain. At night she snuggled down in his bed, totally alone, remembering other nights, nights of passion, of abandon, of giggles, of exploring each other quietly so as not to wake the family. Finally she'd remember Hawaii and weep.

Eleanor and Marcia drove down early on the day of the funeral. Marcia let Eleanor out at the door of the Chadwick's home while she went to park the car. Becca groaned internally as her mother swept into the living room wearing a too-short black dress with black nylons, the outfit topped off with a black Spanish-lace scarf over her newly dyed hair—an interesting hair-color Becca had never seen before. Becca moved across the room knowing she both needed to greet her mother and to save Josephine from Eleanor's all too effusive sorrow.

"Hello Mother," tears welled up in her eyes as Eleanor turned and began gushing over Becca in "your new widowhood." Fight this as she may, Becca sought her mother's hugs: they had been, after all, her main source of solace during her childhood after Andy died but she was appalled by Eleanor's appearance. She broke away quickly and centered herself.

"How was the trip down?" Becca asked. Just as Eleanor started to answer Marcia entered the room looking fragile and apprehensive. Becca went to her sister.

"Oh, honey," Marcia said as they hugged, "oh, honey," she repeated sobbing.

Eleanor and Marcia's responses were so predictable that Becca smiled and said, "Hey, I'm the one who lost a husband, not you."

Marcia laughed through her tears and blubbered, "Don't make me laugh now!"

When they left for the church, Becca rode with the Chadwicks: Eleanor and Marcia followed in Marcia's car. The large, neo-gothic building held no memories for Becca and that left her free to use the time to prepare for the events that would follow. She sang at the right times, stood and sat on cue, greeted friends appropriately and felt numb. To keep her confused emotions in check, she established significant distance between herself and Eleanor.

After the service and the internment, a large group returned to the Chadwick home for a reception. Eleanor kept introducing herself to various political figures, alternating heavy tragedy with her usual inappropriate flirtation. Marcia smiled, looking both sweet and lost. With steely self-preservation, Becca clutched the flag that had been on Greg's coffin as she steered a course through this event.

A little homunculus sat on Becca's shoulder and kept up a semi-detached commentary: 'Good. You remembered that name just in time…Walking slowly is a nice touch… The dress is working, it's appropriately demure… Here comes

Greg's lecherous old roommate, careful, he's invading your space... He's such a bastard… Withdraw your hand but no, you may not spit in his face.' The voice also provided strength. Once when she almost lost her temper, was about to spew a dreadful verbal tirade triggered by a small, innocent remark, the homunculus simply said, 'Stop, Becca. Now!' She complied.

Marcia and Eleanor left when the reception broke up. Becca felt relieved and sad as she watched them go. She wished their relationships were different but had no idea how to change their long established patterns

That evening after dinner with just the Chadwick family members and Greg's lawyer present, they read the Will. Becca, still holding the flag firmly, sat on the couch next to Nancy. Greg left the bulk of his estate (inheritance from his grandfather) to Becca with a few items to other family members. Josephine twisted her handkerchief and pursed her lips but said nothing. If she could have challenged Becca's claim, she never did. Becca breathed a sigh of relief. She didn't care much about the money though having it would give her security. She just wanted these events over. She sat quietly still clutching the flag just below her heart.

5

Becca stood at the open bedroom window watching the lightning of distant thunderstorms prowling the Kentucky hills across the Ohio River. The air stirred as the storm approached arriving at 4:15 a.m. She visualized Greg's coffin holding his 'remains' in his new grave in the Chadwick plot overlooking the river. Rain would rearrange the loose dirt; gradually the earth would incorporate his casket. Her mind wandered to her father's grave in Craigmoor. The tension of these past five months eased as grief crashed around her. Tears drenched her face; gravity pulled her down; she curled up in a ball on the floor. Alone. Abandoned. Again.

Three hours later she awoke. Everything hurt in this muggy heat. Stretching her muscles she headed for the shower and let the water pummel her neck and shoulders and then slither down her body.

'Southern Ohio at its summer worst: you never get dry.' She stepped out, tried to towel down, swiped her towel across the fogged mirror and glimpsed her reflection. The eyes surprised her. The face—a bit asymmetrical, not bad looking, topped by her short, dark, wet curly hair—looked foreign. A long suppressed idea popped up full-grown like Topsy. Until now, her identity existed (with Eleanor's and most of the world's encouragement) in connection with people or abilities or stereotypes: Andrew's daughter, Eleanor's daughter, Marcia's little sister, a math whiz, a member of this or that group, a dancer, a scholar, a troublemaker, a Marine wife ambivalent about Vietnam. But a person? Who lived here? Did some separate entity named 'Becca' exist or was she just a stitched together jumble of roles, relationships? Her mind cleared. She must discover who she was and fight for her life. Steam clouded the mirror again.

After breakfast she said her good-byes: quick hugs, encouraging words—an exit insuring maximum harmony and minimum pain. As she and Nancy drove down the long driveway, the memory of a childhood toy popped up in Becca's head.

"Remember those little Chinese finger traps?"

"Those woven things you stuck one finger from each hand in?"

"Yea. Well, that's sort of how I feel: I'm moving out of Greg's family, your family, kind of slowly so none of us gets trapped, hooked. But I'll keep the name Chadwick."

Nancy parked at the Avis Rental Car Office as tears filled her eyes.

"I'm glad you'll keep Chadwick. I know it'll never be the same but I don't want to lose you. Greg…" she chocked, swallowed hard. "Becca, I don't know what to say. There is a certain Chadwick craziness and you're good for us."

Becca chuckled. "Yea, your family crazies and my family crazies balance out." Becca fumbled with a Kleenex. "Look at you. Neat tidy tears: and me, nose running all over the place. All this week I've wondered 'How do Nancy and Josephine do it? Cry without nose-running.'" They both laughed through their tears.

"It's not much of a saving grace but I'll take it. Thanks for being here and for loving Greg and us."

"Let's not get maudlin. I have to drive to Dayton." Becca got out of the car—her sunglasses placed strategically over swollen eyes—retrieved her suitcase and walked to the driver's side. Nancy reached out, they held hands briefly and then Becca turned and walked into the Avis office, signed for her rental car and drove north to her Mother's home in Dayton.

Eleanor, Marcia and Becca spent the afternoon at the country club while Biff and Marcia's husband, Jack, played golf. Both the temperature and the humidity pushed 100. In the dressing room, Eleanor gasped and Marcia raised her eyebrows when Becca changed into the red and white bikini Greg bought her early in the Hawaiian fiasco.

"That's an awfully skimpy suit for a recent widow," Eleanor's 'appearances are everything' voice remonstrated.

"And," Becca replied wearily, "the only one this widow owns."

"What will people say?" Marcia stretched the vowel in 'say.'

"Well," Becca eyed herself in the mirror, "people who know me will say I'm thin. People who don't may ask 'Who's that?'"

· Other Places ·

"You look indecent," Marcia rebutted primly, adjusting the skirt on her ruffled, one-piece, totally prepubescent-looking swimsuit.

"For what I've been through, I look damned good."

"Well, if that's what you want to wear…" Eleanor began condescendingly but caught herself as Trudy Evans walked in. Married and childless, Trudy and her husband owned one of Dayton's most successful women's clothing stores. Becca admired her style and no-nonsense approach.

Eleanor and Trudy exchanged greetings and Eleanor began her standard baby talk introductions of Marcia and Becca—first names only. Becca cringed.

"Of course I know your daughters." Trudy greeted Marcia, turned to Becca. "I'm so sorry about Greg's death, Bec. If there's anything I can do, either now or when you go back to Seattle let me know."

"Thanks. The past few months have been rough."

"Well you look good, if a bit thin. That suit's grand. Hawaiian?" Becca nodded. "Don't get locked into widow's weeds. It's difficult now but your life's out there, before you. Remember that." She patted Becca's arm affectionately and moved to her locker. Eleanor, Marcia and Becca exited onto the porch overlooking the first tee.

Turning away from the rolling hills of the golf course, they approached the pool area. The summer noise sounded like an orchestra tuning: always different yet always the same. Marcia's ten-year-old son, Philip, and eight-year-old daughter, Cynthia, ran to join them. Children splashed and swam, dove and jumped from the boards, calling distracted mothers repeatedly to watch their exploits. One change since Becca's childhood: the club now demanded that all children under 18 leave the pool for ten minutes each hour allowing a delicious 'child-free' time when adults could actually swim.

As the whistle blew, Becca tossed her cover-up into a lounge chair and dove into the now almost abandoned, mildly cool water. After four lengths, she climbed out, wiped off, brushed her short brown curls back from her forehead and flopped into her chair. Becca, Eleanor and Marcia talked lightly. A young black waiter in his neat uniform of black slacks, white shirt and black tie, came by to take their drink orders. All the waiters were black. Even in childhood, this 'plantation system' at the country club had rankled Becca. She'd left southern Ohio a decade ago and the racial stratification now slapped her in the face. The afternoon lolled on: they talked, sunned, played cards, drank lemonade and occasionally swam. After the whistle blew at 4:00 to clear children from the pool, Eleanor pulled on her swimming cap.

"Becca, would you like to swim?"

"No thanks, Mother. Not right now."

"Well, if that's what you want…" Eleanor walked away.

Marcia leaned over. "Mother wants to talk to you," she said in earnest, hushed tones.

"Then she can say 'Becca I want to talk to you' and not ask if I want to go swimming. I'm not up to all this damned second guessing and game playing."

"You're ungrateful. You should be nice to Mother." Marcia grabbed her swim-cap and trudged away.

'*Should* and *nice*,' Becca thought, 'are two words I'm trying to understand in a new, less guilt-provoking way.'

She closed her eyes and relaxed. MIA was behind her. She'd survived the funeral, remained civil. Greg was dead: the marriage over. She'd never know if they would have divorced. The Will gave her some money. Being single again felt strange, brought anxiety: the game had changed and her old insecurities lurked just below the surface. Images, fears, fantasies and memories tossed in her head. Trudy Evans had encouraged her, reminded her that she had a future, a life 'out there before you.' She'd finish graduate school but, beyond that, where was 'out there?' She had to get a job and discover who she was. Becca dozed.

Something cast a shadow across her. She awakened. Shading her eyes before opening them, she quickly recognized his silhouette against the sun.

6

"Hi."

"Hi. Just learned you were here," Steve flipped his towel next to her chair, leaned over and kissed her cheek—his lips too close to her mouth, the kiss too long—and sat by her side. He ran his hand gently down her arm, took her hand: a simple gesture between old friends?

"Awful news about Greg." Steve looked genuinely concerned and something more. With Steve, there was always something more.

Becca felt the first stirrings of 'person specific' sexual longing since Greg went MIA.

"Yes, it's such a waste." They talked. Then he took her address and stood to leave.

"If I get to Seattle on business, I'll buy you dinner." He gave her another too long kiss, squeezed her shoulder. "Take care."

She watched him walk slowly to his car feeling furious, violated and aroused. They'd known each other forever. He was five years older, an occasional juvenile rutting partner when she was in high school and he in college. Beyond shared upbringing in a social group focused on the country club, they had little in common. But something primitive pushed their hormones into high gear around each other. Life threw them together every few years leaving them both rattled. She hoped he'd never call: dinner with this married man 'old friend' would be terribly unwise.

At five thirty Eleanor, Marcia and Becca dressed for dinner. The club oozed mid-twentieth-century-upper-middle-class American society. No blacks, no Jews, no women need apply. No non-northern Europeans, no Asians, no Hispanics. Few Catholics. White. Male. Monied. Protestant. She'd grown up here, spent holiday dinners here and called the black waiters by their first names. The comfortable chairs, gracious surroundings, pastel walls, damask drapes, indirect lighting and String Quartet bespoke air-conditioned elegance available for an entrance fee if one survived the vetting process. Would the country ever live up to its promise of greater equality? Becca wondered as she studied the menu. Friends dropped by the table, exchanged greetings, offered condolences. Sitting in her perfect black dress, Becca felt fragile. The waiter came for drink orders.

"Nothing, thank you," Becca smiled at the young man and resumed her conversation with her nephew, Philip.

Eleanor reached across the table, patted her arm.

"Come now, you must join the festivities," Eleanor glared at her, smiling.

"I really don't want anything to drink, Mother." Becca tried to control her rage. "And I'm uncomfortable with the term 'festivities.'" Their eyes met and Becca saw Eleanor's 'I-will-not-tolerate-this' look. "Please, Mother, let's not argue about something this silly."

"I," Eleanor stated regally, "am not creating the argument. Civilized people at social gatherings drink cocktails before dinner and refusing to join in is rude."

"Oh, lord, Mother. I just don't want a drink tonight, okay?" The waiter fidgeted. Becca felt sorry for him.

"Bring her a sweet Rob Roy and I'll have a Manhattan." Eleanor said coldly. After taking their orders, the waiter retreated rapidly. Becca shook her head.

"I won't drink it. It's a waste."

Eleanor hissed, "People will think you're an alcoholic and I don't intend for my friends to think my daughter's an 'alchie.'"

"Better one who doesn't drink than one who does."

Marcia's forehead wrinkled and she bit her lip. Caught between the opposing forces of her mother and her sister, Marcia busied herself with her daughter, Cynthia.

When the drinks arrived Becca pushed the Rob Roy to the center of the table where it spent the evening next to the fresh flowers, a mute reminder of unresolved conflict.

The food, excellent as always, far surpassed the conversation. Jack and Biff talked golf, stocks, the weather and conservative Republican politics. After her third Manhattan, Eleanor became, predictably, seductive toward any man who passed by. She laughed too much and inserted inappropriate comments. Becca talked to Philip and Cynthia about swimming. Cynthia wanted to train for the Olympics. Marcia and Jack encouraged Philip, discouraged Cynthia. Becca encouraged them both.

"Honey," Eleanor gushed to Cynthia, "you don't want to train hard, you'll get all muscle bound and become so competitive the boys won't like you."

Biff chimed in. "That's right Cindy. You should just stay a sweet little girl. You don't need too much college, like some here."

"I just don't want her to experience too much failure," Marcia said looking worried.

"I can only afford training for one kid and that's for Philip," Jack opined.

"I've got an idea: hire a trainer for Cynthia and then she can coach Philip since she's the one who really wants to do this." Becca knew she was being evil and didn't care.

"Great idea, Aunt Bec," said Philip. "That would solve everything."

The adults pushed food around on their plates and changed the subject but Becca's defiant streak continued.

"You know, Biff," Becca spoke slowly, "speaking of educational opportunities for women, before my great-grandmother would marry my great-grandfather she insisted he agree that all their children could go to college. All three girls graduated from Bates. Breaking new ground comes naturally to Cynthia." Eleanor would be irritated that she called him 'Biff' but it felt more honest than 'Daddy.'

"Yes and two of them ended up old maids," Eleanor remarked pointedly.

"Being single beats a bad marriage. I'm not sure that I want to remarry."

"Of course you'll remarry," Eleanor slurred.

Suddenly, Becca felt trapped, wanted to scream at all these people: 'how can you sit here like this? People are dying; men, in your name and using your tax money, are crawling in the slime of Vietnam. They are coming back in pieces, in body bags. You are eating and drinking and laughing and I AM JOINING IN!' Tears formed as she pushed her chair back and stood.

"Excuse me." She walked calmly from the room, out the door and to the pool. The heat, after the air-conditioned clubhouse, relaxed her. The underwater lights made the outlines of the swimmers dart unevenly through the turquoise water. Tree frogs croaked loudly. Lightening bugs lit up and then darted away. Leaves rustled as a small breeze dragged streamers of clouds across the face of the moon. Bats darted through the night. Becca leaned against a tree and systematically relaxed the muscles in her neck, shoulders and upper back. She closed her eyes and concentrated on a point in front of her forehead breathing evenly. After a few minutes she felt calmer and sat in a lounge chair. Cindy came out fifteen minutes later.

"Aunt Becca?"

"Hi, sweetie. Want to sit with me and watch the swimmers?"

"Are you okay?"

"Since Uncle Greg died I'm sort of up and down. Remember when your kitty was hurt?" Cindy nodded. "I'm sort of like that. I just need to lick my wounds, eat some food, sleep and be left alone sometimes. I'll get better."

"I loved Uncle Greg; I miss him, too."

"He was special." They sat quietly for a while.

"Tell me more about my great-great-grandmother. She sounds nifty."

"She was. Her name was Elizabeth Rebecca and everybody called her Libby. I don't know much but I'll tell you everything I know. Ask your Mom, too. She'll remember more."

7

Something swooped down screeching, "You must SEE!" then retreated. Becca raced to escape as the figure, now beatific, evaporated. "See what? Wait!" It left. Her throat froze. Abandoned, again. Like crystal breaking, something whole shattered.

Eyes closed, now awake. Inhale, exhale, pause. She felt like pebbles on a beach at low tide: moving back and forth, ebbing and flowing, unconnected things tumbling over one another. Higher on the beach there'd be reprieve from such relentless motion; further out to sea a gentler rhythm swayed. But here she experienced constant battering. 'Odd,' she felt, 'to discover my *self* as colliding pieces.' She glimpsed her board of directors for the first time.

"Dr. Harvey, I can't exactly explain it. It's like I'm a group. Not multiple personalities more a committee around a table. I recognize parts. There's 'academically successful Becca.' Bright, clever, seldom factually wrong, seeks approval and rewards: often a royal pain in the ass, but productive and focused.

"There are others, some I don't know: just sitting quietly doing Heaven knows what. One does the basics: gets up, eats, brushes hair, dresses, drives—is having trouble sleeping.

"There's a sensual, sexy 'me.' Someone I need to know better, trust more. Dangerous if I ignore her.

"And this tyrannical little girl. Jesus, Harvey, she is so strong, controlling, demanding, pounding the table! But she's not nasty. She protects me but I don't have a clue what she protects me from."

"Who do you mean by 'me'?"

"Me. Rebecca. The woman you're talking to."

"Then who is 'she'?" Becca started to talk. Harvey stopped her. "Not an explanation: a name. Who is 'she'?"

Becca's eyes searched the abstract painting on the opposite wall. After a minute she said quietly, "The little sucker."

"Tell me about 'the little sucker.'"

"She protects me: but I don't know which 'me' she protects or what she protects me—or maybe 'us'—from. She's always alert: always defensive. Scared."

Stepping off the bus, Becca panicked. 'Where am I?' Time spun dizzily. 'My apartment: I live here. Okay.' Stumbling to the entrance, breathing hard, she unlocked the outer door, took the elevator to the fifth floor and entered her apartment. Inside she leaned against the closed door. Home: safe. It was dinnertime. She'd analyze data tonight. She collapsed onto the couch: a month since the funeral. She showered, wrapped herself in Greg's terrycloth robe, ate leftover chicken and a limp celery stalk. Vietnam led the evening news. She yanked the cord to silence the TV and the cord broke. She crumpled to the floor, weeping.

Rich decided "gaunt" won this week's 'word for Becca' contest. His 'final four' were: scraggly, scrawny, emaciated and gaunt. By this macabre game, he tracked her progress. He and Jenny fed her dinner once a week following Jenny's advice: 'Touch burn patients only when necessary.'

"I followed a guy the other day because his pipe tobacco smelled like Greg's. Crept around, crossed streets and entered an unfamiliar building just to smell that damned pipe. I'm going nuts, Harvey."

"I doubt it. You're grieving. Smell is a very primitive sense. Years from now you may react to scents that remind you of Greg."

Becca tried to listen. His words tumbled around. He sounded sincere but his life remained unaffected by the raging crap she dealt with daily. She watched his mouth move, his benign expression continued.

'You silly ass,' she thought, grabbing her purse. His voice trailed off as she stood, walked to the door, down the hall, went down the elevator and out onto the sidewalk. Rain splashed her face as the acrid smell of steamy asphalt flipped her mind back to a day, decades ago, when she was in the first grade. Caught in a thunderstorm on the way home from school, terrified and soaking wet, she raced up the street with tears streaming down her cheeks. Eleanor wasn't home, the key under the milk-box was missing, she hid in the bushes shaking with cold and fear for thirty minutes. Abandoned. Again. That was her second major realization that she traveled, naked and alone, in a very risky world.

Rain continued as she drove home, parked, got her mail and entered the elevator. Reading a letter from Aunt Hildur, Becca pushed the laundry room door open. Her dry clothes sat neatly stacked on the folding table; the new tenant stuffed wet sheets into the dryer.

"I took 'em out," he said over his shoulder.

"Thanks." She scooped up her laundry; her leopard bikini underpants sat on top.

"Mrs. Thompson said your husband was killed recently in Vietnam. I'm sorry," he turned and faced her. He had a medium build, dark hair with receding hairline; stood about 5' 10", wore a mustache and a University Hospital Faculty white coat. Nice dark eyes.

"Thanks," she replied, "me too. He was MIA for months so I'm relieved he's not going through torture though I hate that he's dead. Oh, shit. Why am I saying all this?"

"Sometimes the white coat does that," he smiled easily.

"Yea, but prattling on to strangers isn't my style."

He held out his hand. "Bernie Franklin. Now we're acquaintances."

She readjusted her laundry, shook his hand. "Rebecca Chadwick." The leopard underpants fell to the floor.

He picked them up and dropped them onto her laundry.

"Thanks," she said for the third time and left. Entering her apartment, Becca felt elated, silly. The scene in Harvey's office returned: less than an hour ago she felt depressed unto death, now she felt giddy. Grief: the word slithered around. It felt like walking on a peat bog never knowing when the ground would cave in. Becca hated Ferris wheels, roller coasters and surprises. Grief fused all three experiences.

The refrigerator contained a can of tuna, ½ tomato and some wilted lettuce. She spread these ingredients on a plate and sat down to finish Aunt Hildur's letter. Hildur moved through life easily and stated things well. Becca would accept the invitation to spend Thanksgiving in San Francisco with Uncle Mike and Aunt Hildur. Eleanor might fuss but Dayton was too far. She put down the letter, finished the tuna. Washing her dinner plate, she promised herself she'd go through Greg's things this weekend.

Saturday dawned a sparklingly clear Seattle day. She went to the Pike Place Market for salmon and vegetables, then to the University Medical School Library where she copied two articles and checked out Harlow and Woolsey's *Biological and Biochemical Bases of Behavior*. Returning to her apartment, she opened both the sliding door to her Lanai and her bedroom windows to get a good cross breeze, tuned the TV to some Big Ten College football game and started working. Opening the closet door, she reached for one of Greg's suits and emptied the pockets: a clean handkerchief, a couple of generic ticket stubs and a dime. She took the suit to the living room and put it on the couch. A few trips and a few more miscellaneous bits of pocket debris later, all his suits lay on the couch. She removed his shirts from hangers and folded them. Next she yanked sweaters off shelves along with his shoeboxes and organized it all on the living room floor. Finally she dragged the drawers of underwear, pajamas, hiking and camping gear and sorted through things as football fans—the action had shifted to Kansas or Colorado—cheered teams on. She set out three boxes. There were the things she would keep, things for the local church thrift shop, a box of items to send to the Chadwicks. His hiking and camping gear she'd take to the Brents tomorrow and her friends would come and take what they wanted.

By four, she had finished. Exhausted and hungry, she poured herself a glass of milk. The TV now broadcast one of the Arizona schools playing some team with red jerseys. Her hands shook as she buttered toast. The chore hadn't been a bad as she'd anticipated but she felt morose: no one would ever again spend that much time dealing with the remnants of Greg's life. By completing this last task, Becca knew she had severed threads that held her to him. Once she moved these things out, only his jewelry, books, desk items and photographs would remain.

If she hurried she could get the things to the church thrift shop by five, then load the car with the stuff to take to Brents tomorrow. By 6:15 her major tasks were complete. She pushed the box for the Chadwicks against the wall and started through his jewelry. By now she'd become desensitized. She sifted through these last fragments. Only a few items, like splinters, demanded attention. The football games were over so she turned the TV off. When she finished, a little after eight, relieved and tired, darkness surrounded her. She remembered the salmon she'd bought and wondered if she had the strength to fix it.

The doorbell rang. She'd not let anyone in through the building security system so she approached the door's peephole cautiously. Bernie Franklin stood in the hall smiling.

8

"Hi."

"I saw your light, hope I'm not interrupting."

"No, I just finished a project."

"I finally got away from the hospital ten minutes ago and I'm hungry as a wolf. If you'd like to join me for Chinese, we can go to Tai Tung. Sound reasonable?" He tilted his head, sort of wrinkled his nose.

He's cute, she decided. Not good looking but cute.

"Sure. I haven't eaten yet."

"Shucks, I figured I'd get off cheap."

Becca laughed. "At Tai Tung you will. Give me 20 minutes to shower and change."

"After the day I've had it'll take me 30. See you in about a half an hour."

With few people waiting at the restaurant, they got a booth—private enough to talk, not so isolated they'd be forgotten. After soup, they devoured barbequed pork, egg rolls, sweet and sour shrimp, chicken-almond sub-gum chow mein with soft noodles, beef and mushrooms with Chinese vegetables on mountains of rice and washed it down with hot tea. They recited their educational litanies and somewhat truncated personal histories. After a lull in the conversation, Becca talked about her day.

"I went through Greg's stuff today," she said pushing a shrimp with her chopstick.

"How was that?"

"Not too bad: very little drama. No huge emotional scene. Old theatre stubs, cufflinks I gave him that he never liked: stuff. First date concert program. Personal things left…"

"…after someone dies." He finished her sentence gently. She looked up and nodded. They continued eating quietly.

"Why aren't you married?" Becca asked suddenly.

"Good Lord you're blunt, Chadwick."

"Well, I'm curious and I don't do the 'batting-eyelashes' stuff convincingly."

"I was for seven years until last year: college sweetheart, no children. The relationship worked on campus but not well in real life. Took awhile for each of us to admit it. I love medicine, always wanted to be a doc, got hooked on hematology-oncology. I spend hours with patients, over books and doing research. I want a good medical career and the rest of the time I want to do what I like: fish, ski, climb and sometimes eat Chinese with a pretty woman. I'm not a fan of marriage: friendship, love, sex. Fine."

"Good Lord you're blunt, Franklin," she mimicked. They laughed.

"And I'm REALLY bad at the 'batting-eye' stuff," he said. "Come on, let's go. It's late and I'm exhausted."

Outside, the cold wind whipped around them. Becca clutched her sweater and Bernie slipped his arm around her and kissed her cheek lightly.

"It'll start raining tomorrow and not stop till June," she said, leaning against him.

"Then aren't we fortunate to have had our first date on the last nice day?"

At her door, Becca shrugged. "Well, thanks…" He cut her off with a longer, more interesting kiss.

"We'll do it again. Now I need sleep. I have a big conference next week and work is crazy. Besides, we both need more time." He kissed her again and headed down the hall.

"Goodnight, Bernie."

"Hey," he called over his shoulder, "do you really wear those things?"

"What things?"

"Those leopard things." He grinned, waved, stepped around the corner and disappeared.

"You pervert," she laughed.

Too keyed up to sleep, she read one of the articles she'd copied this morning, turned off her lights, opened the drapes and watched the city sparkle. She'd done the job of clearing out Greg's stuff. The dinner with Bernie was nice. She headed for bed remembering Peggy Lee singing the song 'Is that all there is?' Sometimes life's stark aloneness frightened her. She'd cut many connections with Greg today and done it with remarkably little pathos.

She remembered that her first year at college she'd forgotten the anniversary of Andy's death. Always before, at home, Eleanor marked the day with ritualized drama that, Becca figured, Eleanor needed. Becca remembered looking at the calendar three days later and realizing, 'damn, I forgot.' Then for a few minutes she felt guilty she had forgotten. Now, after today, she knew Greg would recede: slip into background and no amount of artificial resuscitation would bring him back. A peculiar stab of sadness hit as she realized that her recent intense grief had diminished. She'd enjoyed her evening with Bernie and went to sleep breathing the lingering smell of his aftershave.

9

Among the joys of single living, Becca realized as she ate salmon for breakfast and read the Sunday paper, was feeling free to eat salmon for breakfast. Later, she drove to the Brents' house and, walking in, dropped an ice ax onto the couch. "There's a whole lot more in the car." Three of her colleagues went out and unloaded the gear. Jenny came up and hugged her.

"You look better. How'd yesterday go?"

"Not too bad. It feels funny: only my stuff in the closet. It's done."

"You did it, that's the important thing. Want some coffee? A doughnut?"

"Coffee, yes: doughnut, no. I feel stuffed. I had my salmon dinner for breakfast." Jenny raised an eyebrow. "A friend stopped by last night and we went to Tai Tung, ate my favorite chow mein and about a dozen other things."

"A friend?" Jenny poured coffee as Becca nodded. "That's all I get, 'a friend'?"

"New doc at the med center, Hematology Fellow. He lives in my building. Nice guy. Maybe I'll have a doughnut." Taking a big bite of a sugar coated doughnut, she sauntered back into the living room. Rich and Jenny exchanged a glance.

"Might need to add 'saucy' and 'kicky' to this week's word list," she said *sotto voce* as Becca walked away, red mini-skirt swinging gently against her opaque black tights.

Guys fingered items, asked questions about pieces of gear. Within an hour everything was gone, even his old skis and torn backpack. People talked, drifted away carrying fragments from the mosaic of Greg's life. Becca reached for her coffee cup, saw her hand shake.

"Too much caffeine," she said.

"Maybe just 'too much' period." Jenny replied softly.

"If you're around for Thanksgiving, plan to join us," Rich offered.

"Going to San Francisco to visit my Aunt and Uncle."

"I didn't know you had family out here." Jenny looked surprised.

"My real father's brother and his wife. My father died before I was three: Uncle Mike and Aunt Hildur kept Marcia and me anchored into the Morgan family. He's a doc, very bright and pretty conventional; she's a no-nonsense Swede, retired Professor of Nursing, does private duty work sometimes, runs three miles a day. Terrorizes her sons but I really like her. I'll turn in the first draft of my dissertation before I go."

She left twenty minutes later. Rich walked her to her car. "You look good today."

"Thanks. Up and down like a yo-yo but I guess that's not terminal."

"Human," he gave her a thumb's up and backed away as she drove off.

She spent the rest of the day editing her dissertation and, after the late night news, watched the city lights. What, she wondered, would have been the result if Homo sapiens had developed right hemispheric dominance instead of left hemispheric dominance? Would spatial orientation be primary and language just an important, but secondary, function? With a reverse in dominance, most people should be left handed, only about ten percent would be right handed. Would people shake left hands? How would things be different? Would the world be in this increasingly crowded pickle as 1970 approached? All the fields that came together in Speech-Language Pathology fascinated her: the brain, the nervous system, language as a system and how it developed in both the species and the individual, the details of human psychology and how disease and injury damaged function. Even at her lowest, the complexity and order of human communication intrigued her.

"Harvey, I walked out last time because I couldn't stand another minute of you talking about my grief. You're so distant. What do you know about my grief? You sound like you're dissecting a bug. Don't you ever react?"

"What were you feeling when you walked out?"

"Oh, for crying out loud. This is Becca: remember me? I don't *feel* about things, I *think* about things. What is all this 'feeling is superior to thinking' crap? You sounded cold and totally rational. I wanted out. I'd heard enough." Silence.

"Becca, close your eyes and tell me what's happening in your muscles."

She complied. "Tight. Shoulders, neck, arms, chest, legs."

"Now relax them, one muscle group at a time. Take your time."

Becca went through the technique, breathing deeply, relaxing on exhalations.

"Feeling isn't superior to thinking; you need both. I believe we can control our responses and that muscles are key. Too much tension and you're in a 'fight or flight' mode: feel angry, frightened, defensive and mad as hell. In childhood, you learned defensive responses so you respond that way a lot. I do care, Becca but I'm not tense and frantic. True, I can't feel your grief but I know it's there. I try to give you information because you do think so much. I want you to use information to break into old patterns and relax."

"Sometimes, when I remember to use this stuff, it helps. The other day after working on my dissertation I felt really good: focused. Then I remembered Hawaii and tightened up. So I stopped, took some breaths and relaxed. And I thought, 'wow, maybe I can do this.' Do your colleagues agree with this?"

"Many do. Some are sure I've 'gone native,' took too many physiology courses, got seduced by synapses and neural transmitters." They sat quietly.

"Speaking of seduction, do you suppose I'll hear from Bernie?"

"Do you want to?"

"I guess so."

"But not sure?"

"He lives in my building. That's a complication. Some of my male grad school buddies have suddenly become fussy big brothers: like I don't know to come in out of the rain. It's awful. I finally told one of the worst offenders to get out of my office, out of my private life and zip up his prurient little mind. He got angry and is now ignoring me which is blissful."

"What did you *think* about telling him off?"

Becca laughed. "Thanks, doc. Actually I felt something: I felt invaded, violated."

"What if Rich did that?"

"Rich wouldn't do that."

"We can all do that. What if Rich did that? How would you react?"

"Ignore him, joke, clam up, evade. Maybe answer his questions. He's my friend."

"Would you feel invaded?"

"Yea, but Rich has rights, doesn't he? Don't friends have rights?"

"To invade you? Maybe you fear losing a friend so much that you'd let him walk all over you? You have the right to protect your borders and the right to whatever your feelings are."

"But if I told Rich off he might…" Becca stopped.

"Abandon you?" Dr. Harvey asked. Becca nodded. "Like Andy did? Leaving you with Eleanor in charge…"

"She did the best she could," Becca shot back.

"Maybe. But you needed better and the result is the fear and anger you live with, the defensive, protective 'little sucker' who is terrified and now, as an adult, how you distrust yourself."

"Can I learn to be better?"

"Of course. You're already learning."

"I've never told anyone this but I think I chose this life. I've had this memory forever: Marcia and I are someplace with a bunch of people and this group is deciding we should all be born and I don't want to. Then I just sort of say 'Oh, all right.' But I wasn't happy about it: resigned and rebellious. Once I agreed, it just happened. I didn't have to agree. But Marcia convinced me. Does that sound crazy?"

"In other cultures people believe things like that, I can't prove it either way. It's your memory, do you believe it?"

"Sometimes. And that sobers me. If it's true," she prepared to leave, her time up, "then somehow I've chosen to go through this." She stood and smiled. "Makes you part of the plan, too."

10

Wrapped in a peach colored blanket and balancing her coffee, Becca looked out over San Francisco. The rising sun glinted from countless windows under the morning-glory-blue, Thanksgiving Day sky that arched toward the bay. Tucked away up in the familiar fourth floor bedroom of Uncle Mike and Aunt Hildur's house, Becca sat by the window. She visualized the three floors below her, each blending carefully chosen colors and artifacts from Mike and Hildur's lives. An enormous portrait of an American Indian woman grinding corn hung on the living room wall providing the core colors used throughout the entire house. Haunting shades of gray, blue, rose, peach and pale green reappeared in various rooms: the effect lingering long after conventional colors would have grown tiresome. Uncle Mike's study, a paneled, dark leather and mahogany space, held stacks of medical books, journals and manuscripts in process.

The Morgans chose to relocate to San Francisco after Mike's stint as a Navy Medical Officer during WWII. They'd lived in this house ever since. Becca felt welcomed here as she padded downstairs to refill her coffee. Uncle Mike had gone to the hospital and Aunt Hildur and Goldie, their current Golden Retriever, were running.

Heading back to her room, Becca stopped on the second floor and sat on the camphor chest facing the stairway wall covered with framed photographs. At the top left hung Mike and Hildur's families. Becca recognized her grandparents and great-grandparents and a handsome photo of her father. Moving on, Mike and Hildur's wedding picture followed by selected shots of the boys, vacations, graduations, rites of passage that all tumbled neatly down the staircase wall spreading out on the main floor to more recent photos: her cousins' weddings, their children and ending with Mike and Hildur's recent trips. Becca loved these photos.

The front door opened, Goldie bounded in and charged up the stairs. Aunt Hildur followed, pulling off her gloves and headband.

"I hope you've left me coffee," she said. A few minutes later, full mug in hand, she joined Becca. "Sleep well?"

"Here, always." Becca scratched Goldie's neck.

Hildur took a long sip and leaned against the wall. "Sometimes the warmth on my hands is as good as the taste." The quiet Thanksgiving morning was punctuated only by the thumping of Goldie's tail.

"I know I'll never have a wall like that. That may be silly but it feels sad."

Hildur watched Becca. Her nurse's eye saw need and strength, confusion and independence, intelligence and uncertainty. Some things in Becca reminded Hildur of Andy.

"What makes you say that?"

"It's so tidy: one lifelong love, one marriage and family. I always wanted that and now I won't have it." She sipped coffee.

"Life is not a series of photographs. You'll have your own continuity. No matter who comes and goes, the main character remains, beginning to end."

"Some of the sadness has Mother's fingerprints all over it. Like I'm supposed to build a wall like yours, like she couldn't and ended up building a shrine to 'Andy the perfect husband and father.' Trouble was he was dead, gone and unavailable and Marcia and I were infected by her need. I feel myself modifying my relationship with Greg: turning it into something it wasn't under the guise of 'build the perfect wall of pictures.' In Hawaii, Greg and I had a terrible fight and I feel myself trying to believe it didn't happen. But it did. And now he's dead.

"Sometimes being single again is freeing and sometimes it's awful: insecure. I don't mean to dump all this on you but you're one of the few sane women I know. Aunt Hildur, what am I gonna do?"

"Live. Mourn. Get through this. Finish your degree. Get a job. Try to stay focused. Ask for help when you need it."

"That's a tall order."

"Yes, but you can do it. You're strong: accept that in yourself. You won't always do things perfectly. That wall of pictures: nobody there lived perfectly, the cast of characters change, people kept moving forward."

Becca studied the wall. "Who's that?" Becca pointed to a picture of Hildur, Mike, Great-Aunt Annabelle, Andy and some young woman on the rocks in Maine.

"Becky Ziminski."

"Becky who?"

"Ziminski. Your father's college sweetheart."

"Is that why mother periodically freaks about my name? Rages if I'm called 'Becky'?"

"Um hum. Andy adored her. We all figured they'd marry. Even Great-Grandma Libby approved. Then it was off. Later Andy met your mother.

"Eleanor felt threatened. She never knew Becky but she knew the history, maybe more than I do. Then your dad was diagnosed with Hodgkin's and your mother got pregnant again. He wanted a girl named with the Whitman family names; she wanted a son. You came along and got the names but she insisted on a different nickname." Hildur smiled. "My mystical Eastern friends would just say 'karma is karma.'

"Now, let's get dressed and put the turkey in the oven before church."

Aunt Hildur had a rule: 'visit my house on holidays and you go to church with me.' It seemed a small price. Hildur, while serious, remained sane and happy about religion. She embraced an eclectic blend quite central to her life. They attended the Thanksgiving service at the small, local Episcopal Church Hildur preferred. Becca sat, stood, genuflected, read and sang: alert for unexpected cues. Hildur smiled, knelt and prayed for the world, the church, the needy, the departed and, this day, especially for her niece.

11

Hildur settled into her recliner and sipped a brandy. "This is a special time: everyone but the overnight guest gone, food stored, dishes washed. Relax by the fire."

They reviewed the day: the food, the guests and the football. Then the conversation turned to family. After a pause, Becca asked vaguely, "What was Libby like?"

Mike leaned back, sipped brandy. "As a grandmother, they don't come any better. I was closer to her than Andy—he was closer to Grandpa Bert. She and I were more attuned. She never went to college but had a fierce intellect." He reminisced. Becca floated in his warm sea of words, memories, images, bits of stories, threads of names, places, odd snatches of conversation, flotsam washing ashore like debris from a sunken ship. Later, remembering the evening, Becca recalled feeling warm and full, content in the flickering firelight, Aunt Hildur's hands knitting, and few details of Uncle Mike's reverie.

At midnight up in the peach-colored room, Becca snuggled down and thought about her great-grandparents, glad to be in their family, hoping she had inherited some of their good sense and strength. She considered making notes about what Uncle Mike had said but never did.

Twice during the night, Goldie padded upstairs and checked on Becca. Satisfied, her sentinel's duty complete, the dog returned to her bed in Mike and Hildur's room.

12

December 10, 1969

"Marcia, listen," exasperation increased as Becca walked to the end of the phone cord. "I'm sorry Mother's pissed I went to visit Uncle Mike and Aunt Hildur."

Marcia continued her classic, detailed explanation about 'our duty to Mother,' all the things Mother's done for us, how one Christmas wasn't much to ask and 'all I'm giving is sisterly advice.'

"What?" Becca replied in mock amazement, "No 'when-you-have-children-then-you'll-understand' chorus? Has the recent burial of my dead husband made some impression on the continuing saga: 'The Morgan Sisters Living Life?' Marcia, get this straight: I'm staying in Seattle over Christmas. I'll work, study and be with friends. I'm not flying anywhere and if you and our often cockamamie Mother fly out here, I will not invite you in."

Becca teetered on hysteria as she dropped the phone into its cradle. Staring out the window, watching the red lights blinking on the three TV towers on Queen Anne Hill, she began to relax her muscles. Marcia and her mother tried to push her into a dependent, prepubescent form she refused to assume. Escape or be destroyed. Drown or be eaten.

December 24, 1969

They arrived after nine o'clock, unpacked the car and started a fire in a very cold stove. Bernie hauled bedding and clothes to the loft, stashed skies, poles and snowshoes by the door while Becca arranged food, heated a skillet for steaks, prepared pans for vegetables and mulled some wine. After the fire caught, they ate chips and drank wine while the steaks sizzled to perfection. They'd rented the 'no-frills' cabin on the Tye River for ten days.

December 25, 1969

"I feel like a duck with these snowshoes on."
"You look like one, too." Bernie trudged off. "Come on, Daffy!"
"Aren't there instructions?"
Bernie stopped, scratched his head in a very professorial way, called back, "Just remember Newton's first three laws of motion: they cover it." He made a large, whole arm gesture. "Move, Chadwick."
"Remember Newton's first three laws," she muttered under her breath, "you always say stuff like that." She waddled off, forcing her feet forward, tripping, weaving, willing herself upright and desperately trying to review Newton. '1. A body at rest remains at rest and a body in motion keeps moving. 2. One object moves another body in the same direction the first is traveling and—oh, shit!—something else. 3. For every action there is an equal and opposite reaction.' She had no idea if Newton helped but, during the concentration, she caught on. Suddenly her body felt centered, feet moved better, arms swung more smoothly. He waited in a bright, sunlit clearing.
"See, Chad. Newton works—till you get to relativity."
She grinned. "What's the second part of the second: the one about a body moving another body in the same direction?"
"Look it up, you'll remember it longer."
"Don't you know?" Her voice half teased.
He took off his sun-goggles. "Of course I know, Becca, but rely on yourself. Not on me. Not on anyone."

December 31 1969, 11:30 p.m.

Flickering light from the fireplace skipped and danced up the walls, playing shadow-games on the beams and roof. Warm and tired, she traced idle designs on Bernie's back as he slept with his head against her neck. She felt their nude bodies from her neck down to where his right big toe brushed her left calf. He never forced sex. He enjoyed her, enjoyed himself, encouraged and responded to her desires and caresses and, by so doing, managed to please them both. She felt physically relaxed, mentally alert. Part of her still believed that in a sexual relationship she should want marriage ('should' writ large as a cultural imperative). Another part sensed that marriage might not be necessary; her comfort level for that idea vacillated.

Concentrating, she felt the sheet move as they breathed. Deep within her, a shadow person existed, familiar yet foreign. She reviewed the process of human life: first two cells, then 4, 8, 16, 32, 64, 128, 256, 512… the marvel of exponential growth. Even now, within her adult body, cells reproduced all the time. What if every cell in her body suddenly doubled? Or created a negative of itself: Becca existing simultaneously with an anti-matter Becca. Who was this woman who enjoyed Bernie as her lover, accepting and giving, without demands? Was this healthy? Could she maintain it? Did she want to? No possessive scenes or outbursts? Or had they chosen each other precisely because, at the moment, neither could tolerate more than this 'arm's-length share my body, my bed, my mind with no commitment' relationship?

Firecrackers exploded at a nearby cabin. Bernie roused, shifted and mumbled, "Happy New Year."

Becca replied, "Happy New Year." She curled around him, wondering what she knew about him and herself this first day of 1970. '1. I care for him but don't want marriage. 2. This confuses me. 3. Maybe I need to get beyond Newton.'

As she closed her eyes, Greg smiled through her keyhole-memory from their first date. She pictured a clown holding helium balloons, put Greg's face inside a yellow balloon, had the clown release the strings and watched them float away. She smiled and slept.

February 3, 1970, 3:00 a.m.

> *Grief lays down marks*
> > *trails*
> > > *like dry river beds in deserts.*
>
> *From high enough*
> > *we'd know*
> > > *the map of our sorrows.*
>
> *And yet, a grief too great*
> > *to be contained by ancient tracks*
> > > *must dig new paths*
> > *and leave behind*

> *some cutoff ponds*
> *sealed within the landscape*
> *of our being*
> *with no escape*
> *for them or us.*
> *And while these silent pools*
> *sit isolated*
> *from the sea*
> *we rage or cry or wilt.*
> *Oases by long-dead torrents*
> *wither slowly in the sun*
> *until a passing traveler*
> *hardly knows*
> *an ancient lake was ever there.*
> *But scarred landscapes*
> *and scarred hearts*
> *remember.*

Becca toyed with word groupings, alternate terms, punctuation and capital letters. Maybe she should omit all talk of pain or grief: just write about rivers in deserts. Any nitwit should see the connection.

"Who am I?" she asked aloud in the half-lit room.

A confused widow, a graduate student looking for a job, a woman with a nice lover I don't want to marry, a Speech/Language Pathologist and a very bad poet. Those all sound like 'what' I am not 'who' I am. She turned off the light and went back to bed.

February 3, 1970, 1:30 p.m.

Her patient was a 78-year-old retired career officer, two weeks post-stroke, not yet stable. Becca had seen him twice. He understood some things but his expressive language consisted of long strings of gibberish interspersed with angry profanity followed by sobbing. No formal language evaluation could be done yet. Eric Robertson acted frustrated so Becca assumed that he realized he was spewing nonsense and, for her, this was a good sign; he knew he was in trouble. Patients who babbled nonsense, oblivious to their own disability, had a more guarded prognosis.

Walking into the waiting room, Becca recognized Mrs. Robertson from the chart note. 'Attractive, younger than her husband,' didn't do her justice.

"Mrs. Robertson, I'm Rebecca Chadwick. Please come in." They sat in the small interview room in the Neurology Department. "I've only seen your husband twice but the Resident said you wanted to talk."

Felicia Robertson's blue eyes looked tired, her blond hair was swept back into a perfect French twist. She wore an expensive, tailored, light blue suit.

"People keep saying Eric's 'not stable.' Mrs. Chadwick, I don't know what that means." She twisted her handkerchief in tight hands and gazed at Becca.

"It means that how he is today doesn't predict how he'll be tomorrow or next week. For awhile, we'll sound evasive."

"Meaning," Felecia said softly, "you can't tell how he'll end up."

"That's right." Becca nodded.

Felicia leaned back, sighed. "I married Eric 26 years ago, I was about your age; he was 56. My family told me the age difference would become more difficult. It hasn't been easy but being 30 to 56 was different from 52 to 78." Felicia resumed her earlier posture minus the handkerchief wringing. "I don't know why you got this. You seem more open, less defended than the doctors. I'm usually not like this."

"You're dealing with difficult things: sudden illness and uncertainty. When communication's impaired life gets more stressful. I'll be working with your husband and we'll want to keep you informed and involved. If you want to see me our secretary can arrange times, she knows my schedule."

Felicia stood. "Your secretary called you Mrs. Chadwick but you aren't wearing a ring. Are you married?"

The question surprised Becca. "I'm a widow."

"I see." Long pause. "I'm sorry."

Becca watched Felicia Robertson's impeccably groomed back move away as she heard a chorus of internal, competing messages. She evaluated their professional interaction, filed away some details and wondered if the Robertsons could use counseling. Then 'the little sucker' exploded: 'she doesn't have the foggiest idea—what does she mean: "I see." What does she "see"? And what right does she have to pry into my private life?' Finally something like a moan arose deep inside. Becca finished her chart note, grabbed her jacket and purse and left.

February 3, 1970, 3:30 p.m.

"I'm like a circus clown balancing plates on sticks. Most of the time I don't get caught in internal conversations."

"What was the moan? Heard it before?" Dr. Harvey asked.

"Nope," Becca closed her eyes. "Low sigh. Primordial."

"The little sucker?"

"No, she just screamed at Felicia. Got really mad. I don't know why. This woman has things 'together' compared to many wives of stroke patients."

"Then why the rage?"

Becca glared at him. "I don't know Harvey. You tell me."

"I don't know your answers. The 'little sucker' may, or at least point the way. Can you get inside that anger?"

"All Mrs. Robertson said was 'I see,' then she paused. Then: 'I'm sorry.' Jesus, Harvey, widowhood before thirty deserves more than that! What did WWII rate? 'Hum. Dreadful shame.' I wanted," Becca felt her throat tighten, "I needed…" She snapped her chair into an upright position. "Shit, Harvey. It doesn't make sense."

"It may to 'the little sucker.'"

"This is crap. I'm not going to let you manipulate me into something totally nuts." Snatches of dreams, whiffs of memories sped by like the images from a train window as it raced by another train going the opposite direction: flickering patterns, familiar but blurred. The dream-bird screamed again 'you must see' but faded as a hidden, black secret sealed over tightly.

"Becca, what's going on?"

"You want to hurt me. You want me to tell you something, even a lie, just so you win."

"Win what? Hurt you how?"

"All I know about 'the little sucker' is that she protects me. I don't know more. It's muddled. Maybe just hormonal high jinks. Maybe reaction to Greg's death: sort of post-traumatic stress by proxy. War: men die and women survive: maimed. Maybe I just create stuff. You know when I told you I chose to be born? Harvey, you know that's absurd. Maybe this other—" she waved her hand dismissively, "is all boloney. I've been through rough times, I have my dissertation to defend, job interviews next week. I have plenty to do other than worry about some mythical figure I may have invented for drama."

"I won't pass judgment on whether you chose to be born but right now some part of you is terribly defended. Becca, what's so awful? Why all the rage and terror? Even if she's an hallucination, why dream up 'the little sucker'?"

"It's like a big, dark well; it's blank." She paused, right fingers moving aimlessly over the back of her left hand. "It's there but I've never gotten close enough to look into it."

"But something exists."

"Yea. Like a sick dream where things roll over you and paralyze you. Like something's going to happen and you can't scream. But not like I know this chair or Bernie's body or the taste of an apple. Vague, shadowy: curtains blowing at night. More like mist than rain."

"Let's try something. Close your eyes and try to look out through other eyes, 'the little sucker's' eyes."

Suddenly, Becca flung herself out of the chair. "Not gonna do that. Time's almost up and I have work to do." Gathering her things, she danced through a speedy exit ritual, straightening her clothes, checking for keys. She nodded and fled.

He'd seen it before: tight muscles, movements clipped like an old film running too fast, he could almost smell her fear. In his notes he jotted 'I may have seen the grown up version of her protector, the little sucker, just walk out. Protecting her from what?'

March 6, 1970, 4:25 a.m.

Becca slept, breathing fast, her eyes flickering. Images revolved like galaxies in her brain. One spark caught her attention and pulled her into a dark metaphor. Crawling on damp ground, the little sucker's hands and legs moved swiftly toward the dark stain on the ground. 'That's a hole.' She knew about holes. Creeping to the edge, puppy-like, hesitant, peeking in then pulling back. Far away, at the bottom, lay a gaunt, emaciated baby, staring up with unresisting eyes. 'The little sucker' knew her task: keep the baby protected, hidden and alive. Slowly, the image disappeared as a dense fog flooded Becca's sleeping mind and the wounded baby remained safely in the well. Becca rolled over and adjusted the sheet.

April 10, 1970.

"Two good offers: different balance of responsibilities. Both decent starting salaries, not much research support. Both places have dreadful winters, so what? This is your first academic position, what more do you want?" Rich bit into a doughnut and sloshed coffee into his 'Good Morning Daddy' mug.

Becca looked around. She had removed all personal traces from their joint office: no pictures, no small accumulation of private items, no post cards, nothing remained to identify her. Rich's desk exuded personality: family pictures, a trilobite imbedded in a million year old rock, little flags from exotic drinks, 'we love you Daddy' homemade valentines.

"True," Becca said, exasperated. "But I'm paralyzed. How do I make this decision? How do I leave here, leave you and Jenny, Bernie and Dr. Harvey? How do I choose between Madison, Wisconsin and Missoula, Montana? Madison's closer to my family."

"Distance doesn't make any difference. You can…"

"Oh yes it does. Even Einstein says space bends close to heavy bodies and my family are real heavy bodies."

"You can't stay here. Jen and I'll be leaving next year, you'll never have more than you do now with Bernie—sex with little closeness. That won't get you through another winter."

Becca protested but Rich waved his doughnut at her. "And something else from the new physics: everything's always changing. Don't let chances pass you by while you sit trying to remember lines from some half-forgotten poem.

"Your problems, Chadwick, are, first: you aren't hungry enough—three mouths to feed and a mortgage would help. And second: nobody prepared you to live on your own. The lights come on and you freeze like a rabbit. You have two good offers. Flip a coin, throw a dart, look up the July average temperature and choose the highest but for God's sake, choose."

April 18, 1970.

She signed the contract with the University of Wisconsin, wrote a letter to Missoula, dropped them in the mailbox, and walked briskly to Ocean City to meet Jenny for Dim Sum.

After they'd selected items from the carts, Jenny raised her cup of tea.

"Here's to Madison."

"Thanks Jen, but I'll skip the tea. One more drop of caffeine and I'll explode."

"Okay," Jenny said taking a big bite of Hum Bow, "but that's no reason to starve."

Becca stabbed a shu mai with her chopstick. "Do you suppose there's any decent Chinese food in Madison?"

"Nope. Just beer and cheese."

"What if I've made a mistake?"

"You haven't. Wisconsin's a great school. What's Madison like?"

"Midwest. Lakes. Feels familiar. Has pretty good cultural stuff. The campus is hilly. Students look generic—a little grubbier than here."

"And your family? Far enough away?"

"Sometimes I figure the moon wouldn't be far enough away but I have to live on this planet and make my own life."

Jenny puckered her lips. "Um hum. True. Not easy but that's okay. Call when you need me. I'm good at the 'atta girl, do it Becca, yea team' stuff."

"Why do we need it and guys don't?"

"Well, guys do need it. But they're reared differently, pushed to be much more independent much earlier. Given different tasks and rewards. I'll bet you got the 'don't be good in math because the boys won't like you' lectures just like I did."

"Right! But I'm making progress—I no longer even try to wear ruffled blouses."

"Fine. No frilly blouses. Just plenty of challenges about making it in what still clearly *is* a man's world. At least in the US in 1970, women can be more competent, we have better birth control and it's legal." She raised her cup of tea. "Here's to all the women who came before us and made things better."

Becca raised her cup. "To that I'll toast even if all my nerves unhinge." The tepid tea slid over her tongue as she pictured the only photo she had of her Great-Grandmother Libby.

May 15, 1970.

Becca summarized the background of her research, covered the methods and results section and glanced around the conference table at her committee: all males. Two smiled vaguely, two ruffled the pages of her dissertation. The fifth sprawled uncomfortably in his chair, chewed gum and watched the ceiling. She waited. No one spoke. She knew this game: let the candidate talk herself into a corner. She glanced at her thesis director. His advice had been: "Don't defeat yourself. They're being paid; make them work. You know this topic better than anyone. Fritz'll chew gum, stare at the ceiling. He always does."

The two 'smilers' looked at her director. "What questions do you have?"

"If I had questions we wouldn't be here."

'Oh, great,' thought Becca. 'Not even a softball—but he knows this process.'

"Mrs. Chadwick, on page 27 you introduce the early ideas of 'meaning within structure'…" One of the page shufflers droned on.

'Probably only read to page 28,' she thought, but remained relaxed: answered his inquiry.

Fritz scratched his head, asked the ceiling, "Chadwick, how do families, neurologists and nurses do with this system?" She wanted this question, quickly summarized the relevant work and recounted the feedback from co-workers and families.

"My aim is to relate results in ways that people can understand. Most physicians and nurses ignore longwinded, jargon filled reports: they appreciate direct suggestions. When families ask 'How can we help Pop,' I want us to offer real assistance. People need short phrases, key words that provide guidance." Her advisor smiled. Fritz chewed faster. One paper shuffler frowned. She continued.

"Many Speech/Language Reports look like University Seminars and they confuse people. I try to present complicated issues so regular people can understand them."

"The neurological correlates of language disorders cannot be completely described to a second grader, Mrs. Chadwick. I fear you present our information to other professional groups" (meaning 'physicians you want to impress,' Becca mused) "as simplistic."

"Look, we all know 'introduction to anything is selective lying.' We may differ on when and how much to simplify. I use neurological terms when it's appropriate. When physicians see families interacting better, patients being included and responding better as they enter the world of 'brain damage'—a world into which they have been unceremoniously thrown—with hope, a few helpful techniques, then the professionals pay attention. Families need useful guidance."

The discussion ended and she was sent to the hall to wait. She hadn't shot herself in the foot. They might want additional work but she doubted it. She'd learned enough: how to do research, how to ask questions better and when to stop.

The door opened. Her thesis director stepped out.

"Dr. Chadwick, please join us."

She stood, steadied herself and followed him into the room again, her student days over.

Thirty minutes later she walked into her apartment: it looked just as it had when she left this morning. Tonight she and Bernie would celebrate. Tomorrow Rich and Jenny were throwing a party. She'd finish up here during the next six weeks and head for Madison. She looked over the city trying to recall lines from Archibald MacLeish, Kenneth Fearing and Lawrence Ferlinghetti and wondered what it would feel like to jump from this fifth floor lanai. The idea stayed longer than usual. She walked to the bathroom dropping her clothes across the living room. She let the warm water from the showerhead pummel her head and shoulders, soaped her body mechanically. She felt hollow and lost. She'd earned her doctorate. She'd accepted the position in Madison. Greg was dead.

13

July 4, 1970.

Becca pulled over, stopped and got out of her car. Everything ached; heat reflected up from the pavement. A few miles ago, she'd left the Interstate, that marvelous invention that seemed to suck the life out of the small towns it now sped past. She scanned the map: Platt, Canova, Emery, Bridgewater, would they die?

Quail Hill

Pouring orange juice into a cup, she studied the dilapidated house that had caught her eye. She walked passed the old, broken 'No Trespassing' sign and stood under the large tree shading the front porch. One partial wall remained; everything else had sunk down into itself. Circling the remains, the process became clear. First the roof went, then the upstairs collapsed into the main floor that gradually sank into the basement. A jumble of vines and weeds coiled through the wreckage.

The only strong point was the chimney. Surrounded by thick ivy vines, strangled by them actually, neither the chimney nor the ivy could now survive alone. They gave each other form, stability, skeletal strength and stood sizzling together in symbiotic dependence on this South Dakota farmland. What happened here? Who hung the sign? Had there been happier 4th of Julys: with picnics and ice cream? Was the Interstate cause or symptom, disease or cure?

Becca returned to her car as the temperature soared. She stopped early at a motel with a pool, watched the local fireworks while submerged in lukewarm pool water and slept fitfully as the woefully inadequate air conditioner strained to break even.

The next day in mid-afternoon, she entered Madison from the north: somehow that seemed important. In her mind she drew an imaginary protective wall between Madison and her family. The wall began at the southern tip of Lake Michigan, ran through Rockford, Illinois, over to the Mississippi at Dubuque, Iowa and then ended up at Minneapolis-St Paul.

She settled into a motel three blocks from campus, showered, changed and walked to the Student Union. Brightly painted metal tables and chairs cluttered the expansive patio that stretched between the Student Union and Lake Mendota. Couples sat focusing on each other; groups held 'university' conversations: "But Paine didn't say that." "What consequences would you be willing to endure for your beliefs?" "Awful, professor! Grades like a beast."

She walked into the Rathskeller, bought their largest coke, went outside and sat at a shaded table. Surrounded by voices and laughter, she relaxed into the rhythm of the patio. Tomorrow she'd check in with the Department, jump through the administrative hoops, officially become an Assistant Professor and look for a place to live. Today she'd be a visitor, a thirty-year-old brunette widow watching boats sail on Lake Mendota. Welcome to Badger-land.

14

Color splashed across October diverting Becca briefly from her work as she headed from her apartment to her car. Fall disappeared in teaching, supervising, reviewing the curriculum and attending Faculty Senate. Her Chairman also assigned Medical School activities for 'our mutual benefit.' She felt like a fish attacked by cats. When to do research? The question braided itself with 'how to survive teaching' and 'what about an outside life?' Arriving at her office, Becca made a firm resolution to walk each noon and enjoy fall's beauty; it lasted ten minutes.

"Good morning, Dr. Chad," the secretary's condescending voice chirped.

"Good morning, Linda. Any messages?"

"Two students dying for your attention. The Merrimac called. 'Consult by noon with report.'"

"The Merrimac?"

"Dr. Fischman, the wicked witch of Otolaryngology." Linda slapped three phone memos on the counter. Becca mumbled thanks and headed toward her office. Linda's passive-aggressive behavior toward her—carefully never displayed before the male faculty—had become as predictable as the flowers on her 'I'm the perfect secretary' desk.

Becca had met Dr. Nicole Fischman three times. The encounters had gone well but she understood the nickname. Dr. Fischman, forty something, tall, grey-blond hair pulled back severely, little makeup, dark suits and plain blouses, sensible shoes, half glasses perched on a slender arched nose, was as alert as a hunting cat. Becca called the number, got the nursing station, arranged to see the patient at 11:30. 'At least my afternoon's lecture's ready,' she thought. 'Lord, will I ever adjust?'

The patient, a sixty four year old, post laryngectomy, heavy-smoking farmer had his room littered with crumpled papers on which were written emphatic commands to his harried wife. The TV blared, the man fumed, threw the electrolarynx across the room when Becca suggested he try it. She spent fifteen minutes with him, promised to see him again and left. As she wrote her chart note in the small conference room Dr. Fischman walked up.

"Well?"

"He's angry, frustrated, rejected the electrolarynx and esophageal speech—I demonstrated both. His wife seems scared of his disease, his anger, the future. But not of him."

Dr. Fischman looked at her sternly. "How long will it take to get him his own electrolarynx and what services are available in his hometown?"

"We should be able to get him an electrolarynx in a couple of days if you order it—"

"Doesn't your department stock them?"

"No more. It has to be ordered on these forms." Becca placed three copies of the order form on the table. She wanted to hand them to Dr. Fischman but didn't trust her hands not to flutter like trapped birds.

"More damned paperwork."

"But I'm not sure he'll accept it. Of course, in the next couple of days, he may bury himself under crumpled paper: that may help our cause. I feel his wife's an asset. As to esophageal speech, I'll contact the Lost Chords Club and get someone in here ASAP." The stern look continued. "If you approve." Fischman nodded slightly. "I'll find out what's available in his hometown. And either I or one of my graduate students will see him everyday..."

"You, Chadwick. No graduate students: you."

"They need to see patients. They need to learn."

"Then they come with you, they stand behind you, they watch, listen, take notes but they stay away from my patient and his family. Understood?" Becca nodded. Dr. Fischman removed her glasses and rubbed her eyes. "Fine." Becca didn't move. "Something else?"

"In my experience," Becca began, "it's easier if I'm included in a pre-op visit when possible, so I'm not just another stranger making patients feel like specimens. That can get the paperwork started and arrange contact with other laryngectomy survivors earlier."

"My life isn't tidy, Chadwick. I work all days, all hours, short notice. Can you do that?" Becca nodded. "Okay, give my secretary all your phone numbers. We round at 7:00 a.m. Come tomorrow and present your findings." She picked up copies of the electrolarynx order forms and fanned herself. "If you have more of these, bring them."

Becca relaxed. "I salvaged files when I arrived, I've got more. Where at 7?"

"Oto conference room on the second floor. Bad coffee. No doughnuts. We *start* at 7. And thanks, Chadwick." Becca nodded and turned to leave. "What happened to your predecessor? Gracefield? Hairdo like cotton candy."

"I never met her." Becca shrugged. "She didn't get tenure."

Nicole pressed her lips together, shook her head and muttered softly. Then she pulled out a notepad and jotted a note to Esther, her mother-in-law.

The next Thursday evening, carefully following the instructions Nicole had included with her note and dinner invitation, Becca turned into the circular driveway of the Fischman's home.

"You must be Rebecca," Max greeted her at the door.

· Other Places ·

"Everyone calls me 'Becca.' And you're Professor Fischman." Becca extended her hand. He towered over her and, at 6' 4", over most people. Looking up at him through his thick glasses, his magnified eyes made her feel like a bug under a microscope but his warm, inviting smile put her at ease.

"Here, I'm just Max. Welcome."

Becca was the only dinner guest. Max's mother, Esther, who spoke in a heavy Yiddish accent, served an excellent meal.

"This is the best food I've had since I arrived!" Becca commented.

"My secret is the phone number of the best caterer in town. Keeping all three of us and the grandchildren—when they're home—fed and clothed, plus some volunteer work, is my job and my joy." Esther beamed.

Over coffee, Nicole asked, "How's it going on Main Campus?"

"Okay, Dr. Fischman."

"At the hospital, use titles. Here, I'm Nicole. From my vantage point, your department's a snake pit for women. Now, how's it going?"

Becca hesitated. "Probably okay. Teaching and clinical work take so much time, I don't know when I'll get research started—a common plea—and there's little money available."

"Then you start without time and money," Max stated bluntly.

"What Max means, Becca, is that nobody in your department's necessarily on your side. Your position's been a 'turnover' Assistant Professorship for years. They rotate promising young females through but never grant tenure. 'Such a shame woman A, B and C didn't make it.' It's 3 to 5 years and out. But the men make it: get support and get tenure. It's politics. Do you understand this?"

After an awkward silence, Becca spoke. "I know there are politics. My stepfather taught Business Courses for awhile at a small college before he switched into banking but he and I aren't close." She spoke slowly, looked at her three hosts while her hands toyed with each other. "I like Speech Pathology and I'm well trained. Before my husband died, I figured we'd build careers together. Now I'm on my own."

"When did your husband die?" Esther asked gently.

"A year and a half ago, in Vietnam."

"I'm so sorry," Nicole's voice held more sympathy than Becca expected. "How are you doing? Are you past the worst of it?"

"I sleep better. I'm not as scared as I was but I know I'm scarred. That's not a very good answer but it's the best I have."

"There's no right or wrong answer, Becca," Esther said sweetly. "Healing takes time."

"The main thing is, can you move on?" Nicole asked. "Really move into your new role?"

"Well, I'm standing, I've got the job so I need to give it my best shot."

Nicole nodded. "Women make predictable mistakes. Many are avoidable. It isn't easy; there are no guarantees. Even those of us who succeed and head departments don't fully understand the game yet but we're learning and we can help. Much of what I know about academic politics I learned from Max and a few close friends. And, without Esther, or somebody like her, succeeding would have been much more difficult."

Max gave his 'women who succeed in academia' speech as Becca listened intently.

"It sounds hopeless."

"Not at all. You have your degree; that's your union card. You're in the door. But you need a plan."

"What," Becca asked seriously, "do I need to know?"

"A lot," Nicole replied. "Tonight we'll start with the basics." For the next hour they mapped out a five-year 'follow the dots to tenure' program.

As they began, Max slipped a stack of 5 X 7 note cards in front of her. "Take notes. You'll never remember all this." They talked about getting research support from the department in polite, tough ways: people she should see about writing grant applications: faculty in other departments who might be helpful. They discussed teaching techniques and how to write good, quick-to-grade exams. They talked about clothes and people to cultivate and avoid. She needed a mentor; they identified the man to approach and how to approach him.

"Before I turn this over to Mama," Nicole concluded, "you must never, never, never give your secretary the only copy of anything you own—including your shopping list. She will undermine you anytime she can."

Becca blinked. "I've been afraid of that."

"You're right to be."

Esther then suggested a cleaning woman she could hire.

"But there's only me," Becca protested.

"Are your male competitors scrubbing floors, ironing blouses?" Esther became animated. "Becca, if you're serious, get organized. Delegate all the homey stuff. Concentrate on work." The discussion trailed off and Becca left at about 9:30.

A cold wind from the lake whipped around them as Nicole walked Becca to her car. "I can't thank you enough," Becca started, "but I am wondering: why are you doing this for me?" Becca ruffled the 5X7 cards.

"I see some of me in you. I'm sick of watching women marched onto the field, then handed a football and not taught the rules so they fail and the 'old boys' all shake their heads. 'They just can't hack it.' Most men, many unwittingly, act so damned superior. It makes me angry. You've done a good job for me so far. I've never burned a bra or joined NOW so I owe something to the cause. Besides, you're right in front of me."

Becca tilted her head, "What?"

Nicole smiled. "That's an old Jewish mandate; help the person right in front of you." She hugged herself against the cold. "Here's what I tell my kids: 'You can call me at work any time you need me but try very hard not to need me.' Madison's a great place, solid students, interesting patients. It's a beautiful city and a great University. Winter's cold." She held out her hand. "Good luck and call if you need me."

As Becca drove out the driveway she saw Nicole's fingers brush the mezuzah by the door. That simple, faithful gesture startled her: appeared incongruous for this hard-driving surgeon. By the time Becca reached home, her head throbbed. After placing the 5X7 cards on her desk, she swallowed two aspirin and some vitamin C with a glass of orange juice. She looked over her schedule for Friday, reviewed her lecture notes for her 11 a.m. class, reread the 5X7 cards and went to bed.

Friday rushed by. After work, she went to the University Bookstore, bought herself a three-year calendar and a 'thank-you card' for the Fischmans. That evening she created her 'first three-years' plan incorporating her notes from the Fischmans with the information the University had given her during her 'new faculty orientation' meetings.

Early Saturday morning the ringing telephone stabbed Becca awake. "Hello?"
"Hi, sleepyhead." She recognized his voice instantly: refused to admit it.
"Who's this?"
He laughed. "Steve Montgomery."
"What a surprise, especially at 8:00 on Saturday morning."
"I'll be in Madison by 11, you can show me around. You have three hours to rearrange your schedule. Had business in Minneapolis yesterday and I'm on a big driving circuit. I leave Madison Monday for Chicago and then home. So today and tomorrow belong to us."
"Look, I'm busy and…"
He wasn't listening. "And I'm up early because I want to see you. Decide where we're going for lunch. I'll arrive about 11."
"I really AM busy."
"I know. You have three hours to be 'really busy' and then I'm going to save you from yourself. I want to see you; you want to see me. Make the arrangements. Bye for now."

'Damn! Just what I need.' His attitude was so cool and self-confident, so 'Steve.' She felt her body responding. 'Shit.' Three hours to write lecture notes for Thursday and Friday and organize her 'get-a-mentor' project.

After a campus walking tour they drank cold beer and tore into 'seared over flaming coals' steak sandwiches at the Brathaus. Leaning forward in the dark booth, Steve took Becca's right hand, raised it gently to his lips, kissed her fingers and licked her index finger.

"Good choice. Very carnivorous." She tried to pull her hand away but he held it firmly. "God, you look good to me." He leaned over and kissed her, pulled back abruptly and took a large swallow from his beer. "So, Becca, how're you doing as an Assistant Professor?"

Confusion and anger flooded through her. Becca didn't want to play 'mouse' to his 'cat.' Always she had been able to keep a protective distance from Steve. Now she felt victimized, defenseless and aroused. Why was Greg dead? Where was good, solid Bernie? Unsupported, could she deal with Steve's power? She felt raw.

"I'm trying to figure that out, to make a successful plan." She related the events of her dinner with the Fischmans Thursday night. "It makes me wonder if I'm in over my head. 'Play it this way, dress like this, don't talk to so and so, finance your own pilot projects, don't teach so well, write easy-to-grade exams, hire help, eat prepared food, don't spend time cooking, limit time with friends, trust no one.' Heck, Steve, who wants to live like that? They're right: my department's never granted tenure to a woman. Most of the men treat me like a pet poodle and all of the Master's level female supervisors—all married with kids who see career as a sideline—avoid me except when they need help. The only other woman with a doctorate is here for one year while her husband does a post-doc in physics. Now enter Steve Montgomery playing lustful, extracurricular games. Steve, I won't do this."

He leaned forward, his eyes no longer taunting. "Then don't 'play,' Becca, be—just be. Lustful? You bet. Extracurricular? When we were younger you never gave me a real chance; then you waltzed off with Chadwick. Game? Never. Not the way you make it sound. Not to me." His eyes flashed. Then the familiar, sly smile slid across his face. "Fischman's right. It's a tough world. You want to win, you've got to play the game."

After lunch, they walked the shore of Lake Mendota between the Union and Liz Waters dorm, hand in hand, arm in arm. They talked and laughed. He kissed her lightly on the neck, the ear. Back at her apartment he kissed her hard, pushing her against the wall, searching her mouth with his tongue, pressing his erection against her. He put his hands around her neck and kneaded her muscles. Stabs like burning metal shot down her shoulders.

"Oh, God," she moaned.

"Your muscles are tight as steel." He walked her to the living room, sat her in a chair and began massaging her neck. After a few minutes he paused, retrieved a joint from his pocket, lit it and held it to her lips. "Here, this'll help."

It had been years since she had smoked dope and she didn't relish the stinging throat, loss of control and altered sense of time it promised.

· Other Places ·

"Come on, lovely. You're just going to 'be' this weekend." He inhaled deeply from the joint, bent down, held her head back firmly, fit his mouth over hers exhaled into her mouth, moved his hand down her neck, across her chest, kept exhaling and fondling her breast. She inhaled the acrid smoke. He moved his mouth away, let his hand slide to her waist, knelt beside her and placed the joint in her mouth. "Good, isn't it?" He licked his lips, smiling. They smoked in silence. He ran his fingertips up the inside of her leg to mid thigh. She moved her legs, inviting him further but he simply watched her, grinning. Drawing the last toke on the joint, he stood suddenly and pulled her up. "Let's go get dinner. I passed a Chinese restaurant on my drive in."

A candle flickered on their table in the back corner of the ornately decorated red and gold room. Fragrances wafted from platters passing by. Becca felt high and disoriented. Away from the University, the restaurant contained an odd mixture of people and they blended in. They concentrated on each other and the food. They laughed and ate, enjoying the flavors exploding in their mouths.

Back in Becca's apartment, Steve lit the two candles on the dining room table, turned on the late show—some absurd 'creature feature'—lit another joint, kissed Becca into a reclining position on the couch and undressed them both slowly. He began touching her quickly, exploring her body, toying with her, almost entering her but then pulling back. Soon his controlled seduction graduated to lust. They rolled onto the floor clutching and releasing each other: trying to escape from their lonely lives. Finally exhausted, they slept. A black and white test pattern remained on the TV.

He left Sunday afternoon at 4:30. Becca showered, washed her hair and reread the notes she'd made at the Fischmans. After a dinner of a toasted cheese sandwich, tomato soup and three glasses of milk, she chose her clothes for Monday (blue suit, yellow blouse) gathered what she'd need in the morning and went to bed. Steve lived hundreds of miles from Madison, got to town 'once or twice a year.' She didn't want this involvement but she ached for closeness.

At 3:00 a.m. she woke drenched in sweat, tears streaming down her face. The shark circled again. She went to her desk and made notes for two lectures. At 6:00, holding her first cup of coffee, she pictured Greg's grave and shuddered.

The winter passed in a swirl of increasing anti-Vietnam War activity; protesters demonstrated regularly. Becca felt torn. 'If the war is meaningless, what's Greg's death?'

15

As mentor, she targeted Gerald Gilbert. Distinguished, nearing retirement, former 'young tyrant' in the field, he produced interesting research, had grown daughters in professional careers, acted the 'absentminded professor' and knew everything. Apparently asleep at faculty meetings, he would cut decisively through discussions, hardly opening an eye or un-sprawling his lanky body. She cultivated his support, sought his advice on funding sources, casually waved a file labeled 'Research Ideas' past his drooping, ever alert, eyes. In early November, he walked into her office and pointed to the file on her desk.

"You have copies?"

"Yes."

He picked up the file. "I'll read 'em."

"Thank you."

Tapping the file with his index finger, he gazed at her, pursed his lips, smiled slightly and turned to leave. "No promises," he muttered waving the file.

The next morning the file, in a sealed envelope, sat in her mailbox. Inside, cryptic red comments splashed across each proposal. Two carried one word: 'NO.' One read 'Possibly later—consider pilot and student project.' A fourth earned: 'Interesting but not as a major study—rework and submit to P for department start-up grant.' ('P' referred to the Department Chair.) The fifth energized her: 'Complete by Thursday according to attached instructions—I'll seek funding at convention.' He would attend the annual professional meeting of the American Speech and Hearing Association. Becca would go for 3 days and was presenting her dissertation. In the envelope were instructions and an additional note.

Good morning.

What you undertake is dangerous. STEP CAREFULLY. Many landmines. Use my typist. She expects two manuscripts ASAP. Keep P informed: he hates surprises.

Good luck.

gg

Becca smiled as she filed the rejected proposals and slipped the others into her briefcase along with two books, a notebook with extra pens and headed for the library.

"Hi, Linda, I'll be at the library," she said as she passed her secretary's desk.

Linda arched one perfectly plucked eyebrow. "I told Fred, the new student, you'd be in. He's having trouble reaching you."

"Have him check my office hours and leave a note if nothing works. Just standard procedure." She tried to sound light.

"You might be nice and wait, he'll be here soon," Linda fiddled with papers.

Becca said calmly, "It's best to meet at a mutually agreeable time."

"I believe, Doctor Chadwick, he's been ill. It won't kill you to wait."

Becca saw this 'no-win' situation clearly and knew their discussion had little to do with Fred. While she wondered how Nicole might handle this, Fred walked in.

"Oh, good, Linda said you might come by. Unfortunately, I can't meet with you now. Let's see if we can find a good time."

"Linda said this was your office hour"

"Sorry," Becca replied, gesturing to the bulletin board with FACULTY OFFICE HOURS posted conspicuously. Linda typed furiously.

"Tomorrow at 10 is perfect," Fred smiled brightly, "I didn't know this list existed."

"Fine," Becca nodded in Linda's direction. "I'll be back after my 'Intro' class."

Becca kicked a rock as she approached the library. People hunched against the cold wind, folded into themselves, moved across the quadrangle going to and from the Student Union, the Historical Society Building and the Main Library or headed up State Street or Langdon. She kicked the stone again. The leaves were gone: the trees bare skeletons. She recognized no one.

She often ate at the Union, stayed at the Main Library or the Medical Library until late. Alicia came every Wednesday, cleaning, scrubbing, washing and ironing clothes, changing linens and leaving a hot dinner in the oven. Wednesday nights became Becca's night to relax. Esther's insight that she needed support was remarkably on target. Even after these few weeks, Alicia's work lifted burdens.

The Wednesday before convention in November 1970, Becca poured herself a glass of Liebfraumilch, served Alicia's chicken stew and sat down to eat. The phone rang. Eleanor felt lonely.

"Biff's at a meeting. You only call on weekends and never write. Marcia comes over every week."

"I'm pretty busy during the week."

"Are you well?"

"Yes, I'm fine."

"Have you met any interesting men?"

"No."

"Well, are you trying? Joining clubs, getting active? You need to advertise to sell," Eleanor laughed huskily.

"I'm busy enough, I've got a lot to do."

"You work too hard."

"And I have a wonderful cleaning lady who even cooks dinner for me Wednesdays."

"For one person? A cleaning lady? Are you so fancy-dancy with all your degrees that you need a cleaning lady? No man will ever want to marry such a spoiled girl!"

"I'm over thirty, Mother: hardly a girl anymore. Look, my dinner's getting cold, why don't I call you later?" Eleanor hung up without responding.

Dumping her stew back into the pot, Becca grabbed her coat and went for a walk. Her breath puffed out like the smoke from locomotive-engine pictures in some children's book: "I think I can, I think I can." Becca remembered Eleanor's dramatic reading voice from long-ago bedtime stories. Hot tears ambled down her cheeks. How had their relationship deteriorated to this? Why did Eleanor always imply that whatever Becca did was wrong?

She shook her head resolutely. "I'm going to get tenure. It's a worthy goal and I'm not going to be tied down by Lilliputian-strings from Eleanor or anybody. Maybe that's how I'll figure out who I am." Her word-breaths floated through the falling snowflakes toward the streetlight.

Back at her apartment, she copied key phrases from her notes about getting tenure and taped them around her apartment. Then she poured another glass of wine, served herself dinner on a clean plate and ate. Now more relaxed and focused, she called Eleanor.

"Are you apologizing?" Her mother's voice sounded petulant.

"My dinner was getting cold. Now we can finish our conversation."

"You hung up on me."

"That's debatable but I wanted to finish dinner and now I have. Did you call for any special reason?"

"Yes, but it doesn't matter now."

Becca took a deep breath and refused to play this game. "Okay. Things are going well here and I hope to get some funding for my research at convention next week."

"Research, teaching, job: you are so dull. What about me? You haven't come to see me. Come visit and we can have some funzie."

"Mother, you sound like you've been drinking."

"You should've married Christopher. He's alive; his mother has lovely grandchildren."

"Christopher? You're joking! When we dated you said, quote, 'He's a nice boy but if you marry him and have Catholic children none of you will be welcome in my home' unquote."

"If you'd been willing to follow your heart that wouldn't have mattered."

"I see. I should have defied you so you'd now have Catholic grandchildren you threatened to disown."

"I would have loved them."

"You have Phil and Cynthia, they're lovely grandchildren. Now, go to bed. Biff will get home soon. Get some sleep."

"But I live only for you, I love you the most."

"I love you, too, Mom. Now go to bed."

Becca hung up, sat for a long time with her head in her hands, then stripped, showered, looked over tomorrow's schedule and went to bed. She slept fitfully. The bird swept down toward her head, screeched shrilly, shouted unintelligibly, swooped lower, ever lower.

After convention she got another sealed envelope.

Chadwick,

Two leads on funding. Cards attached. I introduced you to both at convention. Each will call you. Provide all requested info. Tell P when they tell you to.
KEEP YOUR HEAD DOWN.

gg

She followed his advice and things began to look up as the winter closed in.

Crocuses blooming under the snow gave her the first glimpse of spring in April 1971. Folks said spring would be 48 breathtaking hours and it appeared to be starting on Friday. The weekend loomed, scheduled hour by hour. Pulling into her parking space, she saw him standing with his hands behind his back, grinning boldly and bowing slightly. 'Damn,' she thought.

"You could smile at an old friend," he said opening her car door.

She stepped out. "Look, Steve, I don't like surprises, dropping by unexpectedly isn't a good idea and I have a busy weekend ahead." Resolute. Definite. No-nonsense.

He stepped back, pursed his lips and swung a huge bouquet of long-stemmed red roses in front of her.

"I knew you'd be mad." The roses unnerved her. He closed the distance between them, kissed her lightly and closed the car door behind her. "Now take me, the briefcase and the roses in; put the roses in a vase, me on the couch with a drink, the briefcase by your desk and yourself in the shower. We have reservations at the Edgewater. You have to eat so why refuse a free meal?" He maneuvered her out of the parking lot, toward the security door.

The voices of various members of her internal committee battled in her head. 'Do not let him in!' (The smell of his aftershave mixed with the roses.) 'Why can't he be an occasional lover?' (He took her keys and opened the security door.) 'Are you crazy? First, he's married.' (In the elevator he kissed her neck softly.) 'This is trouble with a capital T. He does drugs!' (She could feel herself responding.) 'Marijuana's not that big a deal.' (They stepped out on her floor, moved toward her door.) 'Illegal and dangerous! YOU AREN'T THAT LONELY!'

But she was.

16

Spring turned to summer and summer to fall. She taught, did research, followed her plan, submitted papers, wrote grants, met occasionally with Nicole and joined an informal female-faculty support-group. Three weeks before Thanksgiving 1971, P requested a meeting.

"Come in, come in," P flashed his 'golly it's swell you're on my faculty' smile. "And you've been awarded a grant all on your own." He sounded like a kindergarten teacher speaking to a slow-learning child.

Becca coughed and nodded thanks.

"Are you ill?" P actually sounded concerned.

"Just a sore throat."

"It would help if you could teach two courses this summer," he came right to the point.

"My contract makes summer teaching optional and I taught last summer. Two straight years of teaching's a lot."

"With Gilbert cutting back, we all need to pitch in. Understand that I" (he emphasized the word) "want to help your career, too. It would just be courses you've already taught."

"My grant will support me and a student without teaching."

"And of course you are up for contract renewal next year..."

Blackmail! They stared at each other. Becca took a deep breath. "One course. Intro Phonetics," she said hoarsely.

"Fine," he smiled broadly.

Becca rose and left P whistling to himself and filling in his course chart. She felt angry and powerless. Things would improve when she got tenure and more grants. She'd make some new contacts at convention next week.

The Saturday before Thanksgiving, she arrived back in Madison from convention having had a very successful trip. The papers she and her students presented went well and it looked like more grant money would be coming her way. By the time she entered her apartment her cough and sore throat had escalated.

Tuesday, she couldn't eat, could barely talk. Liquids felt like molten steel in her throat. Breathing hurt, her fever raged and all nerve endings felt connected to her throat. After struggling through her last lecture of the week, she stumbled to the University Hospital in hazy delirium, staggered down the hall to the Otolaryngology Clinic. Light hurt her eyes as she approached the admitting desk. The nurse knew her and managed to keep her from falling.

"Page Fischman, STAT, to Room 6 and get me a resident NOW!" The nurse said half dragging Becca toward the 'Emergency' cubicle. "Just a few more feet, Dr. Chadwick," she said, pushed Becca into the exam chair and stuck a thermometer in her mouth. "You're burning up."

The senior resident stepped in and took charge. Becca bobbed in and out of consciousness. Sharp sounds smacked into her, chocking and gasping she fell forward sinking toward the floor. Strong fingers grabbed her shoulders; Nicole's face swam before her. Nicole's lips moved but Becca had sunk under waves of pain and heard nothing. Nicole shook her, scowled, moved her lips more and slapped Becca across the face.

"Snap out of it, Chadwick." Becca heard sound now. "How long have you been sick?"

Becca tried to form a word but her mouth disobeyed. She held up two fingers, concentrating carefully.

"Two days?" Becca shook her head. "Two weeks?" Becca nodded and, feeling irrationally proud of this accomplishment, slumped in the chair and slid toward unconsciousness.

"No you don't. Stay with me. Do what I tell you." The sharp voice jolted Becca.

"We're going to examine you and it'll hurt."

'We? Who's we?' Becca wondered. Her head rolled back and three strange heads peered down, one wore glasses. They bounced around, made Becca dizzy so she closed her eyes.

"OPEN YOUR EYES, CHADWICK. I DID NOT TELL YOU TO CLOSE YOUR EYES. DO WHAT I SAY. LOOK AT ME!"

This screaming person was mean: Becca wanted to leave, to sleep. Hands from all directions held her, cold hard things ripped at her throat: she choked, bit down but something blocked her mouth open. Terrified by the hands and loud voice she opened her eyes, saw two of the funny round heads move away before the bright lights blinded her.

Becca awoke in a hospital room, an IV dripping in her left arm. Nicole Fischman was writing in a chart.

"Hi. Glad you came around before I left. How do you feel?"

· Quail Hill ·

"Better," Becca mouthed. Her throat burned. Nicole slid the bedside table with paper and pencil on it in front of her.

"Writing's easier. You have acute epiglottitis and you're lucky to be alive. We did a tracheotomy. You'll be in here a few days then you'll be fine. Your emergency contact listed your Mother so she's been notified."

'Great,' Becca wrote.

"There's the holiday weekend coming up and it will be good to have someone with you. Now when did this start and how did you keep going so long?" Nicole smiled.

Becca wrote: '1. Two weeks ago. 2. With difficulty. 3. You sounded mean. Was I awful?'

Nicole shook her head and pointed to #3. "Delirious, choking, half dead from lack of oxygen, dehydrated, trying to bolt from the chair—model patient. The main complication was that, when we did your tracheotomy, the medical student vomited. We're suggesting he consider psychiatry. For me, just a normal day. Push the nurse call-button if you need anything."

'I'm thirsty,' Becca wrote.

"Start with ice-chips and water then whatever you want. They'll bring you a light dinner. The Resident will check on you later…."

'What?! Not you? Some butcher in training?' Becca scribbled, repressing a smile.

"Touché, Chadwick. I'll be in tomorrow. Get some sleep."

Eleanor arrived late Wednesday. They ate Thanksgiving Dinner at the hospital and Becca went home on Friday. Eleanor cooked meals, rubbed her back, shopped and bought interesting foods. They took walks. Eleanor attended the two classes Becca taught on Monday: commented only that Becca sounded too serious. Later they walked up Bascom Hill. Standing next to Lincoln's statue, Becca asked a question she'd never asked before.

"What was I like after Andy died?"

"Willful. Lost. Hurt. Angry. Scared. You never stopped being scared."

"Did you?" the question just burped out.

Eleanor looked at her feet. "Tough question. Maybe not." She paused. "No, that's not right. I did stop being scared but I've never gotten back to the place on the other side of his death. I'd depended on him so. But you were there, are there, to fill that void and replace him." Eleanor took Becca's arm.

"But I can't do that Mom." Becca stepped back, peeled Eleanor's hand away. "I've never been able to and I'll never be able to replace him and it feels—heavy. Lord, I don't know how to say this: you hang that responsibility on me and your expectations slip around like mercury. 'You must finish your education, Andy would want that.' And when I do, it's 'nobody will want a woman with all these degrees.' After Greg died: 'you must get a good job.' Well, I have one and now 'you should have married Christopher' or 'you're working too hard' or 'you sound too serious.' Mother, I know you love me and I love you but I'd like some support for being who I am. You are pressing hard for grandchildren: like that's the only value I have. I'm not Andy. I can't replace Andy. And part of the problem is that I've tried, I try to fill the void for you and feel guilty that I can't but that's crazy."

"This is a fine way to treat me when I gave up my holiday to come and take care of you."

"I appreciate your coming and I guess I hoped maybe we could at least talk about, try to make sense out of, our convoluted relationship."

"If you didn't want me here, why did they call me?" Eleanor jutted out her chin like a five year old.

"You're my next of kin. I was hospitalized; it was an emergency. They called: that's the system."

"Then maybe you'd better not list me as next of kin—find someone else. And don't talk so much you'll damage your voice permanently."

"I won't injure my voice, you heard what Nicole said."

"You don't know what she told me privately. Mothers talk to mothers. There may be some things you shouldn't know." Eleanor straightened, avoided eye contact, adjusted her coat.

"That's madness. Nicole didn't tell you secrets. My voice is fine. Why do you do this? Why is there always some special secret known only to you? Why do you play this game?"

"You think it's a game? To give up all my opportunities and devote myself to you and Marcia? That's not a game, that's duty. Even if you weren't the son we wanted…"

"Don't throw that at me! You decided to have a second child after you knew Andy had Hodgkin's. I'm just the kid who came along. I'm sorry he died; God knows I've missed him, too. Being without him hurt all of us; but I can't be Andy, I can only be Becca."

Eleanor's gaze skimmed Becca's face. "I never should have named you Rebecca: it's a funny name. I should've called you Andrella, combining our names. Maybe you'd have turned out better."

Becca stood in shocked silence. It always came back to her sex and her name. Suddenly, she laughed.

"What's so funny?" Eleanor demanded.

"Is this about Rebecca Ziminski? Mama, he named me after Great-Grandmother Libby not some college romance."

"Who told you about her?"

"There's a picture on Aunt Hilly's wall of folks in Maine, she's there and I asked who she was. Mama, let it go. I like my name, I'm proud of it."

"Hildur shouldn't keep old pictures hanging around."

"It reminds them of a good time in Maine, it's no big deal."

"You always take her part. You prefer her."

"No, I don't prefer Aunt Hilly to you but I can relate to her, she can help me with some career things and she and Uncle Michael tie me to my Morgan family." Becca reached for Eleanor's hand but Eleanor pulled away. They walked to the car in silence.

Later, as Becca brewed tea, Eleanor asked, using her most innocent voice, "How's Tippy?"

'Oh, shit,' Becca mused, knowing the next chapter: 'Why aren't you like perfect Tippy?'

"About the same," Becca replied evenly. "Worrying whether her 6 year old daughter and 7 year old son will get into Wellesley and Harvard. She's complaining that Hank doesn't make enough money, redecorating her house every year and herself more often. She talks about opening a design shop, which would be great, use her talents and burn energy. We talk regularly. I remind her that single life's no picnic and she reminds me that marriage is complicated. We're good for each other."

"Don't be snide. You're jealous. Tippy's a daughter any mother could be proud of."

'So what am I,' Becca wondered, 'chopped liver?' Instead she said, "Tea's ready."

"Tea, ugh! How boring. Don't you have any wine or bourbon?"

"Of course, I'll get you some wine."

"Will you join me?"

"No, I'll stick to tea. I've been sick and I teach early tomorrow."

"What's the matter, can't handle both liquor and work?"

Becca ignored the comment as she poured Eleanor's wine and her own tea.

The next morning, Eleanor left early. At the car, Becca hugged her and said, "Thanks for coming. Drive safely."

"Well, I'm surprised that matters to you."

"Mother, that's hardly fair."

"Fair?" Eleanor got into her car, roared the motor into action. "Since when is a Mother's life 'fair'?" She closed the window and sped away.

Becca's breakfast pitched in her stomach. Why was it like this? This never-ending verbal knife-fight. Why couldn't she free herself, walk away and stay away? 'Andrella, indeed. Thank heaven Andy won that round.' Becca felt like Brer Rabbit and the Tar Baby: trapped by her own struggle.

Five days later, Hildur put down the phone and walked into Michael's study.
"Becca's right. Eleanor sounds awful."
"Another bad phone call?"
"Yes, she's furious. 'You're trying to steal my daughter, you just have sons and are jealous, you shouldn't have a picture of Becky Ziminski hanging up for Becca to see.' Weird. Becca doesn't appreciate her sacrifices and should list you and me as next of kin."
"Drunk?"
"Drinking, certainly but drunk? Not sure. She never came to terms with Andy's death and Becca and Marcia sometimes look like flies stuck in the emotional spider web she's woven since then." She leaned over and kissed him.
"I'm not sure I've come to terms with Andy's death, Hilly."
Hildur smiled at him. "But you didn't let it freeze you. They all have frozen parts."
He nodded. "You're a good nurse Hilly, now go call Becca."

17

By mid-February 1973, the department granted Becca a second three-year contract. She celebrated with the Fischmans.
"Tonight we celebrate. A toast," Esther raised her glass, "to your new contract."
"You have twelve to eighteen months to prepare your portfolio for tenure." Max added.
"Will our two clinical notes help?" Nicole asked.
"As long as I have enough data-based publications and it looks like I will."
"What's the political landscape like?"
"GG is in my corner but he's only half time now. 'P' acts supportive: I taught last summer and hired his students. The Experimental Phonetics folks will just add up publications; they're pleased I teach a good Intro to Phonetics course. The two audiologists occasionally mutter 'if it's not done with electrodes it's not science' but at least one of them is getting more interested in how the ear connects to the brain which leads him into my area. I'm bringing in grants, publishing and presenting papers." Becca shrugged. "I'm on track."
"Good," Max smiled as he refilled their wine glasses. "How's the rest of your life?"
"What 'rest of my life?' I'm after tenure."
Esther pursed her lips. "We never said break the First Commandment."

Becca looked stunned. "The First Commandment? Fight for tenure wearing a 'Ten Commandments' straightjacket?"

"A what? What nonsense have you been taught?" Esther scrunched up her normally happy face.

Max patted his mother's arm. "Probably some common misinterpretations, Mama. Becca, what's your religious background?"

"We went to a Congregational Church, Sunday school, high school youth group. A neighbor liked to read us Bible stories. A Catholic friend here, a Jewish classmate there."

"And the Ten Commandments? What's your understanding of them?" Nicole asked.

"What's to understand? 'Do this, don't do that.' Walk the tightrope; shut down most human emotions."

Esther rolled her eyes. "We see them as a gift not a tightrope. Our creator reaches through creation and speaks to Moses: 'I created you and I alone know how you can live in joy and peace as I designed you to live.'"

"First," Nicole began, "don't worship anything that isn't the true creator—including an academic position. Second, don't try to represent the great 'I am': it will confuse you." Nicole looked at Max and he continued.

"Third, don't swear an oath using my name unless you mean it. Fourth: Keep the Sabbath holy: six days of work are enough for you, your hirelings and your animals. Fifth…"

"This one is mine." Esther interrupted. "Take care of your aging parents: they cared for you when you were dependent, repay the debt. Six, a bit more complicated than it looks: don't lie in wait for an unsuspecting traveler and kill him. And good old seven: once you are married, keep your marriage vows. "

Nicole spoke slowly, "Eight. Don't take anything that isn't yours: no stealing. Nine. Don't say anything that isn't true: no lying."

"And finally number ten, don't envy: don't even covet what isn't yours." Max ended the list. "Do these things and you'll live well: doing otherwise gets you into a mess."

"See, Becca," Esther concluded, "not a straightjacket: a gift."

Driving home, Becca played the evening over in her head. The 10 Commandments these Jewish friends knew were different from what she'd been taught about these ancient texts.

***** Take-out Chinese-food by flickering candlelight. Incense, wine and grass: his Canoe and her perfume. Hands and fingers playing familiar patterns. Caresses to the edge of pain, rhythms escalating to the madness of release reverting back to self-loathing.

· Other Places ·

***** "I'm sorry," Becca said, genuinely confused, "I don't understand your question." Introductory Phonetics held few secrets. Our mouths make speech sounds in various locations and these places in our mouths are charted against the various ways we have of making speech sounds, producing the tidy 'Place and Manner of Articulation' chart. Simple. Clear. Not to Miss Coleson.

"But if they don't do it that way in Tibet, if they use our [t] for [k] how do we transcribe it? 'Tee' or 'Kay'?"

Becca tried again. "If the *sound* they make is what we define as [k], you transcribe it as [k]. If the *sound* they make is what we define as [t], then you it transcribed as [t]."

"You're not answering my question," Miss Coleson stated pedantically.

Becca tried to speak calmly. "Miss Coleson, I'd like you to reread Chapter Four and come to one of my office hours. Then we can talk more. Now, we need to move on." The class sighed collectively. Miss Coleson was a pain.

"She won't answer my question," Miss Coleson kept repeating in a low voice. Becca stared at her, wondering how to help, wanting very much to say 'Your question has no answer other than what I have given time and again and I will not allow you to delay this class any longer. This is a simple concept in this field: one without which you cannot progress.' Instead, she turned back to the class and continued.

"One of the most important aspects of 'manner of articulation' is voicing. As we've discussed, most consonants come in pairs with both a voiced and a voiceless version…" Becca enjoyed teaching, notwithstanding confused students, and, after four years, taught confidently. Confused students stumped her. As her publication list grew, her grants increased and graduate students sought her for their committees. She was on track to obtain tenure in her fifth year.

***** A group of faculty regulars often ate dinner at a corner table in the Student Union. Occasionally a few of them went to a play or a movie. The women discussed their mutual challenges. Rarely, a skinny guy in Math took her out. Sometimes she ate at the Medical School cafeteria. If a kind of self-conscious seriousness marked the faculty at the Union, frantic intensity drove folks at the Medical School. At either location she'd recognize people, if only to nod. She had made a few friends but remained loosely connected. This evening at the Union, recognizing no one, she settled into a table alone and began grading papers as she ate.

Her fragmented existence stemmed partly from the fact that many couples excluded single females from the general commerce of the married world, and partly from the fact that the single set in her age group, particularly those 'never married,' were an anomalous lot. Occasionally, a newly divorced male prowled around looking for sympathy, sex and strategic planning for weekend child

· Quail Hill ·

visits: not an appealing trilogy. Steve's infrequent short visits acted like a weed, chocking off healthier relationships and demanding nothing of her except rare and finite involvement. She burrowed into her career as focus moved toward fixation and intensity bordered on obsession. Her one outlet was running: she now ran almost daily.

As Becca ate and graded papers, the wind whipped the water into sparkling white caps. She noted Miss Coleson's third-grade cursive writing and wondered vaguely if the young woman might have a brain tumor or be mentally ill. She scribbled a note on the exam: 'Please use my office hours. If none of my scheduled hours work, I'll arrange to meet with you some other time.' She signed it, put the exam in her briefcase and headed for the library: fifty more papers awaited her attention.

***** "No, Steve. I'm swamped." The fact that he'd called her office rattled Becca.

"You always are. I'll be there about 6 tonight and gone by 7 in the morning."

"I won't see you. End of story."

"Bullshit. You'll see me. You know you will. Don't kid yourself. Get out the massage oil, the Chianti, the candles. I'll bring the pizza. It's February and we both need warming. It's Thursday, take a break. If your not there I'll find you. Madison's not that big." A cold chill shot down her instantly straight back as Steve hung up. She stood and walked down the hall.

"P wants you in his office at 4," Linda said, not looking up from her typing.

"Today?"

"Of course today, Chadwick."

"He usually gives more notice."

"He mentioned it the other day. I haven't seen you since then."

"Notes in my mailbox work."

"It's only 2:30, you have time to pull stuff together."

"What stuff?"

"All your tenure stuff. Don't look annoyed. If this were Dr. Fischman you'd break your neck to get there. Show the same respect for your own Chairman. Or are there other aspects to your relationship with Dr. Fischman?"

"Don't be ridiculous." Walking back to her office, Becca fumed. Fortunately she kept her file up to date and locked safely away. What if this meeting ran late? Would Steve show up here? She hoped P would be on time.

"Ah, Rebecca, how good to see you." By the 70's, an unwritten law had developed at Universities: all male faculty referred to all female faculty by complete given names or last names only: possibly a first step toward full acceptance. She shook hands with P and he led her to his informal seating area where he held all his 'chummy' meetings. A good sign?

"We need to have a little chat," he looked at his watch, "but I don't have much time. How're things going?"

"Quite well. I've brought my file and…"

"Oh, no need for that today."

"Linda said you wanted it."

"She must have misunderstood," he looked quizzical. "Actually I want to talk about the clinical supervising staff. How are they?"

The question surprised her. "I enjoy working with them, certainly they're essential for our students. With our high turnover of supervisors we're always bringing someone new onboard and that takes time for the lead person. Only two of our current supervisors have been here as long as I have; most leave after a few years. With our presence at the Hospital expanding, they're working to streamline record keeping. Our current staff is strong and they seek advice at appropriate times."

P looked serious, tapped a pencil on his knee. "Should we put one person in charge of the whole supervisory process? Say, someone with a doctorate who wouldn't need a 'real' faculty appointment: no research or teaching? More a permanent support position, Senior Clinical Director, something like that? Someone who could handle all issues so the 'real' faculty wouldn't be bothered? Give that person an administrative assistant."

Becca wanted to barf. Two sources for this idea popped into her head simultaneously: both were plausible. Either this was just another attempt by some members of the department's male hierarchy to remove her from competition, move her into a totally clinical position (read 'supportive therapeutic work where women belong') or it had Linda's fingerprints all over it. If the former, then the intent was simply part of the eternal struggle to keep women locked into the status of 'lesser beings,' people who should do 'sweet, supportive things' and it needed to be confronted. If the latter, then Linda wanted to sideline Becca into a Clinic Director role and promote herself to Administrative Assistant. Becca pursed her lips and worded her reply carefully.

"Might be a good topic for the whole faculty. If you found such a person, all of us 'real' faculty would love more research time. Do other faculty find the supervisors' requests bothersome? The questions I get seem appropriate. But we could consider a new model." She sat back, hands relaxed, legs crossed and remained quiet.

"Well, er, yes, I see what you mean." P blubbered. "Linda mentioned it might be something you'd want." He looked at her questioningly. She shook her head and smiled faintly. "Then I guess it's a good thing you brought your file. Is it up to date?" She nodded. "I'll look it over. I'm sure we'll consider you for tenure this year. There shouldn't be a problem."

"That's nice to hear. I do enjoy my work here."

"And both the faculty and the students appreciate your teaching and research." P smiled and they stood. As Becca turned to leave, he asked lightly, "Have any supervisors indicated problems with Linda?"

Becca paused. "Why do you ask?"

"When Lois left she indicated there might be problems that I, a man, wouldn't see."

Becca spoke carefully. "Linda didn't grow up in a home that supported education; she never attended college, married early and had children. Sometimes that may chafe a bit. She sees those of us with advanced degrees as privileged. We make more money and do more interesting work. She's a hard worker but sometimes her priorities concern me. Generally, work requested by a man takes precedence over things requested by a woman. I doubt she feels she's appreciated enough. She might enjoy taking some courses, things available to staff with the Chair's approval. She's certainly bright enough and I doubt she'd ask."

"That's a nice idea. I'll talk to her about it." P smiled broadly as Becca left.

Walking back to her office she wondered, 'why don't men think of this stuff?'

She arrived home at 5:45, showered, slipped into her red lounging outfit, lit some candles and poured herself a glass of wine. Steve arrived at 6:05.

"You're prompt," she greeted him.

Balancing the pizza he eyed her silently. "Well, look at you."

"Tonight, we celebrate. P indicated I'd 'have no problem' in a tenure vote."

Steve put the pizza and his briefcase on the table and then pulled her toward him. "Let me be the first to congratulate you properly." Holding her close, he kissed her hard and ran his hands down her body. "Or improperly, as the case may be." He breathed in her perfume. He stood back and, with a sardonic half-smile, took a joint from his pocket.

***** "You won't answer my questions and you make fun of me."

"Sometimes your questions are unclear. I'm sorry if you feel I make fun of you, I don't intend to. I'm glad you've come in so I can spend more time than I can give you in class."

"I'm as important as anyone; you should answer my questions."

"I try Miss Coleson, and you are as important as any of the other 37 students. I must think of the whole class: they understand this concept. During office hours, we can talk more."

"You don't make sense. Now," Miss Coleson sighed and used her inappropriate third-grader voice, "if the people in Tibet use 'tee' for 'kay' how should it be transcribed?"

"The difference between a sound, something spoken by some human being—technically an 'allophone'—and a little written squiggle that we arbitrarily use to represent that sound when we represent it in writing…"

"T and K are not arbitrary, Dr. Chadwick."

"But the written squiggles we use to represent them are arbitrary, Miss Coleson. That is precisely the point. We could assign any symbol to represent any sound…"

Miss Coleson jumped up. "You don't try to understand me. You don't listen to me. You don't help and you don't care." She marched out abruptly and did not turn when Becca called her. Becca stared at the young woman's back; four more students waited outside her office door.

Later, she went to see GG, seeking his wisdom.

"Some students never understand basic concepts. Maybe she shouldn't be here. If she fails, she fails. It isn't kindness to keep her here."

"What if she's sick?"

He raised his bushy eyebrows. "You spend too much time at the Med School."

"Really, what if she has a brain tumor or is psychotic?"

"Tell her to go to Student Counseling, send her to the medics, document your actions and treat her like any other student." He dropped his feet from his desk to the floor and sat upright, staring at her. "Damn it, Chadwick. You are not a mother hen! Stop clucking. You want to pat hands and bandage knees? Then you get the hell out of this University. This is 'the major leagues' not a summer camp. Some students don't belong here; some won't make it. Tough. Our job is to do research, push back the curtain of ignorance, chip away the edges of the unknown and teach. In that order. Sometimes women, even strong women like you, drive me nuts. You play too many positions. Let the quarterback, quarterback; let the coaches, coach; play your position and for God's sake leave the spectators in the bleachers!"

Becca's body tensed. She'd never seen him this angry.

"I guess I need to hear that, thank you."

"Hearing it isn't enough, Rebecca," he said firmly, "if you belong here, act on it."

***** "Tippy, what do you mean 'Hank left?' Like moved out?"

Tippy blubbered. "Doesn't want to be married to me. Oh, Becca," wailed her college roommate, "what am I gonna do?"

'Throw a fit and get on with your life,' Becca wanted to say but instead she continued evenly, "Maybe he doesn't mean it. What led to this?"

"Nothing," more waterworks, "out of the blue. 'I'll support the kids and you until you get your business going, I have an apartment. If you want, I'll handle the divorce myself.'"

"Don't you dare let him! Get your own son-of-a-bitch lawyer and get one fast. If he's really leaving, you need money."

"Right," Tippy stated, now focused and clear headed as a judge. "It'll take awhile to get things settled. The kids will go to camp in Switzerland this summer, Hank will be in his apartment and you and I can go to Europe again, like after junior year."

"Tippy, the sheets aren't cold yet. Talk to a lawyer and then…"

"I hired one two days ago."

"Two days ago? When did Hank leave?"

"Three days ago. In Europe you can teach me how to be single again. It's been ages since I looked at another man seriously. We can see everything we missed: all those Italians."

"Whoa, stop re-organizing my life. And 'all those Italians' are fifteen years older, married and overweight. Furthermore, you didn't miss many last time."

"That, roommate, was unkind."

"Hold it. I recall dragging you back to hotels and hustling you into bathrooms so you wouldn't puke on the floor. Let's not rewrite 'our trip to Europe.' We had some good times but I don't relish a second round while you do a long-distance divorce and try to recapture your youth." Silence. 'Oh, shit! I've screwed up,' Becca realized.

Tippy's wailing began again. "I need something for me and us in Europe would be perfect. You can't desert me, too."

"I'm not deserting you."

"How am I going to face the women at the golf club? I won't be a member anymore. It's men only."

"Which," Becca mused, "will drastically reduce the number of emotional scenes in the powder-room."

"Don't be heartless. This isn't funny." Tippy, once again, sounded totally clearheaded.

"I know but you're a yoyo. Stabilize. Take some time. See a counselor."

"We saw a counselor once. It didn't help. The marriage is dead. My ego's a mess. I'm embarrassed. 'Tippy, the perfect, disintegrates at thirty five.' I don't know how to get up 'cuz I've never fallen. How am I gonna get through this?" She was wailing again.

'BY YOURSELF FOR THE FIRST TIME IN YOUR LIFE!' Becca wanted to scream but asked, "Have you called your mother?"

"Have you called yours? Are you kidding? It took three days to call you. I'm a mess. I scrape my head off the ceiling and then hit bottom with a thud. Becca, help me. Go to Europe with me."

Raw pain sucked Becca in. Eleanor knew it. So did Tippy. "I'll check my schedule."

***** "Jenny if one more person says 'Becca you must take a vacation, you need a change of scenery' I'll scream."

"You already are."

"What?"

"You already are screaming." Silence. "How long since you've had a break? And no, professional conferences don't count. You visit us every two years and we talk often but it's always the same: you have some project, some grant application or some paper due. There's more to life than patients with brain damage. There are friends, movies, symphonies to hear, paintings to see. You've become a machine. Greg wouldn't want you to live like this."

"Foul. Low blow. Unfair! Even from you, Jenny. Greg's dead."

"So you die too? No involvement, no interaction? Ice Queen, big brain, computer head? Your life is madness."

"Focused. This Department's never granted tenure to a woman and I'm going to change that. I'm fighting for all women here—"

"Very noble. 'All women' don't want to become robots to gain paper acceptance in a driven world. Hey, Rich is trying for tenure too and he's not this obsessed."

"Jenny, it's the only game in town and it's the one I'm playing. And Rich is male, unfortunately that still makes a big difference. I'm the only one in my department assigned to four committees. Know why? Because 'we need our female faculty member's opinion.' If I complain, I'm not fulfilling my obligations." Her voice sounded weary. "I enjoy eating and see no reason why, just because I'm female, I'm paid less and thus have to buy ground beef. I want some of the expensive cuts, OK? I like doing research; I don't want to do just clinical work, 'women's work.' And people keep trying to sideline me into a subservient role. I'd like to be recognized and get a raise."

"You never spend a nickel. Why bother? As near as I can tell all you do besides work is run. Do you have any social life? Any?"

"There's a guy who comes by."

"Comes by when? Who?"

"Don't pry."

"We care about you, we miss you…"

Becca sighed. "I have to do this."

"No, Bec, you don't. You are making decisions: you are not compelled to do this or do it this way. Take a trip, get away from those damned five by seven cards stuck all over that Danish Modern showroom of an apartment. They're still there aren't they? Those little signs telling you what to do?"

"Yes, Jenny, they're here because I need them: they help. You social workers love self-help stuff—'everyday in every way we're getting better and better.'"

"You're becoming impossible!"

"Oh, Jenny, I've always been impossible."

***** Becca sat huddled in her jacket on the wall by the Student Union patio. The calendar said 'spring' but the cold wind and waves on Lake Mendota disagreed. Saturday, 11:00 a.m., time to repent about the call with Jenny. Why did she cut her friends off? What was happening to her?

Scenes with Tippy in Europe fifteen years ago tumbled around like more pebbles at a tide line. London and the changing of the guard; Brussels, the World's Fair; Paris, Florence, Rome. How young and excited they'd been. Sitting on the curb in Paris, looking up, up, up at the Eiffel Tower outlined against the blue-black, star-studded night sky. Sweltering in Florence's July heat made almost bearable by the Uffizi and gelato. St. Peter's in Rome: Michelangelo's masterpiece of space and art pointing beyond life and death to something else. What was it Max said? 'This great I AM: power beyond power, mystery beyond mystery.' Yes, Michelangelo knew that God.

Curled in these memories, other images lurked: Tippy sick from sherry in London, barfing beer in Brussels, both of them woozy from red wine in France and Italy. During the trip Becca called Eleanor regularly: part of the deal for her support. Feeling particularly miserable one night in Florence, Becca tried to shorten the call but Eleanor wanted to talk to Tippy who lay stricken and barely conscious on her bed.

"Tippy isn't feeling too well: really needs her sleep." Hearing this, Tippy sat up, grabbed the phone and carried on an Academy Award worthy conversation.

"How wonderful to hear your voice… Well, you're special, too… What a great time we're having… Of course I'll take care of Becca… Bye, bye." She threw the phone at Becca and raced to the bathroom with her hand over her mouth.

Eleanor raved about perfect Tippy, more pleasant than Becca. That room, with phone and tiny bath had cost a fortune and Becca always regretted the expense and the phone call. After hanging up, she lay on her bed, tears seeping onto her pillow as she fell asleep. Shortly thereafter, for all intents and purposes, Becca stopped writing to Eleanor.

Musing things over as she watched the waves crashing on Lake Mendota, Becca decided that, now that they were older, it might be fun to return to Europe with Tippy. She did need to get away. They could have fun.

***** "Becca, how wonderful to hear from you."
"More to the point, how are you doing Tippy?"
"Super. Really great."
"That's good, Tippy. Hey, we're in luck. I can get away for July. Hot in Europe then, but it's the best I can do."
"Oh, I forgot to call. No can do. Hank's back, all repentant and loving so we're going to Europe together, isn't that super?"
"Yea, I guess so. What happened to the 'dead marriage'?"
"Revived and terribly exciting. Got to dash. Tee time in half an hour. Bye."
"Hope you break par, bye." Becca hung up muttering, "when will I stop playing Charlie Brown to everybody's Lucy?"

***** "Congratulations Associate Professor Chadwick," GG smiled as he stuck his head in her door three days after the announcement. He then continued down the hall, absorbed in his own little world, humming softly.

Becca smiled a tight smile. She felt pleased but continued to reel from other reactions. Eleanor remarked, "How nice, I didn't know you wanted that so much. Will any man even come near an Associate Professor?" Tippy 'had to dash.' Marcia brushed off the news and then accused Becca of distorting Cynthia's mind with dreams of competitive swimming, which, according to Marcia, might imperil her daughter's salability in the marriage market more than good math grades, something Becca also encouraged. Nicole and Max celebrated with her and then began plotting for Full Professorship.

Becca would call Aunt Hildur and Uncle Mike; they would understand.

18

"Tenure accomplished: wonderful. How will you reward yourself?"

Becca laughed. "Maybe take a week off before I assault a Full Professorship. I cleared my July calendar for a trip Tippy and I are no longer taking. Maybe I'll travel then, visit you guys, drive across country, something." Pause. No response. "Aunt Hilly? Are you there?"

"Yes." Pause.

"What's wrong?"

"I'm scheduled for surgery Monday: breast lump. Probably nothing. Just hard to plan ahead, which is silly for a nurse of my age."

"I'm sorry. I don't want you to be sick. Can I do anything?" Becca's voice caught and she felt unsteady.

Quail Hill

"On Monday, send prayers or positive energy whichever you prefer and plan to come in July. I'm strong; I'll be fine. And I really am proud of you. Now I have to catch a bus or I'll be late for an appointment. Uncle Mike will call you Monday."

"I love you Aunt Hilly," Becca blurted.

"I love you too, Bec. Bye for now." The line went dead. Becca stared at the receiver in her hand; she wanted to say something profound and healing.

Becca flew to San Francisco July 1, 1976. The morning of the 4th, Goldie pushed her muzzle into Becca's face delivering a morning wake-up slurp.

"You are disgusting," Becca giggled pulling the covers over her head. Goldie danced, woofed, dove repeatedly at Becca's pillow. "All right, I'm getting up." She pulled on shorts, T-shirt, well-worn running shoes. Goldie bounded down the stairs. "Shh, quiet you horse." Becca dashed downstairs and through the second floor hallway flicking the coffeemaker on as she flew past. She hurried to the front door where Goldie waited and wiggled expectantly. Becca noted their reflections in the full-length mirror as they exited; they were both grayer.

Returning an hour later, she found Hildur and Michael in the kitchen. Goldie roared in, slurped water, inhaled breakfast and leaned, panting hard, against Hildur's leg.

"She's following my pace better; we walk the first few minutes and the last few but she wants me faster in the middle." She poured herself coffee from the thermal pot on the counter.

"Lovely day," Hildur commented, idly scratching Goldie's head.

Michael looked out over the city. "Two hundred years later, what do you suppose the founders would think of what we've done with their dream?"

"Good and bad. More action than dream: they were people of action," Hildur's voice sounded thin.

"The dream came first. All the founders' rousing words, you read those early documents and they pull you in," Michael replied.

"Which led to action and continues leading to action, both good and bad." Hildur and Michael eyed each other: raw power abutting raw power. Then they smiled and raised their coffee cups in a mock toast.

"As always. Now, I have to get to the hospital. What's planned for today?"

"First, Becca and I go to church…"

"Hey, that's only Christmas and Thanksgiving," Becca kidded.

"I changed the rules: all holidays now. Besides, it's Sunday."

"She's always changing rules, Becca," Michael said as he leaned over and kissed Hildur's forehead, "been doing it for years."

"Making them better. We'll join the noon picnic next door; tonight you can take us out."

"Like to the Top of the Mark and the reservations I made last year?"

"Oh, Michael, you are a prince," Hildur's smile melted away the ravages of her illness.

"I get it right sometimes," he smiled.

Later, leaving church, Hildur stopped to smell a rose. "This," she said quietly, "is the hard part: the 'maybe this is the last time' part." Her thin, clear skin looked like crinkled satin.

"Aunt Hilly, you mustn't…"

"No, Becca," Hildur shook her head. "Don't try to cut me off from this moment."

They walked home. "Now, let's go eat hotdogs with our neighbors."

About five o'clock that afternoon, Hildur said, "I'm about 5 minutes away from getting over tired and awful so I'd better take a nap before we head for the Mark."

"Fine, but you're already twenty minutes into 'over tired and awful.'"

"Sometimes Michael, you're too honest." Hildur rose slowly.

"Aunt Hilly, let me help."

"Sit down. Stop treating me like an invalid. I need a nap. If I want your help I'll ask."

"But I could help…"

"Helping when you're not asked is often an exercise of power," Hildur's weary, didactic voice continued. "I love you Becca. You don't have to 'do' anything." She patted Becca's arm as she left the room and slowly climbed the stairs.

"I don't mean to make her mad, Uncle Mike."

"She's not mad, just tired. We're both glad you're here but this is 'life,' Bec, not a play."

"I want to help her."

"Explain that." Michael played with a pipe he hadn't smoked in decades.

"Well, do things, undo hooks that are hard to reach."

"But she hasn't asked."

"I feel helpless…"

"But she doesn't. Don't rob her of her self-reliance, independence and dignity."

Becca's chest tightened, her throat froze. "But I'm supposed to help: figure out what people want and do things."

"Taught by—?" Michael looked at her through his clear sky-blue eyes.

"Mother. Everybody."

He sighed. "Probably true which doesn't make it healthy, just pervasive."

The next morning after breakfast Hildur asked for help.

· Quail Hill ·

"Today, we'll go through my books. Don't look stricken, I own too many and need to weed through them." Next to the wall of books in her study, Hildur pulled a chair into the sunlight. "Read me titles beginning at the upper left shelf." By noon they had sorted fifteen shelves, leaving three shelves full. Five stacks of books labeled 'Michael,' 'the boys,' 'Becca,' 'miscellaneous others,' and 'to the bookseller' stood by the door.

"Thank you. Now we'll take a cab to the waterfront and have lunch."

During lunch, they talked and enjoyed being together. Then they strolled through art stores where Hildur kept sounding like she was about to buy paintings that seemed frightfully expensive to Becca. Hildur smiled impishly. Her eyes twinkled as they left a store and joined the crush of people on the street. "You're afraid I have metastases to my brain."

Becca laughed. "The idea did cross my mind. You sounded serious. What would Uncle Mike do about a $25,000 bill for a painting?"

"Pay it. It's 'our' money: my earnings, too. The painting's beautiful; we value beauty. But we live within our means so I just look." She swayed a bit and leaned heavily on Becca.

"Aunt Hilly?"

"I'm out of fuel. Better rest a minute and head home. Tonight you can fix dinner."

After steaks, salad (with Hildur's special bacon dressing) and sour dough bread, Mike left for the hospital. Lying on the couch, her head propped up on pillows, Hildur talked quietly.

"There're other things I'd like to give you—letters, your great-grandmother's writing, her family things—but they all disappeared. We couldn't find them in the final move from the farm. Your grandmother had packed an old box for you but it was gone. You should have it but then, you should've had Andy longer, too."

"I wish he'd been around. Mother says I'm like him."

"Hum. Stubborn and often too cerebral for your own good. Happy. Bright. Moody. Single focused at times: adrift at others. You're like him. You'd have fought like caged cats."

"We'd have been the perfect father-daughter combo."

"Don't sugar coat the world. The only place worth living is in reality. See that pewter tea set over there?" She gestured toward a hutch. "It was Libby's. I put your name on it. It's dented—something happened that people smiled about but nobody knows the story. Sometimes the only things that get passed on are the dents." She stood slowly, walked to Becca's chair, smiled for a long moment. "I'll talk more tomorrow. We never share it all: aren't meant to. We live our own lives. Sometimes signposts along the way can help. I've been lucky." She kissed her niece lightly on the forehead.

Later, Becca packed her new supply of books in an old suitcase. *Advice to a Young Wife from an Old Mistress* by Michael Drury, *Thoughts in Solitude* and *Zen and the Birds of Appetite* by Thomas Merton, *The Lives of a Cell* by Lewis Thomas, *The Autobiography of a Yogi, King Solomon's Ring, My Antonia, The Bell Jar, Between Night and Morn*, the *Bhagavad-Gita* and a few others. She flipped through the pages of the little Penguin edition of the *Gita* and found a handwritten note: 'Rest in inner life, be one with God.' Why had Aunt Hildur chosen these books for her? They seemed disparate, unconnected and confusing.

Becca closed the book, turned off the light and watched San Francisco glittering. She fell asleep quickly.

Smiling faces laughed at them on the waterfront, Aunt Hilly wearing a green wig screamed silently as she grew into a giant and then crumpled in a chair as skin fell from her face onto their table. Becca reached frantically for the gobs of wilting flesh trying desperately to repair Hildur's disintegrating face. She saw, to her disgust, the naked bones of her own hands and watched in horror as Hildur's dying tissues wrap around her hands like custom made gloves.

She awoke in terror feeling she might explode.

The next morning, they puttered in Hildur's small flower garden.

"There were always portulaca plants by the door at the farm, Aunt Annabelle planted them," Becca said pulling a weed.

"Libby planted it, too: one of her favorites," Hildur replied.

"She must have been awfully strong and courageous."

"Careful, Becca, don't make her a two dimensional caricature."

"What do you mean?"

"Well, standing up when you're tied to a steel beam may not be the singular accomplishment you suggest. Once she married she had few choices. Work hard or starve: plant, harvest, cook, clean, sew, wash, iron, survive the winter and nurse children. Cultural expectations dominated. Going against the grain took courage. Bert's sisters, Rose and Rachel did that."

"Rose was the teacher, right?"

"Yep. The family's first emancipated woman."

"And Rachel?"

"Your great-grandfather Bert's older sister. She stayed home, took care of her parents, never married, helped Bert and Libby raise their brood and then followed some Guru to India. Bert never forgave her."

Becca's jaw dropped open. "When did that happen?"

"Before the turn of the century."

"Well, I'll be darned. What happened to her?"

"She died in India. Some tale about her spirit visiting Rose or Libby when she died."

"Mystical experiences in those hardheaded New Hampshireites?"

"That's what your grandmother, A.L., told me. Believe it or not, as you wish."

"Do you believe it?"

"Strange things happen. Why make up a story that makes you look gullible?"

"Was Rachel in love with the Indian?"

"I don't think so. She felt he was her teacher so she followed him. That took guts."

"The Quail Hill gang gets curiouser and curiouser."

"All families are curious. Mainly, I think families are more for growth than comfort." She paused. "By the way, how's Eleanor?"

"The same. We talk. Whatever I do she criticizes. What she gives isn't what I need: who I am isn't the child she wanted."

"Your relationship, as they say, 'wants healing.'"

"I can't heal her, stop her drinking, be the son she wanted to replace Andy."

"True, so strengthen yourself. Put new voices in your head to counter her negative ones. It's OK to be a woman. It's fine to be successful, single, make money and hire help. It's even OK to enjoy yourself." She squeezed Becca's hand. "Read my books and love Ellie more. Remember, she lost her husband and had two daughters to rear by herself. The war was on; everything was rationed. She couldn't buy gas or relocate. Her options were limited. She made the best choices she could in the circumstances. Life's never perfect. Now, fix me lunch."

"Some of those books talk about reincarnation and stuff. Do you believe in that?"

"I believe life is eternal and I'm not at all sure what that means. I believe in something great and transcendent and unknowable. The longer I live the less I worry about the details. I believe in science and love and beauty and I believe I'm hungry. Fix me lunch."

That afternoon, Becca flew back to Madison. As she headed out the door, Hildur handed her a tapestry knitting-bag.

"It's a short knit coat: your Christmas present. I've done all but the sleeves. The pattern is in there."

"I can't knit a coat."

"You knit a stitch, then another: string them together and you'll have a coat. Or hire someone at a yarn shop. It's nice yarn and a good color for you."

They hugged, mumbled things like 'maybe Thanksgiving, or next summer.' Hildur watched as the cab drove away and sighed.

Back in Madison, Becca tried knitting a few rows, got angry, didn't want to waste the yarn, felt trapped. Then, walking down State Street, she passed the Yarn Bar and laughed. She hired someone. The night the coat was finished, she called Hildur.

"Aunt Hilly, it's lovely. Thank you for the coat and helping me learn it's OK not to do everything."

"A successful working woman needs a lot of phone numbers and friends. I'm glad you like the coat," Becca could barely hear her aunt's weak voice.

Hildur died in October. Becca didn't attend the funeral; she simply could not get away.

19

Two years passed; her merry-go-round life kept turning.

***** Thanksgiving 1977 marked Becca's second annual trek to Marcia's. Skeleton-trees stood against the gray sky; roasting turkey steamed the kitchen windows. Marcia's worn, totally correct, house depressed Becca. Cynthia and Philip competed with the endless TV football games, Becca watched the snow fall and felt her face slacken into a blank mask, her eyes peering out from deep within. Eleanor arrived like Tabasco sauce on an open wound.

"Funzie, funzie. Mother's here with champagne."

Becca groaned inwardly. Soon the family would begin their Peter and the Wolf-esque holiday game with Becca as the duck. Scanning her thirty seven years, Becca felt trapped in a four dimensional web, granted this space, this time and no more, this role and no other. She couldn't smile with these people (except alone with Cynthia and Philip), remained frozen-faced throughout the holiday. She'd lost some core part. She always felt she failed Eleanor and Marcia yet believed this 'failure' was what they demanded. Without the duck's lament, how could Peter and his pals keep playing?

She thought of Hildur who died two years ago. Aunt Hilly had tried to tell her something, point a way: where? She'd read the books. They seemed foreign: spiritual stuff much of which she didn't understand. Greg's face swam before her.

Eleanor popped the cork and filled glasses as tears filled Becca's eyes.

***** "That's a nice print, Linda," noticing the Monet on the wall as she sorted her mail Monday morning.

"We're studying it," Linda replied authoritatively. "I like the balanced composition."

"You enjoy those classes," Becca smiled for the first time in days.

"Yes, I do. And here's the boss who made them possible."

P walked by, blushed and gave his famous 'aw, shucks' smile. "Actually," he said, "Dr. Chadwick suggested the program. I just filled out the forms."

Linda looked stricken. "But you arranged it," she said desperately.

"As Chairman I had to. But Dr. Chadwick suggested it." He walked on, humming.

Linda scowled in confusion and glanced at the print.

***** "Cynthia, ask your parents." Becca walked to the end of the phone cord and picked up her wine glass.

"They won't give me money for swim camp."

"What does your coach say?"

"That I should go. That maybe I could do something. Aunt Becca, please help me out."

"I'll have to talk to your parent; I can't give you money behind their backs."

"They'll say no. Can't you just give me the money?"

"Nope. Put your mother on."

"She thinks I'm talking to a friend."

"Oh, Cynthia. That makes things worse. Hang up and I'll call Marcia."

Half an hour later the answer remained no. No, Cynthia couldn't go to swim camp, no, they wouldn't accept her money, no, no, no.

"She wants to go and is a good swimmer: let her try."

"Jack doesn't want her to and neither do I. She's too competitive, she needs to be feminine, curb her wants to the needs of the family, not follow her own selfishness."

"So that's it. 'Submissive female must stay home, legs spread, awaiting impregnation by superior male.' God, Marcia, what rock have you been under? The world is changing. Cynthia will have to compete and produce more than children to survive. She needs your support and help. Let me pay. I can and I'd love to."

"We don't want your handouts and don't tell me how to raise my daughter," Marcia slammed the phone down.

Becca downed a fourth glass of wine, wrote a letter to the coach, enclosed a check for two scholarships.

He acknowledged the letter, returned the check stating they had no mechanism to deal with scholarship money for a non-school activity.

***** "You won't remember me. You failed me."

"I remember you, Miss Coleson. As I recall, you earned a D."
"May I come in?"
"I'm about to leave for class, can you come during an office hour?"
"That would be difficult."

Becca hesitated. Miss Coleson had refused counseling. "What can I do for you?"

"When you ruin someone's life, you should talk to them."

"I didn't ruin your life. You earned a D and never tried to retake the course."

"After that they wouldn't let me in the School of Education. I graduated in Social Work. All I wanted was to teach. You destroyed that."

"Things are rarely that simple. You're in Social Work?"

"Don't forget you destroyed my dream but you get everything you want so you wouldn't understand." Miss Coleson wheeled around and stomped down the hall.

Becca shook her head slowly; her shoulders slumped forward. Then she gathered her notes and headed for class. Sometimes it all felt hopeless.

***** Steve's voice sounded brisk. Becca cradled the receiver on her shoulder and picked up the three by five cards stacked by her phone. She flipped through them and read what she had written.

"I won't be here when you arrive and I won't be back before I teach on Monday. I have a conference to attend," she lied. "Do us a favor and stop calling. This is over."

She hung up and prepared to leave: fast. She scooped work into her briefcase, threw clothes into a suitcase, grabbed a bottle of sherry and left. It was off-season at the Wisconsin Dells so she'd get a room easily. Four minutes after hanging up, she drove away. This had to stop. She could no longer tolerate their semiannual drug enhanced sexual encounters. She had to change things in her life.

***** Years crept by. Her Christmas card list dwindled. Picking threads from one research project to another, her work and reputation brought support and recognition. Sometimes her studies felt creative; sometimes she dug furiously like an anal-compulsive caged rat looking for any tidbit to pursue. Clinical work with laryngectomy patients diminished when the hospital hired a full time therapist.

Like pebbles falling through successively finer layers of a sieve, patients and students passed through Becca's part of the system. Dealing realistically without destroying hope grew more challenging. What seemed positive, creative and successful at thirty, often felt cynical at forty. A six-month sabbatical at a leading neurological rehabilitation center increased both her knowledge and her sense of ennui: more brain damaged patients now survived though few recovered fully. While she understood that 'improvement' helped both her patients and their

· Quail Hill ·

families adjust to their 'new normal,' the results depressed her. At times, the happy, smiling faces of young clinicians-in-training terrified her. How could she prepare them for the amount of loss and pain they would encounter: sustain them through careers often isolated from the support team they would need? Then some 'your-work-is-wonderful' type would seek her advice and, despite herself, Becca felt successful.

    The elation from earning a Full Professorship was brief: the relief permanent. The competence she had developed through the discipline needed to accomplish this had produced a steely inner core she had lacked as a younger woman. She rented a larger apartment, tore up all her 5X7 cards and sent the shreds to Jenny along with a Thank You card. She had reached the goal she had set for herself after Greg died and she began to relax. There was another women on the faculty in her department now. Becca knew that, no matter how sloppy her own progress had been, she'd made a difference. One quality she finally accepted in herself was her strength. The University continued, like a relentlessly growing chimera, trying to consume everything within reach but it had not destroyed her. In her role as another cog in that wheel, Becca kept moving and the merry-go-round spun on.

    Miss Coleson's annual spring visits no longer frightened her. Linda smirked less and did her work. Becca's niece, Cynthia, without parental support for the swimming she loved or the engineering she wanted to study, dropped out of college and joined a vegetarian, no marriages, no baths commune in Indiana. Becca felt frustrated that she hadn't been able to help her. Nicole and Max remained friends as their careers wound down. Holidays came and went. She rented a cabin in northern Wisconsin each summer where she read, wrote, swam, fished and became adept at skipping stones on the lake, watching as each finally sank. Mourning her non-relationships with Andy, Biff and Greg she finally rested exactly where she was. Bits of writing—Plato's blind men trapped underground, Eliot's 'The Hollow Men,' Ferlinghetti's 'A Coney Island of the Mind'—sucked part of her into cynicism.

    Looks, however, can be deceiving. Like an underground river working its way beneath dry land, nourishment seeped in. She wrote more poems, ran more seriously and entered a 5 K fundraiser for breast cancer. She bought flowers for her new apartment, snuck into churches to sit quietly and reflect on her life, her father, Aunt Hilly, her mother, her students and patients. During years of work she had developed genuine compassion for patients and their families giving her interactions with them more depth. When her students struggled to learn concepts she found simple, she no longer felt annoyed but became determined to teach better, explain things differently, try to see things as the confused students did and move them forward. One summer, while rereading one of Aunt Hilly's books, a Spanish Proverb, "You cannot give with empty hands," snagged in her mind like drifting river flotsam caught by overhanging branches. The phrase altered her, minutely changing her course, even as the University merry-go-round continued to turn.

20

Becca looked furtively through the peephole, saw Cynthia's profile against the streetlight, flipped on her porch light and opened the door.

"It's after midnight, why didn't you call?" she asked hugging her niece and pulling her into the apartment.

"I wasn't sure you'd want to see me."

"Why wouldn't I?"

"I'm broke, my parents are angry, I left the commune and I want to be an engineer."

"That'll keep us talking for awhile. How long since you ate?"

"Breakfast."

"Sunflower seeds and tofu?"

Cynthia smiled for the first time. "Nope: sausage McMuffin with egg, OJ and coffee. I like your new apartment and your long hair."

"Thanks. I'm making some changes: those two show. How's leftover chicken sound?"

"Great. Then a bath and sleep. I'll need a hairdryer."

"I've got two. I teach tomorrow so sleep-in. My weekend's free."

"Getting into school in engineering won't be easy." Bundled against the chilly breeze, surrounded by swirling October leaves, they drank coffee in bright sunlight on the Union patio.

"I know. I'll need a bunch of pre-engineering courses but at least I didn't flunk out of college: I just left. Mom and Dad blocked swimming but I don't want to go through life wondering if I could have made it in engineering." Cynthia set her teeth. "The biggest challenge will be money."

"As in 'Hello, Aunt Becca'?"

"Yea, I guess." Cynthia stirred her coffee.

"I've got some egg money; you're a good candidate."

"What's 'egg money'?"

"Your great-great-grandmother, Libby Whitman Jones, used her egg money to send her daughters, including your great-grandmother Amy Louise Jones Morgan, to college so it's a family tradition. Eleanor used money from Andy's investments to send your mother and me to college. I don't have children so you're in line for my egg money."

"I'll pay you back."

"First things first. Any idea what branch of engineering, which school?"

"Mechanical, aeronautical. Purdue. MIT. But first I need prerequisites."

"I know a couple guys in engineering I can call. They'll advise you. What clothes do you have?"

Cynthia jutted out her chin defensively looking just like Eleanor. "Jeans, sweats, couple of jackets. What difference does it make? This is engineering not charm school."

"Don't get tense. We'll put something together. Trust me on this."

"Why?"

"I know a few things about how Universities work, especially regarding females. Lots of us talented, intelligent women throw glass in front of our own feet. Competence, while essential, isn't enough: extraneous stuff can lead to unnecessary failure. Appearances matter."

"So I need a suit to meet these dudes?"

"Or blazer, blouse, skirt or slacks. Something that says 'I'm serious, intelligent and prepared to work hard.' The school will set the academic standards. What's in your suitcase?"

"Probably not much that will work. How about your closet? We aren't far from the same size."

"We can check but we'll probably need to shop. At least you're over 21 so your folks can't have me arrested for contributing to the education of an adult. I'll tell them you're here."

"Yea, but let's wait and call on Sunday."

Over the next two weeks they developed a comfortable arrangement. At the Fischman's October Fest, Nicole said, "Cynthia's the best thing that's happened to you in years."

"Why?"

"Outside yourself, outside your field, someone you care about. If I worked with brain-damaged patients and trained students to work with brain-damaged patients fulltime, I'd be around the bend in a week."

"You do more work in a week than I do in a month."

"Different kind."

"Anyway, I'm glad you like Cynthia. She's determined, may get in next semester to do some 'undeclared major, pre-requisite' courses. She's reviewing math on her own now and looking for a roommate."

"Aunt Becca, you're right."

Becca looked up from her desk in her university office and saw a professionally clad Cynthia standing in the doorway.

"Hi. Come in and sit down. 'Right' about what?"

Cynthia plopped into a chair just to the right of the door. "Clothes. I just did the experiment: went to the Library in grubby sweats, took ages to get help. Went home, changed into this, went back and 'Little Annie Fannie' leapt to serve me! Amazing."

The woman approached silently and neither Cynthia nor Becca saw her until she spoke.

"Hello, Dr. Chadwick." Miss Coleson's head swiveled toward Cynthia. "You taking her course?"

Cynthia saw Becca stiffen as concern flooded her face.

"What?" Cynthia stammered. "Well, no, I'm not taking her course, she's …"

"Good. Don't. She's a killer. She kills dreams." Robot-like Miss Coleson turned toward Becca who rose slowly and began speaking gently.

"I haven't seen you in a long time, Miss Coleson. How are you?"

Carefully, Miss Coleson pulled a small black object from her purse and pointed it toward Becca's heart.

21

"Jesus!" Cynthia erupted from her chair diving toward the figure in the door. She sliced her arms down forcefully striking Miss Coleson's forearm just as the gun detonated quietly.

Becca spun backwards, left arm extended, right hand grasping her right side. She crashed into her desk chair, which spun away as she dropped to the floor, falling into a bloody pool that expanded rapidly. She grunted softly.

"*Huh, huh, huh….*"

Miss Coleson dropped the gun, turned and walked swiftly out the door, down the hall and through the department's exit. She was humming.

Cynthia glanced at Becca's glazed, confused expression, heard her gasping and raced down the hall.

Linda sat typing, smirking lightly. "One of your aunt's favorite…"

Cynthia smashed her fist onto Linda's desk.

"Aunt Becca's been shot!" she screamed.

Linda sat stunned, her hands poised over her keyboard.

Cynthia picked up the telephone receiver and threw it at Linda.

" CALL SOMEONE! ACT!"

· Quail Hill ·

As the receiver hit Linda's chest, she grabbed it and snapped into action, automatically dialing the correct emergency number. From then on, she behaved like a perfectly trained drill sergeant: issuing orders, clearing a path for the emergency team and remaining in charge as Becca was carried out.

Pain, Oh, God. Blood, pain…

Sirens blaring, the ambulance sped away. Cynthia and two graduate students raced after it arriving at the Hospital Emergency Room a few minutes later. Cynthia gave what information she could, had them page Nicole and flopped down in the waiting area. The students stayed until a nurse came and told them what was happening.

Hands, rough. Oh, God. Pain.

They whisked Becca to surgery. The vigil began.

Two students trailed Miss Coleson for a block, lost her at University and Park, her neutral form swallowed in the noon crowd of the cold November day. Police found her later. She had taken an undetermined number of pills (stolen from the clinic where she worked), washed them down with liquid weed killer and lay, comatose, in the storage bin of her apartment. Rushed to the same University Hospital Emergency Room, she never regained consciousness. On her desk, two notebooks of garbled, rambling prose cast an eerie light on her troubled life.

"That's me," Cynthia said after the surgeon entered and called her name.
"Your aunt's out of surgery and doing well."
 "What'd you do?"
"Her right kidney was destroyed; she lost a lot of blood; she'll be fine."
"My God! She lost a kidney?"
"She's alive. Your quick action, plus proximity to the Hospital, saved her."
Nicole walked in. "Hello Pittman. How's Chadwick?"
The two surgeons lapsed into a private language full of nuance and punctuated by slight movements of small facial muscles, minor changes in tone. Cynthia stood like a bat before a Picasso: unable to understand the discussion before her. Nicole seemed relaxed when Dr. Pittman left.
"Things look good. Do you have Becca's car keys?" Cynthia nodded. "Then go home, eat, rest. Pittman will call if anything happens. Has anyone from the Department been by?"
"Some students, the Chair, a colleague and Linda who broke down, sputtered and cried."
"We owe her a lot."
"Did they find that woman? Miss Coleson?"
"Brought her in a couple of hours ago, suicide. Terribly sad."

"All the same, I'll sleep better knowing she isn't stalking someone."

"Call me if you need anything." They walked out of the surgical waiting room together: two professional women at opposite ends of their careers.

Back at the apartment, Cynthia ate, called her mother, Marcia, her grandmother, Eleanor, and her Great-Uncle Mike. Stepping into the shower, she remembered how kind Mike Morgan sounded.

22

Cold. Bad taste. Blackness. Open eyes: hard work. Distant blob. Squint. Focus. 'Clock!' Becca felt triumphant. *'1:30. Funny time. Funny clock. Not mine. Better get up…'*

"Uhmm, ahh…" Everything hurt. She licked her lips as someone touched her arm.

"Hello, Becca. You coming all the way up this time?" Blue eyes and an easy smile leaned over her as a hand stroked her forehead.

"I'm cold."

"It's the IVs. I'll get a warm blanket. Know where you are?"

"Hospital?"

"Yep," the nurse tucked the warm blanket around her. "You had an accident, needed surgery and you're OK. How do you feel?"

Becca coughed. "Everything hurts. Blanket's nice."

The nurse wiped her face with a cloth, patted her arm. Simple human touch: someone reaching into this prison to lead her back to the world she didn't remember leaving.

"Thank you," Becca blinked, trying to stay awake and connected.

"You're welcome. Now sleep. You're gonna be fine."

Blackness flecked with afterimages ushered her back into unconsciousness.

Dr. Pittman, surrounded by a crowd of earnest faces, read her chart, made comments, poked a bit, asked questions, assured her she was doing well, held her hand and asked, "What's the last thing you remember?"

"Picking up my mail the other morning. Next, I saw the clock."

"Dr. Daniel from psych will drop by: routine after a shooting."

'Bug under microscope,' she felt, nodding almost imperceptibly.

Pittman smiled. "You're doing well."

Cynthia and Eleanor visited, Max and Nicole came by. The nurses remained upbeat. Becca felt jumpy and anxious. Often she found herself taking tiny shallow breaths while her rib cage remained almost fixed by her tense muscles. Eleanor moved into her apartment, called her friends. Eleanor both crowded in uncomfortably and provided a structure she needed. Uncle Mike's calls supported her and reminded her how 'New Hampshire laconic' he was. He called daily and sent flowers. His focus on reality helped her use that ability in herself.

Tippy peeked cautiously around the edge of the hospital door, saw Becca, with lines in and lines out, propped up on pillows looking at a book. Tippy stepped into the room.

"Except for that dreadful hospital gown, you look almost healthy and much less dramatic than I expected," she dropped a box of candy and a perfectly wrapped package on the table as she sat gingerly on the edge of the bed. "Better than you sounded on the phone so I flew out. If that book's a novel, mark your place for later: if it's work, I'm taking it when I leave." Tippy took both of Becca's hands. "I'd hug you but… Oh God, Becca. I'm so glad you're alive." Tears spilled down both their cheeks as they grinned at each other.

"Thanks for coming."

"Through everything, somehow we're connected. Are you better? Are you eating? When do you get out? How are you and Eleanor doing? And what are you going to do now?"

"Whoa, let's see: I'm improving; I shuffle down the hall dragging my IV pole. I'm eating, should go home in two days and Eleanor left an hour ago, will be back this evening. And what do you mean 'what are you going to do now'?"

"I mean," Tippy said, adjusting herself and reaching for the candy, "just that. What are you going to do? You're a full professor; you've proved yourself and squirreled away a fortune, so hanging around Madison's silly. Why not move on? You encouraged me to open my decorating business, why not make a creative change?" She chose a chocolate and handed the box to Becca.

"You sound like Rich: 'come out west to Santa Veronica State, join my department, work halftime, three-quarter time, travel, relax, take life easy.'"

"Where's Santa Veronica?"

"In California, north of San Francisco, in the coastal redwoods."

"Sounds heavenly. Say 'yes.' Take a year off to travel. Buy a house with enough room for me to visit. Now that that's settled, have a chocolate."

"That's settled? Do I get a vote?"

"Becca, you agonize and fuss and torture yourself analyzing every possible outcome. Tell Rich 'yes,' resign here, sell your dreadful Danish modern furniture, plan a trip and take off. I'll come decorate the place you buy in Santa Wherever."

Becca didn't say anything so Tippy continued.

"You almost died. If Cynthia hadn't been there you'd be in the ground. Life is short. All you've done since Greg died is work. You've accomplished goals most women never dreamed were possible and a whole generation of females is moving forward because you, and women like you, have been grinding away, being beaten up by the system, pilloried by both women and men who've felt jealous and threatened. From now on, your life is a gift. Live it. Enjoy it. Savor it. Now, have a chocolate and tell me where you're going on your big trip."

"My big trip?"

"The one we're going to plan before Eleanor gets here and says 'Hum, I'm surprised you'd want to go there.'" Tippy's impersonation made Becca laugh, then wince in pain. "Sorry. How is she anyway?"

"The same. Thinks you're the perfect daughter. Laments my childless state, vacillates between overstating my accomplishments and discrediting them. She's living in my apartment and, from what Cynthia says, is 'tidying up.' I survived the shooting: the recovery may be more difficult."

"According to my mom you're perfect, too: 'so focused, so dedicated.' Bec, I've been a parent long enough to see there's no way to win: we just muddle through. Our families, both a bit nuts, are good enough. We've had fabulous opportunities: great educations, extensive travel. You and I've have had a long friendship. We each would have thrown the other under the bus a number of times but here we are: bonded." She toyed with a chocolate. "I learn new lessons all the time. When Eleanor called I could hardly breathe. Then everything looked different: Hank, the kids, my business, our friendship, life. It'll fade, but right now I'm really *in* this moment."

Becca smiled and squeezed Tippy's hand. "Yea, I know," was all she could manage.

"So, where are you going?"

"On the big trip you want me to take?"

"On the big trip you are going to take."

"OK. India."

"India? Are you nuts?"

"Isn't that weird, Tippy. I want to go to India."

"Me and my bright ideas. Becca you can't breathe the air in India let alone drink the water. India? Be serious; you only have one kidney!"

"So I'd better go soon." Becca smiled and popped a chocolate into her mouth.

Later that afternoon Becca took a fast read of the redheaded, green eyed, 5'3", 105 pounds, 40ish, well groomed professional woman who walked into her room.

"Hi, Becca, Victoria Daniel, clinical psychology."

"Hi. Didn't expect you till later, sorry, my hair's a mess. You look better than I do."

"No need to apologize. I haven't been shot and lost a kidney."

"I don't remember the shooting but talking about it may be a good idea." Becca sat up.

"Mind if I pull up a chair? I have some time now if you want it."

"Sorry, I should have asked. Sure."

"No need to apologize." Dr. Daniel rolled a high office chair in from the hall, closed the door and perched next to the bed. "I disappear if I use the regular chairs. How's it going?"

"Meaning 'it' as in my life? My health? My lack of memory of Miss Coleson's attack? My future? My relationships? My electrolytic-balance? My renal-functioning? Or the whole sticky mess?"

Dr. Daniel smiled lightly. "Something like that. Start anyplace."

Becca lay back and looked at the square acoustic tiles on the ceiling.

"Loosing a kidney seems unreal. I'm probably angry as hell on some level but I don't feel angry. Numb. Dull. Short-of-breath. Tight. Miss Coleson was so confused and I might have done more for her but I don't know. What I was teaching she did not learn. That may be too simple. Her suicide, like fingernails on a blackboard, grates on my spine.

"My somewhat overly attentive mother's here offering her brand of love which alternately sooths and smothers me. She's rearranging my apartment, badgering my niece to drop engineering. My college roommate's planning a trip I should take and my best buddies from graduate school want me to move to California and I—" Becca sighed heavily. "It's all jumbled up. I'm sorry Dr. Daniel."

"No need to apologize"

"I do that a lot, don't I?"

"In the past 10 minutes I've heard a few. Where's it come from?"

"Let's see. My father was terminally ill when I was conceived and Mother wanted 'a son to replace the dying husband.' Cosmic joke: I'm a girl! My Dad was OK with that but my Mom never adjusted. Lots of pushing and pulling. 'If you were a boy you could do so much' and when I succeeded academically 'how proud your father would have been.' But was she? Hard to tell. He died before I was three and I've never satisfied my mother.

"Enter Greg Chadwick. Gorgeous, intelligent, fun, funny great love of my life. Good first years of marriage and then he's sent to 'Nam. On R&R in Hawaii he says 'get a divorce' he doesn't want to be married anymore. Said stuff about how he'd changed in the war and then he stormed out leaving me in that room, alone. I didn't get a divorce.

"Cosmic joke #2: Greg becomes MIA. Later they find his body, remains: enough I guess." She paused. "That chapter closes—but some things never really end they just keep reverberating. Since then, I've worked.

"And Miss Coleson: bleak, confused young woman. So here I am in a ridiculous hospital gown, wondering why I survived and what to do with my life but also feeling like somehow, deep within me, things are already changing. I'm sorry I'm not clearer, Dr. Daniel."

"That's OK. It's why I'm here."

23

December 1985.

Inhale. Exhale. Relax shoulder, chest and neck muscles. Repeat. Like the stuff Harvey tried. Something she could do. When terror struck and life froze: an action.

"It helps, Dr. Daniel. Remembering to do it is challenging."

"In trauma work I like behaviorist intervention; the 'relaxation response' helps. Working on other issues in your life is up to you. How're you doing, generally?"

"I'm healing. Still don't remember the shooting but know I owe my life to Cynthia and Linda. My relationships with both of them have changed: deepened and become more equals with equals. We all feel the change and it's nice: just women helping women.

"I managed some pleasant days with Eleanor: avoided my ritualistic stand-offs and let her do more for me. We behaved: allowed each other space to be who we are.

"Cynthia told me that when Eleanor arrived she looked at my chaotic desk and simply pulled out sheets and covered it up saying 'Becca would have a fit if I tidy that up but I'll not look at it.' So we both tried. When she left I felt OK. We hugged and I told her how much I appreciated her coming and she just accepted what I said. Now she's back in her life and I'm heading into mine—whatever it's going to be. Maybe I'm growing up: letting go of my twin terrors of either being overwhelmed by her or losing her.

"Dr. Daniel, I made up a 'famous old saying' the other day. It's my new motto: 'You only stick to tar-babies you fight with.' I'm trying to see Eleanor with compassion. She wanted a son: got me."

"Unexpected traumatic events can trigger strange benefits," a gentle smile played on Victoria Daniel's lips.

"The pain from Andy and Greg merge. Love and trust: then abandonment, confusion, terror, incomprehension. In a word—loss. The 'baby in the well' is probably part of me at two and a half who remains hidden in that huge empty place that yawned open in my life when Andy died: tectonic plates shifting leaving a void: 'no-thing' where he had been. Emanating from that hole was need and pain that oozed out like dense fog and penetrated me.

"I wish I understood Greg better. What the hell happened in Vietnam?" Becca stared at the ceiling.

"Daniel, they took out my kidney not my personality. But I'm different. The glue's gone. My cells may drift away, disassociate. I'm sort of floating around watching myself do things—not like hanging from the light fixtures but detached."

"Becca, what do you want now?"

Becca rubbed her eyes and gazed into a middle space, focusing on nothing.

"I want to go to India, move to Santa Veronica, re-integrate my 'self.' And I don't want to teach here next semester. Clinical work, a little research. Take a mandatory 'eight count.' Do a mini-sabbatical studying how other cultures view language development and language problems. Not leave the merry-go-round but slow down. Get the baby out of the well, help the 'little sucker' relax." Becca sighed. "Heal. But I don't have enough pieces yet."

"Nobody has enough pieces, Becca. We always exist in Act 2 and we want to know, quote, 'the end from the beginning' unquote. But all we have is this messy 'middle-ground.' You've suffered collateral damage in your life—as well as the results of your decisions—and that gives you strengths, weaknesses, self-awareness and self-deception. You're better than many, not as good as some. You're healing. 'The decisions we make aren't as important as…'"

" '… how we deal with the consequences of the decisions we make.' Who said that Daniel?"

"I don't remember. But I use it a lot."

Their hour ended. They stood.

"Keep doing the intentional breathing and relaxing. See you in a week."

"Thanks Dr. D."

Diary
Dec. '85.

Dream: Greg, older, gray, weathered rugged laugh-lines. Sailing, smiling covered with salty sea spray. Fisheye keyhole view like our first date but when I opened the door he wasn't there. Back in that apartment there were strangers; I snuck out the backdoor into the alley that became a field of wildflowers. Everything dissolved into a light that rolled toward me fast. I jerked my eyes open and woke up feeling scared. Did my breathing: inhale, exhale, relax.

24

"Welcome, glad you could make it." Becca greeted Professor Gilbert as he took his seat across from her, ordered sherry, rubbed his hands together in an effort to escape the frigid February day.

"An invitation to the Edgewater is rare in my retired world. How're you doing?"

"Recovering. A bit slower."

"Aren't we all."

"I'm on a sabbatical. Studying cross cultural developmental psych, Asian philosophy, seeing our field through new prisms."

"Balderdash." GG sipped his sherry. "I may be old but I'm not stupid. So what now?"

He caught her off guard. "What do you mean?"

GG chuckled. "Really Chadwick. An Edgewater lunch's more than 'thanks for the flowers.' You almost died. Ergo, Chadwick's considering change and wants a mentor's advice."

Becca smiled and shook her head. "I was smart to choose you."

"Dear lady who else? P? Maybe but he was busy as Chair. The others grappled with their own challenges when you arrived. We studied complementary things and I'd given up power so I couldn't lose by backing you. Besides, the idea of really opening the system up sounded fun—you became my Mission Impossible." He drained his sherry, motioned the waiter for another. "You were smart and worth the work. I'm amazed we made it. So what now?"

"Not so fast. You thought I'd fail?"

"Sure." He paused. "The whole system pushed against you. But you got through—not always well—I often wanted to yell at you –"

"You did."

"Not enough," he growled, sipping his second sherry. "Nicole and Max, you owe them."

"I know."

"Good." The waiter took their orders. "So why lunch? What're you doing in comparative psych and Asian philosophy? They're irrelevant to treating brain-damaged adults."

Becca sat forward. "Rich Brent wants me to come to Santa Veronica, small program, some Master's students, local VA that needs an Adult Language Rehab Unit. I'm planning to take a trip to India this fall: reasons are vague but real. I've had it here; my 'Madison time' is over. At the department, I'm an outsider." GG listened. "Any reactions?"

leaving a void: 'no-thing' where he had been. Emanating from that hole was need and pain that oozed out like dense fog and penetrated me.

"I wish I understood Greg better. What the hell happened in Vietnam?" Becca stared at the ceiling.

"Daniel, they took out my kidney not my personality. But I'm different. The glue's gone. My cells may drift away, disassociate. I'm sort of floating around watching myself do things—not like hanging from the light fixtures but detached."

"Becca, what do you want now?"

Becca rubbed her eyes and gazed into a middle space, focusing on nothing.

"I want to go to India, move to Santa Veronica, re-integrate my 'self.' And I don't want to teach here next semester. Clinical work, a little research. Take a mandatory 'eight count.' Do a mini-sabbatical studying how other cultures view language development and language problems. Not leave the merry-go-round but slow down. Get the baby out of the well, help the 'little sucker' relax." Becca sighed. "Heal. But I don't have enough pieces yet."

"Nobody has enough pieces, Becca. We always exist in Act 2 and we want to know, quote, 'the end from the beginning' unquote. But all we have is this messy 'middle-ground.' You've suffered collateral damage in your life—as well as the results of your decisions—and that gives you strengths, weaknesses, self-awareness and self-deception. You're better than many, not as good as some. You're healing. 'The decisions we make aren't as important as…'"

" '… how we deal with the consequences of the decisions we make.' Who said that Daniel?"

"I don't remember. But I use it a lot."

Their hour ended. They stood.

"Keep doing the intentional breathing and relaxing. See you in a week."

"Thanks Dr. D."

Diary
Dec. '85.

Dream: Greg, older, gray, weathered rugged laugh-lines. Sailing, smiling covered with salty sea spray. Fisheye keyhole view like our first date but when I opened the door he wasn't there. Back in that apartment there were strangers; I snuck out the backdoor into the alley that became a field of wildflowers. Everything dissolved into a light that rolled toward me fast. I jerked my eyes open and woke up feeling scared. Did my breathing: inhale, exhale, relax.

24

"Welcome, glad you could make it." Becca greeted Professor Gilbert as he took his seat across from her, ordered sherry, rubbed his hands together in an effort to escape the frigid February day.

"An invitation to the Edgewater is rare in my retired world. How're you doing?"

"Recovering. A bit slower."

"Aren't we all."

"I'm on a sabbatical. Studying cross cultural developmental psych, Asian philosophy, seeing our field through new prisms."

"Balderdash." GG sipped his sherry. "I may be old but I'm not stupid. So what now?"

He caught her off guard. "What do you mean?"

GG chuckled. "Really Chadwick. An Edgewater lunch's more than 'thanks for the flowers.' You almost died. Ergo, Chadwick's considering change and wants a mentor's advice."

Becca smiled and shook her head. "I was smart to choose you."

"Dear lady who else? P? Maybe but he was busy as Chair. The others grappled with their own challenges when you arrived. We studied complementary things and I'd given up power so I couldn't lose by backing you. Besides, the idea of really opening the system up sounded fun—you became my Mission Impossible." He drained his sherry, motioned the waiter for another. "You were smart and worth the work. I'm amazed we made it. So what now?"

"Not so fast. You thought I'd fail?"

"Sure." He paused. "The whole system pushed against you. But you got through—not always well—I often wanted to yell at you –"

"You did."

"Not enough," he growled, sipping his second sherry. "Nicole and Max, you owe them."

"I know."

"Good." The waiter took their orders. "So why lunch? What're you doing in comparative psych and Asian philosophy? They're irrelevant to treating brain-damaged adults."

Becca sat forward. "Rich Brent wants me to come to Santa Veronica, small program, some Master's students, local VA that needs an Adult Language Rehab Unit. I'm planning to take a trip to India this fall: reasons are vague but real. I've had it here; my 'Madison time' is over. At the department, I'm an outsider." GG listened. "Any reactions?"

Quail Hill

He nodded slowly. "You'll always be an outsider here. We let you in. Period. You've battered down the door for the next generation of women who'll walk in like the door never existed. So that job's finished."

"You're talking mega-change." He ticked things off. "1. Cynthia moves in. 2. You're shot. 3. They yank your kidney. 4. Cynthia gets admitted to do provisional work and moves in with a roommate. 5. You take this," he waved his hand dismissively, "sabbatical. 6. You travel to India! 7. You move to California from a big university to, forgive me for saying it, a dinky little school. 8. From MadCity to a small town where you've never lived. Most 'stress scales' would predict 'cardiac arrest' next week."

"I'm healthy but I'm fragmented here, GG."

"OK. You know things you're moving away from. What are you moving toward? What's the draw? Why Santa Veronica?"

"Weather. Pace. Rich and Jenny. My Uncle Mike lives in San Francisco. The opportunity to synthesize 25 years of work."

"You're a full professor. As long as you don't seduce some kid on the 50 yard line during halftime at homecoming, you can do just about what you want to do here."

"True and not true. I'm enjoying studying cross-cultural stuff—and it might be relevant—and Asian philosophy. For the first time in years I'm studying things outside my profession and not feeling guilty."

"Men always do that. You women are so serious—maybe just insecure. You all need a 95% on a test to believe you know anything. Men figure they're competent at about 75%. Must be a 'testosterone-driven swagger-component.' Complicated but someday research will show it's real." GG looked out over Lake Mendota. "Change here. You think St V's is perfect? No Miss Colesons there? No departmental bureaucratic crap? Think again."

"My Aunt Hildur gave me some of her books before she died: strange stuff leading me to other books and this sabbatical. Interesting ideas like 'Environment is stronger than willpower.' If that's true, my job is to create an environment that'll support the life I want. Trying to do that here would take more willpower than I've got. Resigning, selling my stuff, going to a different location will help me break from the driven academic life I've been living."

"Om, om, om," GG intoned. "You are into Asian stuff!"

"GG I'm talking about balance. I almost died. I've spent precious little time thinking about the meaning of life. I've always known mortality is real: you don't have a parent die when you're two and a half and miss that message. It's how I deal with things I want to change. What good's a second chance if I just keep dancing the same old dance?"

"OK. You understand the challenge. Now advice: first, wherever you go you take yourself and you are a member of species Homo sapiens. We have an annoying habit of wanting everything better and nothing different: which makes changing damned difficult. Second, in spiritual adventures, pick a worthy God. There are mind-robbing fundamentalist-nuts in all creeds. And third, life's a journey, not a destination." He looked out the window, watching sun reflect from the frozen, snow-covered surface of the lake. "Has Rich made an offer?"

"Yes." Becca handed him an envelope. After ordering chocolate mousse and coffee, he read the letter. The coffee came.

"Pretty standard. Get more money. Ask sweetly 'how close can you get to that -----'." He wrote a number on the envelope.

"You're serious?"

"Of course I'm serious. He's a department chair, you're his friend: if he can get you cheap he will. Besides, I need to earn this lunch."

"I'll miss you." Tears welled up in Becca's eyes.

"Don't get sloppy, Chadwick. I've toughened you up: don't lose it."

"Must be some spicy food making my eyes water," she replied.

"Better. Now, to my 'mousse chocolat.'"

"Your French is awful."

"But my advice's excellent," he smiled as he dug into his dessert.

25

Stultifying hot, humid air smothered the Ohio landscape in late June. Becca carried a tray with three glasses of iced tea through Marcia's newly redecorated living room (the decorating budget, unfortunately, had not been equal to the needs of the cumbersome old house) and out onto the screened-in porch. Eleanor and Marcia looked up surprised, like small children caught in a conspiracy.

"What is it?" Becca asked.

Eleanor smoothed her skirt, smiled and winked at Marcia who let a slow self-satisfied grin spread over her face as she shifted her position.

"Well," Eleanor began cheerfully, "making iced tea didn't take you long."

"What's going on?" Becca persisted.

"Did you find everything?" Marcia asked, ignoring Becca's question.

(*Suddenly the scene changed. Becca, aged three, stood in another doorway carefully holding the cookies they'd sent her to get. Marcia snuggled next to Eleanor with whom she exchanged guilty looks and then they laughed as they both looked at Becca. Becca felt her cheeks flush in anger. They'd sent her away and then united against her. In the world of 'us' against 'them' Becca had been designated 'them.'*)

"If she didn't, we'd better be careful, Marcia. Remember how she dropped the cookies?" Eleanor and Marcia laughed.

Becca's face flushed.

"We'd better get the tea before she drops it." Eleanor remarked and giggled heartily.

Becca wanted to hurl the iced tea at them, scream 'How dare you! I belong, too. I'm part of this family. Don't cut me out.' She resisted, knew what the response would be: 'can't you take a joke? We're only kidding.' But this behavior wasn't kidding: these weren't jokes. Becca put the tray down carefully, handed out the glasses of tea. She concentrated on the voices in her head as she practiced careful, regular breathing. Inhale. Exhale. Pause. Relax. She sat on an old porch chair and allowed her memory of the old scene to continue replaying.

("Stop it! Stop it! I got the cookies. Don't laugh at me!"

Eleanor's laugh escalated as she stroked Marcia's hair. Marcia sat with her back against Eleanor. She faced Becca and stuck her tongue out.

"Mother, she stuck her tongue out at me!" *Becca's three-year-old voice challenged.*

Eleanor's face froze. "Rebecca Elizabeth, don't accuse your sweet sister of awful things. You are a naughty, wicked child."

The cookies slid from the plate in Becca's hand, the terror of her isolation growing: the weight of her helplessness paralyzing her. Eleanor continued stroking Marcia's hair as her cold eyes glared at Becca.

"Look, Mother, she dropped the cookies," *Marcia smiled up innocently at Eleanor and then they both laughed.* "Baby Becca dropped the cookies," *Marcia's voice taunted. Then Eleanor joined in the obscene, repetitive duet.*

Three year old Becca felt like she'd explode. Then energy from some unknown place drove her from the room.)

Becca sipped her tea, suspended between levels of reality as the present threw her back into that ancient incident and she heard 'the little sucker' ranting.

("Get down! Hide! They hate you. They'll kill you. If they kill you I'll disappear. Just like Daddy. We'll all be dead. Please, baby, please. Get down." Darkness covered the infant who huddled in the bottom of the well. It was the only place 'the little sucker' could hide her.

The little sucker sat hunched over, alone and scared on the edge of the hole. With the baby they hated hidden, maybe they'd leave her alone. Maybe she could be tough enough, wouldn't hurt so much or care so much. Maybe she could just stop feeling.)

Marcia and Eleanor, like hounds after a fox, continued their verbal forays toward adult Becca. She said nothing, simply looked at them through her grown-up eyes and accepted their ridicule. She had survived. She might be distorted but she had accomplished her goals. The 'little sucker' had protected 'the baby' by putting her in the well. Becca blinked and sat absolutely still. With no response from her, Marcia and Eleanor shrugged, stopped their game and began discussing the wallpaper and drapes.

Excusing herself, Becca stood.

· Other Places ·

"Where are you going?" Eleanor asked, her bland eyes watching Becca in a vague, disinterested way.

"California. Then India," Becca moved toward the door. "Via Cincinnati," she added softly over her shoulder as she left the room.

Nancy Chadwick Goddard's imposing Tudor house nestled in the shade of huge catalpa trees that provided only minor relief from the relentless Cincinnati heat. Becca pulled into the driveway, turned off the engine, checked her makeup and stepped out just in time to greet Nancy as she came out the front door. With her golden hair, ivory silk blouse, navy blue Bermuda shorts and coral jewelry, Nancy looked like a Vogue model. Becca, practical to her teeth, wore cotton from skin out, felt comfortable but looked a bit rumpled in the sticky heat.

They both mumbled things like 'it's been too long, you look wonderful, thank you for letting me come, thank you for coming' as they hugged. Becca sniffed and blew her nose while tears streamed silently down Nancy's face.

"Well, that hasn't changed," Becca began. "Me snorting like a bull while you and Josephine managed polite silent tears during the folding of the flag."

"And today's weather isn't much different from that day."

"My memories of Greg's funeral replay like an old newsreel—a tattered black and white photo here, distorted faces, my hands clutching the flag, confusion and grief pulsating in the heat. I watched myself perform from a spot on my right shoulder. Coming here, it all rolls back. I knew I needed to see you before I moved to California."

"I hoped you'd come back one day." As they entered the air-conditioned house Becca shivered.

"How's everybody?" Becca asked, glancing around the pale green and cream interior.

"We're fine. I play lots of tennis, direct the Diocesan Feeding Program, organize the house, our social life and kids and oversee Mother's finances. Tim loves teaching and has a good position at University of Cincinnati. Mother's slower. After Dad died it took her a couple years to find her stride, establish her new place…"

"Dowager Queen of Cincinnati."

"Don't be cruel."

"It's not cruel, Nancy. She is the most regal person I've ever known meaning that she is proper, kind and generous. As a mother-in-law she was tough sledding. She didn't want me."

"Initially maybe, but she changed: understood that you and Greg had good chemistry. When Dad died, your letters impressed her. Since then, she's been genuinely fond of you."

"By then Greg had been dead for ten years and our struggle long over. We've always written and she's shown interest in my career."

"Anyway, you're in her Will."

"That's absurd. I don't belong there."

"That's for her to decide. It's no big deal. A little cash, some jewelry. Let's get iced tea and go to the patio."

"Thanks for letting me come early."

"When you called yesterday I was afraid you were backing out, would skip Cincinnati. That would've hurt and the schedule change is not a problem."

"Things," Becca hesitated, "changed in Dayton."

"Changed how?' Nancy asked as they settled into chairs on the porch overlooking the neatly kept garden. "What happened?"

Becca stared out at the butterflies in the lavender. "Some old memories surfaced and I saw connections I'd never understood. How Eleanor manipulated us: kept Marcia and me apart, kept Biff and me apart. Maybe if Andy had lived she'd have kept us apart, too. She'd say little negative things about Marcia: about her redecorating, about Marcia as a mother. Then she'd cozy up to Marcia and whisper things obviously about me. It was sick and I felt exhausted.

"So here I am to reconnect with all you Chadwicks a couple days early."

"We're glad. Want to know the plan?"

"Sure. I'm big on plans."

"Tim'll pick you up at about 2:00 to go to the cemetery. I'm busy this afternoon. Mother wants you to have time alone with Tim. After Greg died, she tried to run Tim's life but once he stood up to her and declared he would study history and teach at university level, she backed off. But he has deep unresolved pain about Greg."

"We're all civilian causalities, collateral damage of Vietnam—like much of the nation."

"Probably right. Anyway, tonight we'll go to Mother's for dinner."

"All of us? That's a big dinner."

"She loves to entertain and hasn't cooked in years. Uses a catering service she helped establish run by single mothers. She swims everyday and volunteers at the hospital. She's a remarkable woman."

"She always has been."

The thunderstorm broke at 2:10. Rain beat down on the Chevy's windows as thy waited in the cemetery parking lot for the storm to pass.

"Do I look like him?" Tim sounded wistful.

"Same profile but your blond hair isn't like his."

"His college buddy said I look like him."

"I was his wife, not his buddy so I saw him in a different way."

"I always fantasized that you married him to be close to me." Tim laughed. "God, I fell in love with you when he brought you home."

"Pretty normal for a kid that age," Becca grinned.

"Do you ever wonder—if it's really him in the grave? That he's really alive someplace?"

"No," she lied, answering too fast, then continued more evenly. "I try not to spend time on that Timmy. It can't do any good."

"But you've wondered."

"Early on I wondered. It made me crazy. But not anymore. The identification…"

"They could fake that. You know they could."

"But they didn't." The rain stopped and steam sizzled from hot asphalt as the sun returned. Becca opened her door and stepped out. "It's time, Tim. Let's go."

26

Following two more busy days in Cincinnati, Becca headed west. This afternoon the highway before her rolled toward the setting sun like a black ribbon through a green ocean. St. Louis and Topeka lay behind her; Kansas stretched before her lush and hot toward the horizon. 'Staggeringly big, this country.' She reached for her coke. As the miles passed, Becca recycled details of the past two weeks.

First, the strange 'odd woman out' dynamic she felt with Eleanor and Marcia. Real? Just her perception? Selective memory? Eleanor loved her, she knew that but Eleanor's 'best' had been amputated. Had Becca followed a similar pattern after Greg? Stayed aloof from involvement as protection against future pain?

Then, in Cincinnati at Greg's grave, she'd plucked stray grass from the edge of his headstone as a rainbow arced over Kentucky, her feet wet in the rain-drenched, well-kept cemetery. Greg's grave lay flat and smooth, no seams in the grass: an old grave.

That night Josephine gave her a ruby ring: Greg's grandmother's ring. Today, the stone sparkled sending darts of light dancing around the car, bringing her back to the present.

She scanned the horizon: no storms. Maybe she'd get out of Kansas without visiting Oz. A ruby ring wasn't Ruby Slippers but she felt protected and affirmed in her life as a Chadwick. Her time with Nancy, Josephine and Tim had been a gift. She smiled as she drove on.

***** 'You must see,' the bird screeched, diving toward her, its eyes wild, talons extended. 'You must seeeeeeeee.'

'See what? See where? Tell me something useful.' Becca confronted the bird.

Surprised, it swooped past, brushing her right ear and then ascended vertically straight toward the sun. 'Keep looking. See,' it screeched drawing the vowel out in the rapidly expanding space between them.

A siren dying in the night blended with the screeching bird as she awoke. Opening her eyes, the darkness did not change. Kansas: I'm someplace in western Kansas. "Well, I showed him," she said quietly. "Damned bird." Rearranging the sheets, Becca smiled back into sleep.

***** On the drive through the Rockies from Denver to Salt Lake City she reflected, 'If Greg had lived, who would we be? What went on in Vietnam? Do my dreams mean anything? What am I supposed to 'see'? Why did I feel so little at Greg's grave?'

After the long day's drive, swimming laps at the motel pool released some of the kinks. After dinner she turned in early.

***** The little sucker crawled to the hole, looked over the edge and shook her head slowly.

'I knew it. I told you to leave her in there. She's gone and lost and it's not my fault.'

The baby sat by an open grave. 'I'm over here. I'm not lost.'

'You're gonna fall in,' the little sucker moved beside the baby and they both looked into the grave.

'Get away from there,' screamed the little sucker, grabbing 'Baby' by the collar.

***** Just beyond Donner Pass, Becca turned off on the road indicated on the Bhakti Community Map Shampa had sent. Uncle Mike had told her this community planned a trip to India; the founder had been Hildur's friend. Becca had checked in with Uncle Mike last night.

"Do you know these people? Are they a bunch of nuts?"

"I don't know them, Becca, but your Aunt Hilly liked their 'good energy.' I doubt they're a bunch of nuts. Enjoy your visit. Hilly liked spending time there. Come whenever you want to. Just leave a message on my answering machine with the date."

"Do I get to meet Sylvia?"

"Of course, we'll all go out to dinner."

Becca wondered if she should be offended about Sylvia, Uncle Mike's new wife, but figured Aunt Hilly would scoff at such silliness.

'Bhakti Community—Turn Right in 200 yards.'

· Other Places ·

After turning right, Becca concentrated on avoiding ruts in the badly maintained road. An opening in the evergreens and 12 parked-cars indicated she had arrived.

'Please Check in at the Visitor Center.'

Despite Uncle Mike's reassuring words, Becca's apprehension rose. Tension crept into her muscles as fear, that old familiar protector, mounted. Inhale. Exhale. Relax. 'No one can trap me here. I do not need to defend against these people. I can be nice and take the opportunity to practice being less defensive.'

Arriving at the Visitor Center the semi-mystic serenity of the place dissolved in loud printer noise and a man's strong voice yelling at a computer screen behind the desk.

"No, no. Stop! Please, machine: stop! Enough." He hit the keyboard, searched the screen frantically and glanced up. "Hi, I'll be with you when I recapture the gremlins. If you know computers, help me. Otherwise, pray. Please, machine: STOP!"

Becca stepped around the desk, pressed a few keys. The printer's pace slowed and then stopped. She smiled.

A silly grin spread across the man's large, heavy-featured face. "Thank you. I'm Zev Levy. Welcome to Bhakti." Before she could respond Zev, a big man between 30 and 35, put his fingers to his temples, closed his eyes and began swaying from side to side. "No, don't tell me. It's getting clearer. I have it." He popped his hands away, opened his eyes. "You are Rebecca Chadwick!"

Becca scrunched up her face: not sure whether to laugh or run and wondered if she'd stumbled into rehearsals for a new Charlie Chaplin movie.

"I know," he said smiling broadly, "what's a nice Jewish boy like me doing in a place like this? Answer: living with devotion and trying to love God more. "Rebecca Chadwick's the only guest scheduled to arrive today so if that's not you, I sincerely apologize."

"You're right, I'm Becca. It's just, well, you do look a bit more like salami on rye than a member of a vegetarian community."

"The things I've given up for happiness. Welcome. You followed the map; you survived the road; you're in time for lunch. I'll give you a tour and eternal thanks for the computer work. Let's check you in." They filled out the forms; she wrote a check.

He picked up the computer print out and read aloud, "Aunt Hildur Morgan knew Swami, is considering India trip, religious background 'Congregational or Episcopalian,' Spiritual practices 'question mark,' brochure and map sent, scheduled to meet with Swami at 10 tomorrow. Now, what would you like to know about us?"

· Quail Hill ·

"I learned about the India trip from my Uncle. I'm moving to Santa Veronica in California and I'm interested in India so here I am." They walked across a large clearing surrounded by various well-kept, simple buildings.

"That's Isis cabin: Goddess of Fertility. You're booked there."

"Fertility?"

"You want something else? Maybe Shiva? Destroyer of the ego, the Universe?"

"Isis is fine."

"Do you meditate?"

"No, but I try to breathe slowly."

"That's OK. A lot of folks come to take our meditation classes. Shampa, my wife, can talk to you about the India trip later."

"You're married to Shampa? Is that an Indian name?"

"Yes. Swami gave it to her. It means lightening. She grew up in the Bronx: lox and bagels like me." They stopped by a large building. "This is the dining hall and meeting center. Beginners meditate here. We don't have many rules just no booze or drugs and we take off our shoes inside buildings." They entered the dining hall after lining their sandals up with many others. Folks were setting tables, working in the kitchen, a couple of kids played jacks: a normal, happy atmosphere. "The daily schedule's posted there. On a 'personal retreat' like you're on, mainly the meal times matter."

After lunch, Becca checked into Isis #3. So far, so good. She'd meet Shampa at 3:30 to talk about the India trip.

The next morning Zev took her to Swami's house. It stood beside the community's main vegetable garden on the other side of this large, rural complex. The front of Swami's bungalow faced a rose garden full of dozens of old plants in various stages of bloom. As they approached through the garden, Swami unfolded his extremely slim 6'3" frame from his chair, stood gracefully, and offered his hand. He totally overpowered the small porch. With his laughing blue eyes, thin hawk-like facial features, long graceful hands, white hair and dark Indian complexion he looked like a Swami from central casting: only his blue jeans and 'I Ran the Bhakti Community Marathon' T-shirt added appropriate California flavor.

"Hildur's niece, Rebecca. I'm delighted you are here." He extended his hand and smiled warmly.

"Thank you."

"How's the visit going? Are we too strange?"

"Actually," Becca spoke slowly, "not nearly as strange as I feared."

He laughed. "Grace?" he called over the back of his giant rattan chair. "Bring us tea will you please? And sugar. I have a guest." He lowered his voice conspiratorially. "The only time my keepers bring sugar is for guests." He sat back smiling. Something about his intensity made Becca feel as though she were falling through space—a strangely pleasant sensation.

Tea arrived.

27

"Do you," he asked slowly, watching the lump of sugar dissolve in his spoon, "know why you are here?" His laser-like blue eyes pinned Becca like a butterfly in a bug collection.

"Somehow I needed to come: the India trip. But…" she shrugged.

"Yes, the trip," he sipped his tea, his expression softened. "But…?"

Ideas flitted through her mind. "Maybe to meet you and see another way to live. Touch Aunt Hildur: make new connections. Since I was shot it's like I need to build a new grid, spider like. Like I exist in infinite black space, my only light reflected from the thin strands of a three dimensional web that connect me to other people, other points. Now, lots of old familiar lines seem gone: cut or untied. And at the same time, new connections are forming.

"Aunt Hilly's books, new ideas. There's a world I've never explored. I'm drawn to things but suspect hidden dangers. Hildur trusted you; I trusted her." She stopped, sipped tea and looked directly into his eyes. "Why do you believe I'm here?"

He chuckled, sat back, clasped his hands behind his head and looked off into space, past the trees, over the mountains.

"Once, sound and light began. Everything that is now was then—at least potentially—so everything is interconnected in strange, yet basic, ways. We all breathe the same air. In crowded rooms oxygen and carbon dioxide move from lung to lung, slip past permeable boundaries, circulate through us nourishing us and then we breathe out and what's expelled is inhaled by another person. On and on. Doesn't look predictable. I read a book when I was 15; Hildur married your Uncle; they moved to San Francisco; I gave a lecture she attended and here we are together drinking tea. To me, it's no more random than the white corpuscles grouping at a cut on my hand. Yet the corpuscles arrive by what appears to be vague wandering through my circulatory system. In truth, they are pulled into place by dozens of biological processes evolved over eons of time, and my wound heals.

"When I speak of 'soul,' 'God' or 'infinite being' wooing us, pulling us toward a transforming presence or mystical encounter, Westerners go nuts. 'What? My free will isn't totally free? My individualism's not absolute? My 'I' interacts with your 'I' in predictable ways?' Predictable, that is, if looked at from a different perspective.

"I've lived in the U.S. for thirty years but I'm an Indian, a Hindu: I see through my cultural prism; you see through yours. This may sound strange but, for me, there is only one reason you've come: because your path to growth, to freedom and to God requires it. You can ignore your soul's call: we often do. But we each have eternity to listen to our creator's voice.

"So, my new friend, continue to rebuild your web: attach a thread to Bhakti if you wish. Why not? You can always cut it." He leaned forward and poured more tea.

Light from her ruby ring danced across his face as she shifted slightly. "I'm not sure I believe that."

"You asked what I believe not what you believe." His eyes sparkled as a bright smile slid across his face. "That you must find yourself." They sat for a few minutes in silence. "So," he began again, stretching lightly, "what about India? Want to come with us?" He curled back into his chair, elbows on the arms, fingertips lightly touching, chin resting between his index and middle fingers, legs sprawled awkwardly.

"Will everybody meditate all the time? I can't do that. I tried but I can't sit quietly and I'm not sure it makes sense."

"Most people will meditate; you needn't. I will. It's central for me. Do you play an instrument? Golf? Ski?"

"Ski, badly, yes."

"And after your first day on the slopes, were you an expert?"

She smiled. "Even after twenty years I'm not."

"But after a couple of twenty minute attempts you write meditation off." His eyes twinkled as he slid his long grasshopper-like legs across the porch and pursed his lips.

"That sounds stupid," she agreed, "but I won't be a zombie lined up for some controlling egomaniac's forced-march off a cliff." The words tumbled out, unmonitored.

"I certainly hope that is not what's going on here," he replied evenly.

"I'm sorry, I don't mean you, personally. It's just some of this stuff scares me. Zev and Shampa are nice. Most folks here seem fine but some look plastic. Their smiles seem superficial. I won't do that."

"No one wants you to. Some hang onto me, to Bhakti, like Dumbo to his red feather—convinced that, if they relax, deviate even briefly, they'll crash and be destroyed. They're scared that if they stop smiling the darkness they are trying to hold back will absorb them. And, just as Dumbo learned that flapping his ears was his power, they need to learn to trust and to love. Most learn. Your image of rebuilding a spider-web grid in a black void would scare many people but at our best here, we try to be open to mystery and look for the truth in the many creeds. I teach what I've been given. You may find it useful; you may not. You decide.

"For me, in this world we learn lessons and continue our journey. We've only one goal: getting home to God, 'that which is,' transcendent deity, creator. In my framework, you'll get as many opportunities as your soul needs."

Becca exhaled through pursed lips. "So, reincarnation. Holy cow. What am I getting into?" She gazed off into the distance as a bird sang a lemon-sherbet song.

He chuckled. "We've few locked doors, you'll leave in three hours, so nothing very confining." He folded his legs back under him. "Come on, Becca, let's have lunch."

28

After a visit with Uncle Mike in San Francisco, Becca headed north on coast route #1: 'one of America's most scenic highways.' She'd bought a few new tapes and listened to Trappist Monks and show tunes on the harp while inching up the coast.

Glimpsing the Pacific while careening around rock formations and crawling through hairpin turns, Becca experienced the beautiful drive. At Sonoma Coast State Beach she stopped, drank coffee and watched the surf rolling onto the shore under the morning sun. The tide was like breathing: in—out—pause. Ideas skipped through her mind like stones on a smooth lake. Did certain things lock into memory because they got trapped like leaves caught behind sticks in a stream? How much personal freedom existed? You could change your focus but could you, as it were, change trains or only your seat in a given train-car? Or only adjust your position in the seat? Would the trip to India be 'opportunity' or 'danger'? Or, like the Asian character, indicate both simultaneously? If nothing else, India would be something new.

> *'Be not the first on whom the new is tried*
> *Nor be the last to turn the old aside.'*

Her high school French teacher wrote that on the blackboard one day. Everyday for years, her teacher wrote a new phrase, yet that was the only one Becca's mind trapped, dragged around with her like a child dragging a teddy bear. Why?

As she walked in the sun, she pictured Uncle Mike and Sylvia. Sylvia: blond, blue eyed, twenty years older than Becca. Perfectly smooth blond pageboy hair. Jealousy flared. Then Becca laughed. 'It isn't her relationship with Uncle Mike that bothers me; it is just her perfect hair. My whole life I've fought my curly hair: endured jokes, put-downs.' Remembering some particularly painful comments from Eleanor, Marcia and Biff, Becca kicked a shell. Eleanor and Marcia teaming up to attack Becca and then Eleanor enlisting Becca to attack Marcia or Biff: always two against one. What a mess. Are childhood memories so powerful because they're stored first?

She got back in the car and headed north. Fort Bragg. Leggett. On to Jenny and Rich's in Santa Veronica. The moving-truck bringing her few things should arrive the next day.

All the boxes stood empty, broken down, ready to store. A few pictures hung on the walls of the rental house she'd occupy until she found a house to buy. Adjusting the old mirror in the front hall completed things. She watched her reflection and nodded happily.

Her reversed image smiled back. How many relatives had watched their reflections in that mirror? Grandma Amy Louise said Great-Grandmother Libby had had this mirror and probably others before that. The peeling silver backing spoke of age and the buttery walnut frame saluted generations of care. Becca studied her reflection: a bit gray, bone structure holding up, eyes clear and direct. Suddenly she laughed.

"You ass! You dope! Not jealous of Sylvia? Only her hair?" Becca spoke aloud and leaned closer to the mirror. "Get real, Becca. Uncle Mike's your closest link to Andy—the god-man, myth-person; the 'blown out of all proportion star of your life' like Clark Gable in 'Gone With The Wind.' Not jealous that she is closer to him than you are? Not jealous of her ability to love well enough to attract him? Not jealous that they are doing the 'till death us do part' thing? Not still fighting with the 'you aren't married, don't have children so are some kind of defective woman' image that society keeps throwing in your face? Does this ever end?"

"Maybe not but I've brought coffee," Jenny called from the kitchen.

Becca jumped. "Shit, Jenny, you just took ten year off my life!"

Jenny grinned. "Possibly, but you and old dark eyes in the mirror were edging close to unraveling some 'absolute Truth' about modern life that might catapult you into a state far beyond worrying about your being unmarried and Sylvia's perfect hair. So I rescued you.

"Today's Santa Veronica lesson: do not leave the back door standing open if you want privacy. Now, show me what you've done and then we'll go look for curtains."

Five weeks later Becca sat in Rich's office exchanging small talk, wondering why he'd called her. Becca re-crossed her legs. They fell into silence; he bit his lip.

"Something's come up. I need you here the last week you're scheduled to be in India."

Bingo! She sat quietly and did not reply. She'd stashed their letter of agreement in her blazer pocket; that comforted her.

Rich sat forward. "If I'd known earlier I'd have worked something out, but" he raised his hands in helpless innocence. "Sorry, I need you here that week. I've got a meeting."

"Gee, Rich," Becca kept her voice even, her tone light, tried not to laugh, "that's a tough problem you've got but you'll find a solution." She didn't move. He stared at her, straight faced, reached up, removed his little half glasses and concentrated on cleaning them.

"I believed you could be gone five weeks but that's impossible now." Rich glanced up briefly. Becca sighed.

"Wrong, Rich. You didn't 'believe' I could be gone for five weeks, you contracted with me that I would be gone for five weeks." She slid their letter of agreement out, unfolded it and cleared her throat.

Rich interrupted. "I know what the letter says. I'm talking about new circumstances and department needs. I was hoping you'd help me out." He smiled a plaintive, little boy smile.

"Rich, you are my friend, colleague and, in this department, my boss. We have a contract that I will fulfill. As to helping this department, well, by being here I do that. This isn't some Judy Garland—Mickey Rooney movie; I'm not gonna jump up and say 'Let's put on a musical and save the college!'

"You will miss three class sessions of that last week if you are gone. It's listed as your course; I'm there for half teaching credit. Assign an appropriate project and deal with it."

He looked up. "That won't wash."

"Wash with whom? You're the Chair. What's the problem?"

"People are making waves; some think you got too good a deal."

"Chairmen are paid to ride waves. Lower the centerboard and sail! For Pete's sake, Rich. Some of the old boys get pissed at the work I have Paula do but my grant pays her salary."

"You could back off there a little, too."

"Would you like it better if I sat in the corner holding a blue blanket and sucking my thumb? If I back off, they'll say 'tisk, tisk, Chadwick isn't pulling her weight. Where are her grant proposals? Her papers for the May conference in DC?'

"Would we be having this conversation if my first name were 'Ralph'? There are pie-throwers out there, Rich. No matter what I do someone will attack me.

Sexism exists. Jealousy in academia exists. We made a deal. You hired me, my reputation, my successful academic career and you signed a contract that I'll be gone for five weeks. I didn't come here to relive the 1950's, be a brunette version of The Donna Reed Show. I'm here. It's 1986 and I'm going to Thailand and India for five weeks."

"You could just call me a sexist pig and be done with it."

"You aren't a pig. Sexist? Sure. So am I. That's why we need to talk about it. I won't roll over and play dead, bat my eyes and say 'of course, Rich, whatever you say Rich.' Twenty years ago in grad school, I imagined the 'equality-thing' would grow in some nice, genteel way. Somehow we women would be treated equally without a fight. Hasn't quite worked that way. You once told me that, in a knife fight, a person needs to make two decisions: first, that you're gonna win and second, that you're gonna get cut. Furthermore, without the second decision, the first won't happen. Well, I've been one of hundreds of 'point-women' in a dirty little war most people don't even know is happening. Half the time I don't recognize the battles till they're over. I've been cut but I'm on my feet and I'm here. If this position makes me 'point-woman' at Santa Veronica, so be it. Society keeps trying to crush women into smiling, eye-fluttering, submissive ninnies. Not gonna work. I have a contract. You break that and I'm out of here. Now, I have work to do before I leave for India." She stood and headed for the door.

"Santa Veronica hasn't gone through the changes Madison has," Rich said softly.

Becca stopped and turned. "Change the name of the city and that's what my Chair at Madison said 20 years ago. 'Go slowly; don't upset anyone.' Maybe the women twenty years behind us will behave better, will benefit from the fact that the castle's been stormed and the gates are open. Maybe what women like me need to understand is that our generation's job has been storming castles, getting cut, bruised, ground up and, at times, behaving badly. Maybe I'll retire and write my memoir: 'What I Did In The Sex-Equity War,' sell it wrapped in plain brown paper so as not to offend the 'Old Boy's Network' and the Moral Majority."

"You weren't this strident twenty years ago."

"I was young! Is that who you wanted to hire? Confused Vietnam widow? Dance and smile just like Dory Previn's song?"

"No, but…"

"But what?"

Rich paused a long time. "You don't make my job easier."

"Yes, I do." Becca's voice sounded firm but not defiant. "By the courses I'll teach, the program I'm developing at the VA, the grants I have, the papers I write and the interdepartmental contacts I'm making. I'm not out of line here, Rich. I'm playing by the rules and I only get surly and nasty with you. After all these years can't our relationship stand honesty?" Silence draped around them, embarrassing them both, like unnoticed cobwebs suddenly discovered in the presence of guests. She looked down at her shoes and dug her right heel into the floor.

Rich took a deep breath and spoke evenly. "OK. I'll assign projects and we will grade them together. Agreed?"

She looked at him and smiled. "Sure. Just no funny business in the projects."

He chuckled. "I promise."

She opened his office door and started out.

"Hey, Bec?"

"What?"

"Have a good trip."

"Thanks." She walked past the secretaries all of whom suddenly became very intent on their work.

29

Trip Diary. October 1986.
New Deli, INDIA. Amazing to be here. Three days in Bangkok, now India. Bangkok memories: flowers, spirit houses on every building to protect and show respect to the spirits or gods or whatever. NOISE! Thai silk—magic colors like spun glass. The group chants a lot. Sometimes I almost remain calm during meditations.

Went to a Buddhist Monastery where we'd understood we were expected only to learn we were not. No problem. Some unseen supporter provided a huge feast for us (we are about 45 in all) while the monks interrupted their meditation and gave us a ninety-minute tour of the facility: eight of us with each monk-guide. Our guide, a young woman in her brown robe and shaved head, joined the monastery 10 years ago. Before that she worked in a big advertising firm: big money, fast track, jet-set life. 'Then I came here and found joy.'

After the tour we returned to the main room where the feast awaited us: foods I didn't even recognize. I watched Swami and my roommate and did what they did! Then we chanted.

As we were leaving, one nun, with whom I'd chatted and to whom I felt surprisingly close, said 'I'm glad our lives have touched. We'll not meet again in this life but you are in my heart.' Then she bowed using the conventional 'namaste' greeting. (My roommate, Deborah, says it means 'I bow to the God within you.') I felt humble. As we left, a recording of our chanting played over the PA system. The head monk laughed and said 'we've captured your singing to remember the sweetness of your visit.' We left with their infectious joy around us and reentered the undertow of Bangkok.

"Becca, do you have another plastic bag?" Deborah called from the bathroom. "My blouse isn't dry yet."

"Big or little?"

"Probably big," Deborah walked into the bedroom carrying the damp blouse. With graying hair pulled back and trapped at the nape of her neck, large green eyes made larger by her glasses, perfect makeup on a face unafraid of her sixty-five years, cherry red cotton shirt, plaid skirt and Birkenstocks, Deborah Mahoney, once a Catholic nun, now a family therapist, wife, mother and grandmother, destroyed stereotypes. Swami called her 'an old soul.' A committed Roman Catholic and feminist, she said Swami's Hindu meditative techniques strengthened her focus on God. A smile spread across Deborah's face: a smile that looked like a ray of happiness emerging through a crack in the universe. Becca felt a smile brighten her own face.

"Oh, Becca, we're going to the Taj Mahal: to see it, touch it, feel its energy." Deborah was big on 'feeling energy.'

Becca laughed. "Stick the blouse in a bag and the bag in your suitcase. We're due in the lobby."

Trip Diary.

The Taj's 'energy' surprised me. After my first glimpse, I turned and there, reflected in Deborah's sunglasses, were two Taj Mahals floating above her radiant smile. Hope my picture turns out. The Taj's 'energy' does seem to draw you in and spin you around. Purified by the scorching sun it remains century after century: 'I am perfection. Beauty. Love. Death.' Words fail. Silence and awe linger like heavy incense.

Heat. Muddy children begging. Cattle roaming or sprawling in the dust, blocking traffic, nonchalantly swishing flies. Peddlers: wooden elephants, brass bells, cheap ankle bracelets. I felt rude, moneyed and arrogant brushing past them. Begging lepers angered me. I wanted to scream 'this is a treatable disease.' Felt choked by my self-righteousness. India barely feeds itself and I'm indignant that lepers beg? Back in our hotel, hot and cold running water behind a secure, walled courtyard. Confusion yanks at strands of the carefully arranged logic inside my head. I've got a knot in my brain, a toothache in my selfish, brutish Western soul. Such beauty and such chaos coexisting. Brutal poverty and squalor next to so much elegance and plenty. I can barely breathe.

Becca stopped writing. Deborah sat on the other bed, filing her nails.

"Sometimes I can't stand India."

"The sum? The whole of it?"

Becca nodded. "It's so triumphant and so squalid. The total assaults me: shakes my bones. I don't understand what's happening inside me."

"India's an experience. My first trip felt silencing. Intellectually, I knew 'my world view' was just that: *my* world view but, diving into a culture so different was shattering."

"Today I almost started screaming at the lepers and I felt terrible and turned away."

"Why?"

"My God, I felt so guilty: angry with the medical system, angry with the lepers. I have so much and the guides say 'don't give to the beggars.' The hotel staff sweeps poor ragged children away like stray cats. And, if I'm honest, I don't want to touch them; I don't trust them. I hate that in myself but I'm not Mother Teresa; I can't save them all."

"Neither can she. There's a Jewish mandate to the effect that the people you must help are those right in front of you."

"You're the second woman to tell me that."

Deborah smiled and continued. "I find it very challenging but I try to do it wherever I am. Here, I buy sweet limes at the market, pass them out along the way."

"This noon you gave me a sweet lime."

"This noon, you were a needy person right in front of me. Now bathe, rest. I'll take a swim before dinner." She changed into her bathing suit and headed for the pool.

"India, India I love your very dust." The words slipped out as she dropped her towel on a chair, pulled on her bathing cap and dove into the cool water.

30

The full moon cast eerie shadows across the crude path as they picked their way toward the Ganges. A total lunar eclipse would begin in an hour. Deborah touched Becca's arm, stopping her. Behind them, Swami placed a hand on each woman's shoulder. Several shadowy figures stepped past them on the trail. A man, clutching a white-shrouded child's body, led. A woman followed, holding a bit of cloth that straggled from the corpse; others followed her. The group moved like a giant ant: one organic unit carrying their burden.

After the funeral party passed, Swami said quietly, "Yogis and young children aren't cremated, just weighted with stones and sunk in the river."

"But people bathe there, brush their teeth in that river!" The horror in Becca's voice showed on the silver-shadowed face she turned toward Deborah and Swami.

He nodded. "Yes, that also."

Swami's long angular nose and the stars above him spun dizzily above her as Becca's stomach tightened.

"Courage, Becca," his voice commanded.

'Breathe,' she reminded herself. Inhale. Exhale. Pause. After regaining her composure, they moved toward the dock and boarded their boat.

The oarsmen slid the open boat onto the black water. Becca held tightly to the side as they glided past other tourists. On shore, thousands of Hindus gathered and a corporate humming sound, like bees hovering around a hive, rose from them. The murmuring people joining the boat's rhythmic undulation reactivated Becca's dizziness. Breathing steadily she wove a new mantra: 'I'll not be sick, I'll not pass out.'

A sliver of shadow nicked the moon's bright face and the mob entered the water. Sounds surged toward the boats as thousands of pilgrims sought protection in Mother Ganga. Without knowing the language, Becca understood the primal aching, the helpless moan. Protect us, Mother. Protect the flesh you spawned, save us from the vicissitudes of this death-dealing cosmos we inhabit. Hide us tucked beneath your wings, secure against the warm down of your breast, bury us in some safe place, soothe our terror, eliminate our fear, give us what none can ever give: a place where no greater power holds sway, where neither horror, nor image of horror, abides. Save us. Save ME. I, this grand controlling creature that I would believe I am: i, i so small, insignificant and terrified that a shadow creeping across a lifeless, rocky satellite creates gut-wrenching dread.

The episode stirred shocking sensuality. The pull of negative and positive: an ache toward ecstasy that cared neither about the good nor evil of some act but simply arose internally. Becca felt as though she carried within her the same potential tension that rent creation in the beginning, blasted universes open, flung galaxies across space-time, with no turning back until the hunger was fulfilled. Then, the forces spent and sated, these awful, urgent powers would uncouple and once more lie quietly together, panting in neutrality, rocking softly like a boat upon water—waiting.

Sitting taut as a bowstring, Becca heard a small splash, jerked her head around just in time to see in the dim distance the woman's hand release the straggling bit of shroud, a useless, mocking, false umbilical cord that had continued to attach her to the child: a child she could now no more bring back to life than could the crowd push the shadow from the moon. Just then another boat of tourists with cameras pointed and faces stretched white in the eerie light, darted between them and the burial party's boat. Becca's head dropped and she stared down as tears, instantly absorbed, plopped onto her printed cotton skirt, a skirt so colorful by day but now just shades of gray. The impassive, hidden moon continued its slow journey through the sky.

***** Dancing flecks, like grains from distant stars, and a slice of luster wiggled on a rippling surface; it all rolled peacefully within her mind. One small speck of light at the far edge oozed across the surface, slid into form and bobbed up suddenly: a skull, alone at first, and then with shoulders, arms and finally legs from which hung rotten cloth. Becca flinched, rolled over, re-drowned the image in her mind and relaxed, surrounded once again by sweet remembered moonlight on the water. Abruptly, every particle of light shifted, reforming a skull and fragmentary child carcass bound by a rotting sari. No leaky boat's protection now: she fought the downward pull of heavy rocks, struggled as bones brushed by her and closed overhead cutting off the moonlight. Kicking free from her shackles, desperately responding to a cry for life, Becca burst through the surface only to find her nemesis swooping toward her from the sky.

"See!" The bird screamed. "SEE!"

"See what?' she moaned, "bones? Dead children? Why?"

"Not 'what or why,'" the bird spun her backward, sent her tumbling off in space. "See 'HOW,' Rebecca. 'How' is what you need."

Unexpectedly, the bird, now white and gold, merged with a huge expanding star that raced toward her across the universe.

"How?" Becca wondered in a murmured, plaintive cry before colliding with the light.

Expanding outward, spreading through eternity, carried on the atoms of this exploding sun, completely disintegrating, she relaxed into a splintered unitary wonder of the warm and loving 'Great I AM,' led onward by the gilded, transformed bird that had haunted her for years.

"Of course, it's 'How' that matters."

31

Diary
Strange dream after lunar eclipse on the Ganges. 'How' is the message my now gold and white, tormenting bird delivered. Will ask Deborah, my local 'wise woman.'

These entries shorten. India doesn't fit into words or even categories.

****** Becca and Deborah sat on their balcony of their ever so first-class hotel by the Bay of Bengal sipping hot tea. A welcome breeze toyed with the bougainvillea as waves arched their spines and gently rolled their juicy content onto the beach.

"That's it: end of dream. Later, I figured the whole thing might have been a little temporal lobe seizure."

Deborah sat quietly in the high-backed rattan chair holding her English bone china cup lightly. She flicked her eyes from the horizon back to Becca. "Which leaves you—?"

"Wondering if this is about as meaningful as a dog chasing its tail, that my idea that some universal power sends messages to me via an imaginary bird is both terribly egotistical and absurd. It's explained more parsimoniously as a cortical hiccough."

"In a cortex created by—?" Deborah fixed Becca in her gaze.

"By life."

"Begun by—?"

"What difference does it make? Maybe creation just *is* and dreams a way we clean out our brains, like shaking crumbs from a tablecloth."

"So 'How' is not important and there is no God."

"I don't know what anybody means when they say God."

"To quote Teilhard de Chardin: 'God defined is God finished.' That gives me solace. And dreams may be glitches or messages and, for you, 'how' may be important." Deborah gazed toward the horizon.

"Like, how I look at things, see things because it comes along with the insistent 'you must see.' What am I not seeing?"

"Perhaps you're seeing only partially."

Becca kicked off her sandals, slouched down and propped her chin on her folded hands. "OK. Light enters my eye, stimulates my optic nerve and sends electrical impulses to my brain. Patterns emerge, I find a related image and my brain chooses a reaction. That's how I see."

"Yes, with physical eyes. But in your dream, when you exploded into the light, did you 'see' that experience?"

"Not really. I expanded, dissipated and became huge and universal; I became the light. Words don't work: it wasn't scientific or logical. I felt warm. If it's a seizure, why not? If it isn't God but some brain activity, why not?"

"What if this is at least part of something that, for convenience, we'll call God?"

"Burping in the midst of someone's sleeping brain is a strange way to communicate."

"What would you prefer? You've only got a few sensory channels. And at least when you're asleep your defenses are down and you're less likely to drive off the road."

"Look, Deb, maybe Ted Bundy got messages in his sleep: 'go rape/murder brown haired women.' This is a message from God? Please."

"An evil message. From God? Most Christians would say 'no' but a Hindu might say 'evil mediated by a distorted face of creation' or a message from 'low energy.'

"We can point ourselves toward evil. Are you so pure that you've never willfully persisted in a bad habit? Never kept your attention fixed on something denigrating: something evil? Have you never felt the pull—and at least flirted with—something that would gleefully destroy you? And then discovered the strength to move away, turn your back on that 'evil' until one day you realized the awful grip was gone? Aren't there thoughts and actions that tug the corners of your mind and pull at you despite your best efforts?"

Becca pictured nights with Steve. "OK. But is there then only space for total personal self-responsibility? How about biochemical processes, out of balance hormones, faulty wiring in some brains, disease?"

"A complex question." Deborah shifted, put her cup down, and spoke carefully. "It comes down to the premises we choose: the foundations upon which we build our logic and our lives. Which may look more important than they are."

"Sorry, I'm not following."

"Becca, about 500 years ago, the Roman Catholic Church threatened to torture Galileo if he stuck to his theory that the sun, not the earth, was the center of the then known universe. The Church 'won.' Galileo recanted. Mercury, Venus and the Milky Way kept moving. No matter what we believe, the universe, exists. You said 'maybe creation just exists.' Maybe. But I choose—with at least some freedom, I hope—to infuse the Great I AM into creation and to live my life focusing on that point: trying to know, to experience, to be open to a greater reality.

"Now, back to your question: my culture is Western post-enlightenment and my religion is Roman Catholic. I struggle with both. I see the world through those frameworks. I believe evolution is the way God carries out creation—and there may or may not be any 'grand plan.' I believe our bodies develop, before and after birth, so that disease is not only possible but is inevitable. Ultimately, we're designed to die. So, was Ted Bundy a physical freak? Did his environment distort him? Was there interplay of biology with surroundings and internal choices that led him to be the person he became? For me, the combination fits best. And it is entirely possible that what we focus on, what we voluntarily choose to focus on changes not only our minds but our brains as well.

"Anyway, no matter what kind of genetics we're born with and what kind of environment we're reared in, at some point, most of us have to live on our own: parent ourselves. Maybe your bird's message of 'How' will help you create the person you will become from the person you currently are. Maybe 'how' is a key for you: will help you woo yourself to be more open, more loving—because God always calls us to expand and grow. Maybe 'how' you see the possibilities and potential ahead is the message."

They sat in silence watching the waves.

"What would Swami say?" Becca asked.

"Ask him."

"I may but I want to know what you think he'd say."

Deborah laughed. "He'd start talking about unformed galactic gasses wafting through eternity and the first creative moment of AUM. Then he'd hint at something vague about a soul and later he'd discuss reincarnation and lead you through Hinduism, Vedanta and Karma with such expertise you wouldn't appreciate it for many lifetimes. He'd probably end up asking you how your meditations were going and can you sit quietly for twenty minutes yet."

"In other words, he'd say we've all somehow created our current circumstances by our past lives and must live out our Karma."

"Something like that."

"Deborah, do you believe that?"

"I believe in God. I believe Jesus fully expressed Christ and that Saints of all religions know things we rarely glimpse—maybe only when a dream-spun bird explodes us in the sun.

"In the final analysis, my beliefs and Swami's both require personal integrity. We know we need help: that we can be lazy and sinful—we miss the mark—and need love and forgiveness repeatedly. Both of our systems find great joy in God's love and willingness to forgive and both systems say understanding the Creator is beyond the ability of the created. The systems use different words, images and time-lines."

Becca stretched. "So I need to 'see' and figure out 'how,' too."

"Possibly. You decide. We all need to grow and love and be creative and have fun."

Becca slowly shook her head and smiled. "As my niece would say: 'Awesome.'"

32

Baby Becca sat in the well
Cold and alone she'd stayed where she fell
Then flexing her muscles
She jumped with a groan

And decided to lead
Her fragmented parts home.

Quite unexpectedly, without a reason, the Matryoshka doll toppled onto its side and rolled down the stairs. Momentum gained, it bumped hard, cracking in the middle, shedding bottom and top smiling layers that continued on their separate ways, tumbling toward the bottom. When the last sections struck the concrete slab, they split open at the seam and rolled to a stop, top akimbo, leaving the solid-center, tiny, one-piece doll staring at the floor. She blinked, breathed: little wooden lungs expanding in little wooden chest. Life entered with breath.

Tiny bands of fragile, newborn muscles moved. She stood, set the doll pieces up. The key was size and the color of the dresses helped. Growing as she worked, Baby fitted each set together. Pleased with herself, she watched them equalize in size. But 'the little sucker,' the two-piece wooden doll closest bound to Baby's one-piece figure, wouldn't grow.

'You'll get hurt.' The little sucker stomped her foot. 'I've kept you safe and hidden, protected you all these years.'

'But hidden isn't good; it's dark and lonely,' Baby said.

Another figure gently took the little sucker's worried hand. 'It's OK now. Let's dance. Dancing's always good.' (Whose voice? Andy's? Eleanor's?)

Joining hands, all the dolls grew and danced, keeping perfect time to silent music, floating whole once more within the fragile tendrils of Becca's sleeping brain.

33

Calcutta. Fecund spicy smells and musty, rotting aromas steamed from the tarmac. Stars peeked through haze. Within the noise and milling hoards, Becca focused on their guide, pressed herself into the middle of the group. Picking up their luggage, guarding their purses and cameras, they exited the airport and boarded charter buses. Sticky and exhausted, Deborah and Becca slumped in their seats. Beggars, who hung like Spanish moss from the open windows, fell away as, horn squawking, the bus lurched into the chaotic traffic and sped away. Three-wheeled tuk-tuks surrounded them, darting about like rats.

Becca sighed. 'Well,' she felt, 'after three and a half weeks in India, I'm as prepared for Calcutta as I can be.' As the bus swung around the corner, she saw hundreds of people sleeping shoulder to shoulder on what euphemistically might be called a 'sidewalk.' The driver careened by blasting his horn. The bodies, like burlap-covered logs (heads toward the buildings, feet toward the street) repositioned themselves like pigeons on a telephone wire after the arrival of a larger bird. 'My god! How can I be ready for this?' Becca's stomach contracted.

At the hotel, she saw emeralds glittering in the lobby's jewelry-case next to the central patio and flipped like a tiddlywink into another universe. Greeted by smiling musicians, given cool yoghurt/fruit drinks and marigold leis, they were isolated from the world outside. Becca watched the smiling hotel employees wondering where they slept, how they coped.

"Calcutta grew from a city of 500,000 in the 1920's to over 10 million now," the guide droned, "badly stressing the city's infrastructure."

"Understatement of the century," Becca mumbled.

The bus stopped. "I'll lead you to Mother Teresa's Convent," the guide said. "Watch your step, the sidewalk is cluttered."

As they disembarked the bus, children swarmed around but the guide shooed them away just like the local bull swished flies with his tail as he stood, munching steadily, in the offal-littered intersection. By 9:30, the sun already sucked them dry. Two, noisy, stench-filled blocks later, they entered the convent.

Ascending the freshly washed steps, a huge crucifix hung before them. Above it, the words "I Thirst" proclaimed Christ's need; below, "I quench" affirmed the Order's response.

In the terrazzo-floored chapel they knelt on the cool floor. The novices' voices sang praise and love to Jesus above the cacophony of street vendors, car horns and screeching brakes that could be heard through the open windows. After the service ended, the nuns left.

Back in the entry hall, they spoke with one of Mother Teresa's first nuns. Looking at this woman perplexed Becca; she wondered if any distance separated her eyes and soul. Her piercing gaze felt soft, as though she saw everything Becca had ever done yet saw beyond all that to something the nun recognized and valued: something Becca only vaguely knew existed.

They visited an orphanage where the sisters cared for handicapped and abandoned children. One girl plowed into Becca grabbing her skirt. Her dark brown eyes looked up as her slightly drooling mouth mumbled. Becca knelt. The child wrapped thin brown arms around her neck, snuggled up and continued the repetitive sounds. Becca carried, patted and soothed her for 40 minutes. The child dozed. When they left, a nurse took the sleeping child.

"She needs all the love we can give," the young nun commented quietly.

"We leave for Kali Temple at 8:30 in the morning." Swami's mellow voice blended with the low light as they sat for evening meditation. "Kali, destroyer of ego, fights fiercely to free us from self-will and delusion."

· Other Places ·

Mid-way through meditation, Deborah slumped over, perspiration dripping from her face. "See you later," she whispered, using Becca for support as she stood and left. Becca returned her gaze to the panoply of Eastern and Western saints on the altar trying to maintain her focus, to ignore her mosquito-like thoughts, to concentrate on breathing and reestablish her mantra.

"Keep hot tea available," Swami said as Anna, the trip nurse, looked through Deborah's medicines and approved their use.

"Put this in her tea or water and as much sugar as she wants. I'll check later but if you need anything just come to my room." Anna projected calm confidence.

Swami brushed Deborah's forehead gently.

"I'll be alright," she said softly.

"I know, but let us care for you." He chuckled. "Goodnight, old soul," he called as he and Anna left.

Minutes dragged by. The second-hand on Becca's watch jumped from black line to black line reminding her of childhood hopscotch: jump, jump, jump. What's time anyway? What's life? Where's meaning? How?

Deborah's cough jolted Becca awake. "Do you need anything?"

"A little tea. The worst is over." She drank. "I do this on each trip: make silly mistakes. I'm feeling better. Sleep, Becca; you've a big day tomorrow."

Becca held Deborah's hand, wiped her forehead with a moist cloth. As she tended to her friend, Becca felt Eleanor within herself: the tender, loving, nurturing Eleanor who cared so jealously for Becca during childhood illnesses. 'Strange,' Becca realized, 'I seldom remember her that way but that Eleanor is also valid.'

(Images of Eleanor as a young, widow and mother led Becca to a fragile memory: Becca, Marcia and Eleanor huddled in their car in the garage with rain pelting down, lightening streaking around them, thunder crashing in immediately and everything shaking. Becca had closed her eyes but nothing shut out the blinding flash nor kept the tree beside their house from splitting and smashing through the roof of the bedrooms overhead, the place they'd left only minutes before. 'Oh God,' Eleanor's voice had moaned, 'thank you for getting us out in time.' The car windows had fogged up; Becca stuffed her face between Eleanor's side and her Teddy Bear. Marcia's arms held her and Eleanor's arms circled both of them.)

Anna came in at 3:00 a.m. and proclaimed Deborah recovering. "Now, Becca, to bed."

Becca pulled on her nightshirt and slid between the sheets. She slept with the clear memory of Eleanor's arms holding her gently.

34

Becca stuffed sweet limes, apples and bottled water into her purse, small coins into her pocket. Deborah stayed at the hotel.

Diary.

    Bus to Kali Temple: Normal chaos. A Brahman woman passed in a Rickshaw: head high, back straight, hair perfectly in place, looking neither left nor right, sari resting like marble folds on a Greek statue, totally comfortable within her culture. Known and knowing: understood and understanding: at ease, as I might look moving across an American university campus.

    ****** A huge banyan tree spread over them splashing blobs of shade on the hot ground. They hired boys to guard their shoes by the Temple gate. Inside, the sun beat down on the un-shaded red brick courtyard; the heat assaulted their feet mercilessly. Smaller temples ringed the main temple grounds. Visiting a room reputed to have been important to Ramakrishna and Vivekananda, Becca was more interested in drinking water than listening to the guide, found the shade and cooler room temperature more important than last century's religious history.

    As they approached a covered, open-air temple where they would meditate, young beggars moved in. A small girl sat by a column, a baby in her arms. Making eye contact with Becca, she struggled up and, glancing frequently toward the infant, approached the foreigners, hands extended, eyes pleading. Becca handed her a sweet lime, placed some small coins and an apple next to the silent infant. A breeze brushed by as Becca settled herself with her group.

    The child returned to the pillar, readjusted the infant and stared at the fruit. A teenage boy swaggered by, scooped up her booty, slipped some coins into his pocket, bit into the apple and dropped a few coins, the sweet lime and the rest of the violated apple next to the child. The little girl carefully wiped the apple on her skirt, leaned against the column, took a bite and chewed slowly. Becca imagined the sweetness and the texture the child experienced. The girl stopped chewing, put chewed pulp on her finger and placed it on the infant's lips. The baby's mouth opened, bird-like, accepting nourishment.

    Swami sat cross-legged, chanting softly. Becca joined in, secured her purse under her skirt with the strap wound around her leg, closed her eyes, felt her shoulder muscles sag and then a tear—of shame? thanksgiving? confusion?—rolled down her cheek. As they moved into quiet contemplation, Becca gradually let go. The layers of veneer she'd erected between herself and the world, between her soul and pain, between life and the fear of death, peeled away. Turning like a rock in a polishing tumbler, her mind bounced around undefended. Images of Thailand and India sped by: soaring beauty, heat, pungent tastes and smells, the smiling eyes of handicapped children, voices of vendors, haunting music, the sincerity of a Hindu nun in Brindaban lamenting that Becca and her friends, who seemed so nice, should be condemned to live in America, a place so materialistic and, above all, not India. She reheard the Thailand Buddhists laughing joyfully as they played the tapes of Becca's group singing and she tasted once again steaming tea in the early morning in Kashmir as the sun shown on the season's first Himalayan snow. Finally at peace, she slid into a state like nothing she'd ever known.

Swami touched her shoulder lightly. She opened her eyes, unafraid and alert.

"We Hindus will get in line to greet Kali. Meet us by the exit in an hour." Becca nodded and stretched noting that the child with the baby was gone.

Diary. On the bus after Kali Temple. After Swami left, I wandered on the open courtyard and found a spot where I could glimpse a bit of Kali's statue: dreadful, fire-breathing goddess. I stood in the midst of a group, none of whom I knew, packed in a 10 square meter area all moving back and forth from one hot foot to the other, looking, if viewed from above, like a field of wheat swaying in the breeze. Alas, there was no breeze. The line of pilgrims, also swaying, snaked around the courtyard to the entrance of the Kali Temple. The scene felt organic; my individualism dissolved and I coalesced into the group. We were one form, drawn into unity by this strange interaction, held both together and apart by unseen forces: selfless. For a moment, I simply existed.

Suddenly, a man and a woman, both about my height with dark, almost black eyes and chestnut colored skin, stood facing me, looking intently at my face. The man held out his right hand, fingers together and pointing down, at the level of my breastbone. I wasn't afraid but didn't have the faintest idea what to do. I looked from his face to hers and back again. The woman reached out, gently took my right hand, raised it and turned it over so that it lay open beneath the man's hand. He bowed slightly, placed a flower and a small candy into my palm and the woman closed my fingers around the items. They stepped back, bowed low with their hands in the 'namaste' greeting, then vanished into the crowd: swallowed up like raindrops in a river.

Opening my fingers, I realized they had given me the darshan they'd received at Kali's altar: their gift from the Goddess. They gave it to me. How far had they traveled to get here? How long had they waited in that hot line before arriving before Kali's statue so that they could encounter the force strong enough to destroy ego and free one to merge with God? Why give this gift away? And why to me?

Later: Swami said Hindus assume any one they meet is someone they've known in previous lifetimes so, for them, each encounter continues an old acquaintance. Here I sit in a hotel in Calcutta, watching the moonlight reflect from the swimming pool's surface, making notes about a marigold and a piece of candy that I have wrapped in a handkerchief in my purse. I'll take this package home. I'll never absorb what's happened on this trip. We leave in two days. I miss India already.

35

Bangkok. Becca stood at the hotel window viewing the same scene she'd seen a few weeks earlier. She smiled. Red streaks from the setting sun sliced across the city. Four weeks earlier this had seemed so Asian, mysterious, foreign, ancient. Now it looked Western, industrial, modern and familiar. Great clumps of vegetation swept by on the river, pulled loose by torrents from the morning storm. Becca wanted to talk to Deborah but she'd flown to South India to join her husband at Shantivanam, the ashram outside Tiruchirapalli headed by Father Bede Griffiths, a Roman Catholic priest. Becca missed Deborah's wisdom and calm manner.

She closed her eyes and pictured gold and silver threads radiating from her body, connected to bright bubbles—Deborah, Swami, Rich, Jenny, Eleanor, Marcia, Cynthia, Tippy, Hank, Nicole, Max, Andy, Grandma Amy Louise, Grandpa Charley, Great-Grandmother Libby, Josephine, Timmy, Nancy and, in the distance, connected by the tiniest of tiny pure-gold threads, Greg's smiling face. Her hand reached to touch him but the scene changed. Tumbling through her mind, trailing golden thread like a modern Rumpelstiltskin, she linked pleasant picnics by a quiet stream to library stacks, faculty meetings to nights with Steve, arguments with Eleanor to laughter with Tippy and, continuing to connect disparate points, she drifted past Miss Coleman's beige face, spun through the Hawaiian scene with Greg and calmly viewed their love. Breathing lightly she floated over the Ganges dropping a fine silver chain into the water to touch the now decaying body of the shroud-wrapped child. Ricocheting off bits of memory, she arrived back at Kali's Temple, receiving homage from the unknown couple who, in this reverie, spun a brilliant ray as they floated off into an all-enveloping warm light.

'Before all time you belong to me,' a clear bell-like voice rang within her silent mind.

Opening her eyes, she saw the nightlights of Bangkok. Below on the sidewalk, ant-sized people scurried to a shopping mall like corpuscles hurrying to an infection. Exhilarated, cleansed like corn after a heavy summer rain, Becca walked to the bathroom, stripping off her clothes. Pondering her new feelings of balance and connection, she let the pulsing water pummel her body like a pianist's fingers playing on a keyboard.

The group ate their last dinner together in a private dining room. After personal reflections, the leaders gave pre-flight instructions for the morning. Becca felt both present and detached. As she was leaving, Swami touched her arm.

"Let's walk." They went to a grassy patio by the pool next to the river. A breeze rippled Becca's new silk dress across her skin and tugged the free end of Swami's ochre robe making it flutter like a wing. "Well, Rebecca, niece of Hildur, has it been what you expected?"

"How," she sighed, "could one 'expect' what this has been? At times I've felt like Alice down the rabbit hole: any minute the Queen of Hearts will come and shout 'off with her head.' A moment later I'd feel like a spelunker who's blundered into an ancient, unexplored cave. This has been more than I ever could have expected and it will nudge at me for years." In this dim light, at the end of a long trip, Swami looked younger than his 70 years as she watched his chiseled profile. "Thank you for encouraging me."

"You're welcome. Any unfinished business?"

She concentrated on her ruby ring. "I expected to feel a pull to Vietnam to look for shards of Greg. But I don't and I don't feel guilty about it. That love is with me; the 'we' I shared with him is connected but not clawing at me. I didn't expect to feel this wholeness. I've always been a jigsaw puzzle with small bits making up a picture but clear divisions separating the pieces. Now I sense more unity, like a face reflected on water—waves break it up but you know the face is whole no matter how the image dances." She watched the river. "Then there's Deborah. And you. Both special gifts."

He smiled. "God's the gift, Becca. And God's the giver."

36

"How was the trip?" Jenny asked.

"Magic. Amazing. Sometimes disgusting. I'm disoriented."

"Well, it's only Saturday; you don't teach till Monday," Rich commented as Becca retrieved her one suitcase and they headed for the airport exit.

"I stocked your 'fridge with a few things and did a quick sort of your mail. Caroline and DJ's wedding invitation for next Saturday is on the top. You're invited to everything. To quote Caroline: 'Becca will protect me from you.' That's us, her long suffering parents," Jenny reported matter-of-factly.

"I want to watch Rich do 'Father of the Bride.'"

"Not much for me to do: no giving away. This is all very 1986."

"As it should be," Becca said lightly.

"Cool it Rich." Jenny's voice sounded icy. "It's in the Catholic Church."

After the Brents left, Becca prowled around the leased house that felt more foreign than India. "Soon, I'm going to buy a house of my own so I can cover walls with pictures and maps." She unpacked, did laundry, opened mail, ate and fell into bed at 9:00.

Monday morning, flowers blooming in a planter sat on a carefully cleared space at the corner of her desk: 'Welcome back' from 'the Secretaries.' Becca shook her head. Then she stopped. They were the people right in front of her. She turned, walked to Paula's desk and called a happy "Thanks all of you," to the secretaries. Heads bobbed up and smiled.

"We know you'll probably kill the plant so just put it on the windowsill and I'll take care of it," Paula volunteered, looking up briefly and smiling.

"Thanks." Becca returned to her office, moved the plant to the windowsill, returned papers to the desk corner, slapped a post-it with 'Right in Front of Me' written on it onto the pencil box next to her telephone and began opening mail.

"Bingo!" She stood and headed for Rich's office. "Paper accepted for DC conference in May and I'm on the panel I want."

Rich signaled thumbs up. "It's been dull without you, Chadwick."

"How was the seminar?"

"Pretty normal except for the videotaping. They really bitched about that. Being a benevolent soul, I placed that responsibility squarely on your capable shoulders. Tapes are all there with my notes."

"They may hate it but they'll learn. Watching yourself on videotape is the best single technique I know to improve public speaking. It isn't enough just to make them technically competent, we need to polish these students, too."

"Spare me your theories." Rich held up his arms in mock surrender. Then, pointing a finger at Becca he continued. "By the way, videotape me when I'm teaching and you're fired!"

"I'm tenured." She grinned. "Bye, Brent."

"Get out of here, Chad."

Fumbling through lectures, watching student videos while wide-awake at midnight, eating and sleeping at odd hours, she jet-lagged through the week. By Saturday, she'd almost readjusted.

· Other Places ·

Walking four blocks to the church on this crisp, sunny November afternoon, Becca felt her new, Thai-silk dress moving gracefully in the light Pacific breeze. Ushered to the Bride's section, she slid into a pew and looked around. A large wooden Corpus Christi hung starkly against the white wall behind the altar; a red light flickered by the tabernacle. Sunlight poured in the large west windows that overlooked a lower-level, cliff-top patio. The ocean view, bordered by tall redwoods, stretched southwest toward the horizon. A string quartet played. 'Nice architectural blend,' she thought slipping onto the kneeler. After centering herself by gazing at the corpus ('I Thirst: I Quench' she remembered), she closed her eyes and reviewed memories of Caroline's life. 'Guide them,' she prayed, 'to be good together, to grow, mature and continue to love each other.'

After the ceremony, they moved downstairs to the parish hall next to the patio. Balancing a wine glass and a plate of appetizers, she stood shaded by a fir tree on the far side of the patio and gazed at the breathtaking view of cliffs, trees and ocean to the southwest. Turning slowly from the Pacific view, she saw him standing in sunlight by the parish hall windows, watching her. Tall, dark hair, blue eyes beneath bushy eyebrows and a neatly trimmed moustache, his right hand holding a glass, his left hand resting easily on the back of a chair, this relaxed, competent looking man in his blue blazer, white shirt and striped tie simply looked at her. Their eyes met. Neither of them smiled, moved or acknowledged the other. Becca felt heat rise in her chest and spread through her body. Her muscles weakened. Time slowed. She didn't move or look away but just stood, frozen by the clear penetrating gaze of the stranger's eyes.

Two giggling girls raced by, bumping into Becca, spinning her around. She remained upright but her glass fell, splashing white wine onto her dress before bouncing on the grass. Glancing across the patio, a void existed where he had stood. She looked at her dripping skirt.

"Wouldn't you know! Children younger than 16 should be confined," a whiny voice mused. Becca looked up to see a sandy-haired, almost chinless, spectacled man who greatly resembled the Pillsbury Dough-boy standing directly in front of her. "Is your dress totally ruined? It's lovely but, heaven knows, you won't need Thai-silk often in St. V's."

"It's white wine so the damage should be controllable." She looked into his beady, defensive eyes and thought: 'Right in front of me.'

"Your appetizers got soaked but that's no great loss. The deviled eggs will survive anything," he sneered.

She extended her hand; he shook it weakly. "We've not met...."

"I'm DJ's uncle Rob, just arrived this morning and passing through." He laughed a high, constricted laugh. "I drift in, pay homage and leave. Who're you?"

As Becca started to reply, a deep voice rolled over her shoulder.

"This is Rebecca Chadwick, Rob, a new faculty member in Rich's department and longtime friend of the bride's family." She looked up into the blue eyes she'd seen across the patio. "I figured you'd need fresh wine," he added offering her a glass.

"Bradley Abbott," Rob sighed, "my eternal nemesis."

"Just life in a small city, Robert."

"How're things at the wrong end of a cow?"

"Interesting and profitable. How long will you be here?"

"I'm leaving tomorrow. A short-dose of St. V is all I can take."

"Good to see you, Rob. Now, if you'll excuse us, Dr. Chadwick may need a towel and some fresh appetizers."

Before allowing Bradley Abbott to whisk her away, Becca re-engaged Rob.

"Nice to meet you. Now that your nephew is married into the Brent family, I'm sure we'll see each other when you do swing through the area. Travel safely." She smiled warmly at this strange little man.

"Why, thank you," Rob replied in evident surprise. "Ta-ta, Brad," he added, fishing a deviled egg from Becca's ruined plate, and walking away.

She looked up at Brad. "Excuse me, but if it's not too much trouble Bradley Abbott, if that's your name, what just happened?"

"Is that 'just' as in with Rob? Or 'just' as in a few minutes ago?"

The warm sensation spread through her again. Feeling 20 years younger, Becca slid a smile across her eyes. "Try: 'Begin at the beginning and don't stop till you come to the end.'"

He lifted his glass and smiled. "I'll start with Robert. We were classmates from kindergarten through high school. He reminds me of the character Miniver Cheevy: not comfortable in his life. He's bright, socially awkward and, to keep a short story short, a disaster with women. I was on my way over with wine so I cut him out. Upset?" His blue eyes watched her, a smile playing beneath his moustache.

"Well, he was right in front of us and that's the person we're mandated to care about. An introduction and a few kind words seemed the least I could do." Their eyes met again. He looked slightly chastened but intrigued. She smiled and toyed with his interest. "How do you know who I am?"

He laughed a great warm laugh. "This is Santa Veronica. Everybody knows everybody. Rich and Jenny are friends, my kids and theirs are thick as thieves."

As if on cue, Caroline and her maid-of-honor, Amanda Abbott, whom Becca had met at the rehearsal dinner, walked up.

"Come on 'Aunt' Becca, I'm going to tip my hat to tradition and throw my bouquet. Hi, Brad." Both young women, standing relaxed in the tasteful cocktail suits they had worn in the wedding, seemed more mature than Becca had been at their age.

'Changes for women are happening,' Becca mused. She and Amanda exchanged greetings.

"Hi, Dad," Amanda kissed Brad and the two young women strolled off.

"So, if Amanda's your daughter then Jason's your son: the two thieves?" Becca felt a twinge, like an itch from a limb amputated long ago, as she watched Brad's expression soften in the wake of Amanda's presence.

He nodded and looked at her closely. "You OK? Is anything wrong?"

Becca took a deep breath. "They're more mature than I was at that age, which is good. And," she continued slowly, "my father died when I was very young so when I see a father daughter thing like that, I get a bit wistful."

Brad smiled. "Don't wax too lyrical. After her mother died we fought for three years. What you see now is complicated and growing. We're doing better." He stepped back, eyed Becca half seriously. "If you're looking for a father-figure, I won't apply."

Becca smiled. "Not anymore." Then she changed the subject. "You're right, I need to do something about my dress."

He nodded toward the church. "The ladies' room is in there."

"Thanks." They started walking toward the parish hall entrance.

"Like Thai food?" he asked.

She nodded.

"Good. There's one totally fantastic Thai restaurant in town. After the festivities end, want to go?"

She nodded again. They walked easily together.

"What did Rob mean about 'the wrong end of a cow'?"

"I'm a vet: mostly big animals: cattle and horses. Artificial breeding."

"I see. Well, I'd better tend my dress."

He smiled. "See you later."

After Caroline and DJ left, Brad and Becca said their goodbyes to Jenny and Rich (both of whom tried to remain blasé) and walked to the parking lot.

"I figure you didn't drive four blocks to the church," Brad said as he opened the Mustang's passenger door for her.

"You know where I live?"

"Sure, I know your landlord."

Becca looked up quizzically. "Santa Veronica?"

He nodded, flipped his jacket onto the backseat, slid into the driver's seat and started the motor. "It's 30,000 not 6,000. Nonetheless, cozy. Advantages and disadvantages."

"I'm not sure I want everybody knowing everything about my life."

"St. V is sort of like a pair of tight jeans: the attention you get is part of why you choose 'em. Humans are pack animals; we need community but it can strangle a bit."

Becca looked down at her dress. "Well, this human needs to change. A little more precautionary work now may save me big trouble."

He drove toward her house.

"How do you deal with it? The scrutiny?"

"I'm third generation: Grand-dad was a rancher, Dad a vet. After Vet school, I spent my rogue years in Kentucky working with fast horses. But I came back. I like it here. I'm known, comfortable and male. You're new, professional and female; in a conservative western town, that's a lot of baggage. People are tolerant if things aren't shoved in their faces."

"As in: jeans can be too tight?"

Nodding he pulled into her driveway. "Right. And I live out of town not on a main city street. Different cultures: you're 'University;' I'm 'Old Guard,' but that division's breaking down. Go change. This is nothing fancy. I'll wait here," he said opening his door and beginning to get out.

"If you're waiting here, why get out?"

"To open your door."

"Not necessary. We 1986 women are opening a lot of doors."

"I know," he sounded a bit miffed. "But it would be nice. Like a date."

"Like the 50's?"

"Why not like the 50's?"

"Because times have changed. Besides, I'd rather have equal pay," she smiled, shrugged, opened the door and left.

"OK. But don't take long. I'm starved and Rob's right: that food was pretty dull."

37

Their waitress removed empty serving dishes and lit the candle in the brass lantern. "More tea?" she asked. Brad nodded.

"It got dark quickly in India; I'm readjusting to twilight."

"You liked India."

"Um-hum, but 'liked' sounds too simple. The whole experience both confronted and charmed me. Often I wanted to scream at things. Have you been there?"

"Not to India."

"But someplace over there, right?"

"'Nam. Eight months. Wounded, sent home. A long time ago."

The waitress brought fresh tea and Brad ordered dessert.

"You'll love it," he promised, pouring yet more tea.

"If I don't float away first."

"U.S. restaurants have indoor restrooms," he chuckled as Becca slid from the booth.

When she returned, Brad was gazing out the window toward the cliffs.

"Penny for your thoughts."

He looked up. "That color complements you."

"That's not what you were thinking, but thanks."

"You want to know?" She nodded. "Xerxes the First. Know him?"

Becca reached for her teacup and held up her left hand to keep him from talking. Concentrating hard, rummaging through information in her head, following a thin thread through her brain, she unearthed a relevant image. "Persian. Fourth or fifth century BCE. Bridges. Canals. Herodotus mentions him, I think. Right?"

"Very good," he sounded genuinely impressed.

"So why Xerxes?"

"You'll think I'm nuts."

"Try me."

"I've got this memory of him: have had it for years. I'm standing next to him, we're designing and building bridges: massive things, hoards of people, enormous organization, logistical support, etc. It seems real; I smell the food and feel the heat. Not like a film but real. I'm in the center of it, surrounded by it: there. The image pops up occasionally."

"What does it mean to you? That you were there? That it's a memory like other memories?"

"Not necessarily. Maybe I created it when I read about him. Maybe memories linger like iron particles, ingested and expelled by one organism after another, up and down the food chain, in and out of lungs, like electrical bees looking for neurons to tickle. It's a nice scene. I've never tried to drive it away."

"Reincarnation?"

He shrugged. "I don't know. It doesn't make any difference to me. Who I am, how I act now is important. How the universe operates is beyond me. I've got enough challenges and complications: a 23 year old daughter, a 17 year old son, conservative ranchers, rambunctious bulls and cows," he looked at his teacup and added quietly, "to say nothing of a new, female, University professor who just walked into my life."

"Am I a 'complication'?" she asked softly.

"I can handle it."

"But maybe, if I still lived in Madison, that would be better. Right?"

"Wrong." He looked across the table at her, took her hand and stroked her fingers with his thumb. "That would not be better." After a few moments Brad took a deep breath. "Let's head back to town."

The moon popped in and out among the trees as they drove out the other end of Santa Veronica. Brad turned onto a private road, heading toward the ocean.

"That's home," he said pointing to a clump of buildings in a clearing. "House, barns, clinic, big animal surgery. My brother and I practice together, Dad, too, but he's mainly retired. They live another 10 minutes down the main road. This land belonged to Grand Dad." The road ended in a cul-de-sac. Brad turned off the engine. "I want to show you something."

They walked through the trees to a clearing that spread for about five acres toward the edge of the cliff. Becca shivered, pulled up the collar of her jacket against the wind whipping off the Pacific.

"I love this place," Brad stated moving toward the cliff. "Spent hours here as a kid, training my dogs, flying kites, watching clouds." Moving back, he gently pulled her to him for a gentle, easy kiss.

She smiled up at him, moonlight reflecting from her face. "I bet you bring all the girls here."

"I bet I don't," he replied. Their second kiss grew: no longer as gentle or easy.

"Right now," Becca said, a bit later looking up at Brad's face, "I'm still jet-lagged and need to go home."

"Good idea," he replied.

They smiled as they walked back to the car.

38

The next Friday he left a message on her home phone. "Hey, Becca, it's Brad. Jason and I are making pizza tonight. Call or just come over: no guarantee of food after 8:00."

"Where'd you guys learn to make pizza?" Becca asked as she sat in the kitchen watching Brad and Jason clean up. They finished the pizza by 7:30.

Jason grinned. "Mom was Italian. Her folks cook great stuff. I learned from them—spent the summer after she died at their house."

"You teach your Dad?"

"Sort of. He's good at slicing and dicing but he can't make dough; that's my job." Jason moved around the kitchen self-confidently, dried his hands and started down the hall. "I need to check the menagerie, want to come?"

"Sure." Becca followed him into the small room down the hall. Various scratching and cheeping sounds intensified as they entered. Jason reached into cages, changed water bowls, scooped grain and food mixtures into dishes and handed Becca a rabbit with a bandaged leg.

"We've always got a bunch of wounded animals; Dad and I run an informal rescue center. Most critters return to the wild but sometimes they're too limited. Then they 'hang out' by the back woods. Lame rabbits, half-blind hawks, stuff like that. The dogs protect 'em."

"Dogs? More than one?"

"Usually. Right now we're down to just old Rex but that's gonna change, right Dad?" Jason called over his shoulder.

Brad answered from the doorway. "Maybe. But I want to know who's taking care of this pup when you leave for university?"

"Aw, Dad. We need another dog. Rex is getting lame, doesn't run well anymore. Besides, a new pup would perk you up." Jason moved toward the door and began to shadowbox with Brad. Becca put the rabbit back in its cage.

"Maybe," Brad responded, boxing back, "I'd like to simplify my life once you leave. Ever think of that?"

Becca watched them. Brad controlled the relationship physically but they approached the fulcrum of their father-son teeter-totter: each appeared slightly unsure of his ground.

Re-entering the kitchen, Jason stopped the mock fight, swung around the butcher's block and said, "Hey, Dr. Chadwick,"

"You'd better call me Becca, Jason. Your best friend does."

"OK, Becca, got any kids?"

"Nope."

"Been married?"

"Yep."

"Divorced?"

"Nope."

"OK. Widowed. Like us. Ever give more than one word answers?"

"Sure."

"Well, when?" Jason sounded humorously exasperated.

"When folks ask questions that need more than one-word answers," Becca laughed.

"OK. Let's see. When did your husband die?"

"Jason, that's pretty personal," Brad interjected.

"It's OK," Becca said. "If he doesn't get answers from me he'll get them from the Brents. I don't have many secrets." She turned to Jason. "In 1969. In Vietnam."

"Oh. Long time ago. Why haven't you remarried?"

Becca laughed and shook her head. "Maybe I should stick to your 'yes/no' questions."

Quail Hill

"I'll take that as 'none of my business.' Fine. Can you cook a turkey?"

"Sure, why?"

"Thanksgiving's coming; Amanda's staying in the city for her job leaving nobody here who can cook a turkey. Right Dad?"

"Jason, that's enough. Becca may have other plans and may not want to spend the day with three guys who watch football all day."

The phone rang and Jason started toward it. "I bet she likes football, Dad. Don't you Becca?" He picked up the receiver and dragged the 25-foot cord down the hall, chatting easily.

They remained quiet.

"Well, is he right? Do you like football?" Brad asked.

"Yea, I like football."

"And Thanksgiving plans?"

"Jenny and Rich invited me. You know the 'if you're not doing anything drop by' kind of thing. I need to spend time that weekend catching up,"

"Sounds much too 'driven' for a tenured faculty member at St. V's," he said putting his arm around her shoulder. "So, want to cook a turkey?"

"You guys do the rest?"

"Sure. Let's invite the Brents. They bring some, we do some, Dad can supply wine and beer. Everybody pitches in. Football both on TV and in the side yard. Of all the locations, this is the biggest."

"Sounds good." Becca nodded in agreement.

Jason waltzed back into the room. "Dad. The Smith's are going to the cabin tonight to ski and snowshoe tomorrow. Can I go?" He handed the phone to Brad. "It's Mr. Smith."

"Hi, Smitty—Sounds good—Make sure he earns his keep—You want any of our gear? Fine. I'll bring him over." Brad handed the phone back to Jason who finished his conversation and hung up.

"Yes!" Jason accompanied the exclamation with quick jabs in the air.

Becca laughed. "You a winter sport's addict?"

"Yes," Jason repeated his teenage, manic display. "Thanks Dad." Then he turned and, in mock indignation, looked at Brad and Becca. "Hey is it safe to leave you two alone? Do you need me to chaperone?"

"Jason," Brad said in an annoyed parental tone, "get your stuff."

"Just checking," Jason tiptoed past Becca whispering loudly, "Is Thanksgiving on or do we eat TV dinners?"

"It's on," she said.

"Get your stuff, Jason," Brad's voice hung a centimeter short of using his middle name.

"I'll make pumpkin pies," Jason called as he raced down the hall, jumped up and touched the ceiling.

"You're a bundle of talent," Becca called after him

"Smart-aleck," Brad said, pulling Becca into a bear hug and kissing her neck. "Son of anybody you know?"

"Chip off the old block." He smiled at her. "Come with me to take him to the Smith's? Then maybe a movie?"

She nodded. They kissed just as Jason returned, dragging a duffel bag and snowshoes.

"Good grief!" he sputtered, "at least wait till the kid leaves."

39

"Turkey should be ready at 3:00," Becca announced from the kitchen. Jason's pies sat on the kitchen island and, with some hot dishes and salads the Brents and the Smiths would bring, everything was under control as Becca removed her apron.

"It's a lovely turkey prepared by a lovelier cook," Jason said, giving Becca a rapid kiss on the cheek. "Now, you ready for your surprise?"

"This better be good, Jason."

"It is. Dad, you ready?"

"Anytime."

Jason grabbed his jacket, helped Becca into her coat, took the car keys and raced to the door. "Come on, then."

"He's Mister Manners," Becca commented, shaking her head.

"When he's in love," Brad responded throwing a proprietary arm around her shoulder and scooping up the 'Small Animals' bag that sat by the back door.

"He's a motherless teenage boy with a crush on an older woman," Becca replied.

"A crush the size of Texas: I expect he'll grill me about my intentions any day now."

"Maybe ask me about mine," Becca said as she slipped her arm around Brad's waist.

"How, Dr. Chadwick, shall we discover your intentions?" Brad asked as they headed for the car.

Squinting in the bright sunlight, she looked into Brad's blue eyes as he regarded her seriously. "Carefully, Dr. Abbott, very carefully," she replied.

He smiled and kissed her softly on the forehead. "Right." Then they settled into the car.

"OK, guys, what's the surprise?" Becca asked, fastening her seat belt.

"Puppies!" Jason's voice rang out as he maneuvered out of the driveway. "Gorgeous Golden Retriever puppies."

"Oh." Becca remembered the dogs she'd known: her great-grandparents wonderful Irish setters, a childhood friend's Boxer, Hildur's Goldie and her own—now only faintly-remembered but greatly-loved—English Setter that Eleanor got rid of after Andy died. Biff never allowed dogs: too dirty, too wild, too noisy, always 'too' something. Now, for the first time, owning a dog could work. All the houses she'd looked at had space for a dog and her schedule remained under control and flexible enough to include dog ownership.

Riding through the Northern California landscape with these two Abbott men, a turkey roasting and going to see puppies, Becca pondered how she'd arrived here. Last Thanksgiving was a blur of tubes, pain and high-powered drugs with death near and the fear from her still only vaguely remembered assault more terrifying than the loss of her kidney. The doctors, nurses, India, Swami and Deborah tumbled together with Eleanor, Marcia, Tippy, Cynthia, GG, Jenny, Rich, Amanda and Rich Jr. like glass fragments in a kaleidoscope. She studied the back of Brad's head, the wave of his hair. An inner voice spoke: 'Careful: heed your own advice.'

A sign announced: 'The Murphy's—Boarding Kennel, Training Center and Retriever Breeding.' Jason parked the car and Brad waved to Mr. Murphy who walked toward them. They went inside to a warm room that currently held one whelping box; in it were eleven, 10-day-old puppies and their dame.

Jason gently picked up a male with a blue whelping ribbon around its neck. "I'm getting one of the males, maybe this one, but Mr. Murphy and I'll make the final choice when they're 7 weeks old."

Mr. Murphy, somewhere between 60 and 90, bent over and scooped up a little female and handed her to Becca. His green eyes sparkled. "Holding's more fun than just looking. Get to know this little sweetie—she's the pick-of-the-litter." He chuckled as Becca tentatively held the wiggling pup.

"How do you tell the pick of the litter? They all look good."

"We have our ways," Murphy proclaimed.

"Murphy's the most responsible breeder around," Brad said as he examined each pup, making notes as he went along. "He rarely breeds a female more than twice and checks out prospective owners completely."

As Brad and Murphy huddled over the notes, Jason and Becca knelt by the litter watching the pups crawling over and chewing on each other.

"Are you really getting a puppy?" Becca asked.

"Yep, during the 8th week. And I'm naming him Thor."

"What happens when you go away to college?"

"Dad will take care of him. He needs another dog. I'll get a lot of training done. I'm working for Dad next summer so I'll be around."

"Finishing senior year and preparing for college, will you have time?"

"What a grouch!" Jason's tone half kidded. "Look, Becca, some guys swim 4 hours a day, some work on cars, some hang out with chicks. Me, I want my own dog before I leave for college. The perfect time never arrives. I've got 'now' so 'now' has to do. These are beautiful dogs."

Becca agreed.

"Look at Champagne before you go," Murphy remarked to Brad, "I may breed her."

They moved outside and Champagne, a frisky, almost white female bounded toward them. Wagging her tail exuberantly, she followed Brad and Jason into the kennel. Brad examined her deftly moving his hands over her, looking at her eyes carefully, checking her ears, listening to her heart and lungs, checking legs and footpads.

"She looks good Murphy. We'll need a hip X-ray and some lab work but otherwise she looks fine."

Murphy nodded. He watched Becca casually petting Champagne. "Look's like you have a dog-need," he commented.

Becca smiled. "You may be right but I'm renting. When I get my own place, maybe. But I need to learn a lot more about dogs before I even consider this."

"Let's see: Champagne'll be bred in February or so, then puppies in April and ready to go in June. You can find a house, fence the yard, watch Jason train Thor and come out here and learn to work dogs by June. And if you're no good, I won't let you have one." He chuckled. "It's a lot of work but it's worth it. Call me and come observe training. You've got time. Never get a dog on whim: the commitment's too great."

They got back to Brad's house by 2:00. The Brents, Smiths and Abbots arrived and their food offerings were stashed appropriately. In the side yard they played touch football. At 3:00, they took the turkey out and Becca made gravy while everybody pitched in to get the table set, hot and cold dishes onto the sideboard, glasses filled with water, milk, cider, wine or beer. Before beginning to carve the turkey, Brad offered a simple prayer of thanksgiving.

Surrounded by old and new friends in this new community, feeling healthy and centered, Becca sensed a peace that had long eluded her. Only her relationships with Eleanor and Marcia left smudges in her life. Thinking silent prayers for them she wondered how to mend their fractious interactions, or whether having a few fractured-fractious places was part of life's plan.

The Smiths took their children, Jason and Rich Jr. home by 9:30. They were heading for skiing early Friday morning. By 10:30 the Brents left. Becca put the well picked-over turkey carcass into a big pot, threw in celery, carrots, garlic, onions and seasonings, covered it all with water and put it on the stove.

"Let it simmer for about an hour, then turn it off and put it out in the garage, it's cold enough out there for tonight. Tomorrow we'll make soup."

Brad moved close, nuzzled her neck. "Too complicated. Stay. Show me."

She turned and put her arms around his neck. "It'll take hours."

"Maybe all night," he whispered into her ear breathing in the smell of her. "Which sounds good."

Logical objections bubbled up from her deep-seated control needs as her abandonment terror sweep past. She held onto him, steadied herself, allowed her fears to rise and sweep away.

"My surgery scar is really ugly," she murmured, her feeblest, last-ditch excuse.

He took her face in his hands. "Mine too. But firelight softens things." They kissed and moved into the family room. Brad turned off the lights, checked the drapes and adjusted the last log in the fireplace sending sparks up the chimney. They stood looking at each other and then Brad reached over and began unbuttoning her blouse; the silk slid off her shoulders slowly.

Later, when only embers remained, Brad arranged a blanket over them. "Comfy?" he asked brushing her hair from her cheek.

"Relatively," she kissed his chin, "though the floor isn't really my thing."

"I've got a comfortable bed."

She sighed. "Would it start rumors in St. V? My staying?"

"Probably not, but I can't guarantee it."

"So I'll stay awhile, check the soup-pot and head home."

"It's up to you."

"Would you stay at my place?"

"No, but that's on a main street in town. It's private out here."

"I'd rather drive home tonight than sneak back tomorrow."

He kissed her. "I don't want you to go, you know that don't you?"

"Yes, but thanks for saying it. And I don't really want to leave."

Later, arriving at her rented house and slipping into bed, the smell of his aftershave lingered on her skin and she could still feel the imprint of his body as she drifted off to sleep.

40

Noon, the day before Easter, and all her mandatory work completed. Most boxes were unpacked, pictures hung and the new furniture Tippy had helped her choose—during a visit two weeks earlier—had been placed in her new home. Feeling settled, Becca sat in her home office, picked up her favorite book of poetry and turned to T.S. Eliot, read a few lines. Sunlight streamed in the window, warmed her face as she closed the book. She smiled. 'I've known cruel Aprils—may know 'em again—but this year I'm in a lovely place; my life's in order.' She delighted in Eliot's use of language and caught glimpses of her own vague spiritual journey in his poems. She'd been attending the local Episcopal parish and, even though conventional Christian theology felt narrow, the liturgy moved her and the local parish priest, a woman who studied Jungian Psychology, helped her understand the Christian story in new ways. Coupled with her post-India correspondence with Swami and her attempts at meditation, seeking an illusive transcendent 'other' added depth to her otherwise totally rational life.

Becca moved around her new home, touching surfaces, admiring Tippy's careful way of arranging items from her life in visually attractive groupings. The house had two bedrooms and a small study, lots of natural wood paneling and large southwest-facing windows with views down over the town and out to the ocean. It was private, had room to entertain, space for a dog. Plus, the expenses fit easily into her new budget: a budget containing more charitable giving than she had ever committed to before. Experiencing the poverty in India, experiencing the whole trip to India, changed her. Her reading now included some classical theology texts along with modern theologians and mystical things she'd have rejected out of hand a few years ago. Hildur's books had opened her; Swami suggested texts and her local priest encouraged her to explore new territory.

She and Brad—now recognized as a couple—moved easily in their own worlds while spending considerable time together. Jason trained Thor, helped Becca learn about dogs and progressed through high school with moderate teenage anguish.

About 2:00 Becca dialed Eleanor's number.

"Hi Mom."

"Oh, hi, sweetie. How's the house? Have you taken pictures for me yet?"

Becca laughed. "Not yet but you'll like it. Tippy came and helped a lot. How are you?"

"Fine. Getting ready for Easter tomorrow. Wish you could be here but I know that doesn't work right now. Maybe this summer?"

"Maybe. Or," Becca spoke slowly, "you might come out here for a visit in late June. See Uncle Mike and tour the west."

Eleanor paused. "Really? That would be OK? I'd love to."

"Let's plan on it. And tell Marcia hello if I don't reach her tomorrow. Talk to you later, Mom. Bye." Becca hung up. She'd done it: invited Eleanor. After leaving Ohio last summer, she had pulled back—again—establishing greater distance from both Eleanor and Marcia. But that couldn't last forever. Tippy was right: they both had 'good enough' parents. Now, in Deborah's words, Becca needed 'to parent' herself. And that had to include keeping contact with—and working on—her relationship with Eleanor.

Becca looked out the window and drifted back to the nightly ritual when she and Eleanor and Marcia lived together alone after Andy died.

(*"Time for sleep."*

"Please Mommy, just a few more pages."

"It's late and time for sleep."

"Two more pages, please."

"Close your eyes and imagine peaceful things."

"Like what?" Becca would ask, acting out the well-known pattern.

"Light things, bright things, summer things, winter things, happy things, glad things,"—at this point Becca and Marcia blended their voices with Eleanor's—*"and 'where does the white go when the snow melts?' things."*)

Becca smiled at the memory. Eleanor at her best: relaxed, loving, attentive to both of them despite her own fears as she mourned Andy's death while living far from any family and unable to relocate during WWII.

"Where does the white go when the snow melts?" Becca mused softly.

Easter Sunday, after Becca went to church and the Brents went to Mass, they all congregated at Brad's for a feast. Jason and Brad could handle baking the spiral cut ham so Becca showed up with scalloped potatoes, a salad and a huge basket of chocolate bunnies and colored eggs. The Smiths and Brad's brother's family joined them. Before eating, they played a robust touch football game in the side yard with both Rex and young Thor joining in.

Later, after Amanda, the Brents and Smiths left, Brad got a call from a local rancher needing help with a badly injured prize bull.

Brad kissed Becca on the forehead as he headed for the door. "I'll call later."

The Abbott brothers drove away: Brad in his station wagon and Fred in the pick-up, pulling the trailer.

Jason and Becca loaded the dishwasher and did the rest of the dishes.

"Why'd you buy a house?" Jason asked sounding annoyed.

"Because I need a place to live and I want to put down roots here."

"You could've lived with us. Dad needs a wife."

Becca dried her hands. "Jason, what's this 'Dad needs a dog, Dad needs a wife' stuff?"

"Well, he does. I've taken care of him since Mom died but I'm gonna leave soon."

"He can take care of himself; he's a pretty competent guy."

"Yea, but Mom told me to take care of him until he met someone." He turned and looked at her. "You're good for him."

"True, Jason, I am good for him and he for me but we like things as they are."

"That's not how it's should be; it's not what Mom wanted. She left me in charge and I'll be leaving and he'll be alone and that's not what she wanted." He sounded exasperated, defiant.

"Jason, you loved your Mom and she loved you and she meant well by saying that but you can't be responsible for him."

"I promised her. You don't understand," he exploded, "I *promised* her."

"And you've kept your promise. You and Amanda and your Dad all weathered the loss of your Mom. She wouldn't want you to beat yourself up about this. She'd want you to live your life and support your Dad as he lives his."

Jason grabbed a dishtowel and wiped tears from his eyes. "I hate it that she's dead. It's so unfair and permanent. Just ugly."

"I know, Jason. The pain's terrible."

"Sometimes the worst is that I forget things, like her birthday or the day she died and then I feel so damned guilty that I'm not feeling the same pain all the time. I want her back and sometimes I just want to be rescued and not have to go through all this."

"I'm sorry you have to go through this, Jason. Grief is tough. You've been strong and your Dad's strong. Life's about going on: using your strengths. It's usually not about rescuing or being rescued; life's about being committed to living."

"That's easy for you to say. Go live in your house up on the hill, leave him all alone, see if I care. But I promised her. Come on, Thor." The door slammed as they charged out.

Becca started the dishwasher, packed up her own items, wrote Jason a brief note and left. Driving home, she slid the Alleluia Chorus into her cassette player. After Lent, these voices, proclaiming joy, hope and something tenaciously alive in the human heart, touched her deeply.

41

Becca proofread carefully. Someone knocked. She shouted a menacing "Yes?" and threw her reading glasses onto her desk, old feelings of annoyance catching her off-guard. As the door opened, her eyes brushed past the note on her pencil holder: 'Right In Front of Me…' Professor Ken Schneider, chair of the general Speech Department, looked in tentatively.

"Is it safe to come in?"

Becca sighed, then smiled and rubbed her eyes. "Of course. Have a seat. What's the occasion? Usually I'm the one going to your office to get recording equipment."

He closed the door behind him, sat slowly.

"You look tired," she commented.

"What do you know about esophageal speech?"

Tiny red flags, nurtured by over a quarter century of professional experience, started waving in her mind. "More than most people, surely, but it isn't an area that I've worked with much in the past few years. I'm not our department expert and certainly not up on all the latest literature. Why do you ask?"

He sprawled in the chair, put his hands behind his head, pinched his lips together and exhaled through his nose. "Finally got my sore throat checked out. It's cancer."

"Oh, Ken, I'm so sorry."

"I'm going in for surgery next week and I need a favor as well as advice."

"I'll be happy to help in any way I can."

"I know there's a good therapist connected with the rehab department of the hospital and I trust my surgeon so that's really not the issue. The issue is, we can cover my university classes but we participate in the big Public Speaking Contest for High School kids. It's the first two weekends in June. We all serve as judges and have hundreds of students signed up. Trouble is, with me out, we're one judge short. I could ask a local high school teacher but the deal is for the kids to experience college-level judges. I'm hoping you'll fill in."

"Me? Judge public speaking? Ken, I'm flattered but I'm not competent."

"Yes you are. The work you do with your master's students impresses me. Most folks don't realize the difference public speaking makes; you get it."

"You'd have to give me pointers. Teach me what to look for. The guidelines I use for my students are pretty simple. And High School kids? I've never taught that age group."

"So, with some guidance, you'll do it?"

She sighed. 'Right in front of me…' Two weekends in June. "Okay, I'm crazy but yes."

"Thanks. That takes a load off my mind." He paused. "Changing subjects, I hear you may be getting one of Murphy's Golden Retrievers."

"How'd you know?"

He laughed, a wheezy, sore throat laugh. "It's Santa Veronica, Becca. We have one of his dogs. We love her. Have you chosen a pup yet?"

"Tentatively, a little female."

"Named her yet?"

"Crystal."

"Good choice. Well, I'm off. And thanks again."

"Ken, if there is anything else, call me."

"Thanks. I may." He got up and walked away slowly.

Becca resumed proofreading her handout for the paper she'd present next week in D.C.

42

Monday afternoon, circling National Airport, a glimpse oriented her and then she felt lost again. Mid-May in muggy D.C., arriving at the Shoreham her blouse felt sticky, the collar pulling at her neck. Then hotel air-conditioning hit like a Gatorade shower. Goose pimples rose as she walked to her room.

'Many days of this and I'll die.'

She turned the room air-conditioner down, striped and took a shower. Traveling west to east—losing time—always disoriented her. She'd give a paper on Tuesday morning, serve on a panel that afternoon and attend a breakfast committee meeting on Wednesday. After that, she'd attend sessions, renew contacts and sniff out grant money for student projects. The conference would end Friday but Becca wasn't flying home until Saturday afternoon.

Cleaned up, she went down to check in at the conference, then walked out to Calvert Street and headed to Connecticut Ave. She walked briskly past a number of restaurants, picked up a 'to-go' special at a decent looking Chinese place and headed back to her room. After eating and reviewing her paper and slides, she left a wake-up call and tried to sleep.

Tuesday evening, after a busy day she attended the major buffet. The place was mobbed. Elbowing through, she grabbed a Perrier and some shrimp. People nodded, gushed, ignored or looked past her with that 'is there anybody more important than you around here?' non-eye-contact that always surfaces at large professional gatherings.

"An interesting paper, Chadwock. Couple it with some of our 'in-development' computer programs and we'll go far."

"Hello, Spike. Is that a grant offer?"

"If you want it, Chadwock, and if you have enough subjects out there in St. Vitus." Spike Milligan, graying hair askew, peered through glasses thicker than coke-bottle bottoms. He headed the Speech/Language grant program at the National Institute of Neurological Diseases and Blindness.

"Got lots of clients in Santa Veronica. With the U's clinic, the local hospital rehab unit and the VA, we're busy with patients and their families; we spend lots of time helping them work through the aftermath of brain injury."

"Fine, help them all, give personal attention but use the computer programs we've got in development." He smiled up from his 5' 2", fat as a sausage, frame.

"You got something in mind?"

"Collaboration. Your clinical expertise and clients: our computer programs."

"Sounds interesting. You have money?"

He pursed his lips and nodded.

"I'm interested. But you must learn to say Chadwick, Spike."

"Whatever. I'm coming to San Fran soon. My secretary will send you information." He flung his pudgy arms around Becca, stood on his tiptoes and planted a big kiss on her cheek. "You can get to San Fran for a meeting, can't you, or is St. Vitus too far out in the boonies?"

"We can work out a date and I'll get down to the city." She returned his kiss and smiled.

"If I liked women, I'd really love you ChadWICK," he said.

"You say that to all the girls, Spike." He nodded. Becca watched him waddle away. He needed a 'Designed by Andy Warhol' sign around his neck. Such a talented man who worked tirelessly for brain injured folk: one of many unsung heroes in the field.

Wednesday she met with some former students, saw colleagues from Madison, attended a few sessions, had lunch with Spike and his other collaborators and went to the conference banquet. Her tolerance for conferences, hotels, professional crowds and banquet food had diminished with age. By midnight she paced her room, reread *This Week in D.C.*, flipped through channels on the TV and looked through the hotel directory. At 12:15, the phone rang.

"Hello."

"Hi. How's the conference going?"

"Fine. My presentation went well and my panel was great. Feedback's good. One solid collaborative offer from an old friend."

"Should I be jealous?"

"No, Brad. Not of Spike Milligan. How're things out west?"

"The same. Sick cows, wounded dogs, an injured rabbit found by a sensitive 10 year-old girl. Big soft eyes."

"The rabbit or the girl?"

"Both, actually." He laughed. "What's up tomorrow?"

"Probably more meetings. Maybe I'll bug out. I've about had it with people being so intense about little specks of knowledge. 'Whittling nothing to a fine point,' as my Grandpa Charley would've said. Maybe I'll chase some elusive memories, play hooky."

"Sounds like you're off to net butterflies."

"Never. Watch or chase them, maybe. Net them? Never."

"Careful, you may decide to join the 'Wonderful World of Vegetarianism.'"

She laughed. "Maybe."

"Don't tell my ranching friends."

"I won't. How's Crystal?"

"Growing fast. They do at this age."

"I miss you Brad."

"I miss you, too."

"Any word on Ken Schneider?"

"Rich called, said he made it through surgery and is recovering well."

"Good. Drop by the hospital if you can. People often stay away after a laryngectomy. Tell him I'll be by on Sunday."

"OK. Have fun tomorrow whether you play hooky or stay serious. I'll see you Saturday night at the airport."

"Thanks for calling. I'll call Friday night. Take care."

Hanging up the phone, she knocked a 'For Your Travel Needs in the Capitol' brochure to the floor. Lines on the map connected D.C. to Atlanta, New York and Boston. Becca looked at it for a moment and then returned it to the nightstand.

III

The Trip Home

If our encounter with the physical world is perplexing, our encounter with the divine can scarcely be expected to yield to ready rationalization.

~Reason and Reality by John Polkinghorne

1

May 15, 1987

Abruptly, between the 9 and 10 o'clock sessions on Thursday morning, Becca left the conference. She changed clothes, made a few phone calls and walked into the bright, sunlit day. Taking a cab to Georgetown, she wandered her old neighborhood around Wisconsin and N, O and P Streets. On Wisconsin, tawdry head shops occupied previously chic stores while fast food wrappers and cheap wine bottles lined the street giving a heavy, ruined look to this place she'd loved. Walking down P Street past the fine old row houses—their quality intact—she felt better. Morgan's Drug Store looked unchanged but, as she wandered in and checked the tourist map section, a woman called from the back: "I'm watching you."

Becca recalled being given credit here 24 years ago before she'd even asked, the respectful way they'd called her 'Miss Morgan' and smiled about her name matching the store. She sighed, bought a map from the frightened clerk and left. Times had changed; the store had probably been robbed repeatedly

The trees lining O Street shook fragile spring leaves overhead: leaves that looked like young birds trying out their wings. The brick sidewalk felt familiar beneath her loafers. Ahead, on the left, she saw the front steps to the house she'd shared with her roommates, noted the peephole in the front door through which she had first seen Greg. Becca at 23 and Becca at 47 both existed here: held apart by the polarity of time. If she could look through the peephole from this side, might she view the intervening 24 years in receding miniature? Back to youth and innocence: before Hawaii, before death in the jungle, and see their dreams and un-shattered plans? Slowly the memories floated off like milkweed from a dry pod. She walked on, past the red brick Episcopal Church, back to Wisconsin Ave. Catching a bus, she planned her route to the Washington Monument. It would only be a short walk from there.

Flickering shadows under the trees on the path along the reflecting pool created interrupted time, a confused sequence like an old movie: things moved too rapidly or not at all. 'Down the steps of the Lincoln Memorial and to the left' the woman at the Shoreham had said. From this direction it would be on her right. A rising knoll blocked her view. 'You can walk right past it and not see it,' she'd been warned. Moving from the path, she climbed the grass-covered hill. Now, without shade, the sun beat down replacing Chaplin-esque jerkiness with wilting heat and light so bright it bleached color.

People said the Memorial 'rose from the earth.' Not for her. It gouged into the earth like a spear-point thrown by an angry giant. She stopped: shocked by its audacity, its abruptness. It began as a narrow slit of black stone and descended. Moving closer, Becca ducked under the single-chain restraining-fence and stood on the outlying square stones before moving onto the main path's rectangular slabs. She slid silently through the crowd: E 11… E 8… pausing occasionally to read names. A man moved a ladder, deftly rubbed a tracing of a name and then handed the paper to an older woman—a mother, perhaps—who looked numb: sucked dry by the heat and old grief.

A heaving, slightly overweight volunteer, wearing an identification badge and carrying a clipboard, watched Becca, moved parallel to her and hovered discretely. Becca saw legs, arms, the backs of heads, even mouths but made no eye contact. Her gaze slid over names. Thousands of names, row upon row, slab after slab. Each name a life cut short. A person. Dead.

Tourists speaking foreign languages snapped 'I was there' pictures: smiling faces against names of the dead. Becca looked down: ashamed of her anger, ashamed of them.

Slowly she approached 'his' panel. Glancing across it, her eyes suddenly stopped. She gasped; her left hand clutched her stomach and her right hand moved involuntarily to her mouth as wrenching visceral pain stabbed her. Time wrapped around her shoulders trying to pull her down. Sound ceased and slowly, like in an underwater fever-dream, she blinked and tried to move her hand away from her face. The effort required to place her hand on the carved letters of his name exhausted her and the unexpectedly cool stone on her fingertips smashed her back to reality. The volunteer hovered closer but did not interrupt.

"Oh, Greg," she heard her voice say softly. Even here, he stood out: his name more beautiful, more perfect than the others. A montage of his smiling dark eyes and easy laugh flooded her mind. Tears slid onto her cheeks as her face softened into the slow, slightly asymmetrical grin she'd used with him. "Oh, Greg."

She stood back; the volunteer remained vigilant. His name was the last on the line, slightly above eyelevel, its length extending the line a bit. Even here he drew attention to himself: exuded magnetism. Gradually she realized his name had disappeared and she saw her own misty reflection on the black stone. A breeze rustled her skirt and the fabric moving on her thighs felt sensual. Now she switched back and forth between names and reflection, reflection and names:

now catching her image on the black polished stone, now seeing the carved letters. The names remained still, stable, dead. Becca felt alive.

She pulled a handkerchief from her pocket, wiped her eyes, blew her nose and saw a flicker of light from Greg's grandmother's ruby ring dart across his name. 'How fitting.' Having envisioned various dramatic gestures, she knew nothing more was needed. The spark of light reconnected him to her and to his family. It was enough. She smiled, touched his name once more. A puff of wind blew a strand of hair across her face. Her hand slid down the wall, over other men's names, other women's husbands, fathers, sons, brothers, lovers and friends.

"Goodbye, sweet Gregory," she said and turned to leave.

The volunteer had vanished.

2

Walking away from the Vietnam Memorial, the roughness of the letters and the cool sensation of the black marble clung to her fingertips as the breeze continued to tousle her long, dark hair. She wondered when she had decided upon these actions—yesterday, last week, years ago?—but knew 'beginnings' were often difficult to establish.

Her movements seemed generated by a steady, gentle force and she focused her attention on that energy—certainly she could no longer focus on the conference—and realized her unplanned exit would cause only minor readjustments for her colleagues like the brief ruffling of birds when one of their own flies away from a crowded wire.

'Walk. Becca, walk.' She heard a voice in her head, her own voice—finally strong and trustworthy and followed it easily. After leaving the Memorial, she caught a DC cab, returned to the Shoreham Hotel, made a few calls and left a message on Brad's answering machine saying she'd call Friday night. She completed the necessary arrangements, checked out, transferred to National Airport and boarded the flight to Boston with a minimum of fuss. Not that she understood her behavior, far from it, but most of her internal voices supported this decision.

After fastening her seatbelt, Becca leaned back and gazed out the window. She didn't know exactly why she was going to New Hampshire, but knew she needed to get back to times before loss, confusion and betrayal had left her emotionally ham-strung. Maybe the 'successful academician' part of her mind would question her later for such a rash decision, but she had to get to Craigmoor, to Quail Hill, to whatever traces she might find of her Great-Grandmother Libby. The desire

· The Trip Home ·

to reconnect with her father's family had become irresistible like the pull to a first kiss.

She let her mind drift over the history she knew of these people who were so embedded in this country: its successes, its opportunities, its wars, arrogance, beauty, racism, sexism, abundance and wastefulness. Her family. Her country. Her home. 'How do I bring it all together,' she wondered as she closed her dark brown eyes and settled back in her seat.

Fragmented thoughts, like summer clouds, flitted by. She had Libby's names, reversed of course, but the pull felt more visceral than names. Why had her father persisted in using them? Given her mother Eleanor's animosity toward 'Rebecca Elizabeth,' why had he insisted? Especially facing what he faced. There must have been reasons he lashed Becca so firmly to the Whitman side of his family: to his Grandmother Libby who was her great-grandmother. Becca was the last baby Libby greeted, the last to inherit the label 'prettiest one yet' from Libby's lips—and only God knew how many generations *that* family tradition pre-existed all of them.

Her mind snagged on the word God and how she viewed God now: a more open, accessible and intimate reality. She visualized her Rector with her hands held high during the Easter Eucharist back in Santa Veronica, CA. Next she recalled Swami, so tall and thin, standing next to her in Bangkok, his ochre robe fluttering in the night breeze. So many images existed in the mosaic of her life and, weaving through all the pain and fear, some thread was guiding her toward hope and peace.

Landing instructions over the plane's PA system roused her from reverie. Arriving at Boston's Logan airport, she picked up a rental car and headed north into the night.

The next morning Becca's car jolted onto the narrow lane at the base of Quail Hill. Sunlight darted through the trees casting shadows on the rock-strewn fields of her great-great-grandparents' farm. She stopped in a clearing as memory met reality. In the 30 years since she'd been here, little had changed. The white farmhouse a half-mile up the rutted road still peeked over the crest of the hill like a shy child looking over a fence. Becca felt safe. A bloodhound's nose might sniff five generations of her family on this rugged hillside.

Driving on, she stopped by the house, shifted into park, set the brake and cut the engine. Across the lane stood the yellow, two-story, 'new house' (built about 1870) and behind her the big gray barn clung to the edge of the pasture. This triangle of buildings seemed like facets of a crystal. Then she noticed a difference: something missing. No huge black walnut tree: only a stump covered with flowerboxes. Becca caught her breath as though she'd been kicked in the chest. Then, inhaling carefully, she stepped slowly from the car so she wouldn't disturb the scene. In this still world Becca scanned the hills, rocks, chicken coops, orchards, fences. A horse in the big pasture by the barn watched her, switched its tail and flared its nostrils.

She gazed out over apple-blossom time on Quail Hill Farm—a sight she'd never seen—a sight Libby watched annually for 70 years. Time swirled around like dust devils in her mind as she imagined children—from generations now long dead—running, laughing and playing tag beneath the orchard's delicately blooming branches.

Becca felt someone watching her but resisted the pull of those eyes. To acknowledge another person would end this moment and make her an intruder. She smiled; the moment stretched, neutralizing the space around her. Becca felt suspended and then, like unexpected snowfall in the night, thousands of memories piled around her. Scraps of images, like fragments of songs or bits of poems, danced along the edge of her consciousness. A bird sang and, quietly, like the last leaf dropping from an autumn tree, even time slipped away.

Then, abruptly, tugging from the unseen eyes brought her back to this sunny morning in May. The bird sang again as she turned toward the house.

A young girl, about 10, with straight black hair tied in a ponytail and honey-colored skin shining in the sunlight stood quietly by the farmhouse door. She had alert, mischievous dark brown eyes and softly Asian features.

"Hi," Becca said. The child smiled but remained silent. Becca panicked. 'What am I doing here?' She took a deep breath and began nervously. "My great-grandfather and my grandmother were born in this house," Becca gestured awkwardly.

"What's your name?" the girl asked.

"Rebecca," Becca said, surprising herself by using the full, old-fashioned name.

"Rebecca Elizabeth Morgan?" The girl's expression didn't change.

"Why yes. How did you know?" Becca felt a strange adrenalin rush.

The girl giggled, turned, opened the door and disappeared inside calling, "Mother, she's here! I told you she'd come and she's here." A moment later the girl returned accompanied by her mother, a small Southeast Asian woman who moved with grace and confidence.

"Welcome. I'm Van Reynolds and this is Shelly. And you are Rebecca Morgan?"

"Rebecca Elizabeth Morgan," Shelly whispered loudly.

"Yes, I am. But everyone calls me Becca and I go by Chadwick."

"So, you're married."

"I'm a widow."

"I am sorry." Van bowed slightly. "To have a husband die is painful."

"It was a long time ago."

· The Trip Home ·

"Tell her, Mama," Shelly prompted.

"Last fall we found a box of papers marked for you. We didn't know how to contact you but Shelly assured us you would come."

"Papers? For me?"

"Old letters. Diaries. Books. A family Bible. A note on top indicates they are for you. All in an old box way over in a corner of the attic behind one of the chimneys. Shelly said you'd come. Dan and I were less sure but in these matters, Shelly's most often correct." She hugged her daughter and smiled. "I hope you can stay for tea. Dan will be up from the field soon. He will want to see you. Do you know him?"

"No. I never lived here. Is he from Craigmoor?"

"Oh yes. He and his brothers bought these three houses, the barn and farmland about 10 years ago. Their family's lived in Craigmoor for generations, usually closer to town."

The screen door squeaked as they moved into the house. Oriental spices assaulted Becca's nose: not unpleasant, just unexpected. Not the warm cozy gingerbread-smells she remembered: not Libby's kitchen, her great-aunts' kitchen, no kerosene stove or water-pump. Surrounded by thoroughly modern, white appliances, standard store-bought generic cupboards and red Formica countertops, Becca felt lost and somehow violated. She steadied herself and sat in the proffered chair. At least the view out the window down to the valley looked familiar. Light, polite conversation took them through the serving of tea. Then Shelly went and brought the old Filene's box with Amy Louise's aging note slipped under the fraying hemp string.

A truck pulled up; dogs barked; the cab door slammed. Shelly ran out to greet her father. Becca stood as Dan entered. He had a quizzical look on his face.

"Daddy, it's Rebecca Elizabeth Morgan. She came!"

"You don't say? She came way out here just to get that old box you found?" He kissed Shelly on the top of her head and turned to Becca. "Hi. Have we met?"

"I doubt it. I visited here as a child, but," she reached to shake his hand, noticing, too late, that his right sleeve was tied off. He intercepted her right hand easily with his left. "I'm sorry, I didn't notice." Becca felt flustered.

"No problem. It happens. Lost my arm in 'Nam: found Van." He winked at Shelly. "So I guess I came out ahead." He paused, a long New Hampshire pause and stood towering over them, a weather-beaten, muscular and powerful man. "We must've met. Joneses, Morgans, Reynolds go way back. You're Libby's…" his rising inflection pulled her answer.

"Great-granddaughter and reverse namesake."

Dan nodded. "She's a legend. The city girl who survived here on Quail Hill Farm."

"City girl? She was from Craigmoor." Becca's surprise amused Dan.

"A century ago, Craigmoor was the 'city.'"

"Only to New Hampshireites," Becca replied, shaking her head.

"Well, that's who was here. And she survived."

A dog close to Becca pawed for attention. "Reynolds and Setters?" She rubbed the dog's head and looked at Dan quizzically.

"The two have been linked for over a century. There's some story about a rejected dog and Libby or your family but I don't know the details," Dan ventured.

"I do." Becca started slowly. "My Great-Aunt Annabelle told all of us that story. 'One day during a huge thunder and lightening storm, your grandmother and I were in the orchard and I got so frightened I let go of her hand and ran for the house. Little Amy Louise wandered around—she must have been terrified— and fell into a big tub of water. She would have died if Mama's dog, Princess, hadn't pulled her out and dragged her to the house. Then Pa held Amy Louise upside down and hit her on the back and got her breathing again. Probably the best thing that dog ever did and the worst thing your Great-Aunt Annabelle ever did.' I can recite that story in my sleep but never as well as my great-aunt did."

They all stood rather awkwardly, Becca fingered the string on the Filene's box.

Dan broke the silence. "Are there things you'd like to see?"

Becca felt enormous relief. "The barn. And the fields and orchard." She wanted to escape from the house, erase this remodeled kitchen from her mind.

He nodded, took Shelly's hand as they walked out. Becca thanked Van, followed them out, put the box in her car and crossed the road.

The barn, smelling of hay as it always had, provided balance. Walking the steep, narrow stairs to the first-level haylofts brought back memories from when she was two years old.

("Jump, Becca, jump."

Flying through the air, squealing with delight, Andy's strong hands catching her and then both of them rolling back into the hay, laughing.)

Becca closed her eyes, felt again the security she'd experienced with him: a security destroyed later when they carried him from the house and he never returned.

When she opened her eyes, her face felt cold.

"Are you OK?" Dan stood at the far side of the loft.

"Remembering things I'd forgotten." He nodded. Becca composed herself. "My great-great-grandfather built this barn but I don't know anything about him."

"The Joneses were Scots maybe. Or Welsh. Nobody else stubborn enough to attack land like this except the Irish." They headed for the stairs.

"Is the big flat rock still out in the first pasture?" Becca asked.

The Trip Home

"Unless God moved it while we've been in the barn. Let's go check it out." They walked into the pasture; a horse sauntered up, brushed against Dan's sleeve, took the sugar cube from his left hand. "We still use horses and Shelly's becoming a good horsewoman." He smiled at his daughter before she skipped off.

Standing on the large granite outcropping, Becca looked over the sloping fields, listened to the birds, felt the sun's heat even as a breeze tried to wipe it away. "I've never been here in May. I live in California and came East to a convention in Washington. Then I hopped a plane and came here." She turned to Dan. "Sort of a pilgrimage." He nodded. "My husband died in Vietnam. I went to the Memorial." They stood in silence.

"I hear," he said, "it's impressive."

"It's—I guess it is. Stark and painful. You sound scornful."

"Later, people erect 'stark and painful' or 'majestic and agonizing' monuments trying to deal with the loss. Time passes, the pain lessens. What's left glorifies war. Politicians create messes, young boys become warriors, march off to commit murder and mayhem in the name of 'Justice' and 'Truth.' I suspect both virtues weep at the waste. Yea, I'm scornful."

"So, are you a pacifist?"

"Heavens no. I'm just a New Hampshire farmer. I love my wife and daughter, breed a few good Irish Setters and occasionally lament our condition. I'm a member of the species. I hope the rains come and the bombs don't. Who knows? Maybe in 100 years Vietnam will look wise. We've been killing each other since before we climbed out of the trees. Must be something in us demands it. And don't let anybody fool you: war can be thrilling. Men bonded together in a real-life predator and prey of the same species drama. I don't like the part of me that got excited in battle. Maybe it's just hormones ripping around, but it's seductive, that 'Band of Brothers' stuff. If it just weren't 'to the death.' Any specific bullet shatters all the romantic horseshit. And I really hate modern 'technologically efficient' war: destroying thousands of lives and miles of land by pushing buttons. It's obscene."

Becca turned and watched Shelly down by the fence with her horse. "Which leaves us where?"

"Alive. The survivors. Trying to live and love and find meaning. Going to Memorials and making 'pilgrimages' to old farms. Scratching a living from this tight-fisted, rock-strewn land outside of Eden. Thinking too much. Being too serious with strangers."

"You talk a lot for a New Hampshireite."

"This land, this farm, Craigmoor, formed both of us. We share a lust for the place. Like we share losses in Vietnam: things we can't escape. If you lived around here we might or might not be friends but we are bonded. So I talk."

Becca smiled at him. "Thank you." He just nodded. She looked down at the granite beneath her feet. "How big is this rock?" She pressed her toe into a crevice. "Below ground?"

"Who knows? Big as a house, maybe a barn, maybe as small as a truck." He laughed gently. "But one thing's for sure, Rebecca Elizabeth Morgan, I'm never digging it out."

Shelly ran up the pasture to them.

"It is beautiful here," Becca said.

"Yep. Hard land. Stubborn land."

"Let's go see the orchard," Shelly said, leading the way toward the ancient rows of gnarled apple trees.

3

Finding Quail Hill had been easy but locating the cemetery nearly defeated her. Walking up the creaking steps to Craigmoor's general store felt familiar. The sign read 'Owned by Mr. Harold Ford: Established in 1802.' Inside, a man somewhat older than Becca stood behind the long glass cabinet smoking his pipe.

"Good noon," Becca tried to sound friendly. He nodded, sucked his pipe. "Are you Mr. Ford?" Another slight nod as he removed the pipe from his mouth, pursed his lips. "Have you been here long?"

He gazed at her, tapped his tobacco. "Quite a spell."

Becca moved toward him awkwardly feeling both an intimate sense of belonging and the ache of being a stranger.

"My grandparents and great-grandparents all lived here. Charley and Amy Louise Morgan, Bert and Libby Jones –"

He motioned slightly with his pipe, the same motion Grandpa Charley had used to command instant silence.

"Then you're Andy's daughter." He played with his pipe, fixed her with his gaze, a slight smile spread over his lips. "If that curly hair's real, you're his youngest. Named after Libby only reversed." Becca nodded. "What brings you back?"

"I was in Washington for a conference and decided to come see the farm in spring."

"You find it?"

She nodded. "I met the Reynolds. They were welcoming."

"Good people. Tough on her at first, being from away: being foreign."

"I've never been here in May. The farm's lovely."

· The Trip Home ·

"Mainly summers, I recall." He lit his pipe, sucked on it, clasped it in his teeth and talked around it. "That first summer after your Dad died, you and your granddad walked down into town everyday and then up to the cemetery: him with his long, gangly stride and you on your little—what, 3-year-old?—legs, stretching hard to reach his hand and running to keep up. I was maybe 12." He held his pipe, gazed at Becca. "Dad kept telling him 'Charley, you're going to destroy that child if you don't slow down.' Then Charley would scoop you up onto his shoulder and stride on." More pipe play. "Charley and A.L. never got over Andy dying so young."

"None of us did," Becca said quietly. "I'd like to visit the graves but I can't remember how to get to the cemetery."

He gave her directions and then asked, "Shelly give you the box?" Becca nodded. "Not sure what's there. Some things might not make sense even to me. Still, it's marked for you –." His words tumbled out with the metallic ring of coins falling onto the counter's glass top, his inflection implied that Becca was the legitimate, though wrong, recipient for such treasures.

"Perhaps," Becca said slowly, matching his Yankee with remembered fragments of her own, "if Uncle Mike and Mother and I can't figure things out, you'd add your knowledge."

"Can't say I've knowledge: just the Craigmoor storeowner. If you get stumped and if I have time, maybe I'd look things over." Both kept their deadpan, expressionless masks in place.

"That would be most kind, Mr. Ford," Becca replied, feeling more like Libby in the 19th century than herself in the 20th.

"How's your mother?" He asked, staring at the glass counter.

"She's fine. Strong as nails."

"Looks," he said softly, "can deceive."

Becca wondered what he knew about her family and also knew it would be futile to inquire. She made a few purchases and prepared to leave.

"Take a minute to stop by the mill. It's been restored. Belonged to Libby's grandparents or great-grandparents, I believe." His level gaze didn't change as he relit his pipe.

"In the cemetery, where're the main Jones and Morgan plots?"

He chuckled. "Every three feet or so you'll stumble over somebody you're related to, if not by blood at least by friendship or feud. Head east from the front gate, turn north at the big Putnam monument and go up the hill: you won't miss them."

"Thanks, Mr. Ford. And thanks for offering to help with the letters."

"I said 'if I have time.' I've no intention of getting stuck to old papers like a fly on flypaper." He removed his pipe and pointed the stem at her. "You'd be wise to remember that, Becca. History's fine, but we live now."

"I'll remember."

"Make sure you do, Rebecca Elizabeth, make sure you do."

Before driving to the cemetery, Becca walked to the mill. Her memory of it was vague at best but she liked the shushing sound the waterwheel made.

At the cemetery, Becca walked straight to the Morgan plot. Andy's grave lay between some older Morgans (names Becca didn't recognize) and Charley and Amy Louise's graves. Pulling grass from around the headstones, Becca recalled Timmy commenting that both she and Josephine did this at Greg's grave: the hands of the living pruning the ground over the dead. Mid-day sun beat down: the heat and quiet interrupted occasionally by a birdcall.

Becca sat on the grass and pictured the ceremonies that had accompanied these burials. Most recently Hildur's ashes had been interred here. Andy's gray-marble headstone felt smooth as she traced his name and the dates bracketing his life. Beneath her all that remained of his physical being lay enclosed in his casket. She remembered the inscription on a tomb in Florence. It had been in Latin and she'd translated it:

As you are, I was
As I am, you will be.

She sat remembering people who'd come before: these people without whom she would not exist. As they now were, she would become.

She stood, wandered and found the Joneses. Bertie and Libby next to each other: one headstone, two graves. Half of her genetic heritage came from people buried here but her contact with them, her understanding of their contribution to her, had been truncated by Andy's death. Yet, who she'd become—successes and failures—included that death.

She knew four stories about Libby. First, she'd insisted the egg money be set aside of college educations for her daughters—wildly feminist in the 1870's. Second, she had a family tradition of greeting each newborn child as 'the prettiest one yet.' Third, the story about Princess saving Amy Louise and fourth, on someone's birthday one year Libby said she'd have breakfast in bed and retired: just stopped working and from then on did only what she wanted to do.

Becca would discover more in letters and papers: maybe things she didn't want to know. 'Well,' she told herself. 'You have the box. You'll read what's there; you'll tell Uncle Mike and Eleanor.' She looked down at Libby's grave, imagined her skeleton: short and bent by the time she died. She smiled. 'I may even uncover new strengths.'

Wandering back toward the gate, she saw some Whitman graves: John Whitman and another John Whitman and Mavis Tillman Whitman who died young. 'Libby's mother?'

The sun stood lower in the sky; she needed to leave for Logan Airport. Walking briskly through the cemetery, Becca almost stumbled over Louise Putman's headstone. 'Doubt we're related by blood so maybe by friendship or feud,' she thought.

She drove back down to town and then up the hill, past the old Morgan mansion and noted how tall the trees had grown. Leaving town, she watched the 'Welcome to Craigmoor' sign slide backward across her side mirror as she headed south to Boston.

4

During the flight from Boston to Washington, DC (where she would overnight before returning to California) Becca wrote eight pages titled 'Everything I remember about Andy's family before receiving The Box.' Short phrases, little verbal snapshots, names, dates poured out like maple syrup over pancakes on the legal pad she bought at Mr. Ford's. She wanted to record things before new information transformed the script, injected new scenes and modified what she knew. Recording unadulterated memory was, of course, impossible. What she created was a 'fast download,' information she'd stored along the way and now pulled through her life history and current mental status.

At the end of her notes she scribbled: 'Where I am determines what I see: how I'm functioning effects what I allow through. What I feel/want/think shades what I retrieve.' She added her notes to her briefcase and, clutching The Box, prepared to disembark.

Crowding through the airport, Becca felt like a red corpuscle pulsing through known arteries, heading purposefully toward her destination beside other corpuscle-people going, with equal focus, to other places. Trudge, trudge, trudge. On some tele-screen in another galaxy—call it Zebulon—reconstructed by giant computer-imaging devices, what might Earth look like? Maybe like a blue and white sphere orbiting the sun, teeming with tiny organisms that sucked their life from the planet like viruses seen through an electron microscope. The caption might read: 'Homo sapiens: Current malignant strain feeding on planet Earth and occasionally flinging metastases toward Zebulon.' Were these Zebulon scientists wiser than humans? Would they avoid our mistakes? Was over-breeding intrinsic to a successful species: malignancy a byproduct of evolutionary triumph? Was there any hope? Could 'brain' overrule 'hormones?' Could 'reason' quell 'testosterone?'

Retrieving her suitcase from the baggage carousel and clutching The Box tightly, she caught a shuttle to the hotel she had booked for the night. Looking over the Potomac, she watched the brightly lit Capitol gleaming against the night sky as a low moon swam among puffy clouds. After ordering dinner and breakfast from room service, she reviewed her 'Everything I remember' notes. At 11:15 she dialed Brad's number.

"Hello."

"Hi. It's me."

"Where have you been?"

"I told you I might play hooky. I said I'd call tonight."

"You checked out of the Shoreham and disappeared!"

"I went to Craigmoor."

"Great. Explains nothing. What's Craigmoor?"

"Ye 'olde' family homestead."

"That's in New England!"

"Calm down, Brad. New Hampshire to be exact."

"You went to New Hampshire from D.C. and call it 'playing hooky'?"

"Yes. I had a wonderful trip. How're you?"

"Testy because you vanished."

Becca sighed. "I said I'd call, told you I'd see you, as planned, on Saturday." Her voice sounded patronizing. She tried to relax. "And I missed you."

"Fine. You missed me. Don't you feel any responsibility to people?"

"To people or to Brad Abbott?"

"Becca, you knew I might call. What if something happened to you?"

"Come off it, Brad. You also might have flown out to surprise me, sent two-dozen roses. Am I supposed to wait in my room for whatever you decide to do? That's crazy! What if something happened to me? Like I get mugged in Foggy Bottom or abducted from Logan airport by international drug smugglers?" She tried to sound light and funny: then became serious. "In those cases, there are competent law enforcement agencies and Eleanor is my next of kin to whom I sent a card from Craigmoor."

"You're being unreasonable –"

"I'm being unreasonable? Reverse the situation. Any woman acting like you're acting would instantly be branded 'clawing' or 'meddling' or at least 'overstepping the current relationship boundaries.' She'd be portrayed as another example of 'what's wrong with women.' Brad, I'm an adult. I'm a full professor. Don't play Lilliputian games with me. I miss you. I care for you but I own myself."

"OK. Maybe I'm overreacting but I was worried and damn it, whether you like it or not, there is a double standard and men and women are different. You can ignore it but it won't go away; you want to change the world."

Becca's serious, centered voice darted across the connections. "I'm aware that men and women are different. I've never denied that. And I am changing the world, Brad. The double standard and reduced pay for the same work won't go away if we ignore them but they will go away, eventually, because millions of women are chipping away: demanding to be recognized as more equal partners in the universe, to be allowed do the things we're capable of doing rather than just those deemed 'appropriate' for women and to be valued for more than just producing progeny. Which doesn't mean that having offspring is not valuable but does point out that having children is not all women have to offer. More equal treatment may be the planet's last best hope."

Silence.

"OK. So, how was Craigmoor?"

"Wonderful." She told him about the Reynolds, the house, the barn, The Box, the general store, Mr. Ford, the cemetery.

"Is there a secret message?"

"I haven't started reading. I'll begin soon: do more tomorrow and on the trip home."

"Sounds interesting," Brad said. "Bec, I love you." Another silence.

"Brad?"

"Yea."

"This trip's been very personal."

"OK, but try to see my side, too."

"I'm trying but I won't do a 'you big and strong—me little and weak' thing. You understand?"

"Yes, but I'm not sure how to do that."

"We're beginning. We're making our relationship both more honest and more difficult."

"True, but I like challenges. Sleep well and I'll see you tomorrow."

"See you tomorrow. Goodnight." After hanging up, she felt agitated about omitting her visit to the Vietnam Memorial but figured discussing that would work better in person.

It was just 12:30 a.m. in D.C., 9:30 p.m. in California. Not too late to call Uncle Mike.

"Hi, it's Becca. I'm on a big adventure." She recounted her trip noting, as she spoke, that the words she used to describe the experience already tangled around each other, changing things, reflecting different emphases. "So I'm sitting in a hotel, stuff all around, taking inventory. If you have your old pipe handy you can play with it just like Grandpa Charley used to, like Mr. Ford did."

"It's a useful ploy to control situations. Is the handwriting on the note Mother's?"

"Looks like it."

"Then it's the lost box." He paused. "It's rightfully yours."

"Would you rather see things first? You're a generation closer."

"They're yours, Becca. I want to see them sometime, but they're yours."

Quail Hill

"There are things I don't recognize, people I've heard of only vaguely, a bunch of letters tied with a yellow ribbon, for instance. Is the person writing to Libby from India around the turn of the century—the signature may be 'Rach' or just 'R'—is that my Great-Great Aunt Rachel?"

"Probably. Rachel Jones was your Great-Grandfather Bertie's older sister. You may find skeletons in that box."

"About her? What do you know?"

"I never knew her. Story goes she went to visit Matthew and Rose in Cambridge—you know who Matthew and Rose are, don't you?"

"More Joneses. A doctor and a teacher, maybe?"

"My God, is that what it comes to when you've been dead a few years? A whole life dissolves into 'a doctor and a teacher, maybe?' Sorry, Bec, just got caught in a reverie. Anyway, she met a Guru and followed him to India. Quite possibly Bertie never got over it, never understood or forgave her. He may not have known Libby and Rachel corresponded or maybe he figured he couldn't stop Libby from writing and secretly wanted contact maintained."

"Craigmoor must've buzzed. Mr. Ford may know all about it."

"Maybe. But the Fords could spread rumors around like the flu and always act innocent. Small towns and gossip are a bad combination."

"Uncle Michael, you surprise me."

"That I don't like gossip? What kind of a family do you think we are?"

"Well, I'm learning more. Will you help me if I get stuck?"

"Of course and don't give Mr. Ford anything before I've seen it."

"Fine." Becca hesitated, squeezed the next words out like the last toothpaste from a tube. "Uncle Mike, I went to the Vietnam Memorial."

"How was it?"

"Not what I expected. Interesting architecture. Strange to see Greg's name there: cut into the stone with those thousands of other names. So cold."

"Are you OK?"

"Yea. I'm stronger. It was so long ago but his name on the wall plowed into me. I felt terribly sad. So many names: such a waste. I'll lose myself in work when I get home."

"Speaking of which, how's the new house and how was the conference?"

"House is great. You and Sylvia need to come up again. Mother may visit in June. The conference was good, my paper went well and I'll be coming down to San Francisco a few times a year for a collaborative project."

"The bed's always available. Bring Brad. I like him."

"I like him too, Uncle Mike."

"Have a safe flight home."

"Will do. Love you, Uncle Mike."

· The Trip Home ·

"Love you, too, Bec." Michael hung up and stood looking at the phone: snared by old memories like an innocent bird caught in an unseen net.

With the packets of letters lined up, Becca checked the books for dedications and publication dates. Expecting some reference to Rachel in the small *Bhagavad-Gita*, she found only a short message: *"Discovered in India by our nephew Capt. Russell. First read by me summer 1865. Fascinating. John Ely."*

Who were these people? This predated Rachel's going to India by decades. After reading and re-reading very old, cryptic post cards from India, Becca felt like a deflated balloon. Nothing made sense. She showered, went to bed and slept fitfully until her wake-up call dragged her from a bizarre anxiety dream in which the bird screeched down at her repeatedly. Her neck hurt and her airways felt plugged by too many days of breathing hotel air. She washed her face, dressed and looked at one of the books while eating her room-service breakfast.

Fragile, with a worn leather cover, the book looked like one of the oldest things in the box. Sipping coffee, Becca opened the front cover carefully. The ink looked brown and the pages beige and stiff, almost brittle.

'This book belongs to Rebecca Elizabeth Tillman: Personal and Private'

A tingling sensation moved up Becca's spine and she became acutely aware of clothing touching her skin.

Dear Diary,

J says we must leave Massachusetts for Canada. I prepare to move. The boys and 2-year-old Margaret believe their father absolutely and look forward to a grand adventure. Thus, I'm alone in my concerns. J thinks he cannot succeed here, has tried since independence and been thwarted. I wonder. So we leave. I do hope I'm mistaken about my condition.

RET June 10, 1798

Dear Diary,

Providence smiled on us. God answered my prayers for J is content investing in the mill with his brother and it is prospering. Our former life seems far away. The church and school in Craigmoor are small so my responsibility to the children's education is great. Our home is large and we've hired a couple named Putnam to help. My Prayer Book and Bible provide solace but I miss old friends and the ocean. Oh, how I miss the ocean. J's brother, wife and sons are our only family here.

RET August 4, 1798

Dear Diary,

My long silence speaks of work and our growing family. Baby P lived only a few hours. My grief was deep but a healthy daughter arrived last month. If Mama were here, she'd proclaim her 'the prettiest one yet.' In her absence, I did the honor silently and then, one day Margaret peeked into the crib and said the phrase herself. I wept with joy and pride. I am a fortunate woman. J has strength and wisdom and treats us well. The mill thrives and the boys help. M and I manage the garden—good crops of peas and beans this year—the cows and chickens. L taught us to make a nice cheese and insists on growing many flowers. We're fortunate to have the Putnams. Our life is good.

RET September 26, 1800

Becca refilled her coffee cup, drank some orange juice and bit into a roll. The spongy-soft, Kleenex-textured dough squished flat in her mouth. "I bet RET never ate bread this bad." She smeared butter and purple jam on the roll and flipped ahead in the book.

Dear Diary,

M and R's daughter survived her first winter. Mavis' disposition is more placid than my children but she is bright and keenly interested in things—just quiet and content. If a toy falls away, she watches it calmly. I'd give her a good dose of my temper if I could: do both of us good. Possibly she'll help me be calmer though how we'd have survived without my willful energy, I do not know. R and the boys work the mill. Caring for J occupies much of my time. M is prudent and attentive. I am blessed in many ways. The Church helps me focus but there are things I believe the Congregationalists imprudently cut from the Anglican root; I hold my tongue. J's illness takes a toll on us all: his useless right arm and leg and difficulty talking present constant reminders of lost ability. He weeps in frustration. I must be strong. Please, God, sustain us.

RET July 25, 1825

Becca closed the book, stood and walked to the window. These familiar symptoms of left-brain damage, things she'd studied and worked with daily for a quarter century, arced across time strengthening the bond she felt with Rebecca Elizabeth Tillman who lived, loved and wept in Craigmoor with someone identified as 'J' who must be her husband.

There was a 'Margaret' but was 'M' also Margaret or someone else? Were 'the boys' destined to cast just this faint, plural shadow or would other writings provide names? She glanced at her watch, closed her suitcase and, before leaving, flipped to one of the last entries in the diary. The handwriting, while familiar, appeared fragile as words scuttled across the page like crab tracks on a beach.

Dear Diary,

Mavis brought Elizabeth Rebecca to visit. 'Libby' seems strong and very quiet. I hope she isn't too reserved. Life can be difficult if one is too quiet. What will her life be? Margaret will be a good grandmother though she won't know that for a long time. Mavis looks pale. She has been cooped up too long. Does John help enough? He's a fine husband and should be an excellent father.

The sun is out but it is cold. I'm ready for spring. I've lived here in Craigmoor for 50 years but I still miss spring in Virginia. It is odd: things of childhood cling like bits of seaweed on a shell.

RET Feb 20, 1850

"My God," Becca said aloud. "She greeted Libby; Libby greeted me. And thank you Rebecca Elizabeth for using names! This must be 'Libby' my great-grandmother, greeted by her Great-Grandmother 'Rebecca Elizabeth.'" She shook her head, shivered and glanced at her watch. She really had to leave.

5

After checking out and securing her luggage and briefcase at the desk, she left for one last sentimental trip. First, she bought a large, sturdy canvas bag with brightly painted DC scenes on it, put the old Filene's box and her purse in it and flipped the shoulder strap over her head so the bag hung on her right hip.

Next, she taxied to the Corcoran Gallery, found her favorite statue, The Veiled Nun. Like a watercolor in stone the face was veiled, appeared mirage-like in the white marble, suggesting a haunting identity for this young woman caught between secrecy and exposure, her private soul only slightly hidden. Twenty-five years had not altered the sculpture's mystery.

Finally, she arrived at the National Gallery and snaked her way through room after familiar room heading toward Henri Fatin-Latou's Portrait of Sophie. The painting calmed her. Its quiet, monochromatic beauty was both centered and dignified. As Becca stood looking at this masterpiece, one of the guards smiled at her. As she left the room, they spoke briefly.

"She's my favorite," Becca said. "I've remembered her often since I moved away."

· Quail Hill ·

"Beauty, and the memory of beauty, lighten the load on days heavy with too much toil and worry," he responded. "She's one of my favorites, too."

She walked to the Gallery's high-ceilinged portico, took a seat and watched people. Reaching into her purse, she removed a letter she'd randomly chosen from the packet tied in yellow ribbon and carefully opened the two crinkly, fragile pages.

My dear Libby,

I am delighted at the news re: A.L. and C. She's such a gift to all of us. My prayers are with you—tell her for me if you are able to do so without discomfort.

How to describe my life and help you understand my decision? Years ago you chose B and life with us while R went to college. Does anyone not have moments of regret, not mourn for choices not made? And are the three of us women not supremely blessed by the choices we've made? My staying home with Ma and Pa, you and B and the children brought me great fulfillment. And moving on, coming here, brings me closer to the core truth I've sought all my life. It's like following the scent of an unseen flower.

Living here is so 'other.' The colors, spices, fragrances, vegetation and animals (monkeys everywhere!) all so different from things we grew up with. Sometimes I'm overwhelmed with being so far away, yet I know I'm where I belong. Here, often surrounded by statues of Hindu gods and goddesses, I touch the heart of Christ in a new and deeper way.

Calcutta is a beautiful city and, since our dear Swami left us, we spend much time here with our community centered at the Kali Temple—the home for Swami's teacher, Ramakrishna. Meditating in shaded areas, it's as if I'm surrounded by divine love and see my Guru's face smiling before me, urging me on, giving me strength when I've none of my own.

Many in the community call me 'Ama.' Imagine: barren Rachel, called 'Ma.' Some see in my traveling so far, my tenacity in following our Guru and trying to fit in an example they admire. Yet, truly, I only do as my soul demands.

You wrote of the many gods here: it can appear that way. However, at best (and a religion should be viewed at its best and not only by bad things done by foolish or ignorant followers—though those aspects mustn't be over-looked) each 'Deity' represents a slim facet of God, never to be confused with the totality which is a reality no human can understand. Kali, for instance, confronts us with her terrifying strength: she who can destroy our self-will, our grasping greed, our idolatrous delusion, is both powerful and good: purifying us. As a Christian devotee, I feel her energy in Christ's agony in Gethsemane: the awesome power necessary to turn one's human self over, totally, to the will of God! I have not, as some may think, left Christianity behind but I have opened myself to a larger view of The God That Is: the great I AM of the Hebrews, the more open cosmos of the Hindus, a God that is truly ONE. Not my idea limited by my mind, my religion and my understanding but transcendent and immanent in ways we, as creatures, can never fully know. It's difficult to put these ideas into words.

I will never again see Quail Hill at Christmas, never hold you and B again but I send you my love and my joy. Whatever the cost, I must be here. As you chose life as a farmwife and thus have endured the winter storms when we huddled close, fearful during days and nights marked only by howling winds and a ticking clock. Our minds contained a memory of light, of the heat and fresh foods of summer, sustaining us through the darkness. Christ does not promise that we'll always walk in the light, only that when darkness comes, He will be there, our brother, our friend, our guide: with us.

Scan the snowy hillside, smell Mama's roses for me this summer, kiss B silently for me. May God bless us and draw us closer to Himself.

With great love,
R   20 Dec. 1904

Becca sat quietly in the cool patio: stunned. She refolded the letter and returned it to her purse. She remembered the Kali Temple: the couple standing before her giving her their darshan and then disappearing into the crowd, saw again the small child holding the apple. Phrases from the letter fluttered in her mind like apple blossoms falling in a breeze. She stood, lifted the canvas bag and heard her own footsteps resound from the marble floors.

Ninety minutes later she checked in at her departure gate at National Airport, and settled into a seat. She needed to think.

Until now, Rachel seemed a distant tragic/romantic runaway who broke free from New Hampshire chasing a dubious passion. Now, Becca felt sobered and deeply touched by this unorthodox woman. Rachel's path consisted of work, duty and focus while Becca's life felt scattered. Then she understood that Hildur had sent her on a quest seeking icons: women and phrases she could use to pattern herself, supports that would be, as Rachel had written, "urging me on, giving me strength when I've none of my own." Becca's career, her profession, had provided the most stable structure but Hildur had opened her. Between Greg's death and her fledgling relationship with Brad she'd avoided deep intimacy. These past few years, and especially since the shooting, she'd modified her life. It felt like there were forces guiding her: forces she didn't understand. Did the twin poles of structure and freedom, independence and community, teacher and student, self and other move around like subatomic units: predictable yet free with the balance constantly realigned, readjusted, modified? Did 'life' push toward anything specific?

6

She pictured Greg and Hawaii. Could she understand their fight differently? Recognize his pushing her away as less to do with her than with his situation in Vietnam?

"Dr. Chadwick?" Becca looked up. "Oh, it's really you." A neatly coiffed stewardess slid into the seat next to Becca's canvas bag. "You won't remember me..."

"Yes, I do," Becca interrupted, longing for a pipe to play with to buy time. "You got a Master's at Wisconsin and both your names have double letters." The woman smiled and nodded. "You took a job in a rehab center. Judging by the uniform, that didn't work out."

"Yes and no. Holly Miller then, now I'm married. You warned me about the job, said I'd be too isolated in a one-woman show. You were right."

"You burned out?"

"Flamed out, crashed. After two years I couldn't take it anymore. The patients and their families I might have managed but the administration! Always see more patients, cut appointment times, do more paper work."

"Holly, I'm sorry I wasn't there for you when you needed support."

"But you were. That's what's so fun about seeing you."

"I was? How?"

"When I wanted to quit I remembered what you'd said about doing what you feel fulfilled *doing*. About how you felt it would be cool to be a famous anthropologist but you didn't want to sift through East Africa. What you liked doing was teaching and working with people who had complicated problems. So I figured what I wanted to be was a healer but what I liked to do was travel and interact lightly with lots of people. Voila! Stewardess."

"How's this working for you and your husband?"

"Great. He's an engineer; we have two boys. Here," she pulled out the pictures. Becca 'ah-d' and 'oh-d' appropriately and, after a few more minutes, Holly excused herself and left. Becca watched her walk to the counter, speak with the agent, turn, wave and move confidently into the crowd.

So many young clinicians burned out in the current maelstrom of health care: a terrible waste of talent and training. Becca decided to set up a system to give more support to recent graduates. She could develop the idea in Spike's project.

Moments later the agent at the counter called her name. "Thanks for answering my page. I need to change your seat."

"Is there a problem?"

· The Trip Home ·

"Not for you. We have a mother with an 8 year-old stand-by for Economy: one seat, next to you in Economy and one in First. I'm bumping a Business to First and you to Business, putting mother and son together. Hope you approve."

"Thanks. It's not even my birthday."

"You're welcome. Flight's full and everybody's happy. Holly said you saved her life."

"Holly has a flair for the dramatic."

"We've noticed that, Dr. Chadwick. Have a nice flight," the agent smiled and handed her a new boarding pass.

The plane moved into position on the runway. As the motors roared, it strained like a stallion against the controlling hand of a strong rider and, when the pilot finally released its trembling energy, raced down the runway. Airborne, the plane began a steep climb and retracted the landing gear. Becca watched the Capitol Building and felt herself untangling from her past in D.C. Light reflected from the wing, briefly dazzling her, as they swung onto their westward course and began chasing the sun in a race they couldn't win.

The larger seat in Business allowed her to spread some of the contents of the box on her tray table. The man next to her ploughed through endless sheets of numbers frantically wielding a yellow highlighter. Her own obsession with old letters shouldn't raise any eyebrows here. Maddeningly, few letters had envelopes thus often denying exact dates and locations. Much of the handwriting appeared eerily similar. Many writers used initials exclusively making Becca grind her teeth and vow never to refer to anyone by initials again. Some letters were signed carefully 'Miss Amy Middleton' a name she had never heard in her life. Why were these letters even here? Who were all these people? She lifted a page and began reading.

> *Dear Mama and Papa,*
>
> *K and I are well. The campus is lovely. She's helping me learn the routine. Our instructors are excellent and demand much. Miss Amy would approve.*
>
> *My roommate, Lucy Cabot, and I study together and play tennis. We are both inclined to physical activity and will both teach.*
>
> *I cannot thank you enough for the sacrifices you have made to give me this opportunity. I will try to live up to your expectations and will repay you over my years of teaching. Now I must to bed. We rise early.*
>
> *Love,*
>
> *Your Ab*
>
> *P.S. Thank the chickens for the egg money.*

· Quail Hill ·

No date and no location. 'Ab' might be Great-Aunt Annabelle at college. Where. Colby? Bates? Uncle Mike might know. 'Miss Amy' might be 'Miss Amy Middleton.' Becca jotted notes on a 3X5 card. Sipping tomato juice and looking out the window she remembered her own first weeks at college: meeting Tippy, signing up for classes, feeling independent and fragile. So many different moments in a life, like the chips of stone, mirror and colored glass used to make a mosaic: how you arranged things determined the design.

Becca forged through ten totally mundane letters from 'Ab' to 'Mama and Papa': the weather, people identified only by initial, Miss A. and Prof E showed up regularly, talk of studying hard, etc. A thick letter pulled from much later in the 'Ab' stack was a treasure.

25 Sept 1920, Cambridge

Dear Mama,

We are excited about the amendment giving women the franchise. I know you agree. Auntie R's efforts go back decades. Did you know she met both Miss Anthony and Mrs. Stanton? Her quiet determination, all the while being a dedicated teacher, to work for the cause, was remarkable. She'd say "When we get the vote, women must put it to good use and bring an end to war." As you know, I worked for the vote these last few years but it takes less courage now than it did for Miss Anthony and Auntie R in her youth. Will women in the future appreciate the sacrifices and struggles to obtain this privilege? I hope so.

C is well but occasionally we see the War took a toll. He swings between being mellow and more mature and being too distant. A.L. tries to do things he wants but he sometimes rejects kindness. Michael, always a dependable, steadfast boy, continues to do well but Andy is too willful. C does not always have the strength or patience to be the father he needs and A.L. is too gentle. So it falls to me to discipline him. He's loveable and has winning ways but his temper and his tendency to rely on his native intelligence rather than applying himself annoy me. He's probably like Papa was as a boy so I do not fret too much.

C and I had a dreadful row the other night. I talked about the franchise and C grew agitated, said it was silliness dragging women into things they had no business in. Both Katy and A.L. remained mute but I couldn't! I fear I treated C as though he were a bad boy in my class. The silliness, I said, was men who wanted to waste half the talent God created by keeping women limited. He asked if I believe all women will vote well and I replied, "I don't for a moment believe that all men vote well." Then we all laughed for I sounded just like Auntie R and even C misses her. Following in her footsteps made my own teaching career much easier. Truly I see I've spent my life following people: you and Papa, K, Auntie R. How fortunate I've been. Walking a path's easier than clearing the woods. All started by you and Papa and the chickens.

It's late and I must to bed.

Best love, AB

'What a gift,' Becca thought. 'Knowing a personal, family response to a great event.'

After the in-flight meal, Becca investigated further packets of letters. One slim group, wrapped in a piece of paper, appeared unlike the others. When she unwrapped them, three envelopes tumbled into her lap, one landed face up. She stared at the handwriting, read the words 'Eleanor Sherwood Morgan.' Becca's face flushed; her hand shook as she turned the other envelopes over. 'Marcia Louise Morgan' was carefully scripted on one and her own name, just as he'd written it on her birth announcement, appeared on the other. Moments passed. Suddenly she realized she was holding her breath and sucked in air noisily. Hearing her rapid inhalation, her seatmate stopped his yellow pen in mid-stroke and looked up. She smiled wanly and he returned to his numbers. Inhale, exhale, pause. Inhale, exhale, pause. At base, life always came back to this simple repetitive pattern.

She opened the envelope, slid out two pieces of ivory bond paper and scanned each page as one would view a painting: getting an overall impression before beginning a detailed study.

17 June 1941, Craigmoor NH

Dear Rebecca Elizabeth,

As I write, you sleep in the next room. Your sister, Mother and Grandparents are out walking. I cannot know when you will receive this letter but I want to tell you some things that are important to me. Maybe they will find a cure for Hodgkin's and I'll live longer but that's unlikely so I write. Even at 15 months you show a passion for life and a very strong will. Your Grandpa Charley said last night you are like me: headstrong from the start. Your Grandma pointed out I got that from him. True, we Morgans are strong willed but you and I get strength from the Jones side, too. (You have influences from the Sherwoods, but information and guidance concerning those, your Mother can provide.) Your Great-Grandmother Libby, for whom you are named, and your Great-Grandfather Bert were extraordinarily focused people. Never doubt that you come from a sturdy and dedicated family and Libby remarked on your strength and determination when she met you last summer.

I love you. I am sicker now than when your sister was little so I do not have the same strength I did then but love is not diminished by physical weakness. In

Quail Hill

fact, it may be enhanced by it. I see the beauty and fragility of life better when my body is slower and I'm not racing to the next prize, the next experience. I hope you will see a great deal of life, spread your wings and fly long distances. The women in my family are strong; they are trailblazers. Pursue education. It has been a key for this family: a lantern that guides us into the future. Never stop learning. Keep your heart open and loving. In the end, love may be all that counts.

There is a balance between exploring edges and maintaining stability, pushing back boundaries and learning from the past. I'm an explorer, a pusher. You may be, too. That's a challenge for a girl but you can meet that challenge. Just don't be afraid. I'm not very religious but in the Bible, when God sends angels, they always start out saying 'Don't be afraid.' So there must be something in us that tends toward fear and we need to overcome that tendency.

Try to balance seriousness and joy, work and play, exercise and rest. No matter how long we live, at the end, it seems short. Use your life well. Your mother is stronger than people think she is. She will be your primary guide and will be a good mother. After I die, she will have a bigger job than she signed on for and that may challenge her. I trust Uncle Mike and your grandparents will be there to help.

I hear you calling now, 'Beba Widdabit' and, as your Grandpa notes, "when Becca says 'Daddy! Up!' it's an order, not a request."

With very great love,

Daddy

Sometime, while she read, a stewardess pulled the blind, the general lights went off and a movie started. The bright, focused beam from her reading light illuminated the pages in her hands. In a surrealistic split, Becca experienced two personas simultaneously: the mature woman reading and the 15 month-old waking up in the crib and demanding attention. She felt calm, stunned, thankful and terribly sad. She refolded the pages, slipped them into her purse, turned off the reading light, leaned back and closed her eyes as tears rolled down her face.

Her mind drifted back to Craigmoor, looked more closely at the Morgan home she'd barely noticed as she drove by on her recent trip. She recalled the bedrooms Andy referred to: pictured the small desk at which he would have been writing, the crib in which she would have been sleeping. Andy had understood the challenge for her: even back then. 'Beba Widdabit' she heard Marcia's voice echoing down the decades, bouncing off other walls: 'Beba Widdabit.' Marcia, the sister with whom she had such a complicated relationship, had stubbornly held her in the family when she wanted to flee. Marcia accepted the rules and

The Trip Home

reacted frantically when Becca didn't. Marcia held onto her: not always gently, not always happily but Marcia held on.

Faces passed by. Eleanor at her best and worst: open, raw, loving and too exposed to the world to live without a mask, a role. Then, a young widow frightened by thunderstorms yet needing to protect her daughters. Eleanor having secrets with Marcia about Becca, with Becca about Marcia, triangulating, controlling by withholding funds and desperately trying to pass on a lifestyle and life patterns many of which Becca rejected out of hand. Eleanor continually wrestling with her own anger and grief while sending the message 'why is Andy dead and you alive?' And always Eleanor, in her own confused way, loving her.

She saw the tectonic plates of history shift and heave under her family tree. RET dealing with an unwanted move to Craigmoor and J's illness. If 'Mavis' was Libby's mother, then her death was another disruption. Rachel left for India. C returned from WW I less able to parent. More recently the rift of her mother's young widowhood, of WW II and the changing roles of women that sliced across Eleanor's path creating rupture, distance and panic. In her own life, Andy's death, Eleanor's ambivalence, Greg and Vietnam and Hawaii. Yet there were the strengths: the women trailblazers, the quest for education, the 'holding things together against great odds.' Just one branch of one family lurching along, scrabbling across this landscape trying to move forward: building on the past while moving inexorably into the future—ready or not. Becca felt commitments to both Eleanor and Cynthia, the past and future. She was one woman with both negative and positive attributes just like everybody else.

Becca's mind drifted back to Craigmoor; sitting in her crib, she rubbed her eyes with her chubby 15 month-old hands. 'Daddy! Up!' she demanded and smiled into Andy's face as he obeyed. Memory? Illusion? A fantasy woven from the word-threads of a long-lost letter?

She opened her eyes, wiped the salty tears from her cheeks. The movie ended, people opened the shades. The man next to her was now reading <u>Newsweek</u>. Squinting against the sudden influx of light she saw snow on mountains. Not far to San Francisco.

Learn and love and don't be afraid: lovely message from Andy even 40+ years later. She felt no anger at the delay. She smiled and pictured Deborah and Swami: 'karma' they'd say. The letter arrived now so she'd use it now.

Between flights she prepared brief explanatory letters for both Marcia and Eleanor, got envelopes and stamps, enclosed their letters from Andy in the two packets, rechecked to make sure she had not used initials anywhere, and dropped the packets in the mail.

She left Uncle Mike a message on his answering machine, washed her face in the restroom and ate a Snickers bar as she waited at the gate.

The small commuter plane to Santa Veronica felt cramped after Business Class. The view from the window during the flight up the coast provided lessons in geography and geology that Becca always enjoyed. Tectonic plates produced remarkable landscapes here and, from the air, it looked peaceful: only on the ground did tremors smash, terrorize, and kill.

7

As she walked to the luggage carousel, a ground attendant holding a sign with her name on it caught her attention and handed her a note. She opened it as she retrieved her suitcase.

Hi Sweetheart,

Welcome home! Sorry I'm not here. Fritz Johnson's cattle have something strange going on so we are all racing to his ranch. Car is in the lot. Will call later. If I get back tonight, how about a late Thai dinner?

Keys enclosed.

BRAD

Becca smiled. Only in such a small airport could you leave a car without specifying a location. She enjoyed the drive home, entered Santa Veronica and saw the ocean sparkle in the distance. Her house already felt like 'home.' She unpacked, put the Filene's box on her desk, stripped, walked into the bathroom and stepped into the shower. Hot water streaming down her back renewed her. Wrapping her head in a towel, she noted the steam-covered mirror that reflected only obscure blobs of color with fuzzy borders. Was any pattern ever clear for more than an instant? Did anything really begin or end?

She pulled on her jogging clothes, pinned her hair back, went to her study and untied the string on The Box. 'This box belongs to Rebecca Elizabeth Morgan' written in her grandmother's neat, turn-of-the-century handwriting clearly marked her ownership. She lined up the packets of letters (each tied with a different colored ribbon), removed RET's diary and the volumes marked LIBBY'S BOOK I, II AND III and put them on the nightstand by her bed.

'The women in my family are very strong… Pursue education…' Andy wrote. He'd even vaguely foretold Eleanor's struggle after he died. But the U.S. hadn't entered WWII when he wrote the letters so he didn't know of the added pressures of rationing.

· The Trip Home ·

Becca wandered into the living room and ran her fingers across a small antique table she'd inherited from Great-Aunt Annabelle. She loved feeling the smooth wood and watched her reflection in its shiny surface. She imagined the graves on the hillside in Craigmoor. So many. Remembered the Wall: Greg's name among so many names, her reflection among so many reflections.

Wherever she'd come from, she belonged here. New commitments and new professional directions, even a 'volunteer' side-trip into judging high school public speaking, helped anchor her in Santa Veronica. The new house, her own house; her puppy, Crystal, would need training, love and care; a growing network of people including Brad, Jason and Amanda provided structure for a more balanced life. She picked up her keys, nodded to her image in Libby's old mirror. "You're doing OK, Rebecca Elizabeth," she said and walked out the door.

Early evening by the sun: three hours later according to her pituitary: both a hundred years ago and tomorrow in her mind. Exercise helped with time-change. She drove to the cliff above her favorite running beach, one of the few where rock and patches of sand alternated. At the top of the steps she watched the sun move lower in the sky. She remembered Rich's words from years ago: "Graduate school will end like a fireworks display with the last sparkler fizzing out while you're trying to remember lines from some half-forgotten poems. Your life's out there." Well, she'd gone 'out there' and made a successful career and now she was creating better patterns. Much this past week felt like distant, half-remembered poems: familiar yet incomplete. Maybe she was beginning to 'see' life more directly: learning 'how' to live better. She would organize the material, find out what made sense and let the rest slip through her fingers and scatter like sand. She would not become a slave to the past but use it to help her, as Deborah said, 'parent herself.'

She started down the weather-beaten steps as the sun, an orange globe shimmering on the western skyline, sank toward the edge of the world. She visualized ancient maps and how, at the far horizon, the mapmaker would write: 'Here Be Dragons.' Maybe now, with more knowledge, she could stop fearing imaginary dragons.

Becca wondered, as she often did at sunset, whether the universe would end in fire or ice. If, physicists speculated, there isn't enough matter in the universe to create sufficient gravity to stop the current outward expansion and pull everything back into 'a big crunch' (creating unimaginable fiery heat and probably leading to a new 'big bang'), then everything would just keep drifting out, out, away, away, cooling slowly until finally coming to rest: a frozen, static, eternal, dead wasteland. (She balanced carefully on the half-rung of the next-to-the-bottom step and hopped onto the beach.) The sun, now partly swallowed by the ocean, sent wavy patterns of light gleaming around itself like a halo. Did it matter, fire or ice? Somehow, fire seemed more acceptable. While virtually everything would be destroyed, something new should arise. All creation frozen static in one dreadful final nanosecond of eternal 'now' seemed frightful. Fire followed by rebirth offered possibilities that dovetailed easily with the elusive concept of 'eternal life' that has been part of humanity's consciousness for a long time.

"But," Becca said aloud to the deserted beach, "it's out of my hands. If you want my opinion—YOU, the great I AM, That Which Is, God, Christ, the Word, Buddha, Transcendent generative force behind/within all, unmoved mover, uncaused causer, reality, Truth, Allah and any of the million other names by which we've tried to tame your eternal elusiveness—here it is: I, Rebecca Elizabeth Morgan Chadwick, vote for fire!" She smiled. 'Fire' allowed hope.

She stretched her legs, rolled her shoulders, swung her arms in great circles and shook her body loosely before coming to a relaxed and centered standing position. A run would feel good and a late Thai dinner with Brad would be, as Biff might say, 'just the ticket.' It had been a long day. Becca jogged slowly across the beach. Then, reaching the firm, moist, hard-packed sand next to the water's edge, she accelerated and 'hit her stride' as the last sliver of sun slipped below the far horizon. The soles of her running shoes left faint impressions in the damp sand.

The good that is possible in the new creation is a different good, for it is based on the coming-to-be of a different relationship between God and the world.

~*Reason and Reality* by John Polkinghorne

Libby's Family Tree

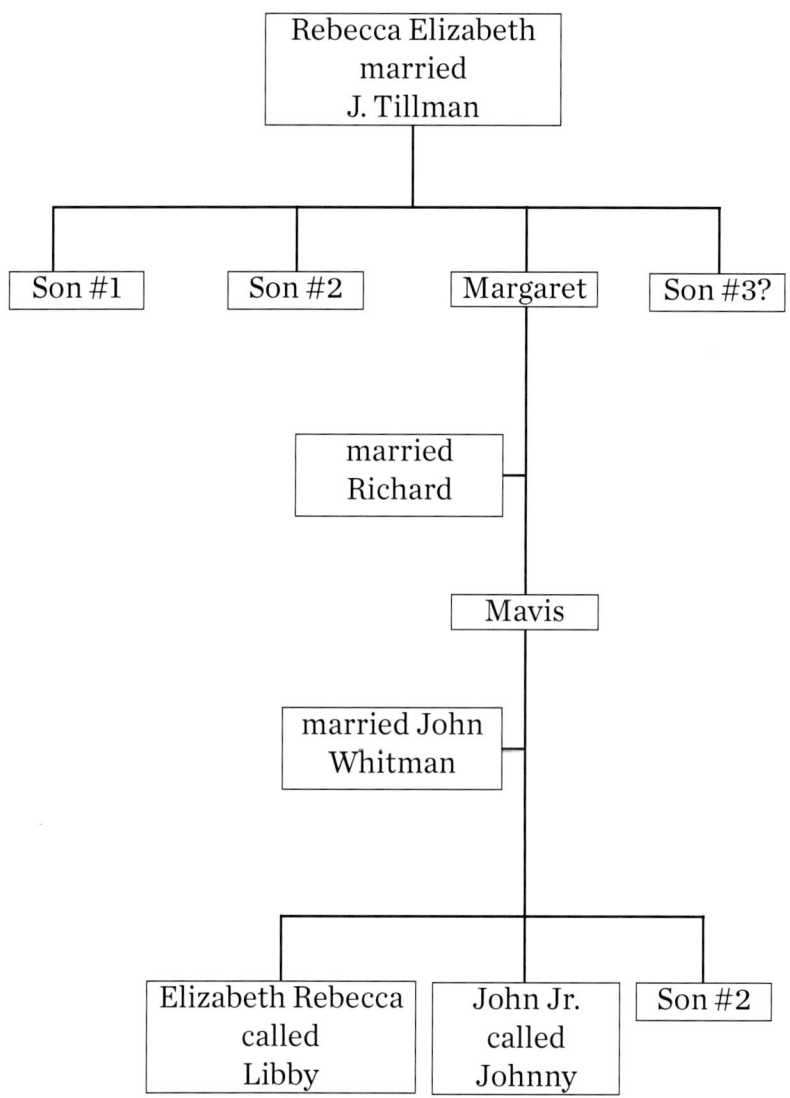

Bertie's Family Tree

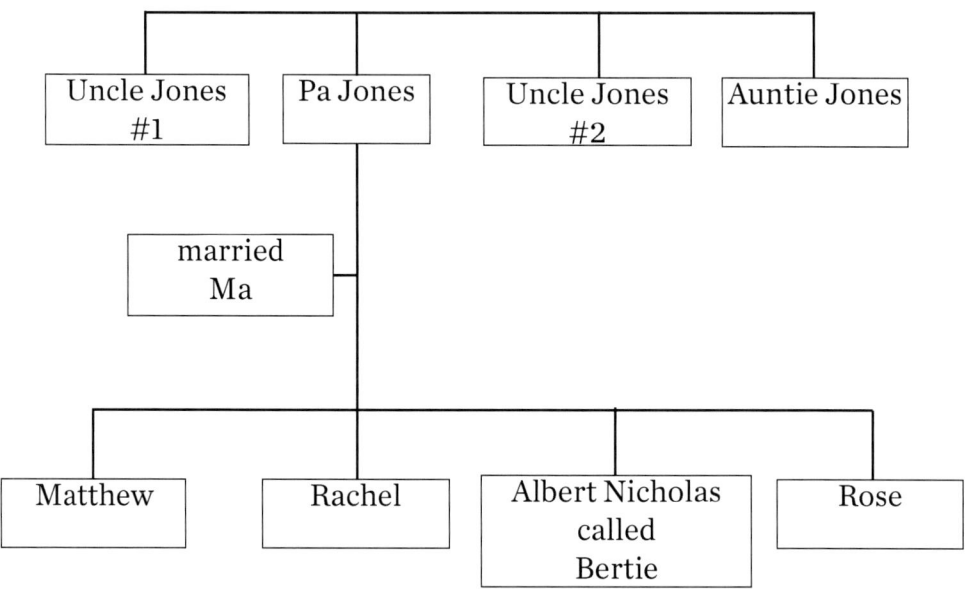

Libby and Bertie's Family Tree

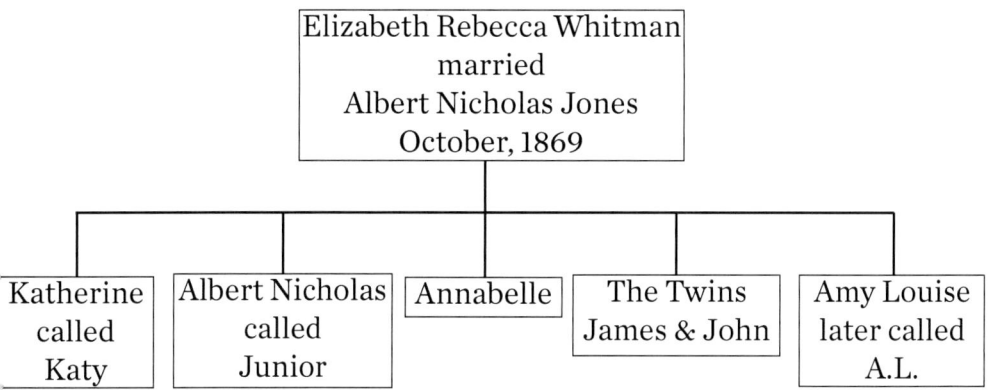

Amy Louise Jones and Charley Morgan's Family Tree

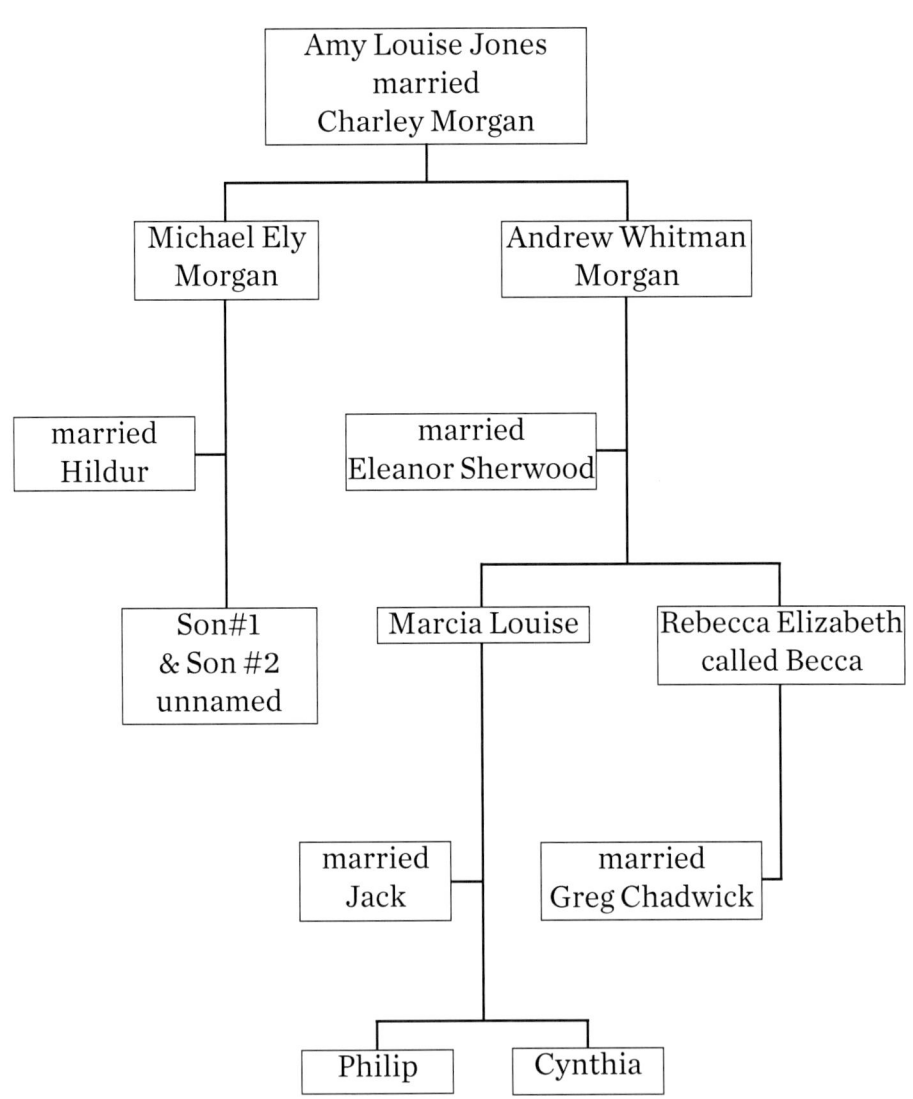

About the author

BARBARA MORRIS ATCHESON is a storyteller from a family of storytellers. She earned B.S. and M.S. degrees in Speech Pathology/Audiology from the University of Wisconsin in Madison, WI and a Ph.D. in Communication Disorders from the University of Washington in Seattle, WA. She has had a long and varied career in Audiology and Speech-Language Pathology. In *Quail Hill*, she draws heavily on her experiences teaching at various Universities and Medical Centers.

She and her husband, a retired Episcopal Priest, currently live in Seattle, WA with their Golden Retriever, Holly. The Atchesons lived in Belgium for most of the 1990's and have traveled extensively in Europe, Israel and India.